A Spell for Saints and Sinners

Also by Emily Carpenter

Gothictown

Burying the Honeysuckle Girls

The Weight of Lies

Every Single Secret

Until the Day I Die

Reviving the Hawthorn Sisters

A Spell for Saints and Sinners

Emily Carpenter

kensingtonbooks.com

KENSINGTON BOOKS are published by

Kensington Publishing Corp.
900 Third Ave.
New York, NY 10022

All Kensington titles, imprints, and distributed lines are available at special quantity discounts for bulk purchases for sales promotion, premiums, fund-raising, educational, or institutional use. Special book excerpts or customized printings can also be created to fit specific needs. For details, write or phone the office of the Kensington Special Sales Manager: Attn. Special Sales Department. Kensington Publishing Corp., 900 Third Ave., New York, NY 10022. Phone: 1-800-221-2647.

ISBN: 978-1-4967-5058-7

First Kensington Trade Edition: April 2026

ISBN: 978-1-4967-5059-4 (ebook)

10 9 8 7 6 5 4 3 2 1

Printed in the United States of America

The authorized representative in the EU for product safety and compliance
is eucomply OU, Parnu mnt 139b-14, Apt 123
Tallinn, Berlin 11317, hello@eucompliancepartner.com

For my Low Tiers

Edie

Help me sit up. Against the pillows, just like that. Now don't start with that shaking your head. And stop crying. I got to tell you something.

My little Budgie. My girl. You know I have given you all my worldly goods . . . this house, the business . . . but there's something more I have to give you. A gift I'm afraid is gonna be a burden to you. But I've got to hand it over. If I don't, sure as shootin' more pain and heartache's gonna follow.

Evil upon evil . . .

It's the pirates you have to look out for. You hear me, girl? Pirates, every which-a-way. Just scanning the horizon for a ship to take . . .

Budgie, come here. I remembered what I wanted to tell you.

A long time ago, there was a wrong done to me. I told myself that I should forgive . . . keep silent, but that was a mistake . . . and because I didn't speak, the darkness grew. Now, here I am at the end, and I see it all. I see the Great Balance—the shining gold scales that measure every good and wicked thing—and it's all wrong.

Do you understand, Budgie?

The Christians say a false balance is an abomination to the Lord. What they don't say is that while it's the rich who falsely weight them . . . it's the least of us, the poor and the weak, who have to right them. That is what I'm asking you to do, little bird.

Right the balance . . .

Now listen to me, my Budgie. Listen closely. You must *do it in the light. You must* always *stay in the light. If you don't . . . if you stray off the path, into the shadows, that's where danger is.*

There are pirates out there, you know . . . in the dark. Pirates who'll see your light and wanna snuff it out. They'll shadow you, girl, flying a flag that belongs to another. Listen to me. They'll sail closer and closer until they spot your weakness. And that's when they come in for the kill.

You gotta watch for the pirates. Their false flags. You gotta be careful . . .

Do you hear me, Ingrid? Are you listening?

I wish I could explain it all to you, but I'm so tired right now. I'll say more when I've had a rest. I promise.

Just do your spells for good. Always for good, Budgie.

Do 'em for the pirates. Sure, why not?

Do 'em for the saints and the sinners . . .

Chapter 1

If Ingrid White's checking account at First Chatham Bank of Savannah hadn't held the alarming balance of $36.08, the two guys without an appointment would've never made it past her front door. But she was a witch—a psychic-witch, technically—and she'd seen enough of how the universe worked to know that just because you made a rule didn't mean you wouldn't need, at some point, to break it.

The guys were no more than twenty or twenty-one. *Boys*, she thought when she saw them, even though she wasn't much older, just twenty-three herself. They were probably students at Georgia Southern, or the University, maybe fraternity brothers. Definitely C students. They had *average* written all over them.

But they had money, that much she could see, just from the way they were dressed. Vineyard Vines shorts, Sperry deck shoes, and crisp oxford shirts they probably sent out to be laundered. Even though they looked freshly showered, their eyes were watery and red, and they still smelled of the previous night: tequila, sweat, and sex. Somehow, they'd made their way down to the southern part of Savannah's historic district, blocks from the tourist epicenter nearer to the river. She might as well snag them before somebody else did.

They were good for at least two hundred and thirty-five, she figured, eighty for each of the two palm readings, and maybe an extra seventy-five for an aura session. They wouldn't tip; she'd bet every penny of her last $36.08 on that. But letting them in was still a better idea than sitting here at her table, scrolling her phone, waiting for several thousand bucks to miraculously drop in her lap.

She asked them to sit and, in the time it took them to manspread on her green velvet settee in her anteroom, she'd assessed their auras:

Stupid. Shallow. Cruel.

She'd seen that last part immediately, that they were bullies, the minute the taller of the two had opened his mouth to ask if she "had something—*wink, wink, ha, ha*—extraspecial for them." She understood the clumsy double entendre.

Filthy cockroaches, she thought. *Hiding in dark places, scuttling in the daylight, allergic to real, authentic human contact.*

She envisioned herself stomping them into a smear of guts with the thick soles of her well-scuffed combat boots, over and over again. Then, thinking of Edie, she amended the fantasy, and instead imagined Litha discovering them, snatching them up in her sharp teeth, and gently batting them around for hours with her hypodermic-sharp claws before finally crunching down on each, a late-afternoon treat. She smiled at that.

She took their credit card information and did the readings. Gave them her very best. Okay, eighty-five percent of her best. They ended up paying two-forty, but not after sniggering throughout both readings, as well as making more unfunny sexual jokes.

Afterward, though, she didn't know what came over her. It wasn't anger necessarily or resentment of the boys. It was more that she was tired. Tired of holding back. Tired of playing nice. Tired of trying to make her grandmother proud. As she opened the door, she stopped the first young man with a hand to his chest.

"You've broken your mother's heart," she said quietly to him.

He froze, looked down at her hand, then back up at her. Fear flickered in his eyes.

"That's why she searches," Ingrid said. "It's not your father's fault. It's that she's lost her child."

His face seemed to melt, and in the way his eyes softened, there was a brief glimpse of the child he must've been at one time. She saw his innocence, his eagerness, his loving side. But then the curtain closed, his face hardened again, and he pushed past her.

Out on the sidewalk, Ingrid could hear his friend asking what she'd said. He didn't answer, just turned around and shot her a look that felt like bullet fire.

"Fucking bitch," he said to his friend, then spat on the ground and walked away.

Chapter 2

In the small parlor where she did her readings, she sprayed the marble-topped table with lavender oil cleaner and wiped it down. The wrought iron door of the cozy anteroom was still propped open to the sidewalk—something she'd done earlier that morning when she'd been feeling optimistic about the river of abundance that was—*definitely, absolutely, finally*—flowing her way.

But this was the new Savannah, and optimism didn't pay the bills here. Not like it had in the old version of the city—that quirky Shangri-la tucked away on Georgia's coast, which had been her grandmother Edie's home. In the mid-nineties a wildly popular book came out—*Midnight in the Garden of Good and Evil,* usually referred to by the locals as "that best-selling book"—and changed all of that. The book, then the movie, built a kind of mythos around the town, one of cheerful transgender cabaret stars, reckless gigolos, and murderous debutantes, and it drew tourists from all corners of the earth to it like a magnet. But the book was never a complete picture of the city. And now, the true artists, the provocateurs of this town, didn't command the main stage. They'd been swept off the streets and into the gutter to make way for the real show: money.

The new Savannah was buffed, shiny, corporate, and ridiculously expensive. A postmodern, gentrified, Airbnb- and Uber-infested playground whose rents were now out of reach for many of its own citizens. Savannah was the plain girl who had, after getting her glow-up, immediately dropped all her weird friends.

There were still pockets of the old city left, but there was no telling how long these places would last; from time to time, an old restaurant or shop would quietly shutter its doors only to be replaced by a Moe's or Jersey Mike's or simply a placard that read AVAILABLE. Downtown was all Urban Outfitters and Hilton Garden Inns and Starbucks. It made Ingrid glad Edie had lost her grip on reality before having to witness it.

And now, the vultures were circling Ingrid. If she wanted to keep her small corner of Savannah intact—her house and the psychic business she operated out of it—she'd have to somehow figure out a way to pay the property tax bill that was coming due next month. She was many thousands of dollars shy of having the full amount, and things weren't looking good. Even after she'd sent Miles out with more flyers.

Ingrid walked out to the sunny sidewalk and glanced up and down the street. There was no one in sight. She looked at the chalkboard sign that proclaimed MISS EDIE'S PALM AND AURA READING in careful chalk calligraphy letters. Her grandmother had done business on this street, in this same town house that faced what used to be Calhoun Square but was now Taylor Square, nearly every day for more than fifty-five years and been able to easily pay off the mortgage on the place back in the eighties. She had been a fixture in Savannah for decades. Now it seemed like no one remembered her.

Five years ago, when Edie got sick, Ingrid had taken over the business. It had been a struggle to convince Edie's regulars to entrust their psychic needs to an eighteen-year-old, but she'd managed to replace the clients who left with new ones. And then, two years ago, Edie died. She left her granddaughter the town house, free and clear of any encumbrances. But Ingrid was young and financially untrained and had been ignorant of the ever-inflating size of the property taxes levied on the well-located house. The realization had been a shock.

The small amount of cash Edie left her had been eaten up in that first year on a new furnace, foundation repair work, and the taxes. Since then, Ingrid lived in a state of near-constant panic. The place was falling down around her ears. She could barely keep up with the utilities. She felt the burden of the money she would soon owe every single day. How naïve she'd been, in so many ways. Naïve and foolish. No wonder her business was failing. What kind of psychic-witch loses her grandmother's fully paid-for house? A bad one, that's what kind.

Now, as Ingrid, squinting into the glaring midday sun, surveyed the house, a whisper of dread threaded through her. The place might look magical at night, in the moonlight, behind the lacy veil of Spanish moss, with the streetlamps and the flickering ghostly gaslight of the huge brass lantern above the front door casting shadows over the pink plaster. But right now, in the unforgiving light of day, it just looked like a dump.

"Ahoy there!" Miles's golden-haired head, tied with a faded green bandanna, appeared on the roof of the town house. He was holding onto one of the fourth-floor gables, like the seaman he was raised to be. He was shirtless, his lean torso gleaming as golden as his hair in the burning sun, and even from the street she could see his startling, light blue eyes. Turquoise as the Caribbean.

Slight but sinewy, tanned beyond what his fair complexion should be, Miles had worked on his father's shrimping boat right up until the man had lost it in a legal dispute. Now at age twenty-six, in exchange for a room on the third floor and whatever food she had in the fridge, he helped Ingrid keep the place running. But just barely. The town house was bigger than it looked, and he could only do so much. And he had another job that kept him busy enough—leading historical and ghost tours for a local outfit in town.

They'd met after Ingrid had found a Moonlight and Magnolia Tours brochure tucked into the garden-level, iron door of her town house and decided a ghost tour was the perfect place to meet tourists and rustle up some more business. She'd been assigned to Miles's group, and they'd hit it off immediately. It was only a week later when she asked him to move in.

They had a unique friendship, she and Miles. Close, but not in a romantic or sexual way. Just real, true friendship. He was a generous soul. Guileless, upbeat, and giving. He would drop whatever he was doing when she asked for help or a favor or even just something to drink. And while she always sensed that she fell short of reciprocating his particular form of ardent, fiery commitment, she still felt a deep connection to him.

He always had looked a bit to her like he could've been living in another century. Maybe kidnapped by Blackbeard to swab the deck of *The Queen Anne's Revenge* and terrorize merchant ships. Poor Miles. Born to the water. Lost on land.

But he was her other half. A fellow traveler in this harsh, often cruel world. He made her feel less alone in this new Savannah without her grandmother. They would always be there for each other, no matter what.

She squinted up at Miles. It was so hot. She could feel her dress, made of an unbreathable polyester chiffon and purchased at the Goodwill, sticking to her. Drips of sweat were already coursing down her back, tributaries forming a river down her spine and into her ass. But she'd never dream of wearing shorts. Edie hadn't approved of dressing casually for work.

Edie also revered the hot Savannah sun. The sun, the light,

was female, she'd always said. The sun was their Goddess, not a male entity like some believed. The moon was male, only able to reflect the glory of the Goddess. Edie's beliefs weren't like anything Ingrid had read in witchcraft texts or teaching, but they made sense to her. Right now, though, Ingrid wished the Goddess would take it down a notch.

"You're going to need a new roof," Miles shouted down at her. "I did what I could with the extra shingles, but the flashing's a mess. Even the decking is rotted through . . ." He held his hands up, apologetic.

"Okay." She nodded.

"Don't worry about this ship, though. She ain't gonna sink. She's got good . . ." He swung a hand around his head, trying to think of the word. "Um, the heavy stuff, down in the hull?"

"Ballast," she supplied.

"Oh yeah!" He crowed like a lunatic rooster. "She's got good ballast. The heaviest of the heavy, you know? It's you, sitting down there at your table, pulling down all the power of the Goddess." He shook his head. "You're holding it down, Miss Ingrid. You're the ballast."

"All right," she said with false cheeriness. "Okay." She really was starting to dread these pep talks of his. In the end, it wasn't him who had to pay the tax bill.

Miles turned back to the rotting roof.

"Hey—" she yelled up at him, suddenly feeling bad for taking his support for granted.

He appeared again, a grin lighting his eyes. "Hey!"

"Be careful up there."

"Hey," he said back.

She squinted up.

"Those guys give you any trouble?"

She waved him off. "Couple of college dummies. No big deal."

He gave her a look that said he didn't buy it. He knew her so well, which sort of annoyed her. Still, she wasn't about to confess what she'd done. Basically, gone down a dark path and imparted information to a client that, while true, should've been delivered in a far more sensitive way, if at all.

She had been given a gift, the same gift Edie had. She was supposed to use it wisely, not to make a stupid kid feel bad about his life. Not for revenge or any other selfish goal. She was supposed to stay in the light. Edie had told her how important that was the day before she died.

Ingrid knew better.

She just had to buckle down and do what was right.

Chapter 3

Out of the corner of her eye, Ingrid saw the sheer lace curtain in a window of the town house to the right of hers flutter and drop. Behind it, Gloria Ledieu's powdery white face, blue-black hair, that slash of coral lipstick was visible for a brief second. She'd obviously heard the exchange between Ingrid and Miles.

Dried-up, Bible-quoting vampire, Ingrid thought darkly.

Once, when Ingrid was a little girl, Gloria had told Edie she didn't know how Edie could worship Satan and not be afraid of going to hell. Edie hadn't deigned to answer her, but later, when Ingrid asked her about it, she said who had time for someone who didn't know the difference between a pagan and a Satanist, for Pete's sake?

Lately, every time Gloria ran into Ingrid and Miles outside their houses, the old bat said in a pinched, high-pitched, baby voice that she'd buy Ingrid's town house if she ever wanted to sell. She sometimes added that she was praying for them.

Gloria probably couldn't wait for the whole roof to cave in on Ingrid and Miles so she and her red-faced husband, Harmon, could unload their much plainer brick town house next door and buy Ingrid's prettier place. In fact, Gloria Ledieu was probably on her knees right that very moment, before that framed picture of Blond Jesus she had hanging in her living room, practicing her own form of witchcraft—that old Bible magic known as "name it and claim it"—telling God she wanted the place for herself.

Dear Lord, how does a Satan worshipper like Ingrid White deserve to live in such a historically important piece of property? With such intricate ironwork? And plaster ceiling medallions and herringbone oak floors? It's blasphemy, Jesus, that's what it is . . .

Ingrid was glad there was no foot traffic. She wasn't in the right frame of mind. She went back inside and pulled the iron door shut with a deafening clang. She hoped the neighbors heard it, that it had scared the bejesus out of Gloria Ledieu and knocked Blond Jesus off the wall, falling right on that judgey noggin of hers.

Maybe it had given her other neighbor, Dean Remington, a fright, too. Such a fright that one of his precious eighteenth-century French porcelain soup dishes slipped from his pale, elegant fingers and shattered into smithereens on his waxed floor. Old Dean wanted her house as well, so he could make it into an Airbnb that his much-younger husband could run instead of modeling or acting or whatever the guy pretended to do while he actually smoked weed all day by the soaking pool in their manicured courtyard.

But no one was getting this place.

No one.

It was Ingrid's place of business. Her home and her birthright from the last remaining family member she had. This is what the Ledieus and Dean Remington and his lazy husband could never understand. She didn't care how the paint peeled, or the roof leaked. They would carry her out of this place dead before she gave it up.

She closed the inner door, letting her head rest against it. She closed her eyes. All she had on the books for the remainder of the day—a gorgeous Saturday in May, Memorial Day weekend—was a single bachelorette party. One single bachelorette party, when every hotel, bed-and-breakfast, and Airbnb in the city was fully booked. When downtown was crawling with tourists. When no one could get a seat at The Grey or Saint Bibiana or The Olde Pink House, she had one measly bachelorette party.

Despair crashed over her. She was fooling herself to think she could keep her neighbors or anyone else who had enough cash away from this place. She was going to lose her home. It was only a matter of time.

She pushed away from the door. Her hands were shaking, her breath coming out in short, scary puffs. A panic attack. She could feel it coming, and the fear of that was almost greater than the original fear. She had to calm down before the bachelorette party showed up. Otherwise, she couldn't hear anything the Goddess had to say to her. Her readings would bomb, and if that happened, there was no chance of a tip.

Her panic grew. She owed the Chatham County tax commissioner $8,900 in exactly one month. What was she going to do?

Nothing, right now. Right now, she had to calm herself. She looked around the room where she received clients—her grandmother's parlor—and catalogued all the things she saw in the calmest way she could.

Pink marble table (in the center of the room) . . .

Moss-green velvet Victorian settee (by the door) . . .

Threadbare, mismatched armchairs (flanking the settee, there since 1969 when Edie first opened up shop) . . .

She breathed in and out, slowly and steadily. There used to be a grass rug covering the pine floor back then, but when Ingrid had gotten Litha, the cat had scratched it to ribbons, and Edie'd had to throw it on the curb. When her grandmother had taken to her bed, confused from the cancer, and refusing to eat or bathe, Ingrid had dragged a dusty Turkish rug out of one of the guest rooms and down the stairs.

Edie . . .

Edie, where are you? I need you . . .

And yet her grandmother did not appear. Ingrid stood and walked farther into the depths of the garden level, through the warren of bare brick and pine floors that had been Edie's storage rooms. The cramped bathroom had a single light bulb that cast a sickly yellow glow from the ceiling, a corner sink with a crumbly rubber stopper on a chain, and a toilet that sounded like a 747 taking off when it flushed.

She splashed her face with water and looked hard at the medicine cabinet's corroded mirror. She looked paler than usual with shadows under her deep-set hazel eyes. In this light her eyes looked dark and depthless, full of fear. Not good. Not the kind of aura that drew clients in.

She smoothed the curtain of light brown hair that hung around her narrow face, the bangs that lay across her forehead. She swiped under her eyes. Lifted her hands up beside her face and swished outward, brushing away the nasty stuff those boys had brought in with them. *Brush, brush, brush.* All the negative energy moved away from her. Moved to another place. *Wave, wave, wave* in the good, the light, the fortune.

She closed her eyes and pictured Edie. Not the Edie at the very end who lay in bed, thin and gray, hands like claws, with her mouth hanging open, teeth unbrushed because she fought Ingrid's attempts with the toothbrush. Not the Edie ravaged by a cancer of the lungs that made the doctors frown in bewilderment because, not only had the woman never smoked, she hated the smell of cigarettes.

No. She pictured Edie the way she was when Ingrid first came to live with her.

Edith White had been short like Ingrid, with birdlike arms

and long, loose, gray hair held back by twin gold barrettes. She had kind brown eyes and pleasantly wrinkled, pink-as-a-bunny-rabbit skin. The day Ingrid arrived, Edie was wearing a shapeless linen dress, a lavender mohair sweater, and Birkenstocks with moisture-wicking socks. She'd welcomed Ingrid with three brisk kisses, one for each cheek and one on the forehead. Then she had served her a plate of warm gingerbread topped with whipped cream.

Ingrid was six years old and at the time, nobody had explained anything to her. Her mother, Tess, and Tess's nameless boyfriend, not Ingrid's father, had simply dropped her off at Edie's and driven off in a cloud of Dodge Charger exhaust. Edie told her granddaughter that she was there because Edie was a widow and lonely and had wanted Ingrid to come live with her. Had insisted on it, frankly, so many times that Ingrid's mother finally relented and dropped the girl off for a forever sleepover.

But now that she was grown and Tess was lying in a grave somewhere in Florida that Ingrid had never seen, she knew the story was bullshit. A fantasy concocted by a grandmother to make a little girl feel loved. Still, the story made her feel warm inside. It made her love Edie even more.

Eyes closed, Ingrid could see her grandmother in perfect detail. The version who opened the black door of the pink plaster town house when she was six years old, standing alone on the small marble stoop, clutching her nylon duffel bag. Ingrid saw Edie's smile, a smile that bathed her in warm, liquid light. She followed the sharp eyes that darted down to the Dodge idling at the curb, then back up to Ingrid's face. She heard the message they sent: *You are mine now. I will take care of you.*

And she had. She had loved Ingrid and taught her everything she knew. She had left her all her worldly possessions. And she had charged her with a mission, even though that mission remained as murky now as it had when Edie bestowed it two years ago. A bunch of vague talk about righting balances and keeping an eye out for pirates.

It was the cancer talking, she'd convinced herself. Definitely not something she could figure out by trying.

"Edie," Ingrid said now, out into the small bathroom. She mentally bent that very same light that had connected the two of them all those years ago, using it to link her heart to her grandmother's spirit. "We are connected."

The room was still. She could hear Miles banging somewhere above her, up on the roof.

Her brow furrowed as she imagined the light looping around each chamber of her heart, blasting open the valves and shooting directly into her grandmother's spirit. *Help me, Edie. I'm so alone. I don't know what to do. I need your help . . .*

She waited, but the air in the bathroom was still. She opened her eyes. Her face looked exactly the same, except now, there was a distinct bloom of red in the corner of her right eye. Probably a speck of dust from this crumbling house. Great.

She switched off the light in the bathroom and headed back to the parlor. At the old rolltop desk, which had also been her grandmother's, she checked the green-and-gold ledger, where Edie used to record her appointments. It even still had the last few clients Edie had seen before she died, the appointments written on the first few pages in her elegant, slanted handwriting. The ledger was enormous, taking up most of the surface of the desk, with large pages of thick vellum that required an actual finesse when turning them and therefore felt somehow of import. Like she was some kind of medieval mage, thumbing through an ancient codex.

She'd used the ledger when she'd first taken over for Edie, eventually transitioning to the calendar on her laptop for convenience. But that laptop had given up the ghost a few months ago and she didn't have the funds to replace it, so she'd returned to the ledger.

Ingrid flipped the page to the day's date and ran her finger down to the one o'clock line and the name she'd written there.

Sailor Loeffler, bachelorette, 5

As she read the entry, she felt a strange prickling up the back of her neck and over her scalp. Also, at that very same moment, she heard the iron door rattle and whine on its hinges. Then the inner door opened, and sunlight filled both the anteroom and the parlor, almost immediately followed by a heady cloud of multiple brands of perfume.

Ingrid turned toward the open door to greet the party. For a brief moment, she was blinded by the bright sunshine, which made the shadowy parlor look even darker, but then her eyes adjusted, and she was able to perceive the outline of a woman. The woman who stood in front of the others.

Her.

She.

The most important one. The one who mattered.

She stood out from all the rest. *Her . . . she . . .* was tall and willowy and graceful. Dressed in an extremely short, ruffled flower print dress that showed legs, long and sculpted like a ballerina's. Her hair was a cool vanilla blond that spilled over one shoulder and all the way down to her waist. It framed a face made of sharp, smooth, flawless planes with wide-set, startlingly blue eyes. Not merely homecoming-queen pretty, this woman was a real, honest-to-God beauty. When she turned to say something to her friends, the hair swung and wrapped around her shoulders and arms . . .

Salt water and cane sugar, Ingrid thought instantly.

Then the other girls came into sharp focus. Four of them and not girls, actually. Women in their mid-twenties. All beautiful, too, in various ways. Short, tall, curvy. Each impeccably dressed, each bejeweled, carefully coiffed, and expertly made up.

Richies, Miles would call them.

"Oh my God, she's staring at you," said one of them. "She must be seeing something in the spirit world."

There was a ripple of laughter. Ingrid flushed, looked down at the floor.

"Finley." The girl, the leader—*her . . . she*—spoke in the tone of someone who was comfortable being in charge, always being the final word, in both praising and reprimanding. The tittering ceased.

In the sudden quiet, Ingrid looked up. *She* was smiling at her, not with the practiced smirk of an Instagram model but with a pure sincerity. As she did, her eyes crinkled, and her perfectly straight, white teeth flashed.

"Hi, Edie," the girl said to her in a mellifluous voice. "I'm Sailor Loeffler. It's so nice to meet you." She held out her hand, forthright and frank, and Ingrid took it. Squeezed once, gently, then released it.

Weak in the knees. Isn't that what they said when you met your Prince Charming? Ingrid wouldn't know; it had never happened to her. But this . . . this felt like something awfully close to that. Not romantic or sexual. Something much, much more important. Something like destiny.

She finally found her voice. "Edie was my grandmother. I'm Ingrid, actually."

"Ingrid. I love that name."

Ingrid flushed. "Please come in. Everyone."

Ingrid might've said *everyone*, but she kept her eyes on Sailor Loeffler. The words were said to her and her alone, because, in some strange way, in the way Edie had taught her to trust, Ingrid knew that the only one who would ever matter to her in that room, the person who was going to change her life forever, was Sailor Loeffler.

Chapter 4

Ingrid, distracted by her money woes, hadn't realized the Sailor Loeffler in her appointment book was one of *the* Loefflers.

The Loefflers were not just a family, they were Savannah Sauce, the spicy, tangy, peppery condiment everyone in the Southeast (and further afield) put on . . . well, everything they ate. Seafood, beef, chicken, wild game. Barbeque and sandwiches, hot and cold. Whatever was on your plate, Savannah Sauce made it taste better. Some people even dunked their fries in it.

But Savannah Sauce was more than just a condiment; it was an empire. So not only was Sailor Loeffler wealthy, she also belonged to the exclusive, upper echelons of the city's society that people like Ingrid and Miles never dreamed of rubbing elbows with.

Even as Ingrid remembered these things, the minute she set eyes on Sailor Loeffler, she forgot them all over again. Like a disembodied hand sweeping the plastic lever on an Etch A Sketch, *right-whoosh, left-whoosh,* her mind was wiped clean, leaving her brain a glorious, meditative blank. Like how they say if you ever happened to be floating in the void of space, you would hear a peaceful, sustained humming of middle C. It was as if she'd been put in a trance, and all she heard was Sailor Loeffler's perfect middle C.

Sailor was sound and light. The young woman filled up Ingrid's dingy, cramped parlor and bathed everything and everyone inside it with a radiating, pulsating glow. It was both warm and inviting. The kind of light that made you forget about vulture neighbors, caving-in roofs, and soon-to-be delinquent tax bills. The kind of light that, without being too gushy about it, made a person think about possibilities.

About hope.

"Who do you want to take first?" Sailor Loeffler asked Ingrid.

Immediately, the chorus of women behind Sailor sang out—What was she talking about? She was the bride! She was going first!—and pushed Sailor forward. Ingrid smiled and, still pleasantly floating on that sustained, outer space, middle C ringing in her head, escorted Sailor to the back-back room.

What was she doing?

This wasn't where she took clients.

After Edie's death, Ingrid had desperately needed to do something with herself, so instead of doing something nuts like, say, running through Forsyth Park, wailing and rending her garments like some ancient, low-tier Greek goddess, she had cleaned. Swept and scrubbed and polished every inch of every room in the whole house.

And then she'd gotten down to the garden level, the lowest level of the house, which consisted of five rooms: Edie's parlor, where she did readings, the anteroom, where people waited, the bathroom, and two storage rooms, which she called the back-back rooms. The back-back rooms were crammed with boxes and chests and rolling racks of spangled, swingy skirts and peasant blouses, fringed shawls and silk scarves.

Oh, Edie. How full of life and color she'd been. She'd really put on a show in her day. Really leaned into that whole stereotypical gypsy, palm-reader aesthetic. As Ingrid had carefully sorted the costumes, folded them reverently, and put them in stacking plastic bins, which she stored in the smaller of the rooms, she'd finally broken down, sobbing and shaking as she sat on the floor.

Spent at last, she finished the organizing then turned to the larger, now-empty, back-back room. She decided to turn it into her own personal sanctuary, an altar room, so she painted the brick walls a creamy white and borrowed another rug from upstairs, a royal blue Oriental with pink and gold birds of paradise flowers at each corner. In the center of the room, she arranged two white leather chairs on either side of a low Moroccan brass tray table. In one corner, she'd put her favorite floor lamp from upstairs, a large brass and white enamel spray of flowers that looked like it was sprouting out of the floor. Finally, she set up an altar on a breakfront sideboard, covering it with her most treasured relics.

The altar room was where Ingrid meditated and prayed and did all of her most private rituals. She cleaned it thoroughly once a week with lavender oil and Dr. Bronner's, burned incense, and on special occasions, when she did special sun rituals, spritzed perfume from Edie's last remaining bottle of Anaïs Anaïs.

It was Ingrid's most private, sacred space. Miles wasn't allowed in the room, nor was Litha, and she'd certainly never taken a client there. But seeing Sailor Loeffler standing in her parlor seemed to have knocked her off balance. She needed to do this reading somewhere else, in a special place where she could truly address the woman who was standing before her.

Sailor looked around the room. Ingrid could hear a cork pop back in the anteroom and the girls' chatter as they passed around champagne. She shut the door behind them and turned to face Sailor.

"What a lovely space," Sailor said. "Who did it for you?"

Ingrid hesitated. "It's just some of my grandmother's things from upstairs. Why don't you have a seat?" She gestured to one of the white leather chairs and Sailor sat. "Would you like something to drink? Water? Tea?"

Ingrid was acutely aware of her still slightly damp dress that was sticking to her in more than a few awkward places. She could feel the bangs that she'd so carefully smoothed earlier curling at her temples like two little mountain goat horns.

"No, thank you." Sailor glanced around. "This seems like the safest place in the world. It's a little idyll, isn't it?"

Their eyes met then disconnected. Along with being way too tall, too pretty, too perfect to be real, Sailor seemed to be a genuinely nice person. These things surprised Ingrid, although they shouldn't have. Nobody was one thing, were they? *Wealthy, poor, bully . . . witch.* People were complicated.

Ingrid found matches in a box from The Fitzroy Bar on the breakfront. Miles and his little gifts. Like Litha and her dead, velvety moles left on the doormat for Ingrid. She went about lighting the candles, her back to Sailor, as a round of cackling laughter drifted from the front room. Ingrid felt a remnant of that earlier fear swirl around her.

The panic again. What if she couldn't do it—do Sailor's reading? What if her energy was blocked, and she had nothing to say? If she botched this, Sailor would leave and the rest of them would go with her, and Ingrid would be in worse straits than before. They'd give her bad reviews and she'd not only not get any new clients, she could lose the appointments she already had. Her fingers that held the match trembled. The wick caught.

Or . . .

What if she knocked it out of the park?

What if she impressed *the* Sailor Loeffler?

"The wedding's in September," Sailor said, interrupting Ingrid's wild, careening thoughts, and Ingrid realized the match had burned almost down to her fingers. She blew out the match and lit another.

"A little over three months away. We had our real bachelorette last month, in Turks."

Ingrid held the match to the wick of the last candle. It caught and the flame stretched high.

"Turks and Caicos," Sailor went on. "I got us this villa. Spectacular, with a pool and everyone got their own bedroom and bath. There was a butler and a concierge. Yoga every morning . . . or evening, if you wanted. I spent forever planning it . . . spent a lot of . . ." She sighed. "They said they were bored. That there was nothing to do. Can you believe that?"

Ingrid shook her head. She honestly could not. She also couldn't imagine being that rude to anyone who offered her a free tropical vacation.

Sailor let out a caustic laugh. "Don't get me wrong. I love them, I do. It's just, I go to all that effort and the whole time, all they want is some basic bachelorette party in Savannah with the bars and a strip club. Go figure."

Ingrid couldn't resist a smile. It was hard to picture Sailor's fancy friends rampaging their way through town, bearing tumblers filled with cocktails, wearing cowboy boots and tiaras and sashes that read HOT MESS and MAID OF DISHONOR and SHOT QUEEN.

Sailor leaned forward. "They're not from here originally, you know, except Poppy. Her I've known since kindergarten. The rest of them don't really know this place. They think it's what it was back in the nineties. You know, with all that woo-woo mystical stuff they read in the book. All that voodoo priestess stuff. But, I mean, you really think that stuff is better than a five-star resort? Come on. Anyway, whatever. I found one of your flyers in my door, and they were all about it. So here we are."

Ingrid noticed Sailor's gaze had wandered over to the altar. To Ingrid's collection of her grandmother's things. The embroidered shawl. The silver candlesticks, cluster of crystals, jug of grave dirt, and Waterford goblet of water from the Savannah River. There were other things on the altar, too. White tapers, black pillars, the palmetto St. Brigid cross woven by the woman at Forsyth Park's fountain.

"I like your . . ."

"Altar," Ingrid said, sitting in the chair opposite Sailor.

Sailor's blue eyes swerved back to her. "So you're a witch, not a psychic?"

"I'm both."

"You do, like, voodoo?"

"I'm not Haitian or West African. So, no."

Ingrid didn't like getting mired in explaining the details of the particular form of magic she practiced. Edie had taught her a sort of homemade witchcraft, passed down from her ancestors and improvised with every succeeding generation, and more often than not, those conversations usually ended up with Ingrid having to defend why she did some things (prayed to the light) and didn't do others (tarot, for example). Mostly to other women who'd watched *Practical Magic* one too many times and fancied themselves experts.

"Oh," said Sailor. "My mistake."

"May I?" Ingrid nodded toward her lap, where her hands rested, one on top of the other, a mirror of Ingrid's. "Your left first."

Sailor offered her left hand, and, in one quick glance, Ingrid took in the essentials. Soft, smooth skin, the enormous princess-cut, emerald ring, the rounded nails, painted in some type of French manicure, pale pink with narrow brown tips.

And then something strange happened. A flash, behind Ingrid's eyes. A clicking sound along with it.

A picture . . .

A picture taken with a phone then sent as a text. A text slipping into a long chain of words-only messages with a swoop and flashing onto the bright screen of another phone . . .

A series of photos . . .

Bare skin . . .

Slightly out-of-focus breasts . . . small, with peach-pink nipples . . .

Fingers hooked in a black lace thong . . .

Ingrid shivered with dismay and blinked the images away. She hadn't expected that sort of thing, and she really didn't want it. Surely the images weren't connected to Sailor. Maybe some energy leftover from the boys who'd been here earlier. She would start again. Clear her mind and start again.

Chapter 5

"Water hands," Ingrid murmured. "The sign of a highly intuitive, sensitive, and caring person." Ingrid felt a squeeze—Sailor's fingers curling up and tightening around hers. The woman's eyes lifted. She was ill at ease.

Ingrid nodded. "Remember, you determine your life . . . your future. Always. I'm just here to offer encouragement. And maybe a bit of insight."

Sailor let out a nervous breath along with a laugh. "Okay. Sorry."

"No apologies necessary." Ingrid gently spread her hand open again and let the hand, cool and narrow, lie in hers for a moment, attuning herself to the vibrations she felt. They were bold, strong. *Thick.*

Better to focus on what she saw in front of her, not the unsettling, out-of-place images that had first invaded her mind. What a bride-to-be needed was good news.

She traced the line that circled the pad of the thumb. "You have a shorter thumb, indicating you're a bit more on the cautious side, as well as a shorter index finger. You like other people to take the credit, don't you?"

Sailor let out a soft laugh, and Ingrid went through the rest of the fingers and then the palm.

"Your lifeline," she murmured, running her nail along its length, "doesn't tell you how long you're going to live; that's a misconception." She touched different points. "These are increments, or years of your life. Infancy, childhood, ten, twelve, your teenage years. Now here we have your teens, your twenties . . ."

Sailor's eyes were fastened on her.

"Broken lines or islands represent an injury . . . and these intersections that come up from the thumb, those are your guardian angels. People who have died who now look after you from the spirit realm."

Ingrid's voice faltered. She sounded so clinical, like some kind of classroom instructor. Not only that, but she'd suddenly started to feel a little dizzy. Faint and blurry around the edges. The pleasant, trancelike hum that had settled her nerves earlier had stopped, and now she'd broken out in a sweat.

She refocused on Sailor's palm, blinking her eyes a couple of times. "Right here? Did you have a loved one die around the age of eight? I mean, not them. You. When you were eight?"

Sailor shook her head. "My grandmother died when I was sixteen. And the rest of my grandparents are still alive. So I don't know who that could be."

"Oh, well." Ingrid cleared her throat. "I see a bit of an island around that time, too. When you were eight. Did you experience some sort of injury or maybe a hospitalization at that time?"

Sailor cocked her head. "I don't think so. I can't remember any." The light in her blue eyes had dimmed, and there was a set to her mouth and jaw, making her lips purse the slightest bit.

Ingrid might not be able to read Sailor's palm worth a crap, but she could read her face with no problem. She'd been nice to

Ingrid because she was that kind of person, but now the curtain across her eyes had closed. She was over this whole situation.

Ingrid's mind shot out wildly in all directions: *wedding, bridesmaids, Savannah, Turks and Caicos, the blue sea, as blue as her eyes, a boat bobbing over it, sails out, tipping to one side . . .*

Shit.

That wasn't helping one bit, letting her panic churn out a bunch of random nonsense. In fact, it was making everything worse. She was getting more and more flustered. And time was ticking by—*shit, shit, shit*—while nothing was being said. All she had to fill was fifteen minutes, fifteen stupid minutes, and even that had turned into an eternity . . .

Edie, she thought desperately. *Edie, I need you!*

Sailor had, ever so tactfully, started to pull her hand back, but Ingrid tightened her grip. Sailor looked up, a hint of alarm in her eyes—and then Ingrid felt a clean, sharp light fill her, like the blast of a nuclear bomb.

A memory of Edie, one early spring day. Tess had only recently dropped Ingrid off, and she was still feeling shy around her grandmother. At the top of every hour, when the old clock on the parlor mantel chimed, Edie had led Ingrid around the house, to the spots where the brightest block of sunlight shone on the floor. From the stair landing to the kitchen, to the front hall and the back bedroom, they followed the sun's movement across the Savannah sky.

In each instance, the two would stand together in the light, hands clasped, while Edie did a ritual. Not from any book, but one that Ingrid realized later Edie had learned from her own grandmother:

Gather strength,
As the clock waxes.
Gather courage,
As the day wanes.

I gather, you gather,
And what we gather shall grow,
So in the bloom of night, we shine forth.

Now Ingrid sat straighter, the memory of that light bringing a sharp certainty. She inhaled and looked Sailor dead in the eyes.

"Your mother won't ruin the wedding," she said.

The words had propelled their way from someplace inside her, in a way that she knew she hadn't drummed up the thought or premeditated it in any way. And she felt that rush she sometimes got—that singular, unmistakable high she felt when she knew she'd tuned into the right frequency.

Across from her, Sailor looked startled, her eyes gone wide and alert, her body rigid in the chair.

Go, go, go, Ingrid told herself. It was the same thing she chanted on the beach in April when she wanted to run into the cold Atlantic surf. *Don't think. Don't hesitate. Just dive in. DIVE IN!*

"Your mother is a problem, but not an unfixable one," she said.

Sailor's face sharpened into focus. Tears filmed her eyes making them shine. Her mouth opened.

"Your father's the tough one. The one who won't listen, but he loves you. He won't do anything to ruin your day. But he's not the one . . ." Ingrid saw the drooping of Sailor's shoulders, the way her eyebrows had knitted together then raised. "It's your *brother* you worry about, isn't it? The path is laid out for him, but he's still so lost."

Sailor sat back, her eyes fastened on Ingrid.

And now Ingrid was seeing more.

Empty rooms.

A gathering in an office . . .

Fire . . .

The middle C hum had started up again, louder now, a singular note that banished everything else from her brain. Incense wafted through the hum. A whiff of Edie's perfume. Ingrid thought of the four elements represented on her altar—earth, air, fire, water. She saw them swirling together, a holy assembly of the natural order.

She opened her mouth to speak again, but . . . there . . . she could feel Edie in the room. *Raised eyebrow over warm brown eyes. A cluck of the tongue*. A gentle warning. Edie had always taught her that predicting the future with too much specificity was presumptuous. Their job was to interpret, not prophesy.

Ingrid closed her mind's eye to her dead grandmother's face and focused on Sailor. "He loves you, the man you're going to marry."

Sailor sat motionless.

"Ballast," Ingrid said. "You're his ballast."

A moment of utter silence. Utter stillness.

And then, "How did you know that's what he calls me?" Sailor whispered.

Ingrid shook her head.

"He says it's because I keep him steady," Sailor said.

"You keep a lot of people steady, don't you?" Ingrid leaned forward. "You keep your father's business humming. Even though he doesn't see it. You . . . you're a marketing . . . type of person, right? Promotions? Partnerships? But a leader at heart."

"How did you . . ." Sailor started to say, then shook her head with a smile. "Sorry. I guess that's your job. I mean, it's amazing. Actually, I can't believe you just said all that."

Ingrid smiled back at her. She didn't know where that word had come from, except . . . Miles, working up on the roof, had said it, earlier, hadn't he? That might've been why it was in her short-term memory, but she knew it was more than that. Much more. She had connected with Edie.

Now, instead of the disdain, disbelief, and disgust she'd seen earlier today in those boys' eyes . . . that she realized she'd been expecting to see in Sailor Loeffler's eyes . . . she saw something else entirely.

She saw trust.

Chapter 6

The next two hours were a blur.

For Ingrid, it was like surfing, riding the wave that she had unexpectedly caught with Sailor. She read palms and auras in a heady, fevered rush, never knowing what words would come out of her mouth. Edie and the Goddess had seen her need, felt her desire, and together they had granted her this beautiful, blessed favor.

Afterward in the anteroom, the other girls chatted away, laughing and passing around what was left of the champagne. Sailor pressed something into Ingrid's hand.

"Thank you so much."

"That's really not necessary," Ingrid said. Still, her fingers closed around the gratifyingly thick fold of cash.

"You deserve it." Sailor watched as her bridal party spilled through the door out onto the sidewalk. It was still radiating heat but shadier now because of the position of the afternoon sun and the canopy of trees. Ingrid reached out and grabbed her arm.

No! What was she doing?

She couldn't . . . wouldn't . . . shouldn't say that . . .

"She's been sending him pictures," Ingrid said as quickly as she could, before she could chicken out.

Sailor looked like she'd been slapped. She hesitated, her lips parting, then moistened them with the tip of her tongue. She breathed deeply, pressing her lips together again, her eyes following her friends now laughing on the sidewalk.

Oh no. No. You've ruined it.

You've ruined everything—

Ingrid gulped. "I don't know why I said . . . that. I don't want to cause a problem. Sorry."

"It's Finley, right?" Sailor's eyes burned into her.

Ingrid hesitated.

"I need to know. Please. Go on. She's not sending pictures to Jude, is she? My fiancé?"

Ingrid shook her head. "I'm pretty sure it's . . . someone else . . . someone close to you. Sorry," she said again.

Sailor sucked in her cheeks, thinking. After a moment, she shook her head. "Damn it. Shit. I told her to stay away from him. That he was vulnerable. I *warned* her."

"I'm really, really sorry." Ingrid wished she could think of something else to say.

Sailor turned to her. "Don't be. Honestly, there aren't that many people that would do that. Tell me the truth. You're a really brave person, Ingrid."

Ingrid blinked. "Oh."

"I could kill her," Sailor muttered. "She's definitely out of the wedding. I'm done with her. Finished."

Ingrid cracked her knuckles nervously. "Maybe you should give it some thought— "

Sailor looked grim. "Oh hell, no. This isn't her first infraction, believe me. I've just got to figure out a time I can get her alone to tell her. *Fuck*."

Ingrid waited awkwardly, and then Sailor turned back to her

and tilted her head, suddenly regarding Ingrid like she was seeing her for the first time.

"I know it's last minute, but if you don't have anything else to do tonight . . . I'd love if you could come to a party. My engagement party. It's at my house, my parents' house. I'd . . . I'd really love it if you could make it. For moral support."

Sailor's eyes held a pleading expression, and Ingrid knew, with full and complete certainty, that asking for favors was not something Sailor Loeffler usually did. But she was doing it now, and Ingrid felt a delicious frisson of anticipation.

"I'd love to come," she said in a breathy voice.

"Oh." A surprised, relieved smile broke over Sailor's pretty face. "Oh gosh, Ingrid, you will? Wow. Thank you. I really appreciate it."

Ingrid nodded back at her.

"It's at seven."

A head appeared in the open doorway, one of the blondes. "Sailor, come on!" she said. "We need to get back to the hotel to have enough time to prep for the party." Gales of uproarious drunken laughter erupted beyond her.

"Coming." Sailor turned back to Ingrid. "It's the Noble Hardee Mansion on Monterey Square. Southwest corner."

Of course. Ingrid knew where the Loefflers lived. The Noble Hardee Mansion presided over the corner of West Gordon and Bull Street on Monterey Square, a palatial huge cream-and-gold Italianate house with grand windows and miles of cast iron balconies and balustrades. The house was reported to have fifteen fireplaces and had hosted at least one president in its illustrious history.

Ingrid must've walked past the place at least twice a day, every day of her life—or at least since she'd come to live with Edie. In fact, Ingrid had often looked up into the windows of the mansion, trying to catch a glimpse of the mysterious people who spent their days and nights in such grandeur and wondering what the rooms looked like behind the curtains. Wondering, too, how people who lived in a house like that spent their time.

Soon she would know.

"Seven o'clock. I'll be there."

Sailor lunged toward her, wrapping her arms around her in a warm, bracing hug. Ingrid was enveloped by a heady mixture of expensive-smelling body and hair products. She froze, unsure of what to do.

"I had no idea today was going to turn out this way," Sailor said, holding her tightly. "I can't believe it. I really can't. I'm going to tell everyone I know to come see you, I hope you're okay with that. You're going to have more business than you can handle, I guarantee."

"SaySay! Come on!" The same girl who'd stuck her head inside the door before saw them hugging and frowned.

Sailor released Ingrid. "I've got to go. Thank you again, from the bottom of my heart. You'll never know what you've done. And . . ." She leaned in again, adding in a whisper, "Wish me luck."

"Oh. Yes. Of course. Good luck."

Sailor hurried to the door and then she was gone. Ingrid heard a waft of conversation as the women made their way down the sidewalk, just a comment one of the bridal party made as they trouped to their next destination.

"Oh my God, that whole thing was so fucking creepy!"

Finley, she thought, of the black lace thong and the texted pictures. She was the soon-to-be ex-bridesmaid. The one about to be dismissed from Sailor's presence. And Ingrid was going to the party.

Ingrid couldn't help but smile.

Chapter 7

After locking the door and blowing out the candles, Ingrid practically floated upstairs. On the main level of the town house, she stopped in the narrow front hall, Litha twisting around her ankles, rubbing her silky white pelt against Ingrid's skin.

All told, she had come away with $1,235 from the day. With enough appointments in the coming days—which she'd get if Sailor really spread the word like she promised—she'd be able to pay at least part of her tax bill. And maybe that would be okay, if she told them she had more clients coming. Maybe they'd give her a break.

Just like that, Ingrid was living in a new life. Looking at a new beginning. Sailor Loeffler was sending her work. She had said she needed her. Ingrid had done it.

Well, she and Edie together.

Now she surveyed the front hall of her home with new eyes. She saw the mauve and blue striped wallpaper in the cramped entryway, installed back in the sixties when Edie first moved in. It still looked pretty good, in spite of the occasional water stain and peeling strip. The chandelier, original to the house and made of brass and crystal, was missing a few bulbs. The small rug at the door needed a good deep clean. The hall tree resembled a small gothic throne.

What would Sailor think of the place if Ingrid were to bring her up here? If Ingrid were to have a party, something small and intimate and invite just a few people? Even though now these row houses went for millions, they had been built for simple, middle-class workers. The rooms were small and serviceable. A sitting room, dining room, and small kitchen. Upstairs, two rooms and a tiny bath. Third floors, if you were lucky enough to have one like Ingrid, held maybe two more bedrooms. Rarely another bathroom.

She pictured throwing a party at her house. Sailor and her friends, mingling, drinking, listening to music . . .

Stupid. What was she even thinking? Ingrid didn't throw parties. She mostly hung out with Miles's friends. Miles's work friend, Boney. Mari, who cleaned rooms at a couple of B and Bs and led the occasional pub crawl. Fran was a server at Common Thread; Louella drove an Uber.

Anyway, when would it ever be appropriate for Ingrid to have Sailor in her house? She couldn't think of a single instance. Sailor might've gotten carried away because Ingrid had called out a supposed friend for sexting someone she shouldn't have, but that didn't make her and Ingrid friends. Not yet anyway, said a little voice inside Ingrid.

Not yet . . .

She felt arms encircle her from behind, tightening bands of muscle, hairy arms, the press of sweat against her back. The smell of tar, sunshine, and sweaty male body.

"Budgie," Miles said in a singsong voice. Her grandmother's nickname for her. She wished she'd never told him about it. He acted like it belonged to him.

Miles was an ambush hugger, a lot like an overeager, poorly trained puppy. She usually didn't mind the hugging and cheek kissing and nickname-appropriating, but right now, his affectionate behavior was getting on her nerves.

Gingerly, she extricated herself from the hug and put enough distance between them that Miles couldn't spring another one on her. "How much longer for the roof?" she asked.

"I think you've got a couple of months. As long as it's done raining."

It was never done raining in Savannah. She let out a growl of frustration. Why couldn't this house just work with her? Just hang in there until business got better and all Sailor's friends started coming around?

"Want me to fix ramen?" Miles was walking back toward the kitchen. "I can put an egg on it and some chili oil. We have scallions, too."

"I'm going out."

He stopped and spun a slow one-eighty. She couldn't see his expression in the shadows of the long hall, but she could feel his curiosity. She could feel him studying her. She briefly considered lying about it all—Sailor, the fantastically successful reading, the engagement party she'd been invited to that night. She could tell the story in a different way, and he wouldn't push. He wasn't the type to push.

But in the next instant, she saw how knotty that could get. The work it would take to keep Miles from finding out she'd gone to the party. To keep him in the dark about Sailor.

"Sailor Loeffler invited me to her engagement party tonight," she said, forcing herself to sound nonchalant.

"Oh yeah?" He emerged from the shadow and into a pale circle of light cast by the brass sconce between them. Now she could see his face. He simply looked interested, that was all.

She summarized the events of the past few hours. The reading, Sailor's reaction, everything. The whole time she was speaking, his face remained pleasantly blank, his eyes unfocused and looking past her.

When she was finished, he nodded once, vaguely. "You'll eat there, then."

"Miles."

"What?" Now he was focused on her.

"Are you mad?"

"Why would I be mad?" It was impossible to read him, and that worried her.

"You know. Those people . . ."

He pursed his lips and started nodding. "I mean, yeah— "

". . . they're so . . ." She made a face.

He nodded and made the same face. That's what all of their friends thought about people like the Loefflers. The richies. Standoffish, entitled, annoying. They lived inside the mansions. On a different planet, never mixing with the workers. The poors.

"Right." He dropped his hands in the pockets of his dingy, paint-spattered chinos. "They're probably not that different from us, though. Really."

She knew neither one of them believed that for a second. They'd both grown up in Savannah, where the line between *in* and *out* was very clearly marked. The richies were as different from them as they could possibly be.

"I probably won't stay long."

He finally looked directly at her. His bright blue eyes did not hold any malice. If anything, he looked sad. Sad and far younger than his twenty-six years. "It's okay if you do. Litha and I won't watch ahead."

He was talking about *The Twilight Zone.* All one hundred and fifty-six episodes were on YouTube, and they'd made it all the way to number seventy-three. Her heart ached a little. Miles was alone in the world, too. His real mother, a runaway like hers. They'd bonded over that one. There weren't that many people who got dropped off by their mothers for other people to raise.

His adoptive father was a drunk who lost his shrimping boat for violations of harvest regulations. The boat Miles would've inherited at some point. His mother was dead, and he had no siblings or extended family. All Miles had was Ingrid . . . and vice versa. How many times had she told him that since they'd first met? And she'd meant it. Now she felt like she was somehow backing out of some kind of promise she'd made to him.

She touched his hand. "Thank you for taking care of the roof."

He shrugged. "No problem. Didn't have much else going on today."

"You don't have a tour tonight?"

"I gave Boney all my groups."

Miles had been looking forward to eating ramen in front of *The Twilight Zone* with her and Litha. Boney, or "Bone Man," would be who Miles meant. He was called that by everyone around Savannah on account of his shockingly good facial bone structure but also how he supposedly had, in his travels around town, come across the delicate digits of what he claimed was a portion of a human hand from the early 1700s. He carried the hand around in a leather pouch, producing it for his tour groups and telling them it belonged to the famous Yamacraw Indian chief Tomochichi, who worked with General James Oglethorpe, the founder of the colony of Georgia and architect of Savannah (which it did not).

So far, the owner of the ghost tour company had received numerous complaints from customers alleging ghoulish and unseemly behavior on Boney's part, as well as misrepresentation, cultural appropriation, and outright illegal possession of human remains. But with his good looks and theatrical talents, Boney wasn't about to get fired. Women adored him and he brought in a lot of business.

Ingrid peered up the narrow staircase. "I should go shower. I've got to find something to wear that's not filthy." Or torn or cheap looking or that didn't smell like mothballs. Which eliminated practically every article of clothing in this house.

"I'll help you pick something out," Miles offered. "We should look in Edie's closet. You should wear something of hers. It'll be like she's going to the party with you."

She smiled at him, understanding this was his version of a peace offering. He wasn't mad after all. Everything was going to be fine.

Chapter 8

After she showered, they met on the second floor outside the Daffodil Room, Edie's room. They called it that because of the delicate, pale yellow-and-green daffodil paper covering the walls. Ingrid usually kept its door closed, only going in to clean once every other week. She'd certainly never rifled through her grandmother's closet. But today was different.

For so many reasons, Miles's idea felt right.

Now as she opened the door and they tiptoed in, she took in the familiar art deco walnut bedroom set, the bed trimmed in white lace. A pastel of a centaur hung over the black marble fireplace, the one that Ingrid always thought of as "Sexy Mr. Tumnus." On the mantel below sat three silver-framed pictures: Edie with her husband, Ingrid's grandfather. Edie holding an adorable, toddler-aged Tess. Edie, her arms wrapped around a twelve-year-old Ingrid, planting a kiss on her cheek. There was no picture of Tess as an adult.

Miles was already sifting through Edie's closet, eyeing each dress critically. But he kept pulling out laughably out-of-style options: a full-length, double-knit pantsuit; a prairie dress made out of what looked like a patchwork quilt; a white-fringed minidress. Everything was so old and smelled very musty.

Finally, Ingrid found a full-length, pale-yellow silk chiffon slip dress with a kimono style overshirt, both hand-painted with pink and green tulips, that smelled reasonably pleasant, and they agreed this was the best option. While she arranged her hair in a twist, Miles found a pair of white patent leather sandals in the back of the closet. One heel was a bit scuffed, and he pulled up the bottom of his T-shirt, spit on it, and polished the blocky heel.

"Ugh, Miles," Ingrid said. "Stop."

He winked and handed over the shoe. She applied a bit of makeup—blush, mascara, some lipstick—and when she spun before Miles for a final look, he held up a finger.

"Earrings."

She kicked off the sandals and ran down to her altar room. From the jewelry box on the breakfront, she selected a pair of white enameled dogwood blooms, clip-ons, the only kind Edie ever wore. Ingrid picked up her bottle of Anaïs Anaïs, small and white with the peachy flowers that matched her dress and shook it.

There wasn't much left of the perfume, and she probably shouldn't have wasted it on a party, since she tried to only use it in her most sacred rituals, but what Miles had said made her think. She needed Edie with her at the Loefflers' tonight. After all, her grandmother was the one who'd helped her with Sailor's reading that day.

Ingrid carefully removed the cap and sprayed her neck once, then twice, closing her eyes as the mist hit her nose.

Edie, be here . . .

Be with me tonight.

Maybe it was just the dress, but Ingrid could feel her grandmother all around her. She could smell her, and not just because of the perfume. She could also smell the faint aroma of bacon that always clung to her. The cherry almond of Jergens hand lotion. The incense smoke that always permeated the air around her. Edie was here, now, floating above her. Moving through her.

She put the cap back on the bottle, switched off the light, and ran back upstairs. Miles was waiting in the front hall, and Litha was perched on the staircase.

"Want me to walk you over?" Miles's eyebrows converged over his nose. It was bent at the bridge from a childhood accident on his father's shrimping boat. Ingrid didn't know if he'd fallen or been hit by the trawling mechanism. Or been hit by his father. He didn't talk much about those days.

She shook her head. It might be selfish of her, but she wanted Sailor Loeffler all to herself. "I'm okay. I'll be fine," she said, then was suddenly gripped by guilt. She clasped his hand. "Go get the money sitting on my dresser. It's yours."

He shook his head.

"Edie was there for me today, Miles, but you're the reason I had that word in my head—*ballast.* You're the reason I said it to her. The money's yours." She gave his hand a reassuring squeeze.

He opened the front door for her. She walked out onto the stoop, staring at the curving marble steps and iron banister that led down to the street. The street that led to the square that led to the mansion where her new friend, Sailor, waited for her help.

She took each step carefully, mindful of the slightly too-large sandals and chiffon fluttering around her feet. The uneven brick sidewalk in front of the town house glistened. It must've rained while she was getting ready, one of those brief Savannah showers. She stopped. Touched her hair. She felt different somehow, like a new person.

"All gussied up and nowhere to go," called a voice from behind her.

She turned. Next door, Dean Remington, in a crisp, blue seersucker suit and peach bow tie, tipped an imaginary hat to her from his front porch. He looked like a librarian with his head of graying curls and round tortoiseshell glasses.

"I've got somewhere to go," she called back, airily. "Sailor Loeffler's engagement party."

He frowned. "No." *Naw*, it came out.

"Yes," she deadpanned and flounced away down the street past Taylor Square. She might not have a full bank account, but her confidence overflowed. Dean Remington would not be getting her house. Nor would Gloria and Harmon Ledieu. She was going to pay all her bills soon and keep doing what she loved.

Sailor Loeffler had changed everything.

In the distance, she could see cars drawing toward Monterey Square, the southern end, where the Loeffler mansion lay. More people, dressed in suits and evening gowns that sparkled in the streetlamps, streamed down Drayton and Bull Streets in the direction of the house.

When Ingrid reached Monterey Square, she stepped up onto the curb. Ahead, in the center of the square beside the tall, white marble Pulaski monument, she saw Boney standing with his tour group. Miles's group.

Boney was decked out in a black T-shirt, tailcoat, Converse, and top hat, making him look like some kind of goth ringmaster. The group surrounding him was big, at least two dozen people, and they seemed especially boisterous. Probably a bunch of bachelor and bachelorette parties. Boney was holding his leather, finger-holding sachet aloft while he orated. Several of the women in the group were giggling and eyeing him lasciviously. He sent Ingrid a salute and she waved back.

But her conscience panged. With a group that size, Miles would've done well in tips. She was glad she'd told him to take the day's earnings. She should also set aside some time for him tomorrow after work. Make some banana bread and watch *The Twilight Zone* with him. Tell him every detail about Sailor Loeffler's engagement party.

No. She'd do one better than that.

She'd bring him something from the Loeffler house. A gift, like the odds and ends he was always bringing her. Just a little thing, nothing major. A stack of monogrammed cocktail napkins or a book of matches. A reminder that she valued him. That she appreciated his friendship and all he did for her.

She squared herself and lifted her chin, feeling the wisps of her updo tickle the back of her neck. As she walked down the path, past the towering monument, toward the house blazing with light, she caught a bit of Boney's spiel.

"Beware, my friends, beware. Henceforth, you venture onto sacred ground, the domain of those who see beyond the veil, the domain of the dead . . ."

Chapter 9

She couldn't believe she was walking up the stairs to the Noble-Hardee Mansion. The Loeffler mansion. Couldn't believe she was walking through the open doors and into the huge entryway. Couldn't believe she, Ingrid White, was at the engagement party for Sailor Loeffler. At Sailor's special request.

Inside, she took in the space with awe. The house was massive. The ceilings soared; the hall stretched for days. An enormous crystal chandelier glittered above her head. The walls of the foyer were painted in some kind of shimmery, pale green, fairy-tale forest mural with iridescent flowering vines, peacocks, and hummingbirds. The staircase, its ornate banister rising from a heavily carved newel post, was carpeted in a thick Persian runner. She couldn't see any of the rooms of the next floor, but she heard them. There were people all over this vast, ornate house.

"Ingrid."

Sailor, wearing a long, low-cut, plum-colored, silk jumpsuit and dangling diamond earrings, stood to her right. She was holding a pink crystal glass full of some mysterious drink.

"You made it." She rushed forward, grabbed Ingrid's arm with her free hand, and kissed her cheek. A real kiss, not an air one.

A svelte woman in all-black with a sleek bun materialized on her other side. "Good evening, miss. Your drink for the evening?"

"She'll have one of these." Sailor held up her glass. The server nodded and vanished, and Sailor turned to Ingrid with an intimate whisper. "I'm so glad you were able to make it. I was worried for a minute you might think it was some kind of . . ." She trailed off. "I don't know. I'm just really glad you're here. I confronted Finley right after we left your place. She admitted all of it—the sexting—that witch." She caught herself. "Sorry. I didn't mean it that way."

"It's okay." Ingrid was dying to know who Finley had been sending those pictures to, but she didn't dare ask. It wasn't her business. Maybe when Sailor trusted her more.

"This is a really nice party," Ingrid said. "So many people."

"Yeah." Sailor's smile looked grim. "My parents have a lot of friends." The server was at Sailor's elbow again, smoothly transferring a pink glass into Ingrid's hand.

Sailor clinked her glass with Ingrid's. "They created a specialty cocktail just for the event. It's called a We Sail at Sunset. Watch out. There's more tequila in it than you'd expect."

Ingrid nodded and sipped along with Sailor. She realized she was staring at a handsome, older man who had materialized at Sailor's side. He dropped a kiss on the top of Sailor's head. Her father, Ingrid thought. But no, that couldn't be her father. Sailor was grinning at him like a thirteen-year-old girl staring into the face of a beloved, pop-star crush.

"Ingrid, this is Jude Etris, my fiancé."

Jude Etris looked like a young, hip, bald Abraham Lincoln. He had a craggy face with the sharpest set of cheekbones Ingrid had ever seen on a human, and he wore a silky black shirt and cream linen pants and a thin gold link chain around his neck.

"Ingrid's the psychic I told you about," Sailor said to Jude.

"Pleasure." Jude spoke with an English accent, and he pursed his lips as he swept Ingrid with a glance. "I can't imagine the sheer psychic bombardment you must be getting at this very moment. House like this. *People* like this." He smiled wryly and Ingrid liked him at once.

"Jude and I met when he agreed to use and sell Savannah Sauce in his hotels," Sailor said.

Jude gave her a loving look. "When I tasted the white vinegar barbecue, I knew I had to meet the great-granddaughter of the man who invented it."

Sailor rolled her eyes and addressed Ingrid. "Ridiculous."

Jude laughed and kissed her. "Darling, I know you want to play with your friends, but we've got work to do."

Sailor flipped her hair, addressing Ingrid. "Jude's opening a hotel in town. I keep telling him this is a party, not a sales meeting—"

"Darling, every party is a sales meeting." Jude kissed her again, on top of the head, and surrendered himself to the vortex of guests. Sailor hesitated only a second, watching him go with a tender expression. Then she turned and took Ingrid's hand.

"He'll be fine. Come on. I'll show you around."

The house may have blazed with light on the outside, but inside was dimly lit, as shadowy as a romantic restaurant. Each room was lavishly decorated with antiques and crammed with people. Also laden with food. Each room had a theme: low country boil in one sitting room. Tex-Mex in the next. Brunch in the dining room, and pastas and antipasti in the library. A cello played somewhere—the music room, she discovered eventually—and with it, the voices created a raucous symphony.

Following Sailor, Ingrid passed guests, mostly older than her.

The men wore suits or blazers, were red-faced and laughed boisterously. Snippets of conversation jumped out at her. Somebody named Stephen had gotten "the *box* in Vegas for the *game*." Another said Joe had timed his sprinklers to turn on right when the nightly ghost tours arrived at his house. A man spoke loudly about how the folks new to town might accept that they were a part of what the town had become—*the Disneyfication of Savannah*, he called it—but by God, the old-timers hadn't signed up for any of this nonsense.

The women were beautiful and brittle. They wore severely stylish dresses accented with bold jewelry, hair and makeup impeccably understated. Ingrid had the feeling Sailor had carefully chosen who to introduce her to. *Devlin is on the board of SCAD, she restored over one hundred and forty-six historic preservation projects in town; Patty Jo's husband is a judge; Clemmie and Lulu, sisters, know* all *the artists in town.*

"Ingrid runs her grandmother's business," Sailor told them all. "Miss Edie's over on East Taylor. She's absolutely the most gifted psychic-witch in town. I can attest to it."

Recognition lit up most every eye, outright glee in a few.

One woman clutched Ingrid's shoulder. "I adored Miss Edie. I used to see her every week, back in the nineties. She single-handedly got me through my divorce."

"Oh, Ingrid's just as good," Sailor said. "She's booked so far out, I couldn't believe my wedding party even got in."

The woman's expression turned to one of panic. "My God. I must have my girl call first thing in the morning. I didn't realize how much I've missed that sort of guidance in my life. A little more feminine and intuitive than Reverend Fowry."

The other women tittered. Sailor sent Ingrid a sly wink. The first woman peered into Ingrid's eyes, reached out to finger a tendril of her hair. "You're so pretty, dear."

Sailor steered Ingrid away from the ladies and toward the

kitchen. When Sailor pushed open the swinging door, Ingrid was greeted with a sight that resembled the inside of an ant hill. The catering team, all in black and white, scurried about the room, stirring pots, chopping vegetables, depositing empty trays, and collecting filled ones. Ingrid thought she recognized one of the team, a redheaded girl, Sasha. A friend of Miles and Boney's. Recognizing her, the girl seemed startled but quickly moved on.

Sailor had pulled a woman from the throng. She was short, plump, with a dark bob and wore round tortoiseshell glasses on a chunky Lucite chain. Dressed in a plain gray suit with sharp lapels, she stared at Ingrid, a grim set to her thin lips.

"This is our house manager, Mrs. Leimberger." Sailor beamed at the scary woman. "Mrs. Leimberger, I'd like you to meet Ingrid White."

Ingrid opened her mouth to speak but Mrs. Leimberger cut her off. "I have your business address and phone. Is there a personal cell I can have on file for Miss Loeffler?"

"She means me," Sailor said apologetically.

Mrs. Leimberger handed Ingrid her phone. "Input there, if you please." Ingrid typed in her number, then the woman reached around to tap at the screen. "Excellent. And here's the number of Adrian, the family's driver. He'll be the one collecting you for appointments."

Ingrid glanced over at Sailor. "Collecting me?"

Sailor looked at Mrs. Leimberger. "I'll be walking to any appointments I have with Ingrid."

"Whatever you prefer, Miss Loeffler, but we've already had several guests requesting Miss White's number," said Mrs. Leimberger. "Guests who prefer in-home services."

Sailor lifted a tentative brow at Ingrid. "Is that okay?"

"Oh," Ingrid said, startled. "That's fine. I'm happy to provide . . . in-home services. Readings. For anyone." Not that she had ever done such a thing. Not that she even knew the possibility existed. Edie had never gone to clients' houses for readings, she didn't think.

"Excellent." Mrs. Leimberger clicked off her phone. "I also need your bank information—"

"Mrs. Leimberger," Sailor interrupted. "We can discuss this later. After the party."

"Certainly." The woman nodded once, curtly, and smiled.

"On top of everything, as always," Sailor said.

"Have a wonderful evening," Mrs. Leimberger said. "Congratulations on your engagement." To Ingrid, "Miss White. A pleasure."

Before Ingrid could reply, the woman was gone. Sailor looked slightly embarrassed. "I happened to mention to her earlier that we'd had a wonderful reading, and I wanted to schedule standing appointments."

Ingrid's heart leapt violently. Standing appointments meant regular money.

"She's an absolute maniac, but she runs this place . . . this family . . . like a five-star general. Which is sort of a necessity, as you'll see when you meet my mother."

Ingrid nodded, taking it all in.

"It's no big deal, I promise. I do this with my massage therapist, my stylist, colorist, aesthetician, et cetera—basically, put them on retainer. It just makes it so much easier if we can deposit payments directly into your account, and you're always available if I need a last-minute appointment."

Ingrid felt slightly dizzy.

"But if that's too invasive, just say the word."

"No, not at all. That works." Ingrid's body felt warm, but maybe that was from the drink in the pink glass. It was empty now, she noticed, and just as she did, a server appeared, deftly replacing the empty glass with a full one. "Thank you." The server nodded and was gone.

Sailor took her hand. "Come on, let's go upstairs." She pulled Ingrid back toward the cavernous hallway, which Ingrid now saw held its own buffet tables of tiny, jewel-like chocolates in every shape and size. The hall was full of guests now, exponentially louder than before, and before they reached the staircase, a male voice boomed from the crowd.

"Sails, my love! Introduce me to your friend!"

Chapter 10

Ingrid turned to see a tall man, in his fifties, tan and lean, with a head of thick salt-and-pepper hair and a layer of fashionable stubble on his sharp jaw. His suit was a cornflower blue. His white shirt was crisp, unbuttoned to the third button, its sleeves fastened with skull and bones cufflinks. His face was sun-weathered, wrinkled but glowing with good health. A pair of cornflower-blue eyes, the same color as the suit, appraised her with a disarming frankness. He looked like a movie star.

"Daddy," Sailor squealed in a little-girl voice and flung herself at the man. He caught her in one crooked arm and moved his line of sight from her to Ingrid, who found herself suddenly glued to the spot, caught in the tractor beam of his gaze.

"Daddy, this is Ingrid White. Ingrid, my father, Aurelian Stokes Loeffler III."

"Rill." The man was extending his hand now, his lips curling into a languid smile. Ingrid felt herself propelled forward, her hand enveloped in the man's strong, warm grip. "I've heard so much about you, Ingrid."

Ingrid couldn't stop herself from giving Sailor a questioning look.

"I've told everybody about you," Sailor said. "I'm such a tattletale."

"She said you got her dead to rights," Rill Loeffler said. His voice was smooth and deep, tinged with that old Southern-sweet accent people older than her still had. Ingrid felt a little bit hypnotized. "You have a gift. Just like your grandmother did."

Before Ingrid had time to absorb these words and what they implied—he had known Edie?—Rill had pivoted her to face a tall, thin woman who was so strikingly beautiful she almost didn't look real. "This is my wife, Scoot."

The woman was an older version of Sailor. Blond like her daughter, but with a finer, more chiseled bone structure that put Ingrid in mind of some Nordic queen of a European country. Her hair was bobbed messily, and she wore almost no makeup. She wore a blue silk caftan that hit the floor, which was tied with a tasseled gold rope. She held a glass of brown liquid with an orange peel in it.

Bitter orange and woodsmoke, Ingrid thought.

Scoot Loeffler . . . such an unlikely name for Southern royalty. The woman took hold of her wrist and leaned over to air-kiss her cheek. The pungent tang of alcohol hovered around her, and Ingrid felt the edge of Edie's enameled dogwood earring jab painfully into the tender skin behind her ear as Scoot pressed her temple against Ingrid's.

Regal, almond-shaped eyes observed Ingrid. "My dear, I am so honored to meet you. Sailor's told us all about you, and we're just so grateful for your generosity of spirit."

Scoot had the same accent as her husband. The spot behind her ear stung. Ingrid resisted the urge to rub it.

"You *must* do a reading for me." Scoot still held onto her wrist tightly. "I'm absolutely going insane with the wedding planning. My darling baby has demanded not only the world, but the planets as well, and I could use all the forces of the universe to converge on my behalf." She let out a tinkly little laugh.

"Mom—" Sailor said.

"Ever heard of a jade vine?" Scoot went on as if her daughter hadn't spoken. "Endangered, grown in the Philippines, pollinated by bats, and only blooms between April and May. I've been tasked with finding them in September, for a Georgia bride's bouquet, imagine that. Apparently, they're an exact match for my daughter's eyes." She winked as she finally released Ingrid.

Ingrid swiveled her eyes to Sailor. The girl's lips were pressed together in annoyance.

"It was just an idea—"

Scoot put up her hand. "It's what my only daughter wants for her wedding, and I'm going to get it, even if I have to deforest an entire island. As well as hunt down the harpist you want." She turned to Ingrid again. "Her name is Violetta Scarperelli, an Italian prodigy, only fourteen years old. Played at William and Kate's anniversary soirée in Devonshire."

Ingrid nodded, as if Italian harp prodigies and Devonshire soirées were everyday topics to her.

Scoot was still talking. "Listen, this girl right here knows how to play the game. And she knows her father and I are just a couple of patsies. We're too sentimental for our own good, I will admit this." She tipped back her glass, swallowing a deep draught with practiced panache. Her skin glowed. Her eyes burned unnaturally. Ingrid felt a creeping mist of darkness oozing from the woman.

Sailor clamped her mouth shut. In her mother's presence, she suddenly seemed like a very young girl.

"Scoot—" Rill said.

Scoot put out one graceful hand, adorned with an enormous rectangular ruby, in Ingrid's direction, then withdrew the hand and touched a nail to her lips. "You know, Ingrid, I think I remember your mother, Tess. Left town at a really young age, didn't she?"

Rill put an arm around Scoot's shoulders, and Ingrid could've sworn she saw the woman subtly shrug it off.

"Yes." Ingrid drew herself up. "When she was sixteen. She

had me down in Florida and brought me back here to live with my grandmother when I was six."

Scoot let out a hoarse chuckle. "A little rebel child, your mother was. I have one of those myself."

Another sigh from Rill. Ingrid looked uncertainly at Sailor. She was scowling and not even trying to hide it now.

"And your grandmother, Edith . . . now her I remember well. A great beauty, let me tell you. A 'sixties bombshell,' you know—" Scoot's lips pursed, as her eyes swept over Ingrid. She looked surprised at Edith and Tess's progeny. Surprised and a little disappointed.

"I could work on the flowers," Ingrid blurted out of nowhere, "if you wanted. And the harpist."

"Work on them?" Scoot knitted her brows.

"Do a spell, I mean." Ingrid swallowed with difficulty. "Call them in for you." She glanced nervously at Sailor. Her head was tilted slightly, her eyes gone soft.

"Oh, Ingrid. How sweet," she said.

Scoot laughed musically, then covered her mouth with her beautifully manicured nails. "Yes, my dear. That really is lovely of you. And so thoughtful."

Rill took his wife's arm again, blue eyes flashing with something Ingrid didn't understand. "You'll excuse us, won't you, girls? I have a few cranky guests who need tending to."

"Thanks, Dad," Sailor said.

Rill lifted an eyebrow at his daughter. "You owe me. They thought they were going to get the attentions of the guest of honor—" Rill grinned at Ingrid, and she saw, clearly, all at once, how easily he manipulated his daughter.

"Surely I can be off the clock for my engagement party, Dad."

"Loefflers are never off the clock" came his light reply. "But I'll take over for an hour. Y'all go have some fun for me, will you?"

His eye skimmed over his daughter and landed again on Ingrid. He looked at her for one long, unhurried moment. Thoughtfully, as if he was trying to puzzle something out. As if there was something he wanted to say. But then he seemed to think better of it because his eyes moved off her and he steered Scoot into the adjacent room. The low country boil room.

Dazed from the encounter, Ingrid watched him shake hands and slap backs as he somehow, simultaneously, kept his wife tethered to his side. She would've missed it, if she hadn't been watching so closely: the brief moment when Rill Loeffler glanced over his shoulder and sought out her eyes again. Finding her looking at him, too, he held them for a second longer than was necessary.

She felt the air leave her lungs and looked away quickly. Sailor was massaging one temple with her thumb. She let out a huff of annoyance, but it was a very quiet one, and she didn't say a word.

Ingrid suddenly felt extremely hot and dizzyingly uncomfortable. When Rill had mentioned her grandmother, what had that been that Ingrid had seen in his eyes? She couldn't figure it out. Scoot had clearly not been a fan of Edie's. Or maybe Ingrid had just imagined that. And what was that look in his eyes just now when he caught her gaze across the room? If he'd been a guy her age, she wouldn't have had any question. She would've called it interest.

Interest interest.

But Rill Loeffler couldn't be interested in her. Not in that way. He had to be in his fifties. *And* he was married. *And* the ridiculously rich CEO of Savannah Sauce. *And* the father of her new friend. She was imagining things.

Except . . .

Ingrid was in the business of reading people. Had been, since she was a child. She knew she was adept at feeling their emotions, both positive and negative, and if she had to bet on it, she'd just read Rill Loeffler. She heard that deep, Southern voice say her name, *Ingrid* . . . she'd seen the way he looked at her over his wife's shoulder.

It was a thing she did when she met someone new. She connected the person with certain smells. It helped her crystallize her feelings about them, helped her open herself to what the universe wanted to tell them. Earlier today, in her altar room, she'd instantly known Sailor was the sharp, fresh tang of salt water and cane sugar. And now, that Scoot was the smoke of wood fire and the bitterness of an orange zest. But Rill was harder to place. There was something about him that eluded her. Something sweet but dangerously so.

Sailor stood in front of her, holding up a tiny, delicate chocolate dusted with cocoa powder. "Open."

Ingrid did and Sailor popped it in her mouth. The flavor burst on her tongue, sweet, earthy with a zing of something else behind it. "Fig," Ingrid said, surprised. "Infused with . . ."

"Cognac," Sailor said.

Ingrid nodded. Yes. That was it. Rill Loeffler was fig and cognac. Two scents, two tastes, that spoke of money and power. Sensuality and refinement—all things she didn't have any experience with.

All of which felt suddenly, strangely, utterly irresistible.

Chapter 11

The second floor was only a fraction less crowded than the first. People jammed the stairs, the hallway, and all the rooms, only this crowd was younger and dressed in an edgier way. Ingrid saw a lot of black, leather, and metallic.

The conversation seemed more intimate up here, too, laughter drifting out from the groups of people lazily gathered in the bedrooms, leaning on fireplace mantels. Lounging on beds and slumped in chairs. A man seated on a stool at the end of the hallway played a guitar, providing an easygoing accompaniment to the conversation happening, blending in a strange way with the strains of cello from downstairs.

As Sailor led her down the hall, Ingrid saw the door of one room was opened. Through the crack, she could see someone kneeling on the carpet. A young man, his hands clasped over the top of his head, his back bowed slightly. He appeared to be praying.

Sailor hadn't seemed to notice him. "One more set of stairs," she said, clutching Ingrid's arm.

Ingrid knew, theoretically, that the third floors of these

huge, old houses were typically servants' quarters, with small, cramped rooms, crooked hallways, and tiny bathrooms, but of course the third floor of the Loeffler house was not that. It was the real party space.

At the top of the stairs, Ingrid looked down and saw the bright oval of the first floor. The flash and glimmer of the guests darting around below. A roar rose up, too—the clatter of cutlery and clink of glasses. The frenzy of tipsy laughter. Mindless fish, she thought, all of these rich people, tirelessly swimming through the rooms like in a giant aquarium, on the hunt for more, more, more.

"Here we are," Sailor said, beckoning her toward an open door. Her eyes glowed. She seemed proud finally to show Ingrid the portion of the party that actually belonged to her.

They entered a large room painted a rich coffee color. There was a sleek modular sofa and a pool table in the center with a red felt top. A string of Christmas lights festooned the ceiling.

The people up here reeked of money just like downstairs, but in a more understated way. The women had a natural look to them. No makeup, lank hair, and yet, inexplicably, they glowed. The men radiated vitality, too, their skin carefully moisturized, facial hair neat and trim. Ingrid felt overdressed. Foolish, in her updo and clip-on earrings and tulip dress.

She looked around warily. A pool game was in progress. There was a group in the corner playing Uno. Uno, she thought, in disbelief. *So this is what old money did at their parties?* Played children's games?

"Here," Sailor propelled Ingrid to a group of women she recognized. "Poppy, Madeline, Calla. Y'all remember Ingrid, from today."

The women nodded polite hellos.

Sailor drew herself up. "I'm sure you all have noticed Finley's absence. I know rumors are flying, so I want to clear the air right now. Earlier today, Ingrid, here"—she laid a hand on

Ingrid's arm—"confirmed something I already suspected. Without going into detail, Finley broke my trust. I've asked her to remove herself from the wedding party . . . and my life."

Ingrid felt the molecules in the air around her suspend in time as the three bridesmaids' eyes swiveled to Sailor. She draped a protective arm over Ingrid's shoulder.

"I don't know what I would do without this woman. I barely knew her and yet she was willing to protect me. She had my back, and she wasn't afraid to tell me the truth."

The trio blinked—guiltily, Ingrid thought—back at Sailor. They said nothing.

"And now we're going to move on. We're going to celebrate this wedding. Mine and Jude's wedding, and we're going to drink . . . and party . . . and never speak of you-know-who again. Agreed?"

The trio nodded.

"I'm going to go get this amazing woman"—she squeezed Ingrid's shoulder—"something to drink." She strode away, and Ingrid turned back to the group, lifting her eyebrows sheepishly at the group.

"What did Finley do?" asked one of the girls. Ingrid couldn't remember which one she was. "Murder someone?"

They all looked at Ingrid.

"I probably shouldn't say," she said.

"I'm sure we can guess," another one said. "Finley's pretty much always had one goal, and one play to get herself there."

All three primly sipped their drinks.

"This house is really amazing," Ingrid said. "You could get lost in here."

"I mean," one girl said, "if you'd never been here before."

One of the girls scoffed softly. "Madeline. Rude."

"Sorry," said Madeline. Her eyes roved over Ingrid's dress, then she caught herself. "I love your dress. Vintage, right?"

"Yes."

"We're so glad you're here," one of the other girls said quickly.

"We *so* are," Madeline affirmed.

Ingrid fell silent. She turned—the discomfort of standing alone almost unbearable—and saw him. A young man, lanky, blond, tall, standing in the doorway.

The praying man.

He wore baggy jeans, frayed at the hem, and a billowy brown linen shirt that swallowed his thin frame. A silver cross hung on a leather cord around his neck, and he was barefoot. Odd, she thought, at an engagement party. And then she realized he seemed to be walking toward her. She turned back to the girls, almost as if seeking their help, but they had vanished.

She turned back and the praying man was standing in front of her, one hand extended, a heavy silver watch on his wrist.

"Hi," he said. "I'm Cas."

She shook his hand. The eyes were a deep brown. She stared up into them, destabilized by the frank way they fastened onto hers. By the gentleness she found there. But that was all she saw. She couldn't see anything past that.

"Cas Loeffler, Sailor's brother." A smile flitted across his face. It was a wonderful smile, a surprising gift that transformed his thin, sallow face into that of a mischievous boy. Ingrid could imagine him climbing trees. Clambering up the roof of this immense house. Balancing dangerously on an old gutter.

This one walks a knife's edge . . .

The thought came and went like a bolt of silent summer lightning.

"And you are?" the guy asked patiently, even though she saw that he was just being polite. He knew who she was, just like the rest of Sailor's family.

"Ingrid White."

"The witch." He released her hand and dropped his into the pocket of his jeans.

"Sailor told me you're really good at what you do." And now a flash of humor in those brown eyes. Was he making fun of her? She wasn't used to not being able to read someone.

"I try to be." Her eyes fell on his watch, her mind frantically scrabbling for a topic to divert from her job. "I like your watch."

"Thanks. It's an Omega."

She widened her eyes and nodded as if she knew what that was.

"They're pretty sturdy. The Apollo 11 astronauts wore Omega watches on the moon."

"Oh, cool."

"It was a graduation present from my parents. I went to Amherst. Law, jurisprudence, and social thought, in case you were going to ask."

"Oh." Even though she was determined to be dignified, she felt her face flaming. She didn't know anything about what he'd just said. A bead of sweat rolled into her cleavage. "I wasn't."

"Well, that's refreshing. Don't get a lot of that around here." He regarded her with interest. "Also, you haven't asked what I do, which I like as well."

She nodded. She hadn't even thought to.

"I'm actually in the midst of what my dad calls my million-dollar gap year. Living at home. Traveling some. It's driving him crazy. He's pissed that I don't want to work at his company. Or that I don't want to do any job that's just . . . a job."

Ingrid didn't comment. Personally, she'd love to have someone offer her a job at Savannah Sauce with a cushy salary and a nice, fat package of benefits.

Now he looked annoyed. "But I'm seeking divine guidance before I just jump into any old thing."

There was silence as they exchanged wary glances.

"If I can ask . . ." he suddenly said. "How do you do it?"

"Do what?"

"Readings."

"Oh, well . . ." She shifted inside her dress, trying to access a pocket of cool air. "It's a bit like a massage therapist, except in my case the client just sits on a chair instead of lying on a table. I put my hands on them . . . on their hands, and I just . . . feel my way to the answer."

He was intrigued by that, she could see. "So you theoretically press on the tender spots and wait for them to scream?"

"I guess so, but my goal is always to help, not hurt."

"But what if, when you think you're helping, you're actually hurting?"

"I don't know what you're talking about."

"The spiritual world is a serious place. Full of entities who hide their true faces and true motives. Most people don't understand that."

She felt a spike of annoyance. "I understand my job fully. My craft," she added, just because she was feeling mean.

To her surprise he grinned.

"And I don't do baneful magic," she said. "My grandmother taught me that."

"I'm not trying to pick a fight with you."

She shook her head and looked away, wishing Sailor would reappear.

"But could it be the Holy Spirit, do you think?" he asked.

She furrowed her brow at him. *What is with this guy?*

"The one who's communicating to you? Who's telling you things about people?"

"I don't think so. No." She really didn't like these topics of conversation. Witchcraft wasn't an exact science. Power like that could not be quantified. It could not be contained. And it did not respond well to being gamed or manipulated in any way, but she didn't like feeling obligated to defend it. To anyone.

But he was like a puppy with a new bone. "It's just that I've been going to church lately. The Lutheran Church over on Wright Square. You know the Loefflers were a part of the Salzburger religious exiles from Austria. Protestants. Hardcore enemies of the Pope." Two spots of red appeared high on his cheeks. "I'm just wondering if what you're tapping into is God and not some . . . psychic phenomena."

She sucked in her cheeks. "God *is* psychic phenomena."

"You know what I mean. The God of religion. The one you access through prayer and humility and repentance."

She studied him. His needling was really getting on her nerves. He might be a Loeffler, but he was not going to get her to fall all over him and agree that what he did in a church pew and what she did at her grandmother's table was the same thing.

"I connect with light," she said in a slow, purposefully cold tone. "Wherever I can find it."

She didn't say *her*. Didn't add that in her mind, the light was always feminine in form. The Goddess, the One True Will of the Cosmos. And that this Goddess moved with grace through the crooked branches of the live oaks in Taylor Square, filtering into the windows of her house. That she dappled the streets and squares of her beloved city, dispensing her kindness and care to whoever could see it.

He wasn't worth it.

"What if someone comes to you who you can't read? Is there ever someone that the light doesn't reveal?"

In an instant, his frank brown eyes seemed to open to her. Oh yes. Here was the boy behind the man. She saw him clearly now. *There are grievances, a list of them. He's angry at the mother. Yearns to please the father . . .*

"Leave her alone, Cas!" yelled out a man from the other end of the room. "She doesn't want your Jesus!"

Another chimed in. "Don't tell him your secrets, sweetheart. He'll just throw them back in your face at the trial." Uproarious laughter at that, and then someone's low voice.

"The witch trial . . ."

Ingrid resisted the urge to turn and aim a deadly dagger's

glare at whomever had made this last comment. Cas's face burned, and now when she looked into his eyes, she found she could read him easily. He might be religious, but it didn't seem like it was the safety of the rules that interested him. He was drawn to the unknown, unrevealed world. She saw curiosity. A searching spirit deep inside him.

And perhaps a willingness to risk everything in the search . . .

And *that* interested her. It interested her deeply.

Sailor appeared, two cans of White Claw in hand. "Cas, tell your friends their manners suck. This is my party." She threw a disdainful look at her brother. "*My* engagement party and *my* friend."

Ingrid felt warm all over.

"Sorry." Cas looked at Ingrid. "They're actually making fun of me, not you."

"Come on," Sailor said to Ingrid. "Let's get out of here. Let's find Jude."

Chapter 12

They went back downstairs, where somehow in the crush of people, she lost Sailor again and wound up in a smaller room off the hall. It was paneled and lined with books. Not just books, but also a bunch of glass display cases. The cases held strange artifacts. What looked like scraps of metal and wood and frayed fabric, all on caramel-colored velvet, all glowing under dramatic, pinpoint lights.

She walked along the cases, studying the objects until she came to the large desk that sat at the far end of the room. The desk was stacked with files and newspapers and yellow legal pads. A glass beaker filled with black powder hung suspended from a small wooden stand. An uncapped pen, red with gold trim, sat on one pad. Ingrid picked it up, felt its slim heft in her palm, then slid the cap on. It clicked softly, satisfyingly.

Without letting herself think about it, she slid the pen into the neckline of her dress, hooking the gold clip over the strap of her bra. She moved quickly back to the glowing cases. A metal box, about the size of a matchbox, made of what looked like rusty tin, was scratched on the top. Someone's initials. Beside it lay a short knife, with an ivory and brass hilt and short, sharp, corroded-looking blade.

"They're pirate artifacts."

Ingrid turned to see Rill Loeffler, holding a crystal tumbler of whisky and watching her from the open doorway. She blushed furiously, feeling the pen against her breast, but he didn't seem to have caught her petty larceny. He pulled the pocket doors closed behind him with practiced ease and moved beside her. He pointed at the knife in the case.

"That's an eighteenth-century Khanjali dagger, reportedly used by Blackbeard when his cutlass wasn't adequate for the situation at hand. God only knows where he got it in the first place. That right there"—he pointed again—"is a remnant of a shirt from one of the pirates who escaped from his ship during the blockade of Charleston."

If words could swagger, Rill's would be strutting down Bull Street.

"I've been collecting them since I was a boy." He was now moving to the massive, mahogany desk on the other side of the room, where he set his glass down and leaned against the edge. "Every little boy wants to be a pirate, don't they?"

He sent her a smile so warm and so incredibly charming, she felt literal shivers run up her spine. "Everyone in this family disapproves of me." He gazed out the window facing south toward Gaston Street and Forsyth Park. "You don't disapprove of me, do you, Ingrid? Because I own this big house? Because I run a huge company that makes lots of money? Because I buy unreasonably expensive pirate artifacts and lock them away in cases?"

Another smile, this one small and intimate. She felt caught by his gaze. By his attention. But also confused. Not that Rill Loeffler would be the kind of man to manipulate with his charm, but that he would consider her a worthwhile target.

"No," she finally said. "But maybe you should open it up to the public. The tourists would love to see all this stuff. They get so much fakery out there on the tours." She thought of Boney with his little velvet bag.

He sniffed. Tossed back the last of the whisky in his tumbler. "The tourists. They're such . . . an infection. This city was run-down back when your grandmother was doing business, I'll give you that, but it was authentic. Real. Edie would say the same, I bet."

"More tourists mean more money . . . for people like me, anyway. But also for people like you. They buy Savannah Sauce as souvenirs, don't they?"

"Good point." He eyed her. "So, are you making a lot of money from all these tourists, Ingrid?"

She felt her face flame. "I'm making enough." A lie. One that he could obviously see, she was sure.

He cocked his head, studied her. "You're a funny girl, aren't you? Speak your mind, right out. I like that. Would you like some cognac?"

She nodded mutely, and from a crystal decanter he filled his glass and another for her. It was so much like a scene out of a movie that she felt the urge to laugh. She gestured to the test tube on his desk instead. "Is that some kind gunpowder from a pirate gun?"

He was the one to laugh. "That is ash from Mauna Loa, an active volcano Scoot and I visited on our honeymoon in Hawaii. Her souvenir from a gift shop. She was furious they wouldn't let us into the actual volcano to collect our own."

Ingrid wasn't surprised. People like Scoot didn't like to be told they couldn't go somewhere. "It's pretty cool," she said, because she couldn't think of anything else to say and she could tell Rill expected praise for all his special artifacts.

He didn't acknowledge her comment. "I was in love with your grandmother, with Edie. Did she ever tell you that?"

Ingrid felt her heart flip. She looked into Rill's eyes and shook her head.

"I wouldn't guess she would have. Too icky. Old people and romance." He made a face.

Ingrid smiled. He smiled back. Then indicated that she should sit as he sat in the chair opposite. She did.

"This would've been, oh, the early nineties. I was twenty-five, just out of business school, working for my father's company. Being trained for the big desk one day, whenever that old son of a bitch, my dad, decided to die. I was so in over my head, it was actually funny. Had no clue what I was doing. Edie had her set-up over there on Taylor Square—Calhoun Square back then. Where you are now—"

She swallowed. He knew where she lived. Where her business was.

"I went in one day, hoping for . . . I don't know what. To find out something real, maybe? If I really belonged in the business. Who I really was. She read my palm, my aura, whatever." He suddenly looked tired.

"What did she say?"

His bright blue eyes fixed on hers. His voice was low. "She told me I had what it took. That I was worthy of the mantle my father would give me." He seemed faraway now. "It was such a crazy thing. She was the first person who ever believed in me. It was . . . a revelation. It was . . . love, if you want to know the truth."

Ingrid frowned.

"You're doing the math." He waved off her reaction. "She was a forty-two-year-old woman with a daughter. Too old for me, obviously, but I didn't care. To me, she had this secret . . . a skill to living a life that was free. A life that truly belonged to her. It was a skill I wanted." He shook his head as if to clear it. "So we became friends instead of lovers. I asked her to do readings for my friends and family. She was over at the house at least once a week back then, doing readings for my parents, aunts, and uncles, channeling some dead grandmother or auntie, whatever they wanted. She used to dress up like a gypsy back then. Do the whole show with the low-cut peasant blouse. Silk scarf over her hair. Gold earrings. She was gorgeous. Breathtaking, really."

His voice had gone low, gruff and warm. Emotional.

Figs and cognac . . .

Had Edie read him as quickly as Ingrid had? Had she been tempted, the way Ingrid felt herself now? Not tempted to *do* anything necessarily, other than enjoy the sunlight of his attention. It was such a warm place to be.

"Her husband had died," Rill said. "Just her and Tess, you know."

Ingrid winced. Pictured her mother in the boyfriend's Dodge Charger, pushing her out the back seat. *I'll call when we get back to Florida . . .* Tess had never called. Not even once.

"Tess was pretty, too, like Edie, but she was a wild one. A handful." Rill was watching her closely. Too closely.

But Ingrid avoided his gaze. She had nothing to say, not about Tess. It was bizarre to think Rill knew more about her own mother than she did. Hurtful. Just another blow from a mother she'd never known. A mother she would never know.

He leaned forward now, his fingers laced. "Well, all that to say . . . we're so glad you're back. Glad Sailor found you. She's looking at a lot of life changes, my daughter. At some point, she's going to have to grow up and face some hard truths about her place in this family. Truths she doesn't want to hear from me."

"What do you mean?" She felt a bit guilty asking. Like she was betraying Sailor somehow.

"When she was young, Scoot and I were having problems. In our marriage. It affected Sailor. She got sick a lot. Missed school. Always wanted to go with me to the office. She told me she wanted to be CEO of Savannah Sauce." His expression was pained. "I think she was trying to fix it, you know? Fix our marriage. Our family. Me, too, no doubt."

Something tickled the back of Ingrid's memory.

"How old was she?"

He shrugged. "I don't know. Around seven or eight?"

That break in Sailor's lifeline. It wasn't a death. Back when Sailor was young, her family had been broken.

He shook his head. "She's a great little worker, my daughter, and more than competent heading up her region in the marketing department at Savannah Sauce. But she's not built to be a CEO. And even if she was, it wouldn't work. People around here want a man at the head of the company they're dealing with. It has to be Cas. My son. But what can you do? She doesn't want to hear that from me."

Ingrid's mind raced. Her family had been connected with the Loefflers from long ago and still was. Rill had loved her grandmother. And today Ingrid had helped Sailor. And Sailor needed even more help, that was obvious, now that Ingrid had met her parents. This was a family in trouble. There was so much unspoken. So many wounds unhealed . . .

Maybe this was what Edie had been trying to tell Ingrid on her deathbed. She had never really understood what her grandmother meant, but right now, standing in this house, in Edie's dress, in Rill Loeffler's opulent study, she wondered if she'd been led here in some way.

To help Sailor. To help this family. To close a part of a broken circle.

To right the balance.

"Maybe if Sailor heard it from someone she trusted . . ." Rill was saying, his eyes roving her face, like they were negotiating a deal. "We all know how you ladies are. It's only meant to be if your horoscope says so."

Ingrid didn't know what to say.

"Daddy, there you are."

Sailor stood in the open doorway. Ingrid flushed, feeling like she'd done something wrong. She hadn't even heard the pocket doors.

"Ingrid, I had no idea he'd trapped you in his awful museum . . ."

Sailor entered the room. She and her father seemed to dance together, kiss the air lightly, then separate again. Ingrid got the impression of two boxers before a match, rather than a father and daughter.

"I'm so sorry I lost you," Sailor addressed Ingrid. "You better come with me before he drags you into his Blackbeard stories and you vow to never come back here."

She pulled Ingrid up out of the chair, and as they headed out of the study, Ingrid turned back to see Rill, his profile, all noble angles and smooth skin, surveying his collection of pirate paraphernalia. Just before they slipped from the room, he looked over his shoulder at her and put one finger to his lips. She swallowed and turned away.

Ingrid asked for the bathroom, and on her way there, she happened to see Scoot Loeffler, in one of the drawing rooms, setting her empty glass on a mantel and taking another from a passing tray. After she'd finished in the bathroom, Ingrid circled back into the empty room, fished the orange peel out of Scoot's empty glass, and went to find Sailor so she could thank her for the evening.

She felt full and tired and a little bit drunk. She wanted to go home.

Chapter 13

Ingrid woke to Litha's paws gently kneading her shoulder. The room was washed in light, the lace curtains breaking into dancing dots. Ingrid looked over at the marble fireplace mantel. Rill Loeffler's red-and-gold pen and his wife's curved orange peel sat there. Tokens from a magical night.

She stretched, warmed by Litha's purring. Everything was different now. She was Sailor Loeffler's psychic. Her friend. She was going to be picked up in the family car for appointments. Do readings for the richest, most influential people in town. It was a new life. She just hoped it started soon. There were still bills to pay, and she didn't have a single appointment on the books until next weekend.

Last night, when she'd arrived home, the house had been quiet, save the ticking of the grandfather clock in the hallway. There was only one lamp on in the sitting room. Miles had apparently gone to sleep and left it on for her. Ingrid had climbed the creaky staircase, and in her room, changed out of Edie's dress and into a nightgown, then crawled into her bed, instantly falling asleep.

Miles would probably be up now, though, expecting to be filled in on every detail about Sailor's party. She would have to step carefully. Try not to sound too excited about her new position. He was on the sensitive side, kind of possessive at times. She didn't want to trigger any jealousy.

She really and truly did value their friendship above all else. It had started in such a stars-and-planets-aligning way when she had found his ghost tour flyer stuck in her door—with a picture of Miles (cute enough, but not her type) and Boney (seriously hot)—and decided to take the tour. She had been feeling especially down about Edie back then. Missing her more than usual. And, besides that, she desperately needed to drum up new business. A ghost tour would be full of potential new clients.

She arrived early to the meeting spot at Madison Square, a bit before nine that night, right by the William Jasper Monument. Boney checked the QR code on her phone while Miles, standing with a few other tourists and looking like a street urchin out of a Dickens novel, grinned shyly over at her. Later, in the historic Lucas Theatre, when Boney was telling everyone about the ghostly applause a worker had heard once only to find the auditorium empty, Miles showed her something special he'd discovered. A little hidden compartment under the stage, about the size of a shoebox, camouflaged by the molding and gold leaf trim.

He opened it for her with a quick push inward. It had been created, he told her, by the builders of the theater as a hiding place for the theater owner's firearms. A gun that could be easily retrieved in the event of a riot if the movie was considered scandalous or immoral. They'd both giggled at that.

"I've seen you around town," Miles said, as he clicked the secret compartment back into place. "I've always wanted a reading, but I was too chicken. Probably raised too Baptist."

"Oh yeah, no," Ingrid said. "We're not too popular with the Baptists."

"You look pretty harmless to me," he said with a laugh.

"I'm a totally ineffectual witch. You have no idea."

The truth came pouring out of her. She told him about the overall decline of her house, including the most recent disaster, a leak in her kitchen sink. That even though the readings she did were fairly accurate—and even though she regularly did abundance spells—she just couldn't seem to get enough momentum going to stay ahead of the repairs.

She also told him about her mother who had dumped her, then died, and about the classmates who'd called her a devil worshipper. She described Edie's sickness and how, in those last hours, she had given Ingrid a mission that she didn't understand—that she'd almost given up believing in.

It had been such a relief to confess all of it to someone. To admit that, though she still had faith in the Goddess and in Edie's light, things just weren't coming together. That she was alone and confused. That, really, she always had been.

But Miles didn't judge her in the least. He had a difficult childhood, too, he said. His adoptive parents weren't the ideal family either—the shrimper father who was a drinker, the mother, a server at The Olde Pink House, who died too early of a heart attack. When the tour was over, he offered to accompany her home so he could fix her sink, and she agreed. After that night, he never left.

Now she picked up Litha and scooched back against the pillows. Eyes still closed, she rubbed the cat on the spot between her ears and let the polka-dotted morning light wash over her.

The light down here on the Georgia coast was soft and thick—a shy, sticky, secretive mystery. Savannah light rode the tides, changeable, cyclical, and capricious. Savannah light was a trickster. That was probably why she had not quite gotten the hang of it. Why she couldn't seem to get the light to bend her way like Edie could.

Now she chanted softly, into Litha's soft, white fur.

Gather strength,
As the clock waxes.
Gather courage,
As the day wanes.
I gather, you gather,
And what we gather shall grow,
So in the bloom of night, we shine forth . . .

As for Rill Loeffler's pen and Scoot's orange peel, Ingrid hadn't decided yet how she was going to use them. The orange peel would definitely serve a purpose—Scoot was a force to be reckoned with—and although she'd originally thought that she would give the pen to Miles as a peace offering, now she wasn't sure. Something told her she should keep it to herself a little longer. Maybe the memory of Rill's first parting glance. The finger against his lips, meaning she should not tell Sailor what they'd discussed.

She thought about it now, fixing his face in her mind, but it kept melding into Cas's face. Sailor's brother possessed that same magnetic quality. A way of focusing on you and making you feel special. And he'd seemed genuinely interested in how her psychic abilities worked.

The clear, sharp bells of St. John's Episcopal Church chimed seven o'clock. She should get going. Edie's was technically supposed to open at eleven, even though it wasn't like anyone would care if she wasn't on time. It was more about not disappointing Edie, whom she knew was always watching.

Ingrid made her bed, then showered and dressed. She put on a red sundress with pintucks on the bodice, arranging her hair in braids that crisscrossed her head. She pocketed Scoot's orange peel, a vague idea forming in her head.

A way to help Sailor.

Downstairs was as flooded with light as her bedroom, as if the Goddess was laying a double benediction on her. Litha trotted alongside her through the messy space, cluttered with Edie's dusty furniture, crookedly hanging art and plants on every available surface. Ingrid made a face. She really needed to get this place in order. Get it looking like the home of a successful, in-demand psychic-witch.

In the dining room, Miles and Boney sat on rattan chairs around the old, scarred pine table. The surface was covered with watermarks, burns, and gouges that were filled with petrified crumbs from decades before Edie. A lavender orchid boasting a row of blooms sat in the center on a straw mat. Ingrid noticed, for the first time, how the flamingo wallpaper was bubbled from rainwater that had seeped through the stucco and porous Savannah brick into the wall.

She sat and Miles jumped up to get her coffee. Boney smirked at her.

"Morning, princess. How was the party of the century?" He was still wearing his tuxedo T-shirt from last night and his top hat sat upside down on Edie's buffet. Had he slept over?

"It was great," Ingrid said noncommittally. She didn't love it when Boney hung around the house. She liked to keep what she and he did together—the occasional sex—private. And strictly at his dingy apartment which overlooked the river. It only happened maybe once or twice a month, but Boney was always making comments full of innuendo and pretending like he was going to tell Miles. It infuriated her. She wasn't sure how Miles would take it if he found out his two best friends occasionally hooked up, but she was pretty sure his feelings would be hurt.

Miles came back in with a mug of coffee and set it before Ingrid. His hair was sticking up on one side, his blue eyes bright, making him look boyish and vulnerable. He sat in the chair beside her, quivering with energy. Ingrid smiled at him. She could tell he was dying for a rundown about the night, but she wasn't about to divulge anything with Boney sitting here. It felt like her own secret, one only Miles would understand.

She cradled her coffee between two hands. "The party was crazy. So much food." This was a safe topic. The boys loved food.

Miles and Boney exchanged a guilty look.

"What?" Ingrid demanded, eyes darting between the two.

"We sorta hung around the back last night," confessed Miles.

"The back?" Ingrid jutted her chin in confusion.

"Of the Loefflers' house," Miles said.

"Around midnight, while the caterers were cleaning up," Boney explained. "We fucking scored. Mini burritos and shrimp and grits . . ."

". . . jambalaya, pulled pork, lobster ravioli," Miles added.

That's why she hadn't seen him last night. They'd come in after she had. Ingrid gritted her teeth. "Where did you put it?"

"The fridge," Miles chirped.

"Did they see you?"

Miles looked confused. "The caterers?"

"The Loefflers." *Idiots.*

"Hell, no," Boney said. "You think those people stick around to help clean up after their parties?"

Miles touched her arm. "Don't worry, Ingrid. Boney knew one of the girls working, and we were in and out in, like, five minutes. No one saw us. I promise."

"You mean Sasha." She and Sasha weren't close. Sasha had been Boney's unofficial girlfriend before he and Ingrid had started up their little arrangement.

"She's cool," Boney said. "We were in and out." He gave Ingrid a suggestive eyebrow lift.

Ingrid sighed. She really didn't want word getting out that

her friends were scavenging the Loefflers' leftovers. It felt demeaning and pathetic. And it could affect her reputation with them. Would anybody trust a psychic whose friends were a bunch of vultures? She was suddenly sure she wasn't going to give the red-and-gold pen to Miles. He'd already helped himself to enough.

"Tell us about the bash." Boney slurped his coffee. "Who did you meet?"

"Just a lot of business types." Ingrid was determined to keep it vague. Boney always had an angle. Was always coming up with a new scheme to get something for nothing. "Older people mainly."

"Potential customers," Miles said with an encouraging smile.

"Hopefully." She concentrated on her coffee. Miles had put in the perfect amount of sugar and milk. In spite of her irritation, she felt a twinge of affection for him.

Boney was watching her with an amused look. "You simp for the richies, don't you, little princess?"

"Come on, man— " Miles protested.

"You're one to talk." Ingrid stood. "All that dumb stuff you tell them on your tours. Animal sacrifice in the middle of Colonial Park Cemetery? Give me a break."

Boney's eyebrows raised. "I've seen the puddles of blood. Feathers and bones."

"You have not, you liar." Ingrid fixed Boney with a cool look. "And I happen to know your cousin found those finger bones on a road construction project on MLK. There's no way it's Tomochichi, so you can just give it a rest, okay?"

"It's called *creating atmosphere*, Ingrid," Boney said. "*Set design.* Which is what that whole altar room of your downstairs is all about. Don't act like you're above it. We all do it for them."

"I do it for the Goddess."

Boney crowed with laughter. "Oh my God, you're so cute."

She stood, turning to Miles, speaking slowly and purposefully to him and him alone. "I'll tell you everything later. I have to go down and get my room ready right now." Even though she didn't have an appointment.

Boney shoved out his chair. "She's too good for us now, Miles, my boy. Witch to the richies. Next thing you know, you're going to be out on your skinny ass—"

Ingrid tried to look bored. "Shut up, Boney."

"I've seen it happen a million times. One of the richies adopts one of us like some toy they can parade around like a freak show attraction at their parties. To boost their Savannah street cred. *Oh, Muffy, you have to meet my nonbinary friend with pink hair and three septum rings who makes sculptures out of cockroach carcasses—*"

Miles snorted with laughter. Ingrid just shook her head.

"—and before you know it, the innocent little freak starts to think they're somebody special. I'm telling you, it happened to an artist friend of mine. They promised to put on this big, fancy show of all her work, so this girl painted *twenty-six* canvases—that she paid for herself, mind you—and then these asshats ghosted her."

"Miles," Ingrid said. "Get him out." She'd started to flick her hands in that ritual expelling of bad energy. She really couldn't afford to have Boney's black cloud envelop the house today.

"Eventually, Ingrid," Boney continued, "the richies get bored and move on. They drop their new, quirky friend and move on to the next drag queen or tattoo artist . . . or witch."

Without a word, she formed devil horns with her fingers and, palm down, pointed them straight at Boney, sending his negative energy back to him.

Boney waved his hands above his head. "Ohhhh, I'm so scared. She's doing the big, bad finger magic on me."

She turned her back on him and headed toward the stairs that led down to the garden level.

"The richies are bad people," Boney called after her. "I'm telling you, Ingrid—"

"—you fucking dick," she heard Miles say to Boney.

Down in her altar room, she shut the door behind her and locked it. She turned and breathed in the calm of the room. She already felt better in here. Already could feel Edie's spirit hovering in the air. She took her vial of lavender oil and dotted spots of it on her finger to imprint in each of the four corners of the room.

She put the two chairs off to the side and draped a black silk scarf over the low brass table. She carefully set candles, matches, and the orange peel in a small glass dish on the table. In one of the drawers in the breakfront, she found the length of red silk cord that she arranged in a circle around the brass table.

"Green for earth, to the north," she murmured as she lit the candles and positioned them around the red cord circle. "Yellow for air in the east. Red for fire facing south. Blue for water in the west."

The candles flickered in the dim room. She usually played music on her phone, through the little portable speaker, while she did a meditation or spell, but after Boney's nonsense, she decided she wanted the quiet. It seemed especially holy. She only heard the hum of the air conditioner. The soft, steady beating of her heart.

Today felt full of strong magic of its own.

It felt ready for her.

She knelt before the altar and called the corners, invoked the light and Edie and the Goddess. When she was finished, she thought back to the party, to the moment she had met Scoot Loeffler. She heard the words in her head.

Ever heard of a jade vine . . .

The rare Filipino flower that Sailor and Scoot wanted for the bridal bouquet. The one they couldn't find.

Apparently, they're an exact match for my daughter's eyes . . .

It would be the first spell she'd cast to prove herself to Sailor's parents. If she could find these flowers for Sailor's wedding, Scoot would see she was a person to be taken seriously. And more importantly, Sailor would know that Ingrid was fully and completely loyal to her.

She searched for an image of the flower in her phone and when it came up, she expanded it. She laid down the phone and pulled out the curve of orange peel. Lighting a match, she held it at the edge of the peel. A thin line of smoke rose, the scent both citrus and something else that seemed ancient and hidden filling the circle. She stared at the orange and envisioned the Goddess, wreathed in light, seeing this spell that married a mother's love with a friend's loyalty.

"I gather every jade vine that blooms in every forest of the Philippines," she said. "I gather them to the mother, gather them to the mother, gather them to the mother . . ."

She repeated the steps for the harpist Sailor wanted. Found the girl's picture on her phone, burned more of the orange peel, and gathered the young musician prodigy toward Scoot.

The clock ticked on and on, and she seemed to fall into a kind of trance. A dreamy, slippery drifting in the spaces between the seconds. She felt her body lift up, up from the altar, up out of the room. She moved with pure intention outside of the house, high above the city. Maybe she had fallen short of the light in the past because she'd been asking things only for herself. Now she was working her magic for Sailor. And for her mother.

As she floated above the city, she felt like it was finally hers. A kingdom where she ruled as benevolent queen. But only as long as she used her magic for good. To do good. Just like Edie had said.

You must always stay in the light . . .

The sunlight crowned her. The moss on the trees was her train. She felt the briny breeze from the ocean. The current of the river giving her power. She alone would say what happened in her city. She would use the moon and the light, the tides and the river to carry out her will.

She wished she could stay here forever, just like this.

But now something was disturbing her. A clanking sound coming from the direction of the front room. The faint sound of the iron door rattling in its hinges. Someone was trying to get in.

Chapter 14

The someone turned out to be Clemmie Fairburn, one of the women Ingrid had met at Sailor's party the previous night. When Ingrid unlocked the inner door, then pushed the outer iron one open, Clemmie, dressed in a crisp, pink striped shirt, white jeans, and espadrilles, threw out her arms and crushed her into a sweet-smelling, bosomy hug. A huge, quilted Chanel bag slung over the woman's shoulder dislodged itself and swung forward, hitting Ingrid squarely in the ribs, knocking the fuzz from her brain.

"Whoops," Clemmie said, corralling the purse and drawing out a tall, round zippered case made of shiny brown patent leather. It had a scrolled monogram, *CFQ*, embossed in gold on the front. Clemmie waggled the case. "Precious cargo. Sorry for trying to break in. Edie used to keep her door unlocked."

Ingrid's head was pounding now. Maybe from the spell, she wasn't sure. "Did we . . . did I . . . ?"

Clemmie pushed her teased, sprayed auburn hair back from her face. "Oh no, no, darlin'. I don't have an appointment. I just thought I'd pop by and see if you could fit me in. For a reading, just a tiny little baby one, that's all . . . and maybe a cocktail or two, to get the juices flowin'."

Waggle, waggle went the patent leather case, and Ingrid suddenly realized that what she was looking at was a portable bar. She motioned Clemmie back to the parlor.

"Oh. Okay, sure. Would you like to sit?" She checked the clock on the wall. It was almost noon. She'd been lost in her work for hours.

Clemmie bustled past her and sat at the pink marble table like she'd done it a hundred times before, and before Ingrid could light her lavender smudge stick, Clemmie had slapped three crisp hundred-dollar bills on the table.

"Now, I don't want you to get the wrong idea or anything," she said in a honeyed tone. "I only ever came here once or twice when it was your grandmother's." She leaned forward, hand to her mouth. "Good Christian girls don't mess with the occult."

She burst into gales of laughter then busied herself unzipping the leather case and pulling out three pie-shaped flasks inside. They fit together neatly and were labeled COGNAC, WHISKY, and GIN. Each had a small silver cup, monogrammed, as well, that fitted over the top of each bottle's lid. She set out the cups, unscrewed lids, and concocted two drinks. When she was done, she pushed one silver cup toward Ingrid.

"Bottoms up." She tossed back her drink. Ingrid stared mistrustfully at the one in front of her.

Clemmie burst out laughing again. "Oh, darlin', no. It's not all that nasty stuff." She pointed to each flask. "Gin, pear liqueur, and dry vermouth. It's called a Poire Iver." She pronounced it *Poy-eye-ver.* "We really should have tumblers." *Tuuumbluhs.*

Ingrid found a couple of glasses in a cabinet and brought them back to the table, which pleased Clemmie immensely. "Now that's the stuff," she said as she expertly concocted another batch of the cocktail in the glasses. She lifted hers. "Come on, now. Chin-chin."

Ingrid chinked her glass against Clemmie's and sipped dutifully. It was a really nice drink. Refreshing and sweet.

Clemmie swirled her drink and gave Ingrid a conspiratorial look. "Ask me anything. Go ahead. Now that we got the talky-juice flowing."

"Oh," Ingrid said. "It's just that usually in a reading I usually do most of the talking." She gave Clemmie a polite smile, which was meant to show she wasn't trying to be rude.

Clemmie leaned forward. "Honey, Sailor Loeffler's officially adopted you as her psychic, so you're gonna need the low-down. And nobody better to get you up to speed on all the people, places, and things you need to know than me. We're going to be good friends, I bet. And you can give me a reading after I'm done. How's that?"

Ingrid nodded and Clemmie proceeded to tell her literally everything about herself: that she was seventy-six, the heir to Savannah's wealthiest banking family, and had been married at age twenty to an heir of the largest oil company in Savannah. They'd had three children, all girls, who had married, even the one who was "just a darling lesbian" (Clemmie's words).

After her beloved husband died at a very young sixty-four, she found herself romanced by a widower in town, the heir of the largest shipping company in Savannah and apparently hot stuff in the sack (also Clemmie's words). After six years of wedded bliss, he died as well, and now, the recipient of major portions of three family fortunes, she was definitely the wealthiest unmarried woman in Savannah, possibly in all of Georgia.

People might say she'd never done a day of work in her life, but Clemmie liked to say she'd raised two husbands and that was the hardest job in the world.

Ingrid sat immobile with awe. She imagined a cave, an enormous mountain of gold coins, a dragon curled on top, guarding the treasure with a wary eye. She pictured Clemmie in her white jeans and precarious espadrilles wobbling up and ordering the dragon to scootch over so she could sweep a mountain of coins into her giant Chanel purse.

Clemmie then recounted for Ingrid the story of the creation of Savannah Sauce by Rill's grandfather—its success and diversification into a global concern that had elevated the Loefflers from a respectable middle-class family to some of Savannah's most illustrious and wealthiest denizens. Laura "Scoot" Fairburn, a cousin of Clemmie's, had met Rill when they were children, had begun dating him their senior year in high school, and it was always understood the two would marry. Their wedding had been written up in *Town & Country*. After a Hawaiian honeymoon, Scoot had immediately gotten pregnant with Sailor.

Sailor had attended Vanderbilt University, graduated with a 4.0 in business, and returned to Savannah to work in Savannah Sauce's marketing department. Cas had been less of a golden child, struggling through high school then, after five or so years, barely snatching a diploma from the jaws of Georgia College and State University up in Milledgeville.

Interesting. Ingrid could've sworn he'd told her Amherst.

Clemmie said Rill was severely disappointed in Cas's academic accomplishments, but he seemed unwilling to promote Sailor to anything higher than her current director status and continued to try to lure Cas into working at the company. Ingrid nodded along, saying nothing. She remembered Rill's finger on his lips. The way he had looked at her.

"You *must* give me a tour of your house." Clemmie was mixing another round of drinks. "I've always loved this one, ever since I was a girl. And you know what they say about all the houses around this square." She pushed a full glass back toward Ingrid. Her eyes flashed mischief and mayhem.

She meant that they were haunted.

Taylor Square was two blocks northeast of Forsyth Square and rumored to have been a burial site for enslaved African people. It had been desecrated, and re-desecrated, dug up, and built over numerous times. Formerly called Calhoun, the square had been recently renamed for Susie King Taylor, a woman born enslaved, who later became an educator, civil rights activist, and the first Black nurse to serve during the Civil War.

On the west side of the square, the Methodist Church was rumored to have been involved in a bootlegger-romance-gone-awry ghost tale. On the east side, the house at 432 Abercorn Street was a font of endless grisly rumors of child murders, suicides, and ghostly presences. None of the tales had any basis in truth, but that didn't stop the tourist trolleys and horse-drawn carriage drivers from parading tourists past the house, much to the chagrin of the current, long-suffering owners. Throw in the various bloody Revolutionary War battles, yellow fever epidemics, and deadly fires that the spot had seen, and it was no surprise that Taylor Square held a certain morbid fascination for both locals and tourists.

But Clemmie had clearly moved on from thinking about haunted Taylor Square. She was up now, gathering her supplies, organizing the flasks back into the leather holder and dumping everything back into her capacious purse. Her eyes danced around the room, until they finally landed on their intended target: the stairs.

"Shall we?"

Chapter 15

The next thing Ingrid knew, she and Clemmie were standing on the first floor and, to the accompaniment of blaring music, Miles's favored nineties trip-hop, Clemmie was taking it all in. The stacks of roofing shingles on the entrance foyer floor, along with Miles's toolbox, and a roll of blue plastic liner for the roof. There were also shoes everywhere, Miles's battered work boots, Ingrid's sandals, ballet flats, black Converse. The distinct smell of leftover cilantro fish tacos from the Loefflers' party wafted through the air.

"I hadn't really expected guests—" Ingrid began.

"Oh my dear," Clemmie called out from deep in the front hall. "You have no idea. I'm in heaven. *Heaven.*" The woman turned back to Ingrid, eyes wide with disbelief. "Every architectural detail, perfectly intact." She pointed to the ceiling, the windows, the stairway. "I don't think I've seen a house in this town that has been completely untouched, walls intact, moldings and medallions not slathered in paint or varnish, not stripped down to *modernize* . . ." She said this last word like a curse.

"It's the same as when my grandmother bought it—" Ingrid said.

But Clemmie had moved on to the sitting room and was spinning in a circle, her arms outstretched. "Look at these pieces . . ." She was touching things now: sofa, love seat, tables, and chairs.

Ingrid looked around the room in acute dismay. Burger King wrappers covered one chair. A stack of comic books rested on another. Her notebook, pens, colored pencils were strewn across the sofa, from her last session of journaling. Even the surface of the coffee table was obscured by empty Sprite cans, water bottles, and White Claws. Peanut shells littered the rose-patterned rug.

Clemmie fingered the thick drapes on the tall, narrow windows. "You still have the old pulley system windows."

Ingrid nodded. Litha, perched on the back of a tattered armchair, watched Clemmie with mild curiosity.

Clemmie ran a hand over the carved curves of the white marble mantelpiece. "A working fireplace?"

"Yes."

Clemmie tutted with sheer relief. "Just divine." She moved to the dining room where she touched Edie's old pieces, nodding the whole time, as if she was mentally cataloging it all. The table where they used to sit, just Edie and her, eating tuna casserole or mac and cheese and black-eyed peas. Where Ingrid blew out the candles on every birthday cake Edie baked her, age seven to nineteen.

Clemmie reappeared in the arch between the dining and sitting room. "Got any bubbles?"

For one breathless second, Ingrid thought the woman was talking about the bubble bath Edie used to bathe her in, the one that came in the pink plastic bottle. Clemmie sauntered past Ingrid, pushed aside a stack of bills on the ottoman and sat.

Flushing, Ingrid took the bills and crammed them into the credenza drawer.

She turned, to see Miles coming from the kitchen where he must've been hiding this whole time, bearing a bottle of wine in one hand and two relatively clean-looking glasses in the other. Not bubbles but close. Ingrid sent him a look of gratitude.

Clemmie straightened, her eyes bright, knees primly pressed together. The fingers of her right hand tickled the wrinkled, age-spotted skin below the open neck of her blouse. "Who's this?"

"Ah." Ingrid moved quickly to Miles's side. "Clemmie Fairburn, this is my roommate and friend, Miles Drummond."

Miles offered Clemmie the pirate grin he used on his tours. "Thought you ladies might be looking for a little refreshment." He poured the wine into the two glasses, then jammed the cork back in with a pop of his palm and set it on the coffee table.

"What a nice vintage." Clemmie's eyes moved from the label of the wine—something French Ingrid couldn't decipher—to Miles then back to Ingrid. Ingrid felt herself go scarlet again. She wanted the floor to open up and swallow her whole, but it didn't, and Clemmie just drank her wine, not saying whether she recognized the bottle as one served by Rill and Scoot Loeffler at the engagement party of their daughter.

Miles gathered a few fast-food wrappers and sat, elbows propped on his golden-haired knees. Clemmie's fingers continued to play over her chest, as she studied Miles, looking as if she'd like to put a dollop of whipped cream on his head and eat him with a spoon.

"Now, honey," she said to Ingrid. "I want you to know that I go way back with Cousin Scoot, even before she married Rill, and I love her like a sister—"

Ingrid gulped and braced herself for some new revelation.

"—but I'm here to tell you, she's a jealous woman. She keeps score like you wouldn't believe. Memory like an elephant. I'd like to think she's over the whole Edie thing, is what I'm saying."

Ingrid just stared at her.

Clemmie widened her eyes meaningfully. "You know . . . everything that happened with Rill and her—"

Ingrid glanced at Miles. He'd bolted upright and moved to the edge of his seat, interest lighting up his turquoise eyes.

"I'm sorry," Ingrid said, keeping her face very still. "I don't know what you're talking about."

Clemmie sucked down another inch of the Loefflers' French wine then held out her empty glass to Miles, who jumped to oblige.

"I hate to be a tattletale, sugar," said Clemmie who obviously loved being a tattletale, "but thirty years back, when he and Scoot were engaged, Rill fell plumb in love with your grandmother. He was just crazy about her, and there wasn't a damn thing Scoot could do about it. They never got together, per se—Edie was too old for him, and she knew it—but Scoot couldn't accept it. Couldn't just be happy that she'd won. No, that girl was fit to be tied, and I don't think she's ever gotten over it, not even up till the day Edie died."

Ingrid pictured her grandmother on her bed. Her frail body wrapped in the lavender mohair sweater. The hands like claws. The panting sound, gravelly and shallow. Ingrid felt faint.

"She's not right, you know," Clemmie said. "Somebody dropped that one on her head when she was a baby. Scoot's always been mean." She sighed and gulped her wine. She seemed to have lost interest in Ingrid, Miles, the house, suddenly distracted and sad. "But I see Sailor bringing you around, showing you off to all her friends last night. Calling you her new psychic." She fixed Ingrid with a steady look. "Scoot didn't like you being at that party, is what I'm trying to say. And I'm afraid she isn't going to want to see you around anyplace else near the family either. It'll just remind her how, at one time, she played second fiddle to another woman who could tell the future."

The air was still in the room, the silence oppressive, and then there was a sudden chime of bells, mechanical and loud. Ingrid jumped, and Litha meowed and slunk out of the room. Another customer at the downstairs door.

Ingrid looked at Miles. "Miles, would you—"

He jumped up, clearly glad to escape the uncomfortable scene. "I'll tell them you're busy."

Ingrid nodded and he hustled out of the room and clattered down the stairs.

Clemmie topped off her glass. "I'm not trying to be mean, sugar. I hope you know that. But I'm not going to lie. Scoot Loeffler is a snake in the grass. So you just watch your step, all right?"

"Ingrid." Miles stood near the top of the stairs, only his golden curls and the top half of his head showing.

"What is it?" Ingrid's tone was sharper than she intended, but, *Goddess*, did he not get that this was a delicate moment?

"Ingrid, hi! I'm so sorry to interrupt . . ." Sailor Loeffler's head poked out from behind Miles.

Ingrid stood. "Sailor. What are you doing here?"

Sailor edged around Miles and rushed into the sitting room. She held up a small silver gift bag with a tuft of tissue paper poking out of the top. "For you," she said to Ingrid. "It's just a little something. A candle. I hope you like it."

Clemmie squared her shoulders in delight. "Sailor, darlin'!"

"Oh, Clemmie. Hey." Sailor's magnificent mane of blond hair swung around, making her look like a shampoo model. "What are you doing here?"

Miles, staring, hadn't moved from his spot at the top of the stairs.

Clemmie rose, wobbling precariously, and swooped at Sailor, kissing her extravagantly on both cheeks. "Me and Ingrid are just talking about the future, my sweet little cousin, that's all." She went to gather her purse, but Sailor kept hold of her wrist.

"Oh, but you can't go. Not yet. You have to hear the news."

She set down the gift bag, then turned to Ingrid, her face like a sunbeam. "You did a spell, didn't you? Tell the truth."

Ingrid shook her head, confused. "Yes, but just this morning . . ."

"Oh my," Clemmie murmured.

Sailor was practically emitting beams of light. "Ingrid. Mom just got a call from Costa Rica. From a cultivator of exotic flowers. He grows the flowers there. The jade vine I wanted for my bouquet."

Already? Ingrid pictured the orange peel, its burnt rim gone cold on her altar. She felt her body flood with warmth. With light. It's what happened every time she knew a spell worked. She could feel Edie all around her. She wanted to dance around the room and shout her victory.

"He just called her out of the blue," Sailor went on. "He said he heard from someone in the Philippines that she was looking for the flower. He can force the blooms for us in September and have a colleague deliver them in time for the wedding." Sailor was grasping Ingrid's hands, shaking them excitedly. "And not just that . . ." she continued.

"The harpist— " Ingrid said breathlessly.

"How did you know?" screamed Sailor and grabbed her, giddily dancing around the room. "We got the harpist! We got the harpist, too! You did it, Ingrid! You did it!"

Chapter 16

Ingrid went to bed early that night. She was exhausted, her head still throbbing, but the rest of her buzzed with elation. She had done it. She'd found the elusive jade flowers for the wedding and secured the elusive harpist. There was no denying it. Clemmie's warning about Scoot not liking Edie might be true, but the woman couldn't deny what Ingrid had done for her daughter.

This would prove to Scoot that Ingrid held nothing but goodwill for the Loeffler family. She couldn't possibly still hold on to old jealousies after this. Ingrid felt certain of it.

Now, as she lay in bed, she reviewed everything that happened after Sailor left her house. Ingrid had gone to the attic, to look through the old ledgers her grandmother had stacked under the steep pitched roof. Specifically, the ones from the nineties. She wasn't sure exactly what she was looking for. Maybe just a clue from Edie's past that would give her some understanding about her relationship with the Loefflers.

She flipped through the pages, perusing the names of Edie's customers. Random people with random problems, inked beside long-ago dates. As earth-shattering as those problems might have been to each person, they no longer existed now, did they? No problem was big enough to beat time.

She saw a few names she recognized, but mostly none rang a bell. No Loeffler, Scoot or Rill, appeared anywhere in the columns. Then she opened the 1995 ledger and noticed one entry that appeared over and over. That was odd not only for the frequency of appointments, but because there were only initials, S.S., rather than a full name.

She'd found nothing more and putting away the ledgers, had gone about her day. But she kept wondering who S.S. was . . . and why they had come to see Edie so many times. There had been at least two dozen entries. Was it some code name for Rill?

Suddenly, there was a knock on her door. Before she could answer, it swung open revealing Miles. Bare-chested, he wore a pair of too-big, old-fashioned pajama pants that had belonged to her grandpa and carried his laptop. His eyes were dancing.

"I've got to show you something."

She waved him in, and he bounded onto the bed, leapfrogging Litha, who was curled up near Ingrid's feet. He plumped up the extra pillows and burrowed into the blankets next to Ingrid. They did this sometimes, she and Miles, watching TV together in her bed, snacking on popcorn, tickling Litha, and laughing about whatever show they were watching. Sometimes Miles even scratched Ingrid's back until she fell asleep. But it was never anything more than that.

In the beginning, when Miles first moved in and he'd never even attempted to kiss her, she had assumed he must be gay or asexual. But then there had been the nights he'd gone out and hadn't come home until the next day, and when she asked Boney about it, he assured her that Miles did indeed like women and got around quite a bit down at the riverside bars. Apparently, Boney added, Miles was pretty famous for his talents. In spite of not wanting him for herself, Ingrid had been slightly crestfallen, but then she realized how ridiculous that was. The pure, platonic, doggedly loyal way Miles loved her was a rare thing. A gift. She was lucky to have it, and she didn't want any more than that.

Beside her, Miles had propped his laptop on top of the covers and was clicking to a website. A resale site that sold vintage designer stuff.

"Look at that," he breathed. "Look at the price."

A huge, quilted, tan-and-black Chanel purse filled the screen. An identical match to the one Clemmie Fairburn had carried earlier that day at the house.

"Fifteen thousand," he shrieked, as if the numbers weren't right there in black and white.

"I see that." Honestly, she shouldn't allow him to mentally tabulate how much her new friends were worth. It wasn't wise.

"And that's the resale price!"

She fixed him with a severe look. "I know you and Boney were just doing your thing the other night at the party, but if you take anything else from the Loefflers—I don't care if it's buried at the bottom of their garbage can and rotting—if you ever take anything from them again, or their friends, I'll never forgive you."

He clamped his mouth shut.

"They are my clients now, and I have to keep things professional."

"Ingrid, come on," he cajoled.

"I'm not kidding, Miles. You show this purse to Boney and next thing you know, Clemmie Fairburn's Chanel is going to turn up missing."

"He wouldn't do that," he scoffed. "I was just saying that it was wild how much it—"

"Miles!"

"What?" He looked wounded now. He slapped his laptop shut and slumped back on the pillow, pouting.

Ingrid turned up the volume on the TV, an episode of *Medium*. It was far-fetched, but she loved Patricia Arquette and felt that if they ever happened to meet, they'd definitely be friends. She tried to concentrate on the story, but she could feel Miles's aura, a stormy blackish purple, swirling on the other side of the bed.

She spoke again, this time in a calm tone. She needed him to understand. "This is an opportunity for me, Miles. My chance to get in with the people who can actually take my business to the next level. Do you understand what that means? It means I never have to worry about paying the taxes. It means I can afford to fix all the broken stuff, right when it breaks—"

"I'll fix anything you need, Ingrid—"

She let out an impatient huff. "You do a great job with the stuff you can handle, Miles, but I can't have you up on the roof, fixing my flashing, falling and hurting yourself. I would die if that happened."

"You would?" He looked genuinely touched.

"Miles. Of course. And besides all that, I'm talking about securing a place for myself—my business—that will last for decades. That will continue to bring in not just money but . . . other things."

"What things?"

"I don't know exactly." The words had been pouring out of her mouth, with no thought, but now she truly considered his question. "Maybe, I don't know, trips to places we could never afford . . ." She was saying *we* but, in truth, she was picturing herself, wearing a bikini and gauzy sarong, on a tropical beach somewhere, frolicking in turquoise water, turning golden in the sunshine. The person who watched her wasn't Miles.

It was Cas Loeffler.

Or maybe it was Rill. He fit into the fantasy just as easily.

". . . or parties we could throw," she hurriedly went on. "Maybe even one of them will even put me in their will."

Okay, that one was over the top, but it definitely got his attention. Understanding dawned in his simple blue eyes. "Are you serious?"

"Yes, Miles. Dead serious. The Loefflers are my—*our*—ticket to a future we could never reach on our own."

He nodded slowly, turning her words over in his head. This was the way Miles was. You could always see every thought that was drifting through his brain. It was something that both endeared him to her and aggravated the ever-loving stew out of her. But it was true. She was not just looking for a friendship with Sailor or a flirtation with her brother for herself. She was working for them.

"I'm sorry," he said. "For taking all that stuff from the party."

"It's okay. Just don't do it again."

He nodded and snuggled closer to her, dropping his chin on her shoulder. She reached up and stroked his curls. He sighed heavily and draped an arm across her waist. She knew without looking that his eyes had fluttered closed.

On the nightstand, her phone lit up with a text. Trying not to disturb Miles, she reached for it and tapped the screen. A message appeared from a number she didn't recognize.

I prayed for you in church today.

Her heart tightened. *Church.*

She thought of Gloria Ledieu praying to Blond Jesus. A chorus of little girls chanting. *Renounce Satan, renounce Satan . . .*

Below the message, three dots appeared. Her heartbeat went into overdrive.

And then, another message appeared on the screen.

And for myself. That God would be gracious and forgive a sinner for his sinful thoughts.

More dots appeared. She held her breath.

Thoughts of you. Thoughts of us.

Sinful thoughts.

She stared at the phone, breathless, heart hammering now. What the hell?

What the hell was happening?

"Don't stop," said Miles, pressed into the crook of her neck. "That feels so good."

She absently stroked his hair again.

Sinful thoughts . . .

Was it Cas Loeffler? The first time she'd seen the guy, he was on his knees, praying during Sailor's party. What kind of person *prayed* during a party at his house? He was on a new religious kick . . . and definitely someone who disapproved of what she was.

Or maybe it was Rill. It was possible that at the party Sailor's father had seen a trace of Edie in Ingrid, and now he was sort of . . . reliving the past in some way. She didn't know what to make of the message, though. Was it a true confession of guilt and a plea for forgiveness? Or was there something else buried in his words?

An invitation maybe?

Who is this? she typed.

Your sinner came the reply, so quickly she had to swallow a gasp.

She thought for a minute, then answered, **No name?**

Better this way.

And then, a few seconds later . . .

Freer. We can be who we really are.

She put the phone face down so Miles wouldn't notice if it lit up again and turned her full attention to him.

"Bedtime," she said in a singsong voice and gently shoved him off her.

He groaned but grabbed his laptop and went back to his room. When she was convinced enough time had passed for him to have settled into his own bed and drifted off to sleep, she opened up the text thread, lay back on her pillow, and read each line, over and over again.

* * *

The next day, she found it hard to put the Loefflers out of her mind. Sailor, Cas, Rill, and Scoot. Each of them was fascinating for different reasons. Each fought for space in her brain, but, the truth was, only one of them called themself her sinner. Only one of them was texting her anonymously about sinful thoughts. She hoped it was Cas, but she wasn't sure. It could be Rill. Either possibility sort of terrified her but in the most titillating way.

In the end, she had to tell herself to stop obsessing. It was only Sailor who really mattered. Sailor was her friend. Her priority. She needed to remember that.

Ingrid had two appointments that day. Both were tourists, older women from Atlanta and Augusta who looked at her with hungry eyes as she spoke. They probably saw a psychic every time they went on vacation. Some people preferred to keep asking questions rather than acting on the answers they got. Not the most beneficial for them, but at least it was good for business.

After they were gone, Ingrid set about tidying up the shop and thinking about how she was going to reassure Miles. He got his feelings hurt easily, and Ingrid didn't want to upset him by seeming too invested in the Loefflers. Miles was invaluable to her. She resolved that she would be a better friend going forward. She would make him dinner tonight. Watch *The Twilight Zone*, as many episodes as he wanted.

When she went back upstairs, she saw the cleared surfaces, the gleaming furniture, the dim, hushed air that smelled of lemon polish. He'd cleaned up the whole first floor. She was noticing the vacuum marks on the sitting room rug with a twinge of remorse, when he came out of the kitchen, hands in bright yellow rubber gloves and one of Edie's ruffled aprons tied around his waist.

"Ta-da!" he exclaimed, beaming at her.

"You're the best," she said. "I love you." And she meant it.

The gloved hands dropped down by his side. "I love you, too, Ingrid. I'm sorry for the whole purse thing—"

The doorbell rang. Glad for the interruption, Ingrid hurried to answer it. Sailor stood on the doorstep.

"Hi, Ingrid." She flipped her impossibly luxurious blond hair over her shoulder. She wore a man's boxy button-down, untucked over jeans, and expensive-looking loafers. The shirt was blue and matched her eyes perfectly. Rill's eyes, too, Ingrid thought.

"Hi, Sailor." Ingrid squinted in the bright sunlight.

"Sorry I keep dropping by without calling, but this time, I have a good reason." Sailor leaned sideways, peering past Ingrid. She waved. "Hi, Miles."

Ingrid felt him drawing close, hovering just over her shoulder.

"I just wanted to deliver this." She handed Ingrid a manila folder and beamed.

Inside was an official-looking document with an official-looking government letterhead and a jumble of boxes and codes and numbers below.

Ingrid tilted her head. "What is it?"

Sailor's eyes bounced from Miles to Ingrid, a smile playing on her lips. "A receipt. Showing that your property taxes have been paid. And will be, from an account that's been set up for you, for the next three years."

Ingrid felt her heart thud painfully. "What?"

Sailor beamed. "Miles let it slip about your situation—yesterday, when I came over—and I wanted to help you out. To let you know how much I appreciate you. So I paid your property taxes."

Chapter 17

Sailor did more than just pay Ingrid's taxes.

The next day, she also sent a whole crew of workmen—roofers, plumbers, electricians, and HVAC techs—to Ingrid's house to repair every system that was outdated or broken.

Ingrid chewed Miles out for telling Sailor about the money she owed, but it was a half-hearted performance at best. The truth was, she was relieved. And she could see that with Sailor writing checks, Miles suddenly realized Ingrid might no longer require his services. He was scared, which made her feel bad.

Taking pity on him, she assured Miles that it was an old house, that things would continue to break and need upkeep, and of course, he'd always be needed. Still, he refused to be cajoled out of his melancholy mood. He and Litha lurked around with baleful eyes and petulant frowns while the workers swarmed the house. Finally, that day around lunchtime, he stomped out of the house without telling her where he was going.

Ingrid didn't have time to deal with it. She was too busy showing the workers the special quirks of the house, hanging around to make sure nothing got stolen. Not that she actually believed these guys would steal anything. They worked in houses like the Loefflers' and their friends' all the time. Still, she kept an eye on them. She'd been hanging out with Miles and Boney too long to trust anyone.

Later that afternoon, to give her ears a break from the noise of the work, Ingrid heated up some of the leftover Loeffler shrimp and grits, intending to take it down to one of the benches in the shady square. On her way down the front steps, she noticed Gloria Ledieu fertilizing the pots of hideous, spiky plants in front of her house.

"Getting some work done, I see," the woman said.

On the sidewalk, Ingrid turned and lifted her chin. "It's a major overhaul, actually. Long overdue, as I'm sure you know."

"Gracious, all those fellas scurrying in and out." The woman was practically quivering with the need to know more. "Must be setting you back a pretty penny." She let out a giggle to let Ingrid know she wasn't prying, just commiserating.

Ingrid wasn't fooled. "Not me. My new employer."

Mrs. Ledieu's small, sharp eyes glinted. "Employer? You have a new job? Did you close down your business—"

"Sorry, gotta run," Ingrid said sunnily and headed toward the square where she felt the old woman's eyes on her as she sat on a bench and started to eat. When she was finished and heading back to the house, Mrs. Ledieu was gone, but Dean Remington's young husband, Sheffield, happened to be coming out the door of their private courtyard. He was shirtless as usual, tanned and waxed smooth, a pair of pink, rimless sunglasses holding back his cupcake swirl of honey-colored hair.

"Hey, Practical Magic," he called to her. "You going to have us over for a drink when you finish your redecorating?"

Ingrid sighed wearily. "I'm not selling y'all the place, Sheffield."

"I hear you're Sailor Loeffler's new pet." He arched one perfectly plucked eyebrow. "Lucky duck. I wish I could tell fortunes."

"I'm a witch, not a fortune teller." Her voice dripped with disdain. Good Goddess, people drove her crazy sometimes.

"Then you know that the Loefflers are a dangerous bunch." Now he was looking at her in a way she couldn't decipher. Like he wanted to tell her something he shouldn't. "They'll use you up and throw you away. Ask Dean. He knows."

Ingrid sent him a tight smile and headed up the steps. It wasn't her fault that she was actually good at her job, and someone had recognized it and wanted to reward her for it. But it was the unfortunate reality of life—people weren't happy for anyone's good fortune but their own. Well, that was fine. Add it to the list of all the new things she was learning and experiencing, thanks to Sailor.

That evening, when Miles came back for a quick bite to eat before his tour, he apologized for his behavior. "I shouldn't be mad about anything, Ingrid. This is good news for you."

"For us," she reminded him and went to the kitchen to make him something from the leftovers of Sailor's party. A roast beef sandwich on a gorgeous hoagie roll with horseradish and onions. Miles loved sandwiches.

When he had finished eating and left for work, she cleaned up the kitchen, then went up to her room and changed into pajamas. She climbed into bed with her phone and opened her messages, deliberating for a long while. At last, she typed out a message to the phone number that she still hadn't labeled in her phone.

Have you been forgiven? Have you sinned again?

She settled back against the pillows, her entire body tingling with anticipation, and waited for a reply. While she waited, she typed in a contact name.

My Sinner.

The following week, in the midst of the chaos of the renovations, Sailor popped in to go through the house with Ingrid so they could decide a few things: where new wallpaper and fresh paint was needed, which light fixtures needed rewiring, and which ancient kitchen appliances needed replacing. Sailor suggested they drop by Scoot's interior design studio—located on the corner of Bull Street and West Jones—to make their selections.

They met one morning later in the week outside the shop. The shingle that hung above the door read LOEFFLER INTERIORS in gold lettering, and when Sailor opened the door for Ingrid, she was hit with the deliciously cool smell of expensive reed diffusers. *Bitter orange and woodsmoke.* Scoot's aura.

Inside, bathed in soft lighting, vignettes of antique sofas and chairs mixed with modern tables were scattered about. Crystal chandeliers hung from the ceiling. Rugs so old they were almost threadbare covered the floor. Gilt mirrors and huge paintings adorned the walls.

As Sailor inspected the abundant fringe on a pillow, Ingrid's phone buzzed.

I am thinking of a saint today.

Ingrid bit her lip and typed quickly. **I'm thinking of a sinner. Tell me what you're thinking. Give me details.**

"Girls!" Scoot was dressed in another flowing outfit, a tunic and wide leg pants in a creamy ivory silk. Her blond hair was pulled back in a tight bun and her lineless skin shone peachy pink. Blushing furiously, Ingrid dropped the phone into her purse and zipped it closed.

Scoot gathered both of them into an embrace, kissing the air between their cheeks. Ingrid smelled the sharp, sweet scent of liquor.

Ingrid felt a sharp blade of warning cleave the space between her shoulder blades.

Backstabber . . .

The word floated into her head, black letters on a stark white background.

Scoot Loeffler gripped Ingrid's arms, shaking her slightly. "What you've done for us, my darling girl! I don't even know how to thank you! The flowers . . . the harpist? I just don't know how you did it!"

Sailor smiled at Ingrid. "It's called witchcraft, Mother."

Scoot shivered exaggeratedly. "Ooh, witchcraft."

"It's nothing to be afraid of," Ingrid said.

"Oh, don't worry about me. I'm not afraid of anything," Scoot said wryly, and Ingrid had no trouble believing her. "You have a gift, don't you? A rare, special gift." She was studying Ingrid, as if trying to solve a riddle.

Well, Scoot wasn't far off. Witchcraft was a riddle. The seeking to connect to the universe. The aligning of oneself with the Goddess. There were rarely definitive answers. Mostly it was an intuitive game of hide-and-seek, a fumbling in the dark during a storm, with the occasional illumination during a flash of lightning.

She would've said all this if she thought Scoot Loeffler truly wanted an answer. But she saw that Scoot did not expect or even desire a response. Scoot Loeffler was accustomed to answering her own questions.

Now the woman's expression was playful, impish. "We should keep you close, shouldn't we, Ingrid? So this whole wedding goes off without a hitch."

Sailor put her arm around Ingrid. "Mother, she's not a circus monkey. Ingrid's done us a huge favor. We can't just keep asking her to drop everything and do spells for the right buttercream icing."

Scoot eyed her appraisingly. "I don't know. I think she likes doing favors. I think she likes being needed."

Ingrid swallowed.

"As long as we're on the subject of things we need," Sailor said. "Marcella's sent word that she doesn't have time to do the third dress."

"For pity's sake," Scoot huffed.

Ingrid was incredulous. "The third dress?"

"The first is for the ceremony—" Sailor explained.

"Danielle Frankel," Scoot interjected.

"—the second is for the dinner. That one's either the Vera Wang or Loewe, we haven't decided yet. The third is for the reception. For dancing."

Ingrid had no words. She'd only been to a handful of weddings and those had taken place at courthouses or backyards or Starland Yard, the food truck lot. Only one of the brides had worn an actual wedding dress. Not a single one had included multiple costume changes.

Scoot winked at Ingrid. "You know Marcella."

Ingrid shook her head gravely. She did not.

"Oh. Well, she's a designer in New York," Sailor said. "She was at J. Mendel then Carolina Herrera before she went out on her own."

"Anyway." Scoot reached out and playfully pinched Ingrid's arm. "If you could just conjure up a window in Marcella's schedule for us. Maybe her entire client list could get the chicken pox or something, I don't know?"

Scoot tittered. Ingrid smiled grimly. It wasn't really worth mentioning that she didn't do that kind of black magic. The baneful kind. There were a lot of reasons for that, mainly that Edie had never allowed it.

"Shall we head back?" Scoot asked, indicating a cluster of offices in the back of the space.

Ingrid nodded and followed Sailor and Scoot, but she couldn't help feeling she was being led into enemy territory. The lair of a deadly spider.

The word came again.

Backstabber . . .

Chapter 18

Scoot's office was lit dramatically by a variety of lamps, most notably by one that sat on the edge of a burled, inlaid wood desk. It was small and bronze and sprouted four lily-shaped lights. Ingrid smiled at the sight of it. There was one just like it in her house.

The girls sat as Scoot settled herself behind the desk, glasses perched on her nose, and examined her calendar. "I've blocked out next month for you, Ingrid. I've also set out wallpaper books and paint samples on the tables in the showroom. We'll have a look at those later. I just wanted to get an idea of your color scheme."

"My . . ." Ingrid was starting to feel a rising panic, a sort of whirlwind in her chest.

"Color scheme." Scoot enunciated the words slowly like Ingrid's ears weren't working properly.

Sailor leaned forward. "Mother, I wonder if Ingrid might like to stick with the palette her grandmother already had for the house." She sent Ingrid a sympathetic smile. "I know how important it is to you to remain connected to Edie. To feel her presence."

Ingrid gulped, nodding. "I don't mind if you change the colors, though." She glanced at the lily lamp. "I like the colors in that lamp. We actually have one like it in our sitting room."

Scoot laughed gaily. "Oh my dear. No, you don't."

Ingrid eyed her. "We do."

Scoot lifted her eyebrows. She spoke slowly and deliberately. "That's a Louis Comfort Tiffany. It's made with Favrile glass that's over a hundred years old."

The room seemed to suddenly drop in temperature. Beside her, Sailor stilled.

Scoot sucked in her already perfectly hollowed cheeks. "This lamp is a collector's item, an extremely rare example of the early-twentieth century work, worth at least twenty thousand—"

"Mother," Sailor said quickly. "Maybe it's a place to start." She turned to Ingrid. "Is your lamp green, too?"

Ingrid nodded.

Sailor fixed her mother with a hard, purposeful look. "Well, then, there we are. We'll start with that green. Let's go look at those books."

Two hours later, Ingrid was limp with exhaustion and her head throbbed. She had never felt so completely out of her element. Making decisions about things she'd never had the luxury to consider her opinions about was overwhelming.

Thank goodness for Sailor, who noticed how lost she was and jumped in, assuring Ingrid they'd only tackle the main floor and save the bedrooms for later. She proceeded to pick out wallpapers, paint colors, fabric for curtains, and a select few pieces of furniture as well as a whole new collection of kitchen appliances. When Ingrid and Sailor finally left, Scoot promised that when everything arrived, she would personally supervise the installation.

On the way back to Ingrid's house, her stomach pitched like a ship at sea. She tried not to think about having Scoot Loeffler in her home. Or the cost of all the new items.

"All that stuff," Ingrid said to Sailor. "It's so pretty, but I'm worried it's too expensive."

"It's not."

"Come on, Sailor. I couldn't afford anything out of that shop."

Sailor's jaw clenched. "It's my money, *my* trust. And I can do whatever I want to with it. I don't care what Mom thinks. If Dad thinks I don't have any business sense . . ." Sailor pointed a finger at her. "You, Ingrid White, are good business. *That* much I know."

Sailor stared ahead with an expression Ingrid couldn't decipher. Ingrid was afraid, suddenly, that Sailor was angry with her.

"Do you know," Sailor said abruptly in a soft voice, "before the party the other night, I gave my bridesmaids their gifts. These really great Olivia von Halle crêpe de chine robes . . ."

Another brand name Ingrid had never heard of.

"The robes were monogrammed and came with these little room sprays I had created especially for each of them. You know, Poppy likes rosemary, Madeline likes citrus, and Calla likes vetiver . . ." She was getting a faraway look in her blue eyes, that Ingrid had come to recognize as a self-protective measure.

"Sailor?"

Sailor dabbed under her eyes. "It's silly, I know. I was scrolling Instagram and there was Poppy's younger sister, Freya, in a reel she'd made. She was dancing around, doing a makeup tutorial or something, and she was wearing the robe. Poppy's robe."

Ingrid frowned.

"Poppy regifted my bridesmaid's gift, like only *hours* after I gave it to her. I mean, maybe she didn't like the color or the fit. I get that—"

"Sailor," Ingrid said vehemently, "you shouldn't excuse her behavior. It was rude. Inconsiderate."

Sailor looked on the verge of tears. "I shouldn't care so much."

"She's your best friend. Your maid of honor. Of course you care."

That faraway look again. "They're all just so . . . different with me now." She ducked her chin. "Since I met Jude, since we got serious, it's like . . . they're angry with me. Distant. Cold, I don't know."

"*Jealous* is the word you're looking for, I think."

"No. Why would they be jealous?"

Ingrid started to laugh, then realized, with a jolt, that Sailor was being entirely sincere. Her lovely face held an expression of true confoundment.

"Sailor," Ingrid said carefully. "A lot of people wish they had what you have . . . or that you didn't have what you have. People can be really uncharitable that way."

Now Sailor did laugh, but it was a rueful one. "I know I seem oblivious, but I know who I am, Ingrid. I know what I was born with: money, status, my mother's bone structure."

Ingrid grinned.

"But I can't apologize for who I am, can I?"

"No. You should never apologize."

"And I try to do the right thing. I do try to help people when I can." At this she looked at Ingrid.

Ingrid felt her face redden.

"That came out wrong," Sailor said quickly. "I don't mean to imply that you need my help."

"But I do need your help, don't I?" Ingrid said. "I mean, let's not pretend. I was about to lose my house. Lose everything my grandmother left me, including my business. Then you came along."

Sailor's eyes lit up. "No, Ingrid. *You* came along for me. I can't explain it, but from the moment I came into your house . . . into that room . . . from the moment you took my hand, I felt like I finally had someone who believed in me."

Ingrid thought of the night of the party in Rill's study. What he had told her about Edie. *First person who ever believed in me.* Almost identical words to what Sailor had just said. Was it just fate that the past was repeating itself this way? Or had Edie somehow made it happen, made the threads of the two families intersect again?

They crossed Drayton, almost back to Ingrid's house.

"I really appreciate you, Ingrid," Sailor said. "I hope you don't mind me saying that."

"I appreciate you, too," Ingrid replied, meaning it with her whole heart and feeling more hope than she'd felt in years. "There's just one thing . . ." She stopped at her front steps.

Sailor raised her eyebrows.

"There is something I want to do for you."

"You've done plenty."

"Okay, but just tell me—what was the name of the designer you wanted? For your third dress?"

Sailor threw back her head and laughed. "Oh my gosh, Ingrid. My mother is not going to believe this. I love you, you know that?"

When Sailor had gone, Ingrid dug up Edie's wedding veil and went down to her altar room. She smudged the room, cast her circle, called the corners, then laid the veil, brittle and yellow with age, on her altar.

She summoned Edie, summoned the light and the Goddess, ignoring the shame. Maybe she was going too far, sacrificing Edie's veil, but it felt like a worthy gift to offer in exchange for all Sailor had done for her. She'd actually said she loved Ingrid. Loved her. Even if she'd only meant it in a joking way, it meant something.

She lit a match and set fire to the edge of the veil. For maybe the first time in her life, Ingrid felt no doubt in the power that was coursing through her. She closed her eyes, letting one name take over her consciousness.

Marcella.

But something was off. Another name, unfamiliar to her, kept overshadowing the first. She opened her eyes, searching for something more. The meaning behind the other name. Who in the world was Louise?

She shut her eyes again, the smell of burnt tulle filling her nose. It didn't matter. Her job was to go with whatever the Goddess put before her. To dive in, just like she'd done at Sailor's reading. Like she'd done when she called in the jade flowers and the harpist.

All she had to do was trust what she'd been taught by her grandmother, what she'd known and believed in the core of her soul since she was six years old. What could be simpler than that?

The magic was just waiting to be harnessed.

"Louise," she whispered. "I gather you, I gather you, I gather you . . ."

Chapter 19

A few days later, Scoot and Sailor dropped by Ingrid's house to measure all the windows. Scoot was astounded to see that Ingrid did, in fact, own a Tiffany lily lamp identical to the one in her office. Her only comment was to advise Ingrid not to sell it, because it was sure to double in value in the next decade.

"Maybe if she'd sold it a couple of months ago, we wouldn't have turned into some charity case," groused Miles, who was lurking around, eating Quaker Oat Squares out of a coffee mug and watching the women step around the men regrouting tiles on the fireplace.

Ingrid sent him a mild warning look. His jealousy was flaring more and more with the constant stream of workers in and out of the house. Also, whenever she mentioned Sailor.

"Miles." Sailor planted her hands on her hips. "I get that this has been a really disruptive process, but this is not charity. Ingrid did something for me that was so meaningful, I can't imagine I'll ever be able to adequately repay her." She took a step closer to him. "I hope you and I can be friends, too, Miles. I'd really like that."

At the windows, Scoot sniffed quietly.

Miles nodded thoughtfully. "Okay. If you really want to be friends, come on my ghost tour."

"Your— " Sailor looked confused.

"My ghost tour," Miles repeated. "You've never even been on one?"

"Miles," Ingrid said.

Sailor straightened. "No. I can't say that I have."

"And you've lived here all your life?" Miles looked scornful.

"Miles!" Now Ingrid was mad.

Sailor waved a hand in her direction. "He's not wrong. I have lived here all my life, but I don't think I've ever fully seen this town." She glanced at Ingrid. "The beauty of my home. The strength of the people who are the heart of it." She looked back at Miles, her chin high. "The people who make this place what it is."

Miles sent Ingrid a triumphant look. "It's a date."

That weekend, Sailor and Ingrid went on Miles's tour. When it was over, the three walked over to a bar called Artillery where Sailor bought them drinks. Over her vodka cranberry, Ingrid furtively watched Sailor drill Miles about whether he really believed any of the stories he told on the tour.

Miles had finally warmed up to Sailor, chatting companionably with her and cracking jokes about how much better his tour was than Boney's. And, Ingrid saw, it was all because Sailor had made the effort to reach out to him. She was a good person. She really cared, not only about Ingrid, but about the people in Ingrid's life.

Ingrid felt a catch in her throat and had to look away. She didn't want to cry in front of them.

"Wait a second, I have an idea," Miles suddenly said. "Ingrid, you should just move in with Sailor. It's so loud at the house with all the sawing and banging and drilling . . . you said it's been tough to do your readings."

"Miles, stop. You're drunk." Ingrid turned to Sailor. "He's drunk."

"Oh my God, Ingrid. Yes," agreed Sailor. "He's right. You totally should."

"No," Ingrid said. "I couldn't."

"He's absolutely right." Sailor nodded at the bartender for another round. "With all the repairs going on, how can you possibly be doing business—"

"I could keep an eye on everything," interrupted Miles. "And you can work out of Sailor's house—"

Ingrid looked alarmed.

"—or do house calls with all the peace and quiet you need for accessing the"—he fluttered his fingers—"woo-woo."

Sailor's eyes were bright. "And you'd be around to keep me from absolutely losing my mind over my mom."

"And to do readings for you," Miles added.

"To access the woo-woo!" Sailor squealed.

She and Miles high-fived over the table. Ingrid sighed. She'd love to stay at the Loeffler mansion—who wouldn't—but what would Scoot say?

Sailor reached out a soft hand to rest on Ingrid's. "It would be so nice to just have a friend around. I could really use a friend right now, Ingrid. Say yes. Say you'll move in with me."

Ingrid glanced at Miles doubtfully. "And you're really okay with this?"

"Look, I know I've been an asshole." He glanced at Sailor. "And I apologize. I'm just an idiot sometimes. A bit too protective of the people I love."

Now Ingrid's eyes unexpectedly filled with tears. She nodded at Sailor. "Okay. Okay, I'll do it."

"Woo!" Sailor cheered.

"My work here is done," Miles said, and stood.

"No. Your drink just came," Sailor protested.

"Miles, really, you don't have to go," Ingrid said in a half-hearted way. She couldn't deny she was itching to get Sailor alone and discuss their plans.

"I'm supposed to help Boney on this job in the morning. Some deck we're building for this house over on West Gaston." He bent to kiss Sailor's cheek. "It was fun. I hope you come around more. Seriously." He waved and was gone.

Ingrid smiled at Sailor. "Should we, like, go ahead and schedule your readings for the next couple of months? I can also walk you through lots of energy rituals and healing meditations, which might be good before the wedding."

"Nope," Sailor said. She pushed Miles's drink, a gin and tonic, over to Ingrid. "No business talk tonight. I want to show you my Pinterest board for the Marcella dress."

"Oh, okay." Ingrid sipped her drink and accepted Sailor's phone. She scrolled down the board filled with gorgeous and expensive-looking gowns. Ingrid marveled at Sailor's unflagging interest in what she wore. Even with a closet full of designer clothing, the woman never seemed to tire of buying more.

"So Finley's texted a couple times," Sailor said, out of nowhere. "I've just ignored her."

Ingrid looked up from the phone. "I'm sorry. That must be hard."

"Losing a friend, yeah." Sailor looked suddenly distracted. Then she brightened, smiling again at Ingrid. "But I have gained one in the process. Which room do you want to take in the house?"

"Whatever is easiest for you. And your parents, of course." She handed Sailor's phone back. That was what she really wanted to ask. What would Scoot and Rill think about Ingrid moving in? What would Cas think? "I really don't want to put anyone out," she added.

"Oh please, there are nine bedrooms in that house. And my

parents will love having you there. They may be annoying as hell, but they really do want whatever makes me happy."

Unless it was stepping into the role of CEO of Savannah Sauce, the role she'd wanted since she was a girl. Ingrid wondered if Sailor was aware of Rill's final position on the subject yet. Or if Rill really did want Ingrid to break the news to his daughter for him.

"So I'm thinking"—Sailor slurped her whiskey sour thoughtfully—"the red-and-pink room. It's like feminine and traditional but also sort of . . . spicy." She sent Ingrid a playful little shoulder wiggle. "Like you."

"Me? You think I'm spicy?"

"Girl, you are so spicy." Sailor leaned in, conspiratorially. "I think my brother has a crush on you."

"No." Ingrid felt herself going bright red.

"I know. He was kind of rude to you at my party—"

Ingrid let out a noncommittal puff, but she hoped Sailor would say more.

"—but he's gotten into this weird church thing lately, so he thinks witches are like—"

Ingrid braced herself.

"—anti-God or something—"

"I'm not anti-God."

"Oh, I know that, but you have to understand Cas. He really gets into stuff. Like, *into*. When he was a kid, he was bullied at school."

Ingrid tilted her head to one side.

"We went to this really la-di-da private school, and Cas's grade was full of all these little pricks. Cas was always quiet. He liked to draw and read. He wasn't athletic. Anyway, around that time, he found this YouTube channel of a guy, some kind of MMA wrestler who taught all his moves. Cas started wearing this getup to school and calling himself Casimir the Killer."

"Oh no."

"He beat the shit out of these kids. Like, for real." Sailor gulped her drink. "My brother's kind of a weirdo but when he gets a new hobby, let me tell you, the guy does not play."

"I was bullied, too, actually," Ingrid said.

"What?"

"In school. The girls in my class put me in a chair and told me to renounce Satan."

Sailor's eyes got shiny. "Oh, Ingrid."

Ingrid shrugged, trying to seem unbothered. "I'm just saying that kind of thing can make a person . . . seem . . . I don't know, weird."

Sailor looked chastened. "Sorry. I shouldn't have said it like that. I just meant that Cas seems to think he had to do penance for being rich. It's just another way of rebelling against Mom and Dad, renouncing his worldly goods and worshipping God instead of P&L sheets. But I guess it's better than what he was up to before."

Ingrid went still. "What was he up to before?"

But Sailor had gotten distracted by her phone. "Oh my gosh. It's . . ." She trailed off.

"What?"

"It's my dress. For the dancing. Apparently, my coordinator went through our attic at the house, and she found my grandmother's wedding dress from, like, 1960-something, and she's found this incredible seamstress to remake it. Look at the drawing she did." She flashed her phone at Ingrid.

"Sailor, that's amazing."

Sailor sniffed, misty. "It is, actually. She was my dad's mom. Louise. I was very close to her, but she died."

"When you were sixteen."

Sailor looked started.

"You told me in our first reading."

"That's right. You remembered. That's so sweet."

Ingrid couldn't resist a smile. "Of course I did."

Sailor gazed back down at the image on her phone. "I can't even believe I thought Marcella was such a big deal. Louise's dress is so much better. I mean, look at it. It's so retro, but really kind of modern, too. It's perfect."

Sailor glanced up, and when she saw Ingrid's grin, stretched wide across her face now, her mouth dropped open.

"What?" she said. "Stop it! Did you do this? You did this, didn't you?"

Ingrid had only started to nod when Sailor was on top of her, jostling her drink, hugging her so hard Ingrid could barely breathe.

"You're the best! The absolute, fucking best! I love you so much, Ingrid!"

Chapter 20

A week later, Ingrid left Miles and Litha to supervise the renovations and moved into the Loeffler mansion.

The third-floor room Sailor had chosen for her, with its heavy, dark furniture and red-and-pink toile wallpaper that matched the bed linens that *also* matched the curtains, was, in Ingrid's opinion, not so much spicy as suffocating, but she wouldn't have dreamed of complaining. She felt lucky to be so close to her friend. To be living in the most luxurious mansion in Savannah.

In a million years, she would never have imagined it happening to her.

Cas had gone on some kind of religious retreat with his church, so there was no chance of running into him on the many flights of stairs, while getting a snack out of the impossibly well-stocked double fridge in the vast kitchen, or in the spacious theater room down on the garden level. Rill was also gone, out of the country on business.

There were no texts from her sinner either.

* * *

The following week, Sailor announced they would set up an altar room in one of the garden-level spa rooms where Scoot had her aestheticians come and do her many treatments and procedures.

"We need a dedicated place for readings," she told Ingrid. "And your spells."

Together they decorated the room with fairy lights and fake flowers and silver tinsel fringe so that it resembled a middle school girl's clubhouse more than a sacred space. After they'd finished, Ingrid offered to do her first official reading for Sailor since the bachelorette party. She lit the candles, and they sat together in the quiet.

"What would you like to focus on?" Ingrid asked. "Love, health, career?"

"Career." Sailor had a particularly intense look in her eye.

Ingrid felt a whisper of dread twist through her. Still, she tried to clear her mind and focus on the light. Sailor needed her, regardless of what inside information Ingrid happened to possess.

"You're good at what you do," she started. "You're a motivator and a connector. A team builder. You make people want to work hard for you."

That wasn't exactly a secret. Ingrid had experienced all these things firsthand and she'd pretty much said the same in their first reading. Still, other images were appearing in her mind . . .

A top-floor office . . .

Sailor, in a dark suit, sitting behind Rill's desk . . .

She felt the words come out of her mouth as if someone else was speaking them. "September is a big month. And I don't mean the wedding. I mean, for your work."

"Oh my God, really?" Sailor asked. "I'm really having a tough time there. Not with the work—all I have to do is basically sign off on everyone else's good ideas. It's just that I don't feel like my father gets how much I bring to the table. I need to come up with some great idea—I don't know, like a tie-in or partnership or something—that will get my father's attention. I really want to show him I should be CEO. When he's ready to hand the title over, obviously."

"Oh." Ingrid hooked her hair behind her ears, feeling uncomfortable. "I'm sorry . . . it's just that you're really not supposed to tell me everything. It kind of makes it hard for me to . . . hear."

"Oh." Sailor laughed self-consciously. "Good point." Her blue eyes shone in the dim light. "I guess what I need is someone to talk to more than a reading."

Ingrid's heart sped up. She wanted to talk to Sailor, too. Get answers to the many questions she had. For instance, who had Finley, ex-friend and former bridesmaid, been texting with that got her booted out of the inner circle? Did this person like to play a game of "sinner" and "saint"? Was it Cas? Or could it have been Rill?

But all she said was "I'm here for whatever you need."

Sailor frowned. "It's just that I've always been honest with my father about wanting the CEO spot. Lately, though, when I bring it up, he changes the subject or says something like 'That's my baby,' which is just code for *Settle down, you hysterical female*."

Ingrid nodded.

"And he keeps trying to get Cas to come to work for the company, which just kills me, you know? My baby brother couldn't give two shits about Savannah Sauce, and Dad just offered him a spot in the international division. For doing nothing! Which, naturally, Cas turned down because he thinks he wants to run away from home and join the circus. A monastery, I mean. Whatever."

"He really wants to be a monk?"

"Honestly, I don't know what he wants. He barely talks to me anymore. I think he thinks I'm one of them. On their side.

The point is, I can see Dad wants his precious son to be CEO when he retires instead of me. But I'm the one who loves the company. I'm the one who understands my dad—how he wants things, what he likes, the way he wants the company run."

"And you want him to be proud of you." Ingrid remembered the island on Sailor's palm. The break at age eight. For whatever reason, when she was a child, Sailor had felt she was losing her dad and had become determined to hold on to him any way she could.

Sailor looked miserable. "Will you do a spell for me, Ingrid? Like you did for the wedding things? I need a really powerful one so Dad will see me. Really see me."

"Oh." Ingrid chewed her lip. "I don't know, Sailor. I feel like . . . maybe I shouldn't get in the way of you and your dad's relationship, you know? I mean, the situation."

Sailor darkened. "I'm telling you that I need my father to see me as something more than a marketing director or Jude's trophy wife . . . I'm saying that I want him to take me seriously as a part of our family's company . . . and you don't want to help me?"

Ingrid felt shaky suddenly, adrenaline pouring into her body. "Sailor, I'm just saying that it seems like a really complicated family issue. I don't feel right getting in the middle of it."

"I brought you into my home, Ingrid. I hired you because I need you to help me with things . . . issues . . . specifically like this."

Ingrid hadn't been prepared for this at all. Hadn't seen this side of Sailor, the flip from cool to furious in a matter of seconds. It was true Sailor had said she loved her, that she was grateful for her friendship, but in the end, Ingrid was only here to do a job.

To be Sailor's psychic.

"Maybe I can—" Ingrid started to say, but Sailor's phone had just lit up and she glanced down at it.

"Oh *shit*!"

"What?"

"*Shit*!" Sailor grabbed Ingrid's hand and pulled her out of the room and toward the stairs.

Ingrid stumbled over her own feet. "What is it? Where are we going?"

"It's Tuesday, six-thirty, that's what it is," she said grimly. "Family dinner." Sailor charged up the stairs, Ingrid in tow. "We didn't have it last week because Dad was traveling, but he's back now, and when he's in town, the family eats supper together every Tuesday. Cas is back, too."

"Oh," puffed Ingrid, trying not to fall, trying to take in the new information. Cas was back. Rill was back. She was going to see them both. "I'm happy to go out to eat somewhere. Leave you to it."

"Oh no," Sailor said, her grip on Ingrid's wrist firm. "If I have to suffer through this, so do you."

When they reached the main floor, Ingrid noticed the Louis XVI clock on the delicate table in the corner showed 6:07.

"We dress," Sailor said simply and shooed Ingrid up to the third floor while she scurried toward her own room.

Ingrid changed into a simple skirt and blouse, brushed her hair, and washed her face. When she reappeared outside Sailor's door, she practically gasped out loud. In ivory trousers and a blue silk, off-the-shoulder blouse and her hair looking like she'd just had a blowout, her friend looked like she was about to dine at a Michelin star restaurant. Ingrid wished she had brought nicer clothes. Not that she had anything that compared to Sailor's wardrobe.

Before they went downstairs, Sailor walked her through the particulars. Freddie, the family chef, always prepared a huge meal while Sailor mixed the pre-dinner cocktails. Drinks were served in the drawing room along with some sort of canapé. When the meal was announced, the family moved into the dining room. After dessert, they took their after-dinner amaro or Drambuie into the library.

"When Mom breaks open the bourbon, that's when you get out," Sailor instructed. "Exit stage left. Under no circumstances do you drink with her. She will destroy you, reduce you to rubble, tears, a pile of dust, whatever, and you won't even see it coming." She sighed. "What we really need is an anti-Scoot spell, now that I think about it."

Ingrid nodded, relieved that Sailor seemed to have moved past the CEO thing. She hoped she would make it through the night. Did Cas and Rill even know she was living here now? She smoothed her skirt, trying to settle her nerves.

"Nobody makes a Dark and Stormy like my baby," Rill said. He looked more tan than usual, his healthy glow set off by the light blue linen suit and crisp white shirt. He'd been in the south of France, working on some deal there.

When Ingrid and Sailor had arrived in the grand foyer, Scoot had air-kissed Sailor and made a beeline for the bar. Rill on the other hand had taken Ingrid gently by the hands and kissed her on both cheeks. On the last kiss, he had leaned close to her ear. "Look at you, bringing the light to this dark house."

She'd only given him a tentative smile. Did he know what he was saying? Had Edie told him about the power and pull of the light? She couldn't tell, but he'd just sent her a playful lift of his eyebrow and gone to hug his daughter.

Now Sailor rolled her eyes at Ingrid. "Notice how he didn't say if the Dark and Stormy was good or disgusting. Just that I make it in a unique way."

Scoot lifted her glass. "Rill Loeffler, the master of the uncompliment."

"You women need to eat. You're getting snappish." Rill tossed back his drink and steered Scoot into the dining room. Just then Cas descended the stairs, barefoot and wearing what looked like the exact same clothes he'd worn the night of the party. The silver cross glinted on his chest. Fixing a polite expression on her face, Ingrid nodded at him.

"Cas," Sailor said. "You remember my friend Ingrid."

"I do." His eyes traveled up and down her plain skirt and blouse. But not in a way that made her feel awkward. It was like he was simply taking in information. She wondered what conclusion he was drawing.

"She's staying with us for a while. Until the repairs at her house are completed." Sailor handed him a drink.

"Ah," he said, sipping. "The repairs you forced on her."

"I'm really so grateful for everything Sailor's doing for me," Ingrid said.

Cas nodded, and she noticed he kept his eyes on her. She liked it, the feeling that he was studying her. They moved into the dining room, and she realized that instead of saying *We're really so grateful*, she had said *I'm*. She had purposefully left out any mention of Miles.

Chapter 21

Supper, as the Loefflers called it, was served quietly and efficiently by Freddie's assistant, who was dressed in the ubiquitous black uniform, and whose name Ingrid only caught when she deftly arranged a bowl of cold green soup in front of Rill with the skill of a trained server.

"Lovely, Sarita," he said in a low voice, and touched her arm. The young woman smiled but said nothing.

The Loefflers' dining room was formal, wallpapered in a plum iridescent paper with more scenes of nature: willow trees and storks and tiny bridges over clear, blue streams. The chandelier threw a spray of rainbow-colored light across the highly polished furniture and over the meticulously set table. The room was freezing. So cold you could hang meat in it.

Scoot had directed Ingrid to a chair beside Cas, and when she went to sit, he put a hand on her arm to stop her. She looked up at him, shocked at his touch, the first time he'd ever touched her, but she saw he only meant to pull out the chair for her.

"My son, the gentleman," said Scoot, coolly, cutting her eyes at Rill.

Ingrid sat and so did Cas, and then, when she smiled her thanks at him, his lips curved into a smile that made his dark eyes snap. She had a hard time looking away.

Sarita served them the chilled spring pea soup, then a Parmesan soufflé followed by marinated asparagus and snapper over a carrot purée. Scoot drank and talked, intermittently pushing her food to various positions on her plate. Cas didn't say much, nor did Sailor, but when they did speak it was to soothe and placate their mother. It seemed their role was to steer Scoot like an out-of-control bumper car. Rill watched his family interact with a distant, vaguely amused expression.

When she got a chance, Ingrid surreptitiously checked her phone, finding a series of texts from Miles.

Can you come over tonight? I was hoping we could hang out.

We could watch more *Twilight Zone*.

Litha's been acting weird. She's been coughing.

I think she misses you.

Where are the Band-Aids?

There was a feather touch on her thigh and she jumped, looking up. Cas raised his eyebrows at her like she was a naughty child.

"No phones," he mouthed.

She wedged her phone under her leg. The spot where he'd touched her tingled.

Dessert was espresso over ice cream in delicate crystal dishes. By then, Ingrid, thoroughly chilled to the bone, wished she'd worn a sweater. When the plates were cleared and the after-dinner drinks brought in, Ingrid finally summoned the courage to speak.

"You haven't told us how your retreat was, Cas. You went to a monastery up north, Sailor said?"

Scoot swirled the ice in her glass. Rill leaned back in his chair, arms crossed over his chest. Sailor looked uneasy.

Cas turned to Ingrid. "Yes. Michigan."

Scoot blew out her lips. "Pfft. Michigan. Who wants to go to Michigan?"

"Michigan is beautiful," Sailor said.

Scoot held up a finger. "Wait a minute, I take that back. I did go to Michigan once. Mama and Daddy took me to Mackinac Island when I was a little girl. That was *such* a cute place."

Sailor's jaw clenched and unclenched. Cas slowly folded and refolded his napkin.

Ingrid turned to Cas again. "I didn't know Lutherans had monasteries."

Cas nodded. "It's pretty rare. This one's ecumenical. People from all denominations go there. Roman Catholic, Episcopalian, Eastern Orthodox."

"What did you do?" Sailor asked. "Like, pray all day?"

Cas bent forward, warming to the subject. "It's a farm so most of the day everyone's working in the garden, helping out in the kitchen, or chopping and hauling wood. But that doesn't start until the afternoon. The morning starts at five with the Office of Vigils, then personal meditations and Lauds at six. Everyone observes silence during breakfast, then there's Terce around nine, then the Eucharist. After that everybody does their jobs. Sext is at noon, None at two-thirty, Vespers at six, Compline at eight-thirty."

"We did Vespers at camp," Scoot said.

"What are all those things you just listed?" Ingrid asked.

"The monastic offices." Cas's face was flushed. "Prayers that structure the monastery's day."

"That's so nice," Ingrid said. It reminded her of the prayers Edie had taught her, that they prayed as they followed the positions of the sun in the house.

Suddenly Ingrid's phone rang. Loudly. She pulled it out from under her leg. Miles.

"Sorry," she said, and sent the call to voicemail.

"Sweetheart," Scoot said. "We don't bring our phones to family dinner."

"Sorry," Ingrid repeated and, face burning, tucked her phone away again.

"So. You gonna be a monk, Casimir?" Rill asked.

Cas swallowed his water. "I don't have plans to, sir, at the moment. I just went to see what it was all about."

"Because that's one hell of a commitment." Rill was leaning forward now. Sarita smoothly stopped at his chair and removed his empty wine glass.

"Yep."

"They use the sauce on their meat?"

The sauce. He meant Savannah Sauce.

"They're vegetarian, so . . . no."

Rill snorted. "The least you could've done was sell 'em a box. It's good on beans and tofu, too."

"We're in all hypermarkets and specialty chains in Michigan already, Dad," Sailor said, and took a delicate sip of her drink.

Scoot stood up. "Library time. Sarita, will you bring the Blanton's with you?"

Sarita scurried out to the foyer bar. Sailor sent Ingrid a pointed look as the rest of the family stood.

Scoot paused, her eyes glassily focused on Ingrid. "Sweetheart, Ingrid? Have a bourbon with me. I want to hear more about everything your grandmother taught you." She sent a saucy look at Rill.

He moved to her side and caught her by the arm. "Darling, the kids want to go hang out or watch a movie or something, not stay with the old folks."

Ingrid resisted the urge to rub her arms to warm them. "Thank you so much for dinner." As if Scoot had had anything to do with the meal.

"You're welcome, my dear," Scoot said, formal and cold once again. "We're so glad you joined us. And came to stay."

Cas and Sailor headed toward the foyer, Ingrid following. Sailor leaned over to her and whispered, "I'm telling you, we need an anti-Scoot spell."

"Hey!" Rill's voice behind them was like the boom of a shotgun.

Cas, Sailor, and Ingrid stopped and turned, facing the man.

He was eyeing Cas. "Put some goddamn shoes on next time you sit at my table," he said. It was a snarl.

"Yessir."

Sailor took Cas's arm and pulled him out of the room, but Ingrid couldn't seem to make her legs move.

Rill lifted his eyebrows. She stared back at him, trying to comprehend how someone so funny and warm and strong could speak to his adult son that way.

"I know," he said. "I'm a dick. I'm sorry." His eyes bored into hers. "You look beautiful tonight, Ingrid. So much like Edie."

She hesitated, whiplashed from Rill's turn from domineering father to smooth charmer. And still, something warm and needy opened up inside her. It was a compliment only a handful of people in this town could pay her. Not that many people had known Edie well enough. Not that many seemed to care.

"Thank you," she said. Then she headed to the kitchen, where no one would notice the way her lips unsuccessfully resisted a smile.

By the end of June, Ingrid and Sailor were texting each other throughout every day, sharing jokes, gossip, and memes about weddings, witchcraft, and difficult mothers. By this time, Ingrid had also experienced a list of things she never imagined in a million years she would've done.

These included:

Taking a full tour of the Savannah Sauce headquarters, located in a sleek high-rise near the bridge. It swarmed with important-looking people holding files and briskly walking around. Sailor's office was an impressive, all-glass space on the twenty-first floor that overlooked the river. Sailor also showed Ingrid Rill's office and a conference room, a vast expanse of white, glass, and chrome that took up nearly a whole floor and made you feel like you were floating in midair.

Shopping in Atlanta for Sailor's honeymoon wardrobe, which concluded with Ingrid the proud new owner of a gorgeous gown for the wedding, a new pair of four-hundred-dollar, metallic silver sneakers, and a buttery, soft brown leather jacket that fit Ingrid like a dream.

A facial, massage, and private Pilates session with Sailor at the Hotel Bardo's elegant spa, and a private chef's meal at The Grey restaurant with Sailor and Jude that lasted four hours.

Finally—and definitely the experience that took the cake—was a simulated hostage extraction experience on an abandoned army base in South Georgia where she, Sailor, Jude, and a group of their friends were allowed to shoot automatic rifles loaded with blanks at masked actors who were playing paramilitary terrorists. There had been a helicopter and several fake bombs involved, and while Ingrid had cowered behind a bunch of oil drums for much of the time, praying for the whole ordeal to be over, Sailor had taken quite naturally to the action, transforming into a screaming, chest-pounding action hero.

Ingrid got to know the Loefflers' staff as well: Mrs. Leimberger, the Loefflers' house manager, and Adrian, the chauffeur, a thin, older man who wore a black suit and a chauffeur's cap and who Ingrid learned had a son who was earning an MBA in themed entertainment design at Savannah College of Art and Design. Freddie and Sarita in the kitchen. The crew of housekeepers who, daily and meticulously, cleaned every room of the enormous house.

At least once a day, Mrs. Leimberger texted Ingrid dates and times that Adrian would be waiting at the curb in front of the Loeffler house in the family's gleaming black Rolls-Royce to pick her up and ferry her to luxurious mansions or five-star hotels, or once, even a gated compound at the far eastern end of Tybee Island, to do readings for their friends. Clemmie Fairburn, her sister Lulu Hawkes, Devlin McIntyre, Josephine Penski, and several others all clamored for Ingrid's time.

Ingrid quickly learned she was expected to be on call at all times. Her time may not have been her own any longer, but the trade-off was worth it. Every Friday, she got an alert from First Chatham Bank that the exact amount of one thousand dollars had been quietly deposited into her checking account. She marveled every time it happened, even more so because she didn't actually need the cash. She wasn't spending any money to speak of. She ate most every meal at the house or out with Sailor. And Sailor was constantly offering to pay for things. As a result, her bank account was growing by leaps and bounds.

Thankfully, Sailor seemed to have forgotten the whole CEO spell issue—or at least she'd decided to respect Ingrid's reluctance to interfere—and was satisfied with the meditations, moon rituals, and wedding-related spell work that Ingrid led her through.

Miles checked in regularly with a variety of problems such as Litha's loneliness and imaginary illnesses, but they all seemed like inventions to get her attention. Ingrid called him as often as she could, always reminding him that it had been his idea for her to move to the Loefflers' and she'd be home before they knew it. He usually calmed down, but she was getting tired of having to coddle him.

She finally called him one day so she could address the situation head-on. "Miles," she said gently, "I need you to understand that me being here with the Loefflers is part of a bigger plan."

"How so?" He sounded doubtful.

She took a deep breath. "I think it has something to do with the thing Edie asked me to do before she died. Remember? She said I needed to right the balance."

He was quiet for a long moment. "I thought you said it was the cancer talking. That she didn't make any sense at the end."

"I did," she said. "But I think I might've been wrong. Maybe it's nothing, but I feel like Edie wants me here. And if she does, if this is a chance for me to fix things, that will be good for you, too."

That shut him up. He might be jealous of her new position and friendship with Sailor, but he understood Ingrid's loyalty was to Edie first, and he would never interfere with that.

Her love life was substantially different now, too. Boney sent the occasional text that would hint around for one of their "get-togethers," and one afternoon when Sailor had appointments, she did meet him at his apartment for a brief half hour. Most times, though, she gave him the brush-off.

The texts from her secret admirer, her "sinner," were now taking up all the space in her brain. After she'd been living at the Loefflers for just under a month, a new string of messages hit her phone. She'd been getting ready for bed, washing her face in the small bathroom adjoined to her room.

I sin every day because of you, he'd written.

She paused, her face covered in foamy bubbles. Was it Cas, locked away in his bedroom on the second floor? If so, they were so close. Close enough to actually meet in one of their rooms.

Fingers trembling, she replied. **Then you and I should keep our distance.** Not that she wanted that. She wanted the opposite. She wanted Cas Loeffler to come up to her room and take her in his arms.

That won't help. No matter where you are, you surround me.

It was the perfect response, pure poetry, and the words left her breathless. She hopped into bed, hastily propping up pillows behind her. When her phone vibrated with another text, she felt her stomach flip deliciously.

Ingrid. It means Fair, beautiful goddess of fertility.

She waited, holding her breath. A message in another thread dinged, and she checked it.

Come over

Ugh. Boney.

She composed a quick excuse—**I'm in my luteal phase**—and sent it back. Almost immediately her phone dinged again.

What the fuck is that

My period. Go read a book, Boney. Improve your mind.

I want to improve my dick

No.

Her phone chimed again. Her sinner.

My devotion to you is an act of blasphemy.

She couldn't resist a triumphant smile. She nestled back into the large down pillows, thought for a moment, then typed out a reply. She stared at it a few seconds, not sending it, remembering how quickly Finley had been excised from Sailor's life for texting someone she shouldn't have.

But she wouldn't send pictures of herself. This wasn't *that*. This was different. This was something so real and deep, it transcended the normal ways people communicated.

She pressed the blue arrow, sending her reply.

Punish yourself then. Punish yourself for me.

Chapter 22

"The place is yours."

Down in Sailor and Ingrid's garden-level altar room, the two had just completed a psychic attunement ritual and were sprawled out on their backs staring at the ceiling Scoot's team of installers had papered with a dreamy navy-blue constellation design.

Sailor had told Ingrid that every fourth of July, the Loefflers went to Maine, to a large private island owned by one of Scoot's cousins. They stayed in a huge house, what Sailor called a cottage, with thirteen bedrooms, a carriage house, a barn, a beach, and a variety of boats. Sailor described the three-day getaway as filled with tennis matches, bridge tournaments, and more lobster than a human being could eat.

Since the Loefflers would be out of town, Sailor said that the family beach cottage on Tybee Island was available for the holiday. Ingrid was welcome to use it for the long weekend and take Miles or a girlfriend, if she wanted. Although she shouldn't expect too much, Sailor warned. This cottage was built in the fifties by Rill's grandparents, the originators of the Savannah

Sauce empire and humble folk, and hadn't been updated in more than forty years.

"My mom doesn't darken the doors of the place," Sailor said, with an eye roll. "Tybee's a bit on the downscale side for her. Anyway, you should go." She patted Ingrid's arm. "The beach is fantastic and private, and there's a hot tub on the deck."

When Ingrid called Miles, he was ecstatic. "A free beach house?" he crowed. "For three days? Are you kidding me?"

"I figured we could use some time together," Ingrid said. "And a way for me to say how much I appreciate all you're doing, looking after the house. I know it hasn't been easy."

"I'm sorry I've been such a pain. I just want you to remember who you are, Ingrid. Those people may be paying you, but you're every bit as good as them."

"I know that."

"In fact, you're better than them, if you want to know the truth."

She redirected the conversation back to the Tybee weekend. He said he would try to get away. Although July Fourth ghost tours were always jam-packed, and his boss would probably pitch a fit, he thought Mari, who cleaned rooms at several B and Bs and occasionally filled in for him, would welcome the extra work.

The following Friday morning, the pair of them were ensconced in the cool, leathery back seat of the Loefflers' Rolls-Royce as Adrian drove them the half hour to Tybee Island. When Adrian wheeled the Rolls onto an unassuming side street lined with old beach cabins, Ingrid's mouth dropped. He pulled to the end, stopping at a wood-paneled, two-story house which was nearly obscured by a thick hedge of wax myrtle, and cut the engine.

Sailor hadn't been kidding. This place really was low-key.

Maybe the first time that word applied to anything related to the Loefflers.

The rough cedar siding was painted a beachy mint green. Brown shutters flanked the windows. The deck looked weathered, but everything was in good repair. Adrian took their bags out of the trunk and carried them through the hedge, up a set of wooden steps. Dropping them at the door, he handed a set of keys to Ingrid and tipped his hat. "I'll be back to pick you up on Sunday evening at eight o'clock."

When he was gone, Miles gave the cottage a once-over, then Ingrid a look of incredulity. "So this place is ours? For the whole weekend?"

Ingrid shrugged, unlocking the door. "Apparently, they barely come here. Well, Rill does sometimes, I think. Sailor said it belonged to his grandfather."

"The one who started Savannah Sauce."

"Yep."

"What an absolute boss. It's like some kind of badass Ernest Hemingway man-cave."

They explored the whole place, starting with the main floor. It was one open room, a knotty pine-paneled living room and dining room area scattered with matching mid-century modern furniture and seagrass rugs. A huge sailfish arced gracefully over the stone fireplace.

On the other end of the room was a rustic kitchen, with orange Formica countertops and ruffled curtains on the windows. An old, green rotary phone with a long cord hung on the wall. Upstairs consisted of four small bedrooms.

The fridge, in true Loeffler style, was fully stocked with neatly stacked takeout meals from a local caterer, deli meat and bread, and a variety of fresh fruits and vegetables, as well as a selection of eggs and bacon for breakfast. In a small fridge in the laundry room, they found beer and wine. Sailor had made sure every detail was taken care of.

"Such a wild place," Miles said when they were back outside, standing on the deck, drinking bottles of fancy IPAs and watching the waves roll in. The beach was a glorious sight. Deserted and lit golden brown by the sun.

Ingrid turned to look at him. "What do you mean?"

"It's a party house," Miles said. "Mark my words, my man *Aurelian* definitely comes here to party, get high . . . or fuck his girlfriends."

A sharp desire to defend Rill shot through her. "He's a pretty busy man, Miles. He works all the time."

"Well, then he *used* to fuck his girlfriends here."

Ingrid felt a chill travel through her. He wasn't wrong. There was definitely an aura here. The presence of something . . . mysterious. And not altogether good.

She heard a shriek and blinked into focus. Miles had ripped his shirt off and was racing across the sand in the direction of the lapping ocean waves. She smiled. He was such a little boy sometimes, unabashedly joyful at the simplest of things. She checked her phone. Her sinner had texted.

How's the beach house?

She shook her head, smiling a secretive smile.

Perfect. Almost.

He would know what she meant. The one thing missing was him. And she was almost one hundred percent sure that the *him* was Cas.

Another text. **I hate that you're there with him.**

She drew in a breath and slipped back inside the house, pulling the sliding glass door closed behind her. This was something new—Cas being jealous of Miles. Maybe it heightened the drama for him. Imagining that they were doing something illicit. It was strange, but Ingrid didn't think it mattered that much in the end. If it turned him on, if it got her closer to him, who was she to dissuade him? Nevertheless, she was not going to let this opportunity pass her by.

He's my friend, she typed. **What was I supposed to do, come here alone?**

Are you going to sleep with him?

She sighed. It was almost like he wanted her to say they were. Like it was the only thing that kept him coming back to her.

Is that any of your business? she answered.

Every breath you take interests me.

She really was getting the tiniest bit tired of all this game-playing. All this baiting him with the perfectly calibrated kind of response that would tantalize him but not turn him off. Even if her sinner was Cas, even he was only a flight of stairs away from her at the Loeffler house, the reality was that nothing had come of all their heated texting.

The truth was she was tired of working so hard and getting nothing in return. If he was really that jealous, he'd take her out to dinner, wouldn't he? She tapped a terse reply.

It's just something people do, you know. Sex.

I'm better than him. I would make you happier.

Oh yeah? How exactly would you do that?

I could make you come there alone.

She smirked. **Haha, very funny.**

I'm not kidding, came his stern response. **Go upstairs.**

Why?

Because sometimes saints like a sinner to take charge. Last bedroom on the right. The blue one.

She looked up at the ceiling, annoyed. If you asked her, taking charge would be asking her out on an actual date.

Why? she typed. She was being obstinate, she knew. But she was weary of his games.

Just go.

She sighed. Clutching her phone, she climbed the stairs and walked down the hall, to the last room on the right. She pushed open the door. The room was indeed a soft blue. In the corner sat a small twin bed neatly made up with a navy chenille bedspread. On the opposite wall was a framed poster of Tybee Island Children's Maritime Museum. Obviously, a little boy's room.

Cas's room.

Now what? she typed.

See the bed?

Yes.

Lie down on it.

A long pause, then . . .

I want to make you come in my bed.

She inhaled, frozen, staring at the phone. Her heart thudded so hard she felt like it might burst through her chest. And she suddenly started shaking all over. They'd texted some dirty stuff but they'd never, like, actually *done* anything. This was a step further than they'd ever gone. This felt dangerous.

And a little wrong.

She typed back, fingers trembling. **We shouldn't.**

Don't be scared. I'll be with you.

If this really was Cas, had he also been texting Finley things like this? It seemed likely . . . and it had made Sailor furious. So angry, she'd cut her friend out of the wedding.

So did she dare walk the tightrope of drawing Cas out without doing or saying anything that would be considered out of line as Sailor's friend?

She held her breath, thinking through all the possible scenarios. Sailor could never know. She would have to be extremely careful. She would absolutely, one hundred percent, not send pictures, no matter what. She would not be another Finley. She couldn't bear losing Sailor.

She thought quickly. **That other messaging app,** she typed. Those disappeared, didn't they? That would be safer.

She was having a difficult time thinking straight now—about Sailor, about being discovered. About anything other than Cas. Her sinner.

Go into the room and shut the door, he sent.

She did as she was told.

Chapter 23

Saturday was bright, cloudless, and hot. Ingrid spent the day surreptitiously texting both Sailor and her sinner, all the while trying to seem fully present with Miles. The task presented a challenge, to say the least.

Sailor's texts were all pictures of the rugged Maine coast, the abundant spreads of lobster-themed dishes, and selfies of kissy faces, saying things like, **wish you were hereeeeee!!!** and **miss your smooshy faceeeee!!!** Ingrid replied to these instantly with reciprocal gushing.

When her sinner texted her, she had to be more strategic. She would sneak her phone into the bathroom or wait until Miles went for a swim so she could compose something suitably suggestive but also noncommittal. It gave her a little rush, making sure she didn't accidentally send a horny text to Sailor. She hated herself for it, this addiction to adrenaline brought on by a non-relationship with a man, but she couldn't stop herself.

She was addicted to Cas Loeffler.

All she wanted, all she dreamed about, was the day when they would finally be together. When they could look into each other's eyes and finally say all the things out loud that they'd only been able to write. Scenario after scenario played through her mind. She and Cas would dance with each other at Sailor's wedding. Come next July, maybe they would be the ones to frolic on the rocky shores of Maine. She even dared to let herself think ahead to Christmas. Maybe they'd steal away to Aspen or wherever rich people went, for sleigh rides and snowshoeing.

And then . . . the day would come when he would take her by the hand and announce to his family that he had fallen in love with her. Ingrid White, plain and simple, humble and poor. Cas would tell his family that none of those things mattered and the two of them were going to marry. They would all embrace her then, ready to love her, not just because of Cas, but because she'd proven her loyalty to them all.

She'd proven she was good enough to be one of them.

Ingrid Loeffler, Ingrid Loeffler, Ingrid Loeffler . . . She doodled the name dreamily across her mind as she didn't dare do it on an actual piece of paper that Miles might see.

Once they were together, Cas would realize that he couldn't become a monk and reject his family's wealth. He had other people to think of—a woman he loved and maybe even a future family. He would also see that his money could be better used to help people in need.

Maybe he could find something to do at Savannah Sauce that was more fulfilling than CEO. Anyway, once he was established, they would have a wedding, maybe something a little less formal than what Sailor and Jude were planning. It would be simple and sincere, like Cas. It would be full of love . . .

Later that night, she and Miles walked over to a local seafood place for dinner. She fell asleep, her head on his lap, while they watched *Independence Day*, Miles's selection. She only roused herself enough to make it upstairs, shed her shorts, and fall into bed in her T-shirt and underwear where she slept deeply and dreamlessly.

Much later she heard voices downstairs. Voices and music, Kendrick Lamar's "Not Like Us."

She blearily checked her phone. 12:48 a.m. She pulled on her shorts and tiptoed halfway down the stairs where she saw the entire cabin filled with people and the sliding doors leading to the deck flung open. Miles was standing under the sailfish holding up a plastic cup and telling a group of people circled around him a story. Shouting it, over the pounding music.

She clocked a few faces: Boney, Mari, Fran, Louella. Sheffield, her neighbor and Dean Remington's husband, was dancing in the corner with some guy who was not Dean. Sasha, the girl working catering at Sailor's engagement party, was there, too.

Miles had obviously sent up a flare to all their friends—PARTY AT THE LOEFFLERS'—and after their shifts had ended, everyone had come. It was too good to miss . . . a rager at the Loefflers' beach house, a place none of them would ever get the opportunity to see otherwise. Truthfully, she couldn't blame him.

Just then Miles looked up and caught her eye. He lifted his beer in her direction. "She's up!" he crowed.

As a whole entity, the room turned to look at her. Unable to resist a grin, she waved back, and a cheer went up. The next song kicked in, "Princess Diana" by Ice Spice, at which point the whole room started collectively screaming and jumping up and down. And there was Miles, right in the middle of it all, standing still, beaming up at her.

She laughed now; she couldn't help it. How could she not go down and join the thrashing throng? How could she not drink a White Claw, then another, then another and then do a bunch of shots? She could and she did.

As she danced, she told herself she deserved to celebrate. She had finally made it. She had saved Edie's house. Saved Edie's business. And put her own name on the map. Ingrid White was flying in first class now. And everybody wanted to be her friend.

She partied until she was reeling drunk, hoarse from singing, rubbery-legged from nonstop dancing. At one point Boney pulled her close for a sexy slow dance, after which he led her to the bathroom where he locked the door, started kissing her, and put his hand down her pants. She slapped him away.

"Mean girl." He pouted, then narrowed his eyes. "Are you sleeping with somebody?"

"So what if I am? You don't care."

"I mean, no. But also, yes. Kind of. C'mon, Ingrid. I'm not that much of a douche."

Ingrid felt bad. He wasn't a douche. She just didn't have the time to explain everything to him. "I'm just really busy, that's all."

He was studying her closely. "Is it the brother? What's-his-name, the shaggy dude—"

"Cas. And no, I'm not having sex with Cas Loeffler." Not for lack of trying.

"Well"—Boney bent down and kissed her softly on the forehead—"when you're tired of playing with the richies, I guess come find me."

She felt a twinge of melancholy. She did miss the guy. He might be rough around the edges, but at least he was real flesh and blood, and just said straight out what he wanted and when he wanted it. Boney was easy. And he knew how to please. But he didn't hold the same allure that Cas did.

Extricating herself from Boney, she went back out where she continued to drink and dance. At some point, she found herself pulling Sheffield down the stairs that led to the open area under the house, with some vague, drunken sort of plan to explore. The area was on a concrete slab, enclosed with lattice, with a grimy ping-pong table sitting in the center. There was a tiki bar, too, and a bunch of plastic bins stacked in a corner. Sheffield found a golf ball and bounced it over the ping-pong net to Ingrid and she caught it.

"Athletic while drunk. Impressive." He struck a pose, a look of surprised respect on his face. She laughed and bounced that ball back, hitting him in the face and making her collapse in giggles, and after that, things dimmed to a pleasant land of muffled shadows, then finally to nothingness.

Chapter 24

When she woke—in the right bed, thank the Goddess—it took her a minute to remember what had happened.

She was at Rill Loeffler's beach house.

The love shack . . .

And there had been a party.

One Miles had planned. Had they trashed the place? She couldn't remember, but there had been a lot of people, some she had never seen before. She should definitely check. Today was their last day. Adrian would be back to pick them up that night.

She looked around warily. She was alone in the room. Alone in the bed, thank the Goddess for that, too. She grabbed her phone, still on the bedside table where she'd left it before the party. It was two in the afternoon. Six hours until Adrian. She ached for water.

Beside her, in the covers of the bed, lay a picture. A photograph. She brushed the sleep out of her eyes and held it up. It was a snapshot of Edie, on the younger side, maybe around forty years old. She was wearing one of her gypsy costumes, standing on the deck of a house. This house.

Last night's memories lazily swam to the surface. After playing golf-ball ping-pong and screaming out the score like the guy who called the Savannah Bananas games, she and Sheffield had torn open the plastic storage bins. Inside, they'd found a lot of cool stuff. Old martini shakers and ice buckets. Ashtrays. A whole bin of vinyls, which Sheffield went nuts over and said he was going to come back at some point and steal. They'd also found a bunch of old clothes and beach towels, all mildewed and musty. And then she'd found the pictures.

Pictures she couldn't, at the moment, recall in any specific detail—

Suddenly, the door banged open and someone bounded in, then launched himself onto the bed. Sheffield lunged at her, smothering her in a bear hug.

"Practical Magic!" he sang out. "I can't believe I've lived next door to you for a year and a half and never knew how fun you were!"

She felt her stomach roil, then rise. She struggled out of his arms and ran to the bathroom, where she vomited in the toilet. She came back in and regarded Sheffield with watering eyes.

"That wasn't fun," he said. "Hey. Can you tell your cute little boyfriend to give me a chance? Please, please, please, please."

"Who? Miles?"

"He's so yum."

"He's straight," she said. "And you're married."

"Neither an insurmountable problem. I think there's something else. A bigger problem."

"What's that?"

Sheffield threw open his arms and brought them together in a dramatic, fluid chorus girl move, pointing at Ingrid. "He's besotted with you, gorgeous."

"He's absolutely not besotted with me. Trust me. We're like brother and sister." She sat on the bed beside him. Sheffield groaned and fell over, laying his head in her lap. She laughed, then patted his beautiful, honey cupcake frosting hair.

"It's Moroccan oil." He snuggled on her lap, getting comfortable. "What I use to get my hair to look like an angel's. Tell your boyfriend-slash-brother-slash-roommate that I can get him on a movie set if he'll go out with me."

She swatted him. "What about Dean?"

He sighed. "He is so mean. He says I have to get a job. I told him I had a job. Stay-at-home daddy."

"I thought you were an actor or a model or something."

Sheffield rolled his eyes. "He means like real job at a restaurant or a hotel. He doesn't think I show the proper motivation in my chosen field."

"I mean, you do smoke a lot of weed. I smell it all day long."

He laughed. "Ouch." He gazed up into her face. "You and Miles should come over for dinner sometime."

"And let you seduce him in front of your poor husband?"

"Now you feel sorry for Dean? Believe me, you've got this all wrong. You have no idea. He's got plenty of action on the side."

She gave him another swat, but this one was gentler. It was hard not to feel sorry for him. Snotty old Dean couldn't be the easiest person to live with. "Maybe we'll come over. Who cooks, you or Dean?"

"This lady named Zelda."

She laughed and pushed him off her lap. "I need to get going. What's going on downstairs?"

"Everybody left this morning. I stayed in case Miles needed some help holding his hair back over the toilet." He sent her a devilish smirk.

She walked to the door. "Come with me. Help me clean up. You can score some points with Miles."

While Miles picked up trash on the beach, Sheffield helped Ingrid put the area under the house back in order. Plastic bins were opened, upturned, items strewn everywhere.

They'd made a hell of a mess. It looked as if they'd basically staggered around the space, drunkenly flinging handfuls of old photos in the air. She crouched to gather them, and at last, she had them collected into one huge mound.

She organized them by style of print, older to more recent. The shiny rectangular prints—from the nineties, she guessed—that were all taken here, at the beach house, at Rill's many parties. She sifted slowly through these. From the looks of it, the parties had been epic—everyone tanned and glassy-eyed from drink and drugs. All in a state of undress, all with their arms flung over shoulders.

One photo showed a woman spraying a bottle of champagne off the deck. One showed a man doing unspeakable things to the sailfish, on whose long sword hung a woman's bra. A woman held a pan engulfed in flames over the stove. Someone played the bongos by a bonfire. Someone else was naked, head lolling, twined in the arms of someone who winked at the camera. In every picture, everyone was always laughing.

And then she saw them. The pictures of Edie.

Edic sitting at a small bistro table on the deck, doing a reading for someone. Edie clinking a can of beer with a fellow partier. Edie wearing oversized red, white, and blue glasses and holding a lit sparkler.

One made her heart stop. It was of Edie, standing on the deck, in the same peasant blouse and skirt, hoop earrings and bandana as in the picture Ingrid had brought to bed with her. Beside her, a devastatingly handsome Rill Loeffler, shirtless, tan and very young, had his arms wrapped around her and was kissing her cheek. Above them, on the clapboard siding of the house, hung a carved wood sign reading SARGASSUM SLING.

Ingrid studied the picture again. She couldn't put her finger on it, but there was something different about their embrace. Something . . . intimate. Edie seemed so relaxed, her body resting against Rill's. And he just seemed so happy. And then she noticed his hand. Resting lower on her hip than a friend's would.

Resting in a possessive way, like she belonged to him. Ingrid glanced at the wooden sign above them again. SARGASSUM SLING.

S.S.

The entries she'd found in Edie's ledger. So Edie had come here, in the mid-1990s, at least a dozen times, probably as the entertainment at Rill Loeffler's parties. That must've been when Rill fell in love with her. And when Scoot decided Edie White was her mortal enemy.

It was easy to see why. All you had to do was look at the picture. See the expression in their eyes.

At precisely eight o'clock that evening, the house cleaner arrived, a young woman in a pink polo shirt, lugging a bucket of cleaning supplies and a vacuum cleaner. Adrian arrived as well in the Rolls-Royce.

On their way out, Miles and Ingrid passed the house cleaner and exchanged guilty glances. They'd tidied every room in the house, scrubbed the kitchen, and hauled three full trash bags out to the next-door neighbor's garbage cans so as not to raise suspicion when the maid looked in the Loefflers' cans. Ingrid hoped they'd been thorough enough. She didn't want Sailor thinking she couldn't be trusted.

On the drive back, Miles fell asleep, as she googled *Sargassum*.

The first entry that popped up was the government's NOAA Ocean Exploration website. It said that sargassum was a type of algae, "a genus of large brown seaweed that floats in island-like masses and never attaches to the seafloor." Apparently, when it washed up on shore and began to decompose, the rotten egg smell it emitted was considered poisonous, causing anyone who came into contact with it to suffer heart palpitations, shortness of breath, dizziness, vertigo, headache, and skin rashes. If inhaled in concentrated forms, like in an enclosed sewer, it could cause death.

She swiped out of the website, unsettled. What an odd choice, to name your beach house after a poisonous plant.

When they arrived back in town, Adrian dropped Miles off at Ingrid's house, then took Ingrid the few blocks to the Loefflers'. He carried her bag up to the door, depositing it in the entryway and then tipping his hat.

She suddenly felt panicky, wondering if he could tell she been up to no good at the beach house. If he somehow could intuit that in her bag, tucked carefully between the pages of the copy of *Circe*—the paperback she'd packed for the trip but never gotten around to reading—was a photo.

Not the photo she'd brought to bed with her or the one she'd found when they were cleaning up. It was another one, clearly taken the same day, while Edie and Rill were standing on the deck of Sargassum Sling. A photo she couldn't afford for anyone to find in the Loefflers' house.

Because in this picture, Rill and Edie were locked in an embrace, their bodies pressed together, kissing.

Chapter 25

The following week, Mrs. Leimberger texted Ingrid to say that Scoot would be dropping by Ingrid's house on Wednesday to oversee the final installation of draperies, furniture, and appliances and make note of any final touch-ups that might be needed. Mrs. Leimberger called it a punch list, and Ingrid texted her back, quickly and confidently, as if she was familiar with the term.

She was doing a lot of that these days.

She cancelled her appointments for that day and called Miles to ask him if he'd mind leaving the house to her, so she and Scoot could have some privacy. She'd decided she would use the occasion to serve the woman lunch so they could talk. Scoot would see that, no matter what had gone on between Rill and Edie, Ingrid had no ulterior motive. Maybe she would finally accept her.

Wednesday morning, just as dawn was bathing the city in warm pink light, Ingrid collected a few bags of groceries Sarita had set aside for her in the kitchen then walked the few blocks to her house. Litha met her at the door. She picked up the cat, kissed her nose, and went to wake up Miles. After practically pushing him into the shower and out the door, she walked slowly through the house, marveling at all the changes.

Slick new thermostats were mounted on the walls, and the sound of the new, powerful AC unit purred, silently and efficiently cooling the whole house. Every light fixture was polished and in working order. Walls were replastered, floors were sanded and stained. Baseboards, cornices, balusters, and windows had every scratch and nick filled in and painted over.

The dining room had been papered in a jade green and peach floral. Rich chocolate velvet drapes were held back with silk cords. Even the old dining room table and chairs had been stripped, sanded, and refinished.

The sitting room was even more grand, papered in a peach moiré. Edie's old, rose-patterned rug had been cleaned, the chairs reupholstered in fringed chocolate velvet, and vibrant green print pillows of all shapes and sizes were scattered about, one adopted by Litha as her new bed. The kitchen was bright with the new high-end range, fridge, and dishwasher. They'd painted this room a watercolor yellow.

Ingrid went back upstairs and, slipping into Edie's bedroom, breathed in her grandmother's familiar scent. She was glad she hadn't let Sailor and Scoot redo the bedrooms. Some things should never change and that was just the truth. She put her copy of *Circe*, the photograph of Edie and Rill tucked between the pages, on Edie's nightstand, then sat on the bed. She was remembering the way she and Edie would snuggle up before bedtime for a story and a song. For tales about Edie's family from England and how they learned to work with the light.

"I know, Edie," she said now into the still room. "I know about you and him. And I can see why you didn't tell me. But . . . he seemed like he really loved you. And his children are great. Kind and thoughtful. They've taken me in, you know. Given me work and friendship and so much more. I just . . . I hope

I'm making you proud. I'm sorry I didn't hear what you were saying to me back then. I just . . . I hope I'm on the right path now to doing what you said. To righting the balance."

The air didn't stir. But Ingrid knew Edie had heard her. Every word. And Ingrid would wait as long as it took for her grandmother's response. For her guidance.

Scoot arrived looking chic in a nubby tweed dress and matching jacket, a two-man camera crew standing dutifully behind her.

"I thought we'd get some photos for *Coastal Living* or *Veranda,*" she said as Ingrid stepped aside and let her in. "In case they have any interest."

Scoot moved through the house, locked in jittery concentration as she adjusted tables and lamps, shook out drapes until they billowed, and rearranged vases and candlesticks. Different installers arrived to deliver additional items: curtain panels, an upholstered ottoman, a new set of dining chairs. Another assistant who had appeared out of nowhere scurried around rearranging and adorning every surface with glossy books and potted plants.

As the photographer and his assistant began to set up their equipment, Ingrid suggested she and Scoot eat. She escorted Scoot into the kitchen, to the small table set with Edie's fine china and real silver. Scoot sat, smoothed the linen napkin over her tweed skirt, and proceeded to push the shrimp salad Ingrid had made around her plate the same way she did at the Loeffler family dinners.

"Would you like something else to drink?" Ingrid asked.

Scoot was already reaching into her purse. "I brought a little something." She drew out a mini bottle of vodka and poured it into the iced tea. "Here we go." She gave Ingrid a bright, brittle smile. "Cheers."

In response to every subject Ingrid brought up—Sailor's wedding plans, the Maine cottage, Clemmie Fairburn's upcoming

Labor Day bash on Isle of Hope—Scoot would sigh and say something vague like, "Oh, well, it'll all take care of itself. These things usually do," and then push a shrimp to the other side of her plate.

Finally, she excused herself, saying she needed to supervise the photographer. Ingrid busied herself clearing their lunch dishes, and when she finished, she ventured back out to see how the crew was progressing.

The photographer and his assistant were outside, preparing to take a few shots of the freshly painted exterior, but Scoot wasn't with them. Ingrid searched the whole main floor for her with no luck. She glanced up the staircase and was hit with a sharp, dark thought.

She took the steps, two at a time, with mounting dread, and by the time she was approaching Edie's bedroom door, which was ajar now, she was practically running. Ingrid pushed the door open and froze in horror—Scoot, the trespasser, invader, was standing in the middle of the Daffodil Room.

Scoot turned to her with a playful smile. "You naughty girl, keeping such a *delightful* secret from me. What a charming room."

Ingrid frantically scanned the space, assessing any damage Scoot might've done. And yet, nothing looked like it had been disturbed. Everything seemed to be in order.

"I see now why you didn't want to do the bedrooms over," Scoot said in a teasing tone. "You've hidden all the best pieces up here."

"Actually, I just . . . I like the rooms the way they are." Ingrid glanced back at the door. How was she going to get Scoot out of here? The woman did not belong in this room. She was desecrating Edie's holy space with her bad aura.

Scoot was taking everything in with a hungry look. The daffodil wallpaper. The bed piled with white, lacy pillows. The black marble mantel holding the three framed pictures.

"It's absolutely perfect." Scoot drifted toward the window that looked out over the square. "The bedroom set is 1920s, correct? I want to say Italian. Easily worth twenty to thirty thousand."

Ingrid felt such soul-shriveling panic, she almost choked on her own breath.

"Oh, trust me," Scoot said as though Ingrid had tried to argue with her. "I know these things."

"It all came with the house," Ingrid finally managed to say.

"I'm so sorry I didn't take your word for it when you told me about all the treasures you had here. I have to admit, I can be a bit snobbish." She laughed, drifted to another wall, and pointed at sexy Mr. Tumnus. "If I'm not mistaken, this is a Frederick Arthur Bridgman. A study for one of his pastel pieces."

Ingrid gave a little shrug, her lips pressed together.

"You may not know this, but the original was recently auctioned off at Christie's. Quarter of a million." Scoot shook her head. "Sorry. I know money talk is so tacky. But it's just me and you. You won't tell anybody, will you?"

Anybody, meaning anybody important.

"You know, your little boyfriend was right. You could've sold all this if you'd really wanted to pay your taxes." Scoot lifted an eyebrow. "Instead of insinuating yourself into a vulnerable young woman's life and trying to get her to solve your money problems."

Ingrid's mouth dropped open and she heard herself stammering. "I—I didn't know any of my grandmother's things were v-valuable."

Scoot's eyes continued to sweep over the room. "Uh-huh."

"I didn't," Ingrid said hotly. "And I am friends with your daughter because she appreciates what *I* did for *her*. I didn't ask for one thing from her. And I won't."

"What did you tell her that day?" Scoot asked. "Sailor's never said."

"That's private. I don't share what happens in my readings."

"I see." Scoot's eyes raked over her hair, her face, down her body, lost in thought. "Tell me, sweetheart, have you ever channeled her?"

"Who?" Ingrid's hackles rose.

Scoot moved closer to her. "Your grandmother. Edie. You're a medium, aren't you? As well as a witch and a psychic?"

Ingrid felt ill.

"Surely you must communicate with her. She's all you have. I mean, besides that boy you keep around for . . . odd jobs." Scoot winked.

Ingrid opened her mouth. Nothing came out. Now Scoot was right beside her, her face soft and pleading and somehow, at the same time, evil.

"Let me talk to her," she wheedled.

"What?" It was a whisper.

"Edith. I want to talk to her."

Ingrid's throat felt dry and raw. "I . . . I don't think so."

Scoot's eyes flashed with something malicious. "Why not? You know how to do it, don't you?"

Of course she knew how to invite spirits. To channel. But she wasn't going to admit that to Scoot. She didn't do it that often, and she certainly wasn't going to call up Edie simply because Scoot Loeffler demanded it.

"I've never asked you for a reading, Ingrid. Haven't you ever wondered why?" Now Scoot's eyes turned soft, and Ingrid marveled how quickly the woman could transform herself.

"I just assumed you didn't believe in what I did."

"Oh, I believe." Scoot wandered to the nightstand beside the bed and picked up the book lying there. *Circe.* Right where Ingrid had put it, the picture of Edie and Rill tucked safely between the pages.

Ingrid felt a zip of electricity travel up her spine.

No, no, no, no . . .

For one terror-filled moment, she considered snatching the book out of Scoot's hands and running out of the room, but she resisted the urge.

Don't look inside . . .

Scoot inspected the cover of the book. "I've always believed."

Ingrid's hands, hanging at her side, felt like they were the repository for all the electricity that was now coursing through her. Scoot absolutely could not see that photo. It would ruin everything. Scoot would ruin everything. She would tell Sailor. Tell Cas. Throw Ingrid out of the mansion on her ass . . .

But there was a way Ingrid could stop her.

Very slowly she opened one of her hands, stretching it wide and holding it flat beside her leg. Then she folded in her middle and ring finger. *Stop, stop, stop, stop,* she thought, sending the mental message toward Scoot while simultaneously preparing herself for the worst.

Preparing herself to lift up her hand and point the sign of the horns in Scoot's direction.

Chapter 26

"You know Circe was a witch."

Scoot examined the book. Ingrid held herself very still. Held her hand very still at her side.

Don't react. Don't say a word. She doesn't deserve it.

Scoot's lips curved into a smile. "She lured men to her, then cursed them, and turned them into pigs. But I'll be honest. I often wonder about that story. Maybe we have it backward. Maybe the men were pigs to start with, and Circe actually just broke the spell."

Scoot laid the book down again, the picture still safely tucked, undiscovered, between its pages. Ingrid's breath flowed out of her body in a low, even stream. She released the horns and flexed her fingers.

"Ingrid," Scoot said in a somber voice. "There are things I need to know. Things that still . . . plague me, even after all these years." Her eyes felt like two blue, diamond point drills on Ingrid.

"Oh," Ingrid said in a breathless voice.

Scoot licked her lips, looking distracted. "Like how they felt about each other, for instance, my husband and your grandmother. You know she was over at the house all the time, back when Rill and I first met. When we started dating. Rill's parents had discovered her—at another party one of their friends threw—and she'd done really accurate readings for them. They adored her, of course. Used to have her over for their dinner parties and their annual Halloween event."

Ingrid willed her face to remain a stone. For her body to stay still. She could not give anything away.

"Everybody loved Edie." Scoot's voice was soft now. "She was so bright, so beautiful and warm, even I'm not too jealous to admit that. I knew right away Rill had a crush on her. Everybody knew; it was obvious from the way he looked at her. Found excuses to be near her. To say her name . . ."

A faraway, almost dreamy look softened her face. The sharp angles seemed to melt, the icy eyes went unfocused.

"He knew I was jealous, of course. I wasn't very good at hiding it. He stopped bringing Edie to the house in town. Only had her to the parties he threw out at the Tybee place. And I wasn't allowed at those parties. Not by him, nor by my parents. Everybody knew how wild they were. The drinking and the drugs. The types of people invited. The *carrying on*. You know, Savannah, back in the nineties. One big, decadent orgy."

Ingrid said nothing. She felt like she was standing in a field planted with land mines.

Scoot raked her nails through her hair, shaking her head, letting the waves fall into perfect place. "You know how I knew he'd finally given up on Edie? The day he proposed to me. That's when I knew I'd won and she'd lost. But he kept me in suspense all the way until the bitter end."

"But then you got married."

Scoot sent her an amused look. "And you think that fixed everything? It only made things worse. He moped all during our engagement. He refused to help with the wedding plans. He lost interest in sex. Sex with me, at least."

Now Scoot was closing the distance between them. Ingrid

could see how the thick makeup settled into the wrinkles around her eyes and her upper lip. Her mascara flaked and smudged. Ingrid felt her throat closing. Scoot seized Ingrid's arm and shook her hard enough that Ingrid winced.

"You've got to let me talk to her, Ingrid." Scoot squeezed her arm. "I need to know if he ever had any love for me. If there's anything still left for me."

Adrenaline flooded Ingrid's body. Scoot's grip tightened. She couldn't breathe. She couldn't speak.

"Please. Ingrid. I've done so much for you, and I'll keep on doing it, I swear. You'll never have to struggle again, Ingrid—to keep up with bills, to be safe. Just do this one thing for me."

Ingrid's whole body was shaking now. Not because she was afraid, but because at the moment Scoot had taken hold of her, the Daffodil Room had changed. It had gone dark, suddenly doused in shadows and edged with an odor of something sharp and rank and deeply unpleasant.

Then Ingrid smelled something else, beyond the vile thing. Anaïs Anaïs, cherry almond lotion, and the faint whiff of incense. She felt soft, papery skin brush against hers.

Edie . . .

Edie was here.

In the room.

Ingrid let out a short, surprised huff of air. There was a low murmuring sound swirling around her, like someone trying to speak underwater. She closed her eyes, trying to discern the words from the garbled symphony of voices, but it was so hard. There was so much noise.

"Ingrid?" Scoot's voice was like the crack of a gun. "What is it? What's happening?"

So many voices. So many words. Conversations happening in the unseen realm and all around her. And then one voice sharpened and rose above the rest. A sweet voice, talking low. Repeating a sentence over and over that started muffled then grew increasingly clear.

She wished me ill . . .

Ingrid inhaled sharply and her eyes flew open.

"What?" demanded Scoot, gripping her hard. "What did she say? I know she's here. I can see it in your eyes."

Ingrid swallowed. The shrimp sat uncomfortably in her stomach. The stench of old life, of death, of that which had been called back was so strong . . . too strong . . . she was going to be sick . . .

"Tell me!"

Ingrid's mind raced, but she knew not to answer Scoot yet. Because there was more. She waited . . . waited . . . then she heard the voice again.

She wished me dead . . .

It *was* Edie's voice. Her syrupy, old-fashioned, Savannah accent. Goose bumps covered Ingrid's skin and something sour rose in her esophagus.

She wished me ill . . .

She wished me dead . . .

"She sees you." It was all Ingrid could think to say. Not a lie. But not exactly the truth.

"What else?" Scoot asked. "Did she sleep with my husband?"

She wished me ill . . .

She wished me dead . . .

"Did she?" Scoot's voice rang shrill.

"No," Ingrid said. "She didn't." Another lie. Probably. Maybe. But a lie Ingrid had to tell until she knew more. Until Edie told her more.

Because this was it, wasn't it? What Edie had been talking about at the end? Whatever had happened between Scoot and Edie—the thing Edie had wrongly overlooked—was the event that knocked everything off balance.

Ingrid had discovered it, just like Edie had intended.

But now what was she supposed to do? How could she deal

with Scoot Loeffler and still stay in the light? The woman was a force of destruction. She'd spent a lifetime being cruel to her children in so many ways, and now she kept them at arm's length. She'd craved her husband's love and somehow constantly pushed it away. This was dark territory, and Ingrid would need every weapon she possessed to navigate it.

All her weapons.

"He loved her, didn't he?" Scoot broke into her thoughts. "He loved her more than he loved me." Now her eyes were like two rain-slicked stones. Were they tears? Or just the vodka?

"I think . . ." *Tread carefully.* "I think that's a question for Rill, Scoot. Not for Edie."

Scoot darkened. "Fine. Then ask her if she loved him." She lifted her chin, addressing the empty room. "Were you in love with my husband, Edith? Did you want to take Rill away from me? Did you keep him from ever fully loving me? Was it you?" Her voice broke on this last question.

Ingrid's head clanged with Edie's words. They came in a rush now, reverberating through her skull, sending points of searing pain through her eyes. *ShewishedmeillShewishedmedead, ShewishedmeillShewishedmedead . . .*

Ingrid let out a small whimper of pain and protest. It was too much. Too upsetting to imagine. Too overwhelming . . .

"What?" Scoot cried.

"She says no," Ingrid gasped. "She wasn't in love with him." Her eyes met Scoot's but now she didn't shrink from the woman's stare. "She didn't stand in the way of you two. She was never the problem."

Even as the words came out of her mouth—the lies—she felt herself taking that first step. The first step off the path of light and into the land of shadows. And yet she didn't take the words back. How could she tell this woman what Edie was actually saying to her? The truth was not something Scoot was capable of hearing. She would tear Ingrid to pieces. Throw her out of their house. Out of Sailor's and Cas's lives.

Ingrid would lose everything.

Scoot hesitated, then she patted the skin under her eyes and gingerly pulled back the skin on her face. She turned that face, so cold and beautiful and now masked once again with the inscrutable Loeffler expression, back onto Ingrid.

"So I'm the one to blame for the disdain my husband has always treated me with? The distance he's kept between us?"

Ingrid fists were now clenched by her sides. "I didn't mean—"

"No, no." Scoot fixed her with a brilliant, brittle smile. "Don't back down now. It's always better to know."

Ingrid nodded and Scoot moved toward the door. She stopped, turning back.

"Oh, one thing."

"Yes?"

"Don't get too attached to Casimir. He's never actually dated a girl—or a boy, for that matter. He just likes to play with people. Make them love him, make them want what they can't have and then deny them. He seems sweet but he's always been a little off that way."

Ingrid stared at the woman in shock, burning with shame. Scoot turned and exited the room, leaving the door open behind her.

Ingrid didn't follow. She didn't even move. She could still smell that sharp, sour smell, Edie all around her, permeating the air, now with a quiet disapproval. It occurred to Ingrid that the smell, the sharp, unpleasant aroma she sensed, was nothing more than death.

Chapter 27

The renovations complete at last, Ingrid moved back home. Still, inexplicably, Miles's glum demeanor persisted. He was much less affectionate toward her, even cool, and, instead of tidying up, started to purposefully leave messes everywhere in the newly decorated house.

He was just being childish, Ingrid thought. Making her pay for leaving him alone in the house.

She reminded him that it had been his idea for her to move into the Loefflers' home. That everything that benefited her also benefited him, in a way. But still, he was defensive, claiming not to be mad, even though she noticed he didn't deny the distance that had developed between them.

But what could she say? He had reason to be resentful; Ingrid no longer only belonged solely to him. She and Sailor had formed a new and unshakable bond, and the truth was, Miles was going to have to get used to sharing her. Ingrid did her best to be sensitive to his feelings, making him dinner and washing his clothes. She even let the empty cans and fast-food bags lying around the newly redecorated rooms pass without comment—

and, thank the Goddess, after a few weeks, he seemed mostly back to his old self.

The hot, heavy, oppressive month of July passed in a whirlwind. Ingrid's days were filled with appointments with the Loefflers' friends, lunches with Sailor, and the occasional Tuesday family dinner.

The dinners always left her exhausted. Under Scoot's baleful, drunken eye, she tried to avoid Rill's flirtatious looks and engage in a meaningful way with Cas. Frustratingly, he resisted conversation, seeming to be content with the occasional brush of his fingers against her arm or leg. And he always disappeared right after dessert. Ingrid despaired of ever moving their relationship to the next step. It appeared Scoot hadn't warned her off Cas to be spiteful. Cas really did like to play with people.

The sunset cruises on Jude's boat were a welcome respite. The *Do Not Disturb* was actually a yacht—a small one, Jude informed Ingrid, only seventy feet. Ingrid was agog at the polished wood-and-brass interior, the three bedrooms, three baths, galley, and seating area complete with a wet bar. Jude had a full-time captain and staff who ran the vessel, so that whenever they wanted to take a cruise, they could leave at a moment's notice. Since he and Sailor had been dating, he'd kept it docked at the Savannah Yacht Club marina on nearby Whitemarsh Island.

Initially intimidated by Jude's age and crisp English accent, Ingrid had grown fond of the hotelier. Especially when she saw how thoughtful he was toward Sailor. He was always sliding a drink in her hand, always complimenting her appearance, noticing the details of what she was wearing, gently pushing back strands of hair that had fallen in her eyes and tucking them tenderly behind her ears.

He seemed to rely on Sailor's opinion when it came to business decisions as well, asking her what she thought about a new hotel he was considering in Portugal or if he should sign a deal with a vegan, ethically sourced line of spa products even though it would double his costs.

On one particular trip, Cas joined them. They were all stretched out on towels, catnapping in the balmy afternoon sun, when Sailor asked Ingrid all about her grandmother and how she had learned magic. At first Ingrid felt shy, but eventually she told them Edie had grown up in a suburb of Atlanta, the daughter of a cop and a homemaker mother. She spent summers with her maternal grandmother down in Savannah, who lived in a trailer on a dirt road on the Isle of Hope.

This woman—Edie called her Mama Strode—traced her ancestry back to Devon, England, to a people she called the Dumnonii, "the Deep Valley Dwellers." Devon was geographically an unusual spot, with both a northern and southern coast, allowing the light to bathe the land. Before the Romans invaded, the Dumnonii practiced a form of magic Mama Strode called "Ash and Light."

She explained to her granddaughter that the original Celtic deities were not always anthropomorphic, but more often elemental, and therefore she called the light "Goddess." She taught Edie the practice of following the light that had been passed down to her from her own grandmother who spoke with a strange, clipped accent. Mama Strode told Edie she should always live by the sea, where the light was free and unfettered and where Edie could hear her messages.

When Ingrid finished the story, she had glanced shyly over at Cas, lean and languidly resting on his elbows. His shaggy hair and skin looked like burnished gold in the sun. He hadn't said anything in response, but he'd just smiled with that warm, lopsided grin of his, and she felt like she'd received his approval.

That evening, Sailor tried to persuade Cas and Jude to let Ingrid do a reading for them. Cas declined but Jude agreed. They all showered and changed clothes, then, with a fresh bottle of sauvignon blanc, settled on cushioned seats around the teak dining table.

When Jude offered Ingrid his hand, she was surprised by how quickly and clearly she saw his past. The young orphan boy in the north of England, moved from foster home to foster home, overcome with loneliness and fear, but filled with a steadfast ambition.

And then she saw the woman. Beautiful, sinewy, working at a mirrored barre.

Sailor had told her about Jude's first wife who had died young of cancer, and she instantly knew it must be her she was seeing. She hesitated, reluctant to continue, but there was no fooling Sailor.

"Ingrid, what is it? Don't hold back. Please."

Jude sat motionless.

"The ballet dancer," Ingrid said timidly to him. "Ballerina, I mean. I see her."

Jude's eyes clouded, and he sat back in his chair. He glanced at Sailor.

"I'm fine," Sailor assured him, then turned to Ingrid. "Tell him everything you see."

Jude nodded once at Ingrid. "All right. You heard her. Fire away."

Ingrid cleared her throat. "I see something of hers . . . here, on the boat."

Jude looked down at the teak table.

"You're not obligated to— " Ingrid began.

Jude interrupted her, but he was looking at Sailor. "I'm sorry I didn't tell you."

Her eyes were full of love and understanding. "It's okay."

Jude looked at Ingrid. "It's a hat . . ."

She knew before he said anything more. She'd known the moment she'd set foot on the *Do Not Disturb* and seen the hodgepodge of hats hanging on shiny brass hooks in the galley.

There had been an array of baseball caps and men's straw fedoras, but only one woman's hat. A dusty blue-and-cream-colored straw hat with an old-fashioned pleated brim. Too fussy to be Sailor's, who rarely wore hats because she loved the feel of the sun on her face.

Jude's eyes had gone red and watery. Ingrid held his gaze.

"She's glad you kept the hat, and . . . she wants you to know she thinks you've chosen wisely." Ingrid looked now at Sailor. "She's saying maybe you'll have a daughter who can wear it one day."

Jude stood abruptly, disappeared into the cabin, then reappeared holding the hat. He looked at Sailor, then reached out one hand, taking hold of the tangerine wisp of silk that held Sailor's hair back. He wound the scarf around the brim of the hat, tying it in a knot. He looked for a long moment at the hat, then at Ingrid.

"Thank you." He turned to Sailor, pressing the back of his big hand to his eye, sitting back down. "She would have loved you, baby. So much."

Sailor came over and sat on his lap and nuzzled his face. He planted a long and lingering kiss on her lips. "My ballast," he whispered.

Ingrid and Cas exchanged awkward glances and rose, quickly slipping out of the room. Once they were out on the deck, he stood next to her, at the starboard side railing, hands in the pockets of his linen pants. Ingrid watched the wind ruffle his hair.

Cas eyed her and inhaled deeply. "That was . . ." He didn't finish the thought, just let out a long exhale.

"Yeah. Sometimes readings can be intense."

"I was thinking . . ." he started, then stopped. He seemed to be having difficulty with whatever he wanted to say.

She waited.

"It's just that I wanted to ask you something," he finally said.

"Sure. Anything." She held her breath.

"I just wondered . . . what you would say about someone who might want a reading . . . from a psychic, like you . . . but who's religious . . . I mean . . ." He laughed nervously. "Obviously, I'm talking about myself. I don't know why I didn't just come right out and say it. Stupid." His eyes shifted away from her.

She was touched. "I would do a reading for you. I don't see it as a conflict of interest, I guess. And it's not stupid, Cas."

"It's just . . . there are some things I need clarity on. Work. Life, I guess." He seemed to want to say more but didn't.

"Of course."

Now he looked at her again, his dark eyes making her breathless. He held out his hand, and as she took it, the heavy watch on his wrist shifted. His hand was big, nicely shaped, and warm, and she turned it palm up. She traced the lines, listening to the sounds of the wind and the water around them. Opening herself. Asking the light to reveal.

But everything remained a blank . . .

Everything around Cas was murky. Impossible to discern between what was his life and the forces that sought to overpower him. She had nothing.

How could that be?

Was it what Scoot had said? That he was just playing with her?

"I lied to you, Ingrid," he blurted out.

She looked up into his face, brows knit in confusion.

"I told you I went to Amherst, but I didn't. I went to Georgia College."

She almost laughed, she was so relieved.

"So embarrassing. I'm embarrassed I did that, I mean."

She shook her head. "Please don't be. It doesn't matter to me at all. I didn't even go to college."

He smiled. She smiled back then looked back down at his palm. She traced his lifeline. His skin was soft. She couldn't believe she was touching it. She wanted to bend her face to his hand and kiss it.

"What do you see?" His voice was so small, so vulnerable, like a little boy asking for help. She felt a sudden sweep of sadness.

"A lot, actually . . . now."

It was true. After his admission, his hand had opened up to her like a flower, and now she saw more than she'd ever hoped. Cas was afraid—but not of his family. He only feared never knowing himself. She was desperate to say so many things. She wanted to tell him that he didn't have to take on the role of a sinner to talk to her. That he could be himself. That he was enough. But she didn't have the courage to speak.

She kept her eyes on his beautiful, strong hand. "You're not one of them. Not really. That's why you've always felt on the outside. So . . . outside of your house is where you'll find yourself. Beyond the walls of your family's fortress—"

She heard him hitch his breath and looked up at him.

He hesitated for one brief moment, then leaned down and kissed her. His mouth was soft, and his lips opened, his tongue tasting like the wine he'd drunk earlier but also something deeper. More essential.

Incense and salt air.

She thought she'd never felt a kiss like that in her life. It was almost holy. And now he was holding her face with both hands, his body angling toward hers. Against hers. She let out a small moan and lifted herself to him. Wrapped both arms over his shoulders. Lost herself in the kiss they were creating in time with the rocking of the boat.

Suddenly, from his pocket, his phone rang. He pulled away first, and they disconnected. He pulled the phone out and frowned at it. "Sorry."

"It's okay." She was breathless, everything inside her tight and warm.

"It's Dad," he said. "I gotta . . ." He looked forlorn.

"Go, go. I'm fine."

He ducked his head to the phone and walked to the opposite side of the boat. She stood at the railing and watched the last bit of light fade from the sky alone.

Later that night, when Jude and Sailor dropped Ingrid off at her house, Cas stayed in Jude's Porsche while Sailor jumped out and hugged Ingrid fiercely.

"You're an angel," she breathed into Ingrid's hair. "My angel. What would I do without you?"

Chapter 28

In August, a popular movie franchise arrived in town to film for several months. They brought with them an enormous cast and crew from Hollywood, as well as rabid fans from all over the region who hoped to spot some filming in action or one of the stars on their days off.

The air in town seemed to electrify, and the sidewalks were more crowded than usual in the summer. There were celebrity sightings at local coffee shops and restaurants, not to mention the huge bump in traffic for local businesses.

The ghost tours benefitted from the flurry of excitement, too, and one particularly busy Saturday night, Miles's boss said he'd pay Ingrid if she went along to help. Since the Loefflers were enjoying a family gathering on Jude's yacht that weekend, Ingrid declared herself on vacation and told Miles she'd join him. She didn't need the money—and although she was dying to be with Cas again, she knew the crowded boat would be no place for romance. Besides, she really did want to help Miles. To show him that she valued him as much as Sailor.

Boney also had a big group that night and brought along

Mari to assist him. They all gathered at the Jasper Monument in the center of Madison Square. Boney was dressed in his usual skeleton T-shirt, fake leather pants, and black velvet top hat—a ridiculous getup that still somehow managed to make him look like a sexy goth rockstar. The women gathering for their tours kept giggling and trying to catch his eye.

Through the crowd of women, Boney sent Ingrid a lazy wink and then, when she walked past him, let his fingers graze her rear end. She found herself annoyingly turned on and briefly considered promising him a hookup back at his apartment. But then she thought better of it. Part of her liked the idea of saving herself for Cas, even if he hadn't asked her.

She said hello to Mari, who produced a plastic bag full of boxed soaps from the hotel she cleaned and insisted Ingrid take them. Ingrid felt slightly embarrassed at the gift and guilty that she hadn't brought anything for Mari, especially with how well things had been going recently. Ingrid no longer had to worry about money, no longer stayed up at night sweating over tax bills or an empty appointment book. The least she could've done was pick up a six-pack or one of the many candles Sailor always brought every time she dropped by. She would remember next time.

Ingrid and Mari were given the iPads that had all the spooky pictures of apparitions and energy orbs that they were supposed to show at every stop, and the two groups went their separate ways. Miles's group would start at the first spot, the Old Sorel Weed House, and Boney's group would start at Madison Square, intersecting at the midpoint, Colonial Park Cemetery.

During the tour, Ingrid tried to inject some pizzazz and add some of the stories she'd heard from Edie.

In 1967, a teenage girl saw a ghostly dog, supposedly the spirit of Lieutenant Colonel Archibald Campbell's terrier, running up and down the riverfront, barking for its master.

A trio of singing ghosts live in the balcony of the Independent Presbyterian Church.

In the mid-nineties, a tourist attempting to break into the Mercer-Williams House, site of the famous shooting, claimed to have seen the ghost of Jim Williams, who told her that he knew who really *shot Danny Hansford.*

In the Lucas Theatre, after Miles went through his spiel about the ghost audience applauding in the empty auditorium and the guests started to file toward the exits, he pulled Ingrid aside. "Thirsty?" he asked, then pushed on the panel under the stage. Inside the compartment was a small silver flask. He pulled it out, unscrewed the top, and tipped it back.

"Sure." She took a sip—rum—and handed it back to him.

"I got you." He winked at her. "I always got you, Ingrid." Overcome with happiness, she hugged him. Her own, sweet Miles was back. They were okay.

An hour later, the two groups were standing at the iron fence of the cemetery about a dozen yards away from each other. Close enough that Ingrid could catch bits of Boney's spiel.

". . . there's many a morning I've come for a walk in the cemetery and found puddles of blood or feathers, or the heart of a rabbit sacrificed in a hoodoo ritual . . ."

Such bullshit. But she had to smile. Boney had those poor tourists eating out of his hand, and at the end of the night he'd rake in the tips. She was just glad she didn't have to sing for her supper anymore herself. Well, not in that particular way, at least.

Miles was going on about the number of unmarked graves under every inch of the city, so she pulled out her phone and opened her messages. She saw one unread.

You bewitch me in the moonlight.

She caught her breath, a thrill making her skin prickle. She scanned the dark streets around her. It was past ten but the summer weekend meant the streets were almost as busy as during the day. Still, she didn't see anyone nearby.

The cemetery.

She peered past the iron fence and into the shadowy depths of the graveyard. The crooked branches of the oaks dripped with moss over the stone markers, and she strained to search among the graves, but it was frustratingly dark. She couldn't see a thing.

And then a shriek rang out, splitting her ears. One of Boney's group, a teenage girl, was pointing between the bars into the cemetery. Everyone in both groups was now pressed against the fence, gripping the bars and craning their necks.

"She saw a ghost!" another girl said.

Every nerve in Ingrid's body electrified. She clicked her phone.

News flash . . .

I hear the ghost of the Noble Hardee Mansion is roaming the city.

She grinned, biting her lip and pressing the phone to her chest. Now all the people in both groups were practically losing their minds, running up and down the iron fence, a few trying to scale it, all in an attempt to get a glimpse of the ghost. Boney and Miles were doing their best to calm them all down.

He's causing quite a stir, she wrote.

He seeks his temptress.

Her breath caught in her throat again.

He sees her. But it is not enough. He wants to touch her.

Ingrid let out a soft sigh. *Finally.*

Where? she wrote with trembling fingers.

His house.

"What the fuck are you doing, Ingrid?" Miles was standing in front of her, hands on his hips, and on reflex, she tucked her phone behind her back. "They're trying to climb the goddamn fence!"

"What do you want me to do about it?" she asked.

"I don't know—help, maybe?"

"It's your group, Miles."

"Right," he said. "You're too good for this now. Sailor Loefler's best friend and personal psychic."

"What are you talking about?" she snapped. "I came here to help you."

"Then help!" He glared at her phone. "Stop talking to your boyfriend."

The commotion grew louder. She gritted her teeth. "Get off my back, Miles."

He hung back. "Who is it, anyway? Who are you seeing?"

"Nobody. Why do you care?"

"Because we're friends. Best friends who used to tell each other everything. It was always us against the world and now . . . now it's you and *them*." He caught sight of a teenage boy, halfway up the fence and clinging to it like a monkey, and ran to him. "Hey! Stop! Get down!" Miles grabbed the boy's T-shirt and yanked him off the fence. The kid hit the pavement with a grunt.

"Dude!" protested one of the girls.

"Look," Miles shouted to the group. "There's no ghost, so I need everybody to gather around. We've got to get back to the square soon."

As the group began to reassemble, Miles turned back to Ingrid. His voice was softer now. Pleading. "Who is it? Just tell me, so it doesn't feel like we're keeping secrets from each other."

"I'm not keeping secrets—"

"So we can go back to normal—"

"It's nobody."

"Come on, Budgie."

"Don't fucking call me that anymore," Ingrid hissed at him. "It's what Edie called me. Not you. Never you." She pushed the iPad at him, and he took it, drawing back with a hurt look on his face. She looked down at her phone, not caring anymore if he saw.

Meet me in the altar room, read Cas's latest text.

"I have to go see somebody." She took off, trotting in the direction of Monterey Square, feeling Miles watching her as she went.

Chapter 29

She wondered what had changed. She wondered if Cas had gotten tired of playing games, merely texting his feelings, and wanted to finally declare them, out loud, in person, to her face.

Maybe he wanted to ask her on a real date. Maybe he wanted to actually touch her again like they had on the yacht, his real, human fingers on her real, human skin. The thought of it sent chills through her. She could see it all. Cas Loeffler in her arms . . . in her bed . . . hers and hers alone.

From the sidewalk on Bull Street, she pushed open the gate, and then the side door that led into a hallway in the garden level of the house. She was sweaty and out of breath. Maybe she should pop into the bathroom before she met him, if she could feel her way through the blackness . . .

"Ingrid."

She yelped out loud in surprise. He was right here, standing only a few feet away from her.

"You came."

She stopped, her skin prickling in gooseflesh. Because it wasn't Cas's voice that spoke to her out of the dark. It was Rill's.

"What's g-going on?" she stuttered. Where was Cas? What the hell was Rill doing here, waiting for her?

"Follow me."

"I can't. I . . . it's too dark."

A low light appeared. The glow of a phone screen, a dozen feet down at the end of the hallway. Immediately it began to move away from her. Into a room—the altar room. She followed the light. When she reached the door, she pushed it open and entered the room. There was a candle burning, just one, in the center of the altar she and Sailor had set up. Rill was standing just behind it, the shadows from the flame making him flicker in and out like an apparition.

"Beautiful," he said in a husky voice. "As beautiful in candlelight as moonlight."

"Cas just texted me that he wanted to talk, so I— "

"I know what he texted you, Ingrid. I've seen all your texts." He paused. "I found him down here, waiting for you, and sent him back upstairs."

She was quiet, nearly suffocating from the acute intensity of the shame. She felt like a child who'd been caught doing something naughty. Only she wasn't a child, and neither was Cas. And both were perfectly free to do whatever they wanted.

"I'm sorry if this hurts your feelings or embarrasses you," Rill went on gently. "That's not my goal. But you have to understand. I can't have him . . . interfering with you. He is immature and untrustworthy, and he will hurt you. I know my son. And believe me, I'm doing all I can to encourage him to let go of all these childish obsessions. To get out of his head and live in the real world and learn to work like the rest of us. Experience *life*. You understand, Ingrid. You work hard, harder than anybody else in this family. I see how you've kept your grandmother's business alive. Her legacy. She would be so proud of you."

Ingrid said nothing.

"I won't let Cas ruin what you've accomplished. What you've built. For you . . . but also for Edie."

"He wanted to see me—" she began.

"I know you'd like to think that. But I won't risk it. I can't. I care too much about you."

In the candlelight, he stepped closer to her. Looking down on her with the gentlest of expressions, he took her hand.

"I was too young and foolish to see it all those years ago, but Edie was right. She and I didn't belong together. She did me a favor by turning me down. And now I'm doing the same favor for you. I love my son, Ingrid, but you deserve so much more, and so I've told him to leave you alone. Ordered him, actually."

Instinctively, she backed away from him. Glanced down at the candle. Had Cas lit it for her? Had he planned to finally take her in his arms and kiss her here in the altar room? She felt an immense sadness wrap around her.

"You want to say something." Rill watched her.

She felt bereft. Stripped of all she'd been hoping for. She wanted Rill to know what she thought of him. How much she despised him for what he was doing. But she couldn't speak around the sob caught in her throat.

"Talk to me, Ingrid."

"It's not your place," she burst out, "to control your children. You want to keep Sailor from running the company, and you want to force Cas to do it instead, even though it would make him miserable. You think you're doing what's best for them, but you're only going to push them away."

He grinned. Not the reaction she expected.

"You're so much like her," he said. "So sure of your point of view. But you're wrong, Ingrid. You're dead wrong. This family? My children? They are my world. And I will die before I let anyone come in and upset the balance I've achieved."

The balance.

There it was again. That phrase, Edie's words, echoing in her ears, slapping her in the face.

She felt a twinge of guilt. What was she really doing here? Trying to fulfill her grandmother's final wish? Or was she just using it as an excuse to get the one thing that she'd never fully had but always wanted?

A family.

She stared at Rill, furious, but his expression was so tender, so unguarded, that she couldn't help but be touched in some small, hidden part of herself. A tear slipped out of her eye. A soft, nearly silent, sob. She dashed at it, angry, humiliated.

"Oh, Ingrid. Please don't cry," Rill said. "I see you. I can see you want to be one of us."

She shook her head, but he knew he'd hit on the truth.

"That's why I'm telling you this. This is what family does, Ingrid. We tell each other the hard truths. We look out for each other. We protect each other. I'm just trying to protect you. Will you trust me?" He held his hand out to her, and she stared at it. She could see his palm, the lines that creased the soft flesh.

One in particular.

Via Lascivia. The line that rose from the bracelets of life between the mounts of Venus and the moon, indicating addiction, sexual and otherwise. Edie had called it "the line of lust." Rill's was a deep groove that intersected with his lifeline.

She looked back up at him.

Rill, who flirted as easily with her as with his hired help. Rill, who was messing around behind Scoot's back with somebody else when Sailor was just a kid. Maybe it wasn't just the attention he liked. Maybe there was something deeper there. Something destructive.

Suddenly, there was a loud crash above them, then yelling and thunderous footsteps. Reflexively, they both leaped apart and gaped up at the ceiling.

"What the fuck is it now?" Rill growled.

"Mother!" It was Sailor's voice, carrying all the way down from the first floor, specifically, the front hall, to the altar room. There was now a cacophony of voices and the clatter of feet.

"Mother, come back! Someone! Mrs. Leimberger! *Help*!"

Chapter 30

The sound of Sailor's cries sent Ingrid into overdrive, her whole nervous system instantly calibrated to find Sailor. To get to her, to help her, no matter the cost.

She was also, simultaneously, formulating an excuse for what she was doing in the house, down in the garden level with Rill, so late at night. It wasn't time to let anyone else in the family know about her and Cas. Or had Rill already told them? The thought of it made her want to shrivel to a speck of sand.

"You go out the side door and around, then up to the front." Rill blew out the candle. "Let's keep this little meeting between us, yes?"

"Yes." She ran down the hall, slipped out the door that opened to the side courtyard, and let herself out by the gate. Running around to the front of the house, she bounded up the stairs and stood close to the heavy front door. Even before she saw anyone, she heard Scoot's voice coming from somewhere in the house.

"I know what you're doing, all of you!" Scoot was slurring her words, but loudly enough for everyone to hear. "You brought her here to keep me quiet at the wedding! So I wouldn't embarrass you all in front of all our friends! You know when she's around I'll be on my best behavior! I have to smile and pretend that my own family hasn't betrayed me!"

"Mother! Come on. What are you even talking about?" Sailor again. She'd gone into the dining room.

Ingrid pushed open the door. In the vast hall, the chandelier blazed, illuminating her reflection in the long, gold mirror. She pulled up short. She looked like a foraging raccoon, mascara smudged around her guilty-looking eyes, caught out by the trash cans.

She turned and saw Mrs. Leimberger, bare-faced and in a bathrobe, standing at the rear of the hall, appearing to have just come from the kitchen. She held a silver tray of Perrier water bottles and a crystal dish of limes.

Ingrid froze as the woman spied her. She had to be wondering what Ingrid was doing, bursting through the front door like that. Ingrid glanced up the staircase. She spied Cas, his head leaning over the banister, then retreating again.

And then came Rill, charging up from the lower level, jogging through the hall, nonchalant as anything. Past Mrs. Leimberger and Ingrid without so much as a glance at either as he made a beeline into the dining room and the drawing room beyond. The housekeeper's eyes darted between Ingrid and Rill, but there was no time for questions because just then, from the other room, Scoot's voice rose again.

"Wasn't it enough that he never said he was sorry for bringing the *first one* over here, time and time again, to all of his parties? Was it not enough that he never stopped loving her . . . ?"

"Mother—"

Ingrid heard Rill. "Scoot. You're drunk . . ."

"That doesn't mean I've lost my memory. I haven't forgotten what you did! And now I have to hear that my son has *feelings*? I will not abide it! I absolutely will not!" There was an anguished wail, a loud thump, and then an even louder crash.

The sound galvanized both Mrs. Leimberger and Ingrid, the house manager in the direction of the crash and Ingrid back to the front door. She had just put her hand on the ornate brass doorknob, thinking her best strategy was getting the hell out of the Loeffler house and letting the family handle Scoot, when she heard sobbing behind her.

She turned. Sailor, her face in her hands, stood in the hallway. Ingrid hesitated, torn between comforting her friend and putting herself in Scoot's line of fire.

Too late. Sailor had lifted her head and seen her. "Ingrid, thank God, you're here!" Sailor rushed to her, caught her with both hands, clamping her fingers around Ingrid's forearm like forceps, and collapsed in her arms.

Ingrid held Sailor, looking over at the front door. Her only hope of escape. "Shh. It's okay. I'm here."

Sailor lifted her red, tearstained face. "You've got to help me."

Another crash rang out from the drawing room. They both flinched, separating.

"Sailor, what is going on?" Ingrid asked.

"She's lost her mind. She's finally lost her mind!" She fixed Ingrid with a piteous look. "Ingrid, you've got to do something. Tell her that you're truly my friend. That you're here because you only want to help—" Now Sailor was dragging Ingrid toward the drawing room. Toward the sound of Scoot's braying voice and breaking glass.

Ingrid was literally prying Sailor's fingers from her arm. "Sailor, no. No, I can't. She doesn't want to—"

Ingrid felt herself pushed into the drawing room where everyone—Rill, Mrs. Leimberger, and Scoot—turned to stare at her. Scoot, standing on the far side of the room, in a wrinkled green-and-white striped pantsuit set, hair windblown and held back with huge black sunglasses, opened her arms wide, bangles clanking a demented accompaniment.

"Here ssshe isss, the *witch*!" She looked like hell. Eyes glassy, face smeary. She had a drink in her hand—not one of the bottles of Perrier that Mrs. Leimberger had brought in, but a glass from the bar cabinet. Mrs. Leimberger was busying herself near a sofa, sweeping up glass and porcelain shards of whatever Scoot had thrown against the wall.

Rill gave Ingrid a tired, apologetic look and rubbed his eyes with one hand. "Scoot, my God. Can you give it a rest, for the love . . ."

Scoot sloshed her glass in his direction. "You give it a rest. Or do you have the hots for this one, too?"

Sailor turned an imploring face to Ingrid. But Ingrid was not about to say a word. Anything she said at this point was only going to court more disaster.

"Jesus, Scoot." Rill sent a weary look to Ingrid. "Sorry about this."

"Don't you dare apologize to that girl for me," Scoot snapped. "I say what I mean, and I mean what I say. And what I say is this . . . *she*"—the drink sloshed in Ingrid's direction—"didn't make anything happen. I made it happen. All of it. Everything. I worked my ass off to make this wedding perfect, and then *she* bops in and casts a spell and magically, *poof*, the flowers are suddenly available, the harpist is so thrilled to be a part of your special day, and Louise's gown turns up especially for your third and least-important reception dress."

"Mother, Ingrid helped us," Sailor said in a small but staunch voice.

Scoot whirled on her. "She did a *spell*, you stupid, stupid girl. And spells are pretend. The fact that you believe that what she did got you what you want instead of *my hard work* is just proof of how little you care for me!" Scoot thumped her chest, sobbing now. "Your mother, who has been on the phone, emailing everyone, calling in every favor I've ever been owed . . . I have worked my fingers to the bone for you. So you will have the perfect day. But no. You insist it's all because this *witch* did a *spell*."

Ingrid felt something new now. A twinge of anger, black and thick, twisting through her like a snake. This woman had once hated Edie. And it was clear she hated Ingrid now. And neither of them deserved such terrible treatment.

Scoot gave her daughter a look of supreme pity. "Okay, little Miss Delusional, this is where you need to pay attention to what's going on around you. This—this nonsense right here—is precisely why your father won't let you near the C-suite at the office. Because you're gullible. You're weak."

Ingrid caught her breath.

"That's why your father won't ever make you CEO," Scoot snarled.

Sailor looked like she'd been slapped.

"He won't do it because he doesn't think you're smart enough. He thinks you'll drive Savannah Sauce into the ground and lose everything this family has. And you've proven him right by believing *this person* has done anything for you."

Scoot lifted a haughty chin and smiled in triumph at Ingrid.

Chapter 31

Pure adrenaline flooded Ingrid's body. Her own mother had left her on her grandmother's doorstep, but she never imagined a mother could do something like this to her own daughter. Say such cutting, vile words to her face.

It was unthinkable. So cruel, and she found herself wanting to feel Scoot's neck in her hands. Wanting to squeeze until the woman choked on every word she had said.

"For fuck's sake, Scoot," Rill yelled. "That's your daughter you're speaking to."

But Scoot's face twisted in an ugly snarl as she jabbed her finger at Sailor. "You are so easily led astray—"

"Shut up!" Sailor screamed at Scoot. "Just shut up!" She grabbed Ingrid by the arm and pulled her back out into the hall where she collapsed again into Ingrid's arms again, shaking and sobbing like a child.

Ingrid could hear Scoot ranting on to Rill. She caught snatches, words and phrases. *Slumming . . . trash . . . devil worshipping . . .* Ingrid held Sailor as tightly as she could, as if she could physically shield her from the onslaught.

She realized Sailor was talking, babbling over her shoulder. ". . . we were having a great time on Jude's boat, in the marsh, watching the sunset. She was drinking, of course, like always. Cas said he liked you . . . that's what really did it . . . all he said was he liked you . . ."

"That's enough!" Ingrid heard Rill shout in the drawing room.

"I should take care of her," Scoot yelled back. "Fix her little red wagon, just like I did her grandmother."

Ingrid's whole body went rigid.

Fix her little red wagon?

What was that supposed to mean?

Sailor was still talking. ". . . just saying stuff about how Edie was always around before she and Dad got married. How she was supposedly *after* Dad, whatever that means. And then she started in on you . . ."

Ingrid barely heard her, her mind was clicking through the new information so quickly. What had Scoot done to Edie? She wanted to push Sailor off her and rush into the room, grab Scoot, and shake her until the truth fell out.

Sailor extricated herself from Ingrid's hold and sniffed and wiped her face. "Jude wouldn't even come back in the car with us. The whole way back from the yacht club she wouldn't stop. All the way home, she just kept at it. But she doesn't even see the truth. *She's* the one who's delusional. She's obsessed and paranoid."

"Sailor, I'm so sorry." Ingrid forced herself to focus on her friend. Now was not the time to tell Sailor that she'd discovered that it was true that Rill and Edie had meant more to each other than was proper. Sailor's world was falling apart, and she needed Ingrid by her side.

Sailor's eyes were red, her nose was running. She blotted it on her sleeve. "You know her business isn't even real, don't you? Dad just set her up in that space and paid for all the inventory so he could get her out of the house and away from the booze."

Ingrid's brow knitted.

"She doesn't have any clients—other than a friend who occasionally takes pity on her and hires her to redecorate a guest bedroom or a closet or carriage house or something." Sailor rolled her watery eyes. "She's horrible, Ingrid. A nightmare."

"If me being here or being your friend is a problem, I'll back off," Ingrid said. "It's not worth it, Sailor. Not if it's going to ruin your wedding."

"No," Sailor said fervently. "She should be the one to go. She should be the one who has to walk away so the rest of us enjoy what's meant to be a beautiful, loving, family event . . ." She dissolved into tears and Ingrid held her again. "Promise you won't leave me, Ingrid. Promise."

"I promise." And Ingrid meant it.

But now it wasn't just because she cared for Sailor. Now, she realized, she had been brought here—into the Loefflers' lives and their home—for a purpose. She needed to know what Scoot had meant by *fix her little red wagon.* She needed to know what Scoot had done to her grandmother. Because it was clear now. Nothing could be clearer. Scoot Loeffler had somehow hurt Edie.

And, just like Edie had said, Ingrid was the only one who could right the balance.

Sailor was looking at her with a desperate expression. "Can you . . . will you consider doing something for me, Ingrid? Something about her?"

Ingrid frowned. "What do you mean?"

Sailor held her gaze. Her eyes blazed, and her voice was a fierce whisper. "Yes, you do, Ingrid. You know *exactly* I mean. I want you to do something about my mother. Stop her. With a spell."

Ingrid was shaking her head. "No—"

"Yes." Sailor lowered her voice even further. "I know I've joked about it before, but I'm being serious now. I want you to do a spell that makes her stop what's she's doing. Something that makes her just . . . go away. A hex."

Ingrid gave her a horrified look. "No, Sailor. You don't want to do that. I'm telling you— "

"I do want you to do it." Tears were coursing down her cheeks. "I can't take it anymore. I'm so tired of her hurting me. Hurting all of us." Sailor's eyes bored into hers. "Ingrid, I'm begging you. Hex her. Hex my mother."

Ingrid hesitated. They had just entered dangerous territory. A place Edie had warned her never to go. But she couldn't find it in her heart to outright deny Sailor. The girl was heartbroken. Desperate. She heard an echo of Edie just then.

You must stay in the light . . .

But Edie wasn't here. Not anymore.

She didn't understand the full extent of how terrible this woman was.

"I would need a picture of her," Ingrid said.

Sailor only hesitated a fraction of a second before stalking to a nearby table and returning with a small silver frame holding a photograph of Scoot. She slapped it into Ingrid's palm. Ingrid looked down at it. Young Scoot, devastatingly beautiful with long silky hair and half-lidded cat eyes, stared at the camera like she was considering incinerating it to pure ash.

Sailor closed Ingrid's fingers around the frame. The metal edges cut into Ingrid's skin. "When will you do it?"

"I don't know, Sailor. This is a really big deal."

Sailor pressed her lips together. "You have to do it soon."

"I don't know— "

"Then I'll find someone else," Sailor countered.

Ingrid's brow furrowed.

"Someone who understands what's at stake." Sailor's voice was even.

"Sailor. I understand. I do."

"Then do it tonight. Promise me."

She hesitated.

"Ingrid." Sailor's face was a pale mask.

"I promise." Ingrid's voice was barely audible.

Sailor nodded, almost as if she was convincing herself that this thing, this agreement, must be.

Ingrid held the framed photo face-down against her stomach. "I should go."

Sailor walked her to the door and gave her a swift hug. When Ingrid opened it, Miles was standing at the bottom of the steps, looking up at her with an expression of a contrite child.

Chapter 32

He walked her, in silence, back to the house. In the narrow front hall, a meowing Litha rubbed up against her leg and she set the framed photo face-down on a table. Ingrid picked Litha up and buried her face in the cat's thick, velvet fur. A headache had bloomed in her right temple and was throbbing dully.

Miles rubbed the carved newel post with his palm. "I'm sorry, Ingrid. It was wrong, speaking to you like that back at the cemetery. You were great to come tonight and help me out, and I really appreciate it."

She focused on Litha, who had settled into a contented purr. "I can text people, you know. Men. Guys."

"I know you can."

"It doesn't mean I don't love you."

He nodded. "It's just . . . I can't lose you, Ingrid. You're my best friend. You're the only one who understands me. The mother thing, I mean." He shifted. "Dumping us off on other people. Leaving us."

"I know," Ingrid said. "And that will never change, no matter who comes into our lives."

He let out a sound of frustration.

"What, Miles? You have other friends. You see other girls." And she saw Boney, not that that was a subject she was going to get into now. "Why is this any different?"

"Cas Loeffler is just so . . ."

"What makes you think it's Cas Loeffler?"

"Boney. He said you pretty much admitted it to him at the party at the Tybee cabin."

"What?" Her eyes held a challenge. "You think Cas Loeffler is out of my league?"

"No! No. That's not what I meant."

"What, then?"

"Nothing."

But she understood what he was trying to say, even if he didn't have the guts. Cas belonged with the other Savannah. The rich, the powerful, the ones who existed above all the rest of them. If Ingrid ended up with him, she would, in many ways, leave her old life behind. Maybe even Miles.

The truth was, though, she didn't want to lose Miles. He was her best friend, almost her brother, in some strange way. But right now she didn't have time to untangle that particular knot of feelings. She had another, much bigger, problem to deal with.

"Sailor wants me to do baneful magic," she said to Miles.

Miles gaped at her. "What? Are you serious?"

She propped up the framed photo of Scoot on the table, observing it with a worried frown. "She wants me to hex her mother."

He blinked at Ingrid, at the framed photo, then back to her. "But you don't do that. It's black magic, right?"

She shook her head impatiently. "I do black magic. Miles, I've explained this to you. Black magic reverses. It pushes away, subtracts. White draws in." She sighed, suddenly exhausted. "Baneful magic is something altogether different. It's performed to harm someone. Like a curse or a hex. Sailor wants me to hex her mother."

"Are you going to do it?"

Litha, bored now, struggled out of her arms. Ingrid's head was really hurting now. She just wanted to go to sleep. "I promised I would."

Miles frowned. "What about the Law of Three you're always talking about? You said the energy a person put out into the universe returns to them triplefold."

Annoyance flared. "I know."

"You can't do it. You just can't. It's wrong."

"Well, it's not that simple, okay? Sometimes you have to do the wrong thing for the right reason."

She pushed past him into the sitting room, plopping down on the thick, down sofa. She still could not get over how rich people had somehow figured out a way to get nicer, softer sofa cushions than regular people.

He followed her into the room and sat, too. He was still giving her that reproachful, sad puppy look.

She tilted her head back and stared at the freshly painted ceiling. "Stop looking at me like that."

He looked away, then spoke carefully. "Why would Sailor want you to do something like that?"

Ingrid addressed the ceiling. "Scoot's a monster. You should've heard her, insulting her daughter like was she was nothing more than dirt under her feet." There was more, obviously—what she'd said about Edie and about Ingrid—but she wasn't ready to tell him that. Not until she had a clearer picture of what she was going to do.

"Is there anything else you can do instead of a hex? Something that's like maybe half the strength of the heavy-duty thing?"

She rubbed her temples, fingers circling, pressing so hard it would hurt worse than the headache. "I don't know."

"What about a binding spell? Or a karma spell? I've heard you talking about one of those. Then she just gets what she deserves, nothing more."

With her texting secrets with Cas and the secrets with Rill, she wasn't sure if she was all that keen on a karmic spell coming back on her threefold, but at this point, she didn't have that many options.

"A karma spell puts it all back onto Scoot. You're not doing anything to her that she hasn't done to other people."

"Okay." Ingrid wilted. "Yeah. That makes sense."

He reached over and put a hand on her knee. "I'll make us tea."

Just then her phone trilled.

Are you doing it yet?

Sailor.

I need you to do it now, Ingrid. Now.

Mom actually just left the house. I don't know where she went, but I'm not going after her.

She washed her face, drank two glasses of water, and then went into the Daffodil Room to find one of Edie's old nightgowns, a flannel with a rosebud print, that she put on in front of the full-length mirror.

Feeling an unaccountable chill even after dressing, she pulled the lavender mohair sweater around her shoulders. Back on the main floor, the lights were all turned off and front door locked, but she didn't see Miles. He must've gone back out or gone to bed.

Good. She needed some space for what lay ahead.

She retrieved the photo and went downstairs. In the altar room she turned on her one lamp, leaving the room dim and cozy. She put music on, a soothing cello instrumental that always settled her nerves. She arranged the red cord, set out her candles, and lit them. From a drawer she pulled out a small gift box, yellow with a sticker on the lid that read COTILLION. It was the shop where Sailor purchased the scented candles she was always giving Ingrid. Once Sailor had told her it was Scoot's favorite shop. Above the breakfront, she removed a small, oval mirror from where it hung on the wall, and in another drawer, she found a hammer.

She laid out all the tools on her altar and did a quick centering meditation. She chanted softly, lifting up a prayer for her own purity of motives. She knew that the Goddess, the Light, the One True Will of the Cosmos, desired that Scoot Loeffler move in compassion and love for her daughter. If Scoot refused to do that, the Goddess would be aware, and there would be consequences. Ingrid was only here to align with the cosmos and the Will. Align with those consequences and call them into being.

She took extra care with her preparations, getting her mind and body in the proper alignment. Then, when it was time, she knelt and sprinkled salt in the bottom of the Cotillion box. She removed the picture of Scoot from the frame, then laid it flat in the center of the box, on top of the salt, and focused on it, letting the image of the cat eyes, razor-sharp cheekbones, and haughty lips meld into her vision. Imprint themselves on her consciousness.

"As I will, so mote it be . . ."

Her mind reeled backward, remembering a time long ago when she had asked Edie to do another karma spell. It was when she was sixteen years old and feeling particularly angry at her mother, Tess, for dumping her in Savannah.

"What you put out shall return to thee . . ." she said now.

It wasn't that Ingrid didn't love Edie, but it wasn't easy to be the only girl in school who lived with her grandmother instead of her mother and father. Not to mention, having that grandmother be a witch had put Ingrid on the bottom rung of the social ladder. So she'd begged Edie to cast a spell on Tess, thinking any misfortune that befell Tess would make her feel better.

"Let karma be your teacher . . ."

Edie had refused, and made Ingrid promise not to do it herself, but still, in the end, Tess got what she had coming. Four years later Edie learned Tess had run afoul of the law down in Jacksonville and had been incarcerated for writing bad checks. Then a few months after her release, Tess died.

When Ingrid had asked Edie if it was her fault Tess had gone to prison then died, if her wishing misfortune on her mother had somehow persuaded the Goddess to act, Edie had said no, and then she'd told Ingrid that there was no magic stronger than a person's own regrets.

Now, as Ingrid held the mirror over the picture of Scoot, catching the reflection, she wondered if that was true. Maybe she had aligned with the Cosmos back then and just hadn't realized it. She laid the mirror back down on the altar, on a hand towel, then wrapped the towel securely around the mirror. She lifted the hammer and smashed it with three, small, sharp taps. Lifting the towel, she poured the shards on top of the photo in the box. Taking a short black candle, she wedged it into the broken glass, then lit it.

She watched the flame stretch high. "Three by three by three . . ."

This time was different. This time, Ingrid didn't have four years to wait for Scoot's regrets to do their own work. Sailor needed Scoot taken care of immediately before the woman wrecked the most important day of her life. That's where the cayenne came in. She sprinkled the red spice over the candle's flame, and she could swear the fire licked it up, like a cat licking milk droplets from the floor.

"As I will, so mote it be."

She sat back on her heels and continued to chant in the glow of the burning candle, and after a while—she didn't know how long—she realized she was keening. Crying for the little girl she'd once been. Crying for the little girl she saw in Sailor.

She had come too far and learned too much. She would not stand by and let her friend suffer at the hands of this vindictive, jealous woman. Ingrid would fight for her friend—and she would fight for Edie. She would right the balance. She would win.

Let Scoot Loeffler beware.

She was about to get her comeuppance.

Chapter 33

She woke several times during the night, each time feeling strangely adrift. The candles continued to burn down within the circle she had neglected to close. She had lost herself in the spell, dreaming of many things.

Of Edie and Rill, of Scoot and Cas. Of Miles, showing her the hidden compartment under the stage at the Lucas Theatre. There was something in it. Not a flask, but one of Rill's pirate artifacts.

When she finally woke for the last time, she was in her underwear, Edie's nightgown lying beside her in a wadded ball. She felt light, giddy—like she'd been carrying a huge boulder, and the previous night, she'd finally been able to put it down.

She scrambled up and peered inside the Cotillion gift box, now a mess of black wax, glass, and salt. Scoot's face in the photograph resembled some kind of swamp creature—half human, half blob.

She stretched, yawned, suddenly craving coffee. She pulled the nightgown over her head and mounted the stairs to the first floor which was, appropriately for how she felt this morning, flooded with morning light. In the kitchen, she was greeted with the sight of Miles standing at the coffee maker, mug in hand.

He gave her a wink and filled her a mug. "Some night last night, huh?"

She sipped the coffee. Black. Delicious. Just what she needed. She closed her eyes, inhaling the aroma, willing it to fortify her.

"It was interesting, I'll say that much."

"Feeling optimistic?" He looked haggard, almost as exhausted as she did.

"Very." She leaned over and planted a quick kiss on his cheek, and he brightened. "Everything's going to be okay, Miles, I promise."

She took her coffee upstairs and fell into bed, sleeping for four more luxurious hours until ten. Still an hour before she had to open the shop for the pedestrian traffic. Around her, the house was silent and pleasingly dim.

She could hear the sounds of summer outside her window. Revelers, drunken partiers, families taking tours, all braving the thick August heat. She showered, washed her hair, and pulled on a pair of denim cutoffs and gray T-shirt, knowing Edie would have *tsked* her disapproval that it wasn't a dress.

"Not today," she said stubbornly to the air. "It's too damn hot."

Downstairs, she found the house in order and the kitchen tidied. Since they'd had their talk, Miles had kept up impressively with the housework. She really appreciated it, which she should mention. She should always remember to mention the positive things to him so he would know how important he was to her. So he would leave her alone about Cas Loeffler.

In case Cas Loeffler ever happened to talk to her again.

She opened the fridge, but the smell of spoiled food made her wrinkle her nose. She gathered it up and dumped it all in the garbage, putting the plastic containers in the dishwasher. What she really wanted was a slice of hot pizza. Olive and tomato and basil, extra cheese, with tons of hot pepper. And a Coke. And maybe some ice cream afterward.

She would go out and enjoy the sights of the city. Celebrate her spell and making up with Miles. In the front hall, she slid on her battered Converse, Miles's Braves cap, and a pair of outrageously expensive sunglasses that Sailor had bought her. Grabbing her fanny pack, she headed out.

Twenty minutes later she was sitting at a picnic table in Starland Yard, contentedly munching her way through a piping hot slice. She watched a group of kids at the next table over try to ride their golden retriever while their parents ignored them and drank beer.

Her headache was gone, but even after the initial high of the spell had worn off, she was still feeling strange. Like she'd taken cold medicine or napped too long. After she finished the second slice she went and got herself a Modelo. She sat back down to drink it, staring off into the distance, not seeing a thing. Still foggy and now pleasantly buzzed.

She checked her phone. Nothing from Sailor. Nothing from her sinner. Just two missed calls from Miles.

She called him back. "What's up?" She tipped back the beer, reveling in the slide of cool tartness down her throat.

"Did you hear?" Miles asked.

"Hear what?"

"About Sailor Loeffler's mother," he said slowly.

Ingrid bolted upright, feeling her heart kick into a dissonant, uneven tattoo. Her arms and legs felt weak. She pushed the Modelo away.

"What happened?" She tried to keep her voice modulated.

"She was driving—"

"Last night?" she cut in sharply. It sounded like a cry.

"Yes."

"She was drunk last night," she said slowly. "Very drunk. When I was at the house with Sailor." But Sailor had texted that she went out after that.

Where had she gone?

"Ingrid, I know all that. I'm trying to tell you what Boney told me."

The children beside her were screaming now, pulling at the dog to get him to stand still for their pony ride. She was shaking.

"Then tell me," she said brusquely.

"Apparently Scoot was driving, drunk. Out to Tybee, they think."

"Driving herself to Tybee? She never drives herself. *Or* goes to Tybee."

"Regardless, she hit a guy on the sidewalk, Ingrid. A homeless guy. Then she left him and drove into one of the side streets and ran the car off into a ditch."

Ingrid covered her mouth with her hand. Oh God—oh Goddess, oh Edie—what had she done?

What had she done?

"Ingrid?"

"I'm here."

"The guy was hurt pretty bad, and the Tybee police arrested Scoot, but the Loefflers' lawyer set up some kind of deal with the judge. Judge Norwood—"

Judge Norwood. She'd met someone at Sailor's engagement party by that name. Patti Jo Norwood. She'd had sleek cinnamon hair cut in an angled bob. Lots of hammered silver jewelry.

"Wait, Boney told you all this? How does he know?"

"Sasha told him. She was working a charity breakfast thing at the Norwoods' house this morning when the judge got the call. One of the caterers overhead him on the phone."

This was how this town worked. Not only did gossip spread like wildfire through the elite families, it was shot with flamethrowers through other channels as well. And Ingrid had found the network of servers, Uber drivers, housecleaners, and every kind of underpaid support staff to be uncannily accurate when it came to getting their stories right.

Miles was still talking. "Boney said Sasha said that she heard Rill was going to check Scoot into a hospital."

Ingrid could barely breathe. In her line of vision, the children were now pulling on the dog, flinging themselves onto its back and falling off again. The poor dog looked miserable.

"Hospital?" she repeated dully.

"A rehab facility," Miles said. "Like one of those places you go to, so you won't be charged with anything. In Charleston."

Her heart was still racing, skittering away in her chest. And now her fingers tingled. She was having a panic attack. She hadn't had one of those in a long time. Not since the day she'd met Sailor . . .

"You there?" Miles asked.

"I'm here." She didn't know what to say, but she didn't want to end the call. Along with the jittery, suffocating panic, something else had settled on her. A sudden, deep, devouring terror.

"Ingrid, it's not your fau—"

"It is my fault," she cried. "I cast a spell last night—"

"A karma spell," Miles said.

"She hurt someone. She hit a man with her car," Ingrid said, her voice desperate.

Her eyes burned, but no tears came out. Her brain began spiraling down new corridors of thought. It wheeled and switched back, folding on itself. She was so hot. Dehydrated. Her heart was slamming against her chest now. The children shrieked. The parents ignored them. Their own kids. They didn't even look over in their direction.

A thought surfaced. "How is he? The person she hit?"

He hesitated.

"Miles!"

"He's, ah . . . well, he's in the hospital. Boney said he might be dead; he doesn't know."

"Oh no. Oh no. My God, no!" This was a wail. The parents from the next table over sent her annoyed looks. Their kids still pulled at the dog, but now the dog twisted around and yelped sharply.

Something inside her snapped. Ingrid leapt up and in one bounding step was at the group of children, grabbing two of their arms, yanking them away from the dog. "Leave him alone!" Ingrid shouted.

"Hey!" one of the moms said. The man sitting beside her rose up, disentangling his legs from the attached picnic bench.

"Hold up," he said in a gruff voice to Ingrid. He was still holding his beer can. He glowered menacingly like she'd slapped one of the children instead of pulled them off an innocent dog.

Ingrid's rage surged, and she released the two children. "Little shits were torturing your dog. Not that you noticed." She turned and stalked off.

"Hey, bitch," the man called behind her.

She kept walking, then looked once over her shoulder. He was following her. She rounded on him with a glare. Sent the sign of the horns at him so hard she was surprised lightning bolts didn't shoot out from her forked fingers.

He pulled up, an incredulous look on his face. "What the fuck?"

She burst into tears, turned, and ran.

Chapter 34

It was over two miles from Starland Yard to Monterey Square, and she ran the whole way. By the time she knocked at the Loefflers' door, her T-shirt was damp, her hair plastered to her neck. Mrs. Leimberger, in her ever-present gray suit, answered.

"Hi, Mrs. Leimberger. Is Sailor around?" Ingrid asked, panting.

"Hello, Miss White." Mrs. Leimberger stared at her, no expression on her face. "It's been a busy day here."

Ingrid hesitated. "I know. I heard. I just wanted to see how Sailor was doing."

"She's not feeling well. You should go home." Mrs. Leimberger started to shut the door, but Ingrid put out a hand to block it. Mrs. Leimberger pursed her lips. "Excuse me, Miss White. I'm not going to ask you again—"

"Please," Ingrid said. "Please, Mrs. Leimberger. You have to tell her I'm here. Just ask her to come talk to me for a minute. Just one minute. I'll stay out here on the porch."

"Thank you, Mrs. Leimberger. I'll handle this," came a soft voice from behind the house manager.

Sailor appeared in the doorway. She had been crying, it was obvious. Her eyes were red, her face, puffy. She glanced at Mrs.

Leimberger, dismissing her with a nod. When the woman was gone, Sailor turned her gaze to Ingrid.

"What do you want?" Sailor's flat voice matched the look in her eyes.

"I just heard what happened, and I wanted to come check on you. To see how you were doing."

"I'm terrible; that's how I'm doing." Sailor's swollen face remained stony. She hooked her hair behind an ear and sniffed.

"I'm so sorry, Sailor. It's terrible."

"You're right," Sailor said. "It is terrible. And *not* what I asked you to do."

"Wait. No. I mean . . . I don't understand."

Sailor threw a look over her shoulder and squeezed the door closer to her body. "You did this, didn't you?" Her voice was a harsh whisper.

Ingrid's mouth opened, but no words came out.

Sailor's eyes were watery slits. "How can you just *stand there*, on my doorstep, acting like you're so innocent?"

"You asked me— " Ingrid began.

"That wasn't what I meant, Ingrid!" she snapped, then glanced around apprehensively. She lowered her voice. "This is not what I wanted. For her to drive drunk. To hit someone. To almost *kill* them. My mother never drives drunk. She has a chauffeur, for God's sake." Her eyes scrunched up and her mouth opened into an ugly gash. "How could you do this to her, Ingrid? To all of us?"

"I didn't do this. I didn't want it to happen. Sailor, I swear. I would never."

But something had settled over Sailor, an expression that was both somehow upset and at the same time detached. "You did do it. You did it, Ingrid. Don't lie to me. You took her picture from this house, and you did a spell."

A chill coursed through Ingrid. "You gave me the picture. You asked me to do the spell."

Sailor's red eyes drifted past her. She was quiet for a long moment, then said in a steady voice, "No, I didn't."

Ingrid flinched like she'd been hit in the face.

"You stole the picture," Sailor said in an odd, detached voice. "You stole it and did a spell and put some kind of curse on my mother. I don't even know what to say. Our family is devastated."

Ingrid could only search her friend's face, looking for a shred of something she recognized. Looking for a glimmer of her love and loyalty. But she saw only a wall holding back her pain. Her pain and her clear hatred. Ingrid couldn't believe what she was seeing. Was this really how it was going to end? she thought desperately. With such a simple and obvious lie?

"I don't want you coming here anymore, Ingrid," Sailor said stiffly. "I don't want to see you or talk to you." She lifted herself up, drew in a deep breath. "Neither does my brother."

Ingrid's face must've registered her shock, because Sailor started nodding her head quickly, her chin bobbing up and down almost maniacally.

"That's right. I know you've got a thing for him." She sucked in her cheeks.

Ingrid swallowed.

"You know it's his thing. The *sexting*. He's done it with girls in our crowd, but also girls he'd never date, much less marry. It gets him off in some disgusting way. He's also done it to a few of my friends, but they always told me immediately."

Not Finley, Ingrid thought.

"Unlike *you*, who didn't see fit to mention it. But Dad did. He told me he's pretty sure Cas has been up to his old tricks with you."

Ingrid's face was on fire now. She wanted to disappear. Just wanted to be done with this nightmare and be back at home, holding Litha and watching TV with Miles. But Sailor wasn't through twisting the knife.

"Don't worry about it, Ingrid," she said in a low, cruel voice. "It's meaningless. Just a compulsion he has. The nasty compulsion of a dumb boy."

Ingrid started to cry, but this only seemed to strengthen Sailor's resolve.

"I'm getting married in one month," she went on. "I have to concentrate on my wedding. My fiancé. My mother getting well. I won't be needing your services any longer."

Ingrid let out a soft, breathy huff. Sailor smiled. And then she swung the door closed.

It was a full minute before Ingrid could force herself to turn around. Force her feet to go back down the steps and head back in the direction of her home. She felt like she wasn't in her body. That her soul had shrunk down to something hard and small and dry.

She heard the voices. Childish chants echoing in her ears.

Renounce Satan, renounce Satan, renounce Satan . . .

She was a kid all over again. Friendless, a mockery, floating along the shady streets of Savannah like a ghost. Edie was dead. Her mother was, too. All she had left was Miles.

Miles, who remained loyal, fiercely and doggedly loyal. Even throughout misunderstandings and fights. Miles was her only true friend. He waited for her at home right now.

She suddenly realized she'd been gone for almost two hours. There was no telling how many possible walk-ins she'd missed. How much money she'd lost.

She could never do that again.

Everything had changed and nothing at all. Once again, she was on her own.

Chapter 35

As a result of a series of events that occurred in the spring of Ingrid's eighth-grade year, when she was thirteen years old, Edie pulled her out of Hubert Middle School.

It all started with a girl named Destiny Amos. Destiny was a talkative redhead Ingrid sat next to in social studies. Destiny was a born ringleader, organizing trips to the movies, pottery painting dates, and sleepovers like she was a miniature CEO of Pubescent Girls.

Destiny's parents lived in a modest town house on Lafayette Square just one square north of Ingrid's. The Amoses had enough money to send their two daughters to the private Savannah Country Day School, but as her mother had political aspirations to run for Georgia's U.S. Senate seat, she saw the benefits of keeping her in the same classrooms as the children of her future constituents.

Destiny, a precocious girl who could intellectually trounce everyone in every class, occasionally even her teachers, lorded it over the other girls. The girls, in turn, worshipped her. On Valentine's Day, Destiny gave out full-sized candy bars to everyone in her class. For her birthday, she invited every girl in the grade out to Pooler to play paintball.

To Ingrid, Destiny Amos was perfection—the best friend for whom she felt an almost suffocating sense of loyalty. At night, on her bed, Ingrid would imagine possible disasters that she might be called upon to save Destiny from. A freak tidal wave on the river walk that threatened to sweep Destiny out to sea. A hundred-year-old live oak, struck by lightning and about to topple onto Destiny's head. A rogue street sweeper about to squash her friend, that Ingrid would throw herself in front of, sustaining bruises, cuts, and a few broken bones in her selfless sacrifice.

In real life, Ingrid was as loyal as in her fantasies. More than a few times, on the playground, she took on the toughest, meanest boys in her class when they dared to insult her friend, going at them gladiator-style until they ran. No one was allowed to bad-mouth Destiny, as long as Ingrid was in earshot.

Ingrid was beside herself to be invited to Destiny's birthday party and carefully selected a gift for her friend—a pair of nearly new, black-and-white checkered Vans, in Destiny's exact size, that a client had given Edie. After the paintball and present opening, the paint-spattered girls gathered for cake and ice cream on a picnic table at the edge of a muddy field.

"Here's the schedule for tonight," Destiny said. "We're going to watch *Aquamarine* and have snacks, then Ingrid's going to do a séance for us." She gave Ingrid an indulgent smile. "At midnight under the full moon."

Ingrid squirmed. It was only a quarter moon, Destiny was wrong about that, but that didn't actually matter. You could do a séance anytime. And certainly, Ingrid had experienced plenty of séances, but always under her grandmother's guidance. She'd never led one.

Besides that, Edie had always warned her that messing around with spirits wasn't a thing to be taken lightly. Spirits were like dogs, Edie said. They could just as easily give you slobbery kisses as bite your hand clean off.

Ingrid said maybe they shouldn't do a séance, but Destiny insisted. She wanted to speak to Nanna, her only grandmother, who had died when she was in third grade. It hit Ingrid unexpectantly, the shock of what it must be like to lose someone like that, and, tears pricking her eyes, she relented.

In the garden level of Destiny's town house, the girls ate Doritos and guzzled Cherry Coke while they watched the movie. When midnight came, Destiny, wearing a crown she'd won in some Little Miss Something-or-Other pageant, lit a bunch of candles and then instructed the girls to pull their sleeping bags into a circle.

Looking in their expectant eyes, Ingrid's earlier feeling of doubt became full-blown panic. She thought she should probably cast a circle and call the corners but even doing that felt wrong. Like sharing a secret known only to her and Edie.

Under her breath, she mumbled a quick prayer of protection to the Goddess, then told the girls to join hands and close their eyes. She announced to the room that only friendly spirits were welcome and that she wished to speak to Nanna. Destiny's nanna, she added, in case some rogue spirit in the Amos house happened to overhear and get the wrong idea.

The room stilled. The candles flickered. Destiny seemed surrounded by a nimbus of fuzzy light. Now, Ingrid felt the strength and unity of the girls as a fierce circle of its own, linked by their hands and their single intention. All desiring their friend Destiny to reach her beloved grandmother.

For the first time in her young life, Ingrid felt herself taken by the moment, and to her surprise, she floated gently and easily out of her body. She began to see and hear and feel many things. She was only dimly aware of the room, the girls around her, of what she was saying. And boy, was she saying stuff.

Words she couldn't quite string together in coherent sentences. Or at least sentences that made sense to her.

. . . your mother isn't . . . your mother . . .

. . . your sister . . .

Your sister is your mother . . .

Destiny suddenly came into sharp focus. No longer surrounded in the light, she leaned forward, face pale and eyes blazing, and grabbed the front of Ingrid's pajamas.

"Shut up," she hissed in Ingrid's face, then released her. "She's lying!" she announced to the girls, then jumped up and ran out of the room.

The others edged away from the circle, murmuring amongst themselves and eyeing Ingrid dubiously. Ingrid felt herself reeling, a sensation that felt like she was falling off a cliff, scrabbling for purchase. Two girls went after Destiny.

When Destiny came marching back into the room, flanked by her two adolescent deputies, Ingrid knew she was in trouble. Adrenaline flooded her small body, and she tasted something sour in her mouth mixing with the Cherry Coke and Doritos. Destiny's face was shiny and red. The two girls on either side of her, pale and wide-eyed.

"We're going to pray for you now, Ingrid," Destiny said in a dramatic voice. "Because you've got a demon in you." She fixed the rest of the girls with a fierce look. "You were definitely talking to one just now, and I think he's still in the room."

The girls screamed and clutched at each other. One started crying to go home.

But Destiny stood firm. "We have to cast the demon out of her," she insisted, and she pulled a chair into the center of the room. "Sit down," she ordered Ingrid.

Ingrid sat meekly as Destiny directed the girls to use socks and belts to tie her arms and legs to the chair. When they were finished, Destiny produced a Bible from which she started reading. Ingrid didn't really understand what it was saying, but it sounded very ominous. And by now she had to pee so bad it hurt.

"Please let me go to the bathroom," Ingrid begged.

Destiny leaned close to Ingrid's face, enveloping her in the scent of Cool Ranch Doritos. "First you have to renounce the devil. If you renounce him, then you still have a chance to go to heaven."

Destiny got the girls to chant with her: *Renounce Satan, renounce Satan, renounce Satan . . .* Destiny waved her arms, and marched around Ingrid in the chair, holding up the Bible and screaming at the demon to leave her house. She commanded the girls to help her, and they obeyed.

RENOUNCESATAN, RENOUNCESATAN, RENOUNCE SATAN! they all screamed as they marched.

At last, Ingrid was sobbing. Sobbing and renouncing the devil, sobbing and renouncing witchcraft, sobbing and, in the end because she couldn't hold it any longer, wetting herself.

"It's the demon!" Destiny shrieked, pointing at the puddle of urine that dripped off the chair. The girls screamed again, one breaking down in tears. Finally, hearing the ruckus, Destiny's mother came downstairs, broke up the exorcism, and called all the girls' parents to come pick them up.

When Ingrid was finally home, bathed and tucked in her own bed, Edie lay beside her. She stroked Ingrid's hair and sang her favorite old John Denver song, "Sunshine on My Shoulders," in a soft voice. After the song, she muttered something else, some unintelligible words—spells, Ingrid thought hazily, but she wasn't sure because during them, she fell asleep.

The next day, Edie found Ingrid in her bedroom, black candle burning on the floor, chanting an improvised hex intended for Destiny. Edie admonished Ingrid, blew out the candle, and immediately performed a cleansing ritual.

"We don't do baneful magic, no matter how richly someone may deserve it," she explained to the girl, then added, "and anyway, the One True Will of the Cosmos can take care of that girl without our interference. Some pirates fly flags that belong to another."

"What does that mean?" Ingrid asked.

Edie waved her hand like it was irrelevant.

On Monday morning, she informed Ingrid that from here on out, she, Edie, would take care of her schooling.

Chapter 36

The next morning, Ingrid lay in her bed and wondered if it was a reasonable idea to stay under the covers forever.

Miles would allow her a grace period to wallow in her sadness, she thought. He would bring her takeout from Bull Street Taco and Mirabelle. She could maybe count on a week or two, she figured, before he got tired of waiting on her. Before they started dipping into the money she'd saved.

Which she knew would not stretch far.

She would have to get her ass in gear. She had adult responsibilities. An obligation to Edie and the Goddess. She just didn't know how she was going to do any of it without Sailor. She'd come to depend on her—her contacts, connections, money.

A few days later, when the direct deposit into Ingrid's checking account did not appear, the reality of her predicament hit her. If she didn't continue getting just as many, if not more, customers, Ingrid would be back to broke once again, quicker than she even imagined. Besides that, she missed Sailor, badly. She felt sick knowing her friend was angry at her.

Panic enveloped her. Although she had tried to honor Sailor's wishes and not call, this was too much. What was she going to do? Go down without a fight? She couldn't. Trembling, she tapped Sailor's number, but the call rolled straight to voicemail.

"Sailor, it's Ingrid," she said in a breathless voice. "I just wanted to talk to you. Just for a minute . . ."

She closed her eyes. Waited a beat.

"I swear to you on the earth and all the elements, I never intended for anything to happen to your mother. I was only trying to help. To do what you wanted me to do. And . . . I don't mean to be unfeeling . . . but maybe it's for the best, what's happened. Maybe she can heal and get better and . . . I don't know, be the mother you've—"

There was a click, and a robot voice informed her that her message had been erased, but she could wait for the beep and record again. She hung up.

She called again after that—five, six, seven times—each time getting Sailor's voicemail message, each time hanging up. That was when the devastating truth dawned. There was no going back. Her life with the Loefflers, her friendship with Sailor, had been nothing but a brief, wondrous dream. But it was over.

Not thinking to grab her purse or phone, she burst out of the house and headed down the street. She didn't know where she was headed, and when she arrived at Forsyth Park in the dimming light of the early evening, she sat on one of the benches that encircled the fountain and watched the sprays of water jetting out in all directions.

Lulled by the sound of the water, she let the tears flow. Hadn't Edie warned her over and over again of something like this happening? Performing magic, any kind of magic, was a serious undertaking. It was so easy to lose sight of the point of her practice, so easy to let her own emotions cloud her intentions.

But that's exactly what she had done.

She should've talked Sailor out of the spell. She should've been strong enough to do the right thing.

Her phone rang. It was Mrs. Leimberger, talking in a distant, crisp voice, telling Ingrid to cease and desist all phone calls to Miss Loeffler—and if she didn't, Ingrid would be hearing from the family's lawyer, *forthwith*.

Ingrid only uttered one word in reply—"okay"—then hung up, feeling nauseated all over again. She left the park and went home, dully stumping up the stairs to her bedroom. Even though it was only eight o'clock, she immediately fell into a deep sleep.

She dreamed that Edie and she were sitting in Edie's doctor's office. Ingrid was eighteen years old again, holding Edie's hand—or rather it was the other way around because Edie had known there was something deeply wrong with her, and she wanted to shield Ingrid from the blow. Edie's cancer diagnosis.

"I know it's not much comfort," the doctor said to Edie, "but maybe something to think about for Ingrid here. You have what's known as chronic beryllium disease. An exposure to the toxic metal beryllium which probably occurred years ago."

Edie, holding fast to Ingrid's hand, said nothing.

The doctor went on. "We usually see this type of exposure in workers in nuclear, biomedical, electronics, defense, and semiconductor fields. As that isn't you, we might conclude there were other sources. Contaminated soil, perhaps. Volcanic ash. Kitty litter. Is there any sort of contamination like that in your house?"

In the dream, Scoot Loeffler appeared behind the doctor's plush, leather chair. On the doctor's desk, on a wooden stand, was a beaker of gray ash. Scoot plucked it from the stand and dumped it into a silver milkshake cup. She stirred it with a red-and-gold fountain pen, Rill's pen, then poured the concoction into a glass, squirted whipped cream over it, and plopped a maraschino cherry on top.

"What is it?" Ingrid asked Edie. "What's she making?"

As Scoot slid the glass toward Edie, a malevolent smile curled the corners of her lips. "I'm taking care of her." Scoot turned her gaze upon Ingrid. "I'm fixing her little red wagon."

Chapter 37

In the days that followed, Ingrid managed to drag herself out of bed every morning and go to work. Even if her reflection in the mirror told her that she had barely eaten or slept, she forged ahead. She had plenty of clients, friends of the Loefflers and others, who were still coming to her for readings. Apparently, Sailor had not told anyone that her former psychic-witch had hexed her own mother.

But word about other things Ingrid had done for Sailor's wedding had gotten out. Now, when booking a client for a simple half hour reading, they requested spells for all sorts of things: new jobs, new boyfriends, new cars. Ingrid explained to all of them that was not her business model—she wasn't exactly Santa Claus—and soon, the flood of new customers slowed to a trickle.

Ingrid knew she should cleanse herself, meditate, maybe even do a settling ritual that would help her focus on her own healing. But she had no desire to set foot in her altar room. No desire to connect with Edie or the Goddess. She just wanted Sailor back. Sailor and Cas, her new family.

With all the free time she had on her hands, she took to lurking around Monterey Square, baseball cap pulled down low over her face, hoping to catch sight of Sailor. Usually there was no sign of her ex-friend. Only once did Ingrid spot her slipping out of the garden-level door of the Loeffler mansion and stepping into the open door of the Rolls that Adrian held open. The Rolls pulled away, heading north, then turned a corner and disappeared.

One day, Ingrid showed up at the door of Boney's filthy apartment. It was on the second story of an old cotton warehouse that faced the river, above a trinket shop that sold souvenir mugs, magnets, and shot glasses. In the shop there was, of course, the ubiquitous Savannah Sauce shelf, with all the flavors on offer so tourists could take the taste of the town back home. A set of iron stairs on the back wall of the building led up to the space Boney shared with Mari and another guy who occasionally worked at the shop downstairs but mostly sat in his room and smoked the place up with a particularly pungent form of weed.

After enduring Boney's gloating that the richies had dumped her just like he said they would, she accepted his apology in the form of an hour in his bed—although *bed* would be a generous word for the lumpy double mattress that occupied the corner of his bedroom.

It was a relief, losing herself in Boney's embrace. Being with him was the only thing that took her mind off her situation, if only momentarily. And after she told him the truth about what had happened with the karma spell, he gave her his whole stash of weed.

One early Sunday morning, after a night filled with bad dreams, Ingrid got out of bed and pulled on one of Edie's old shapeless linen sack dresses and her lavender mohair sweater. She had a vague idea that if she walked down to Forsyth Park, sat in front of the fountain with her morning coffee, and focused on the sights and sounds of the spraying water, she might feel better.

Out of habit, she went by way of Monterey Square, and nearing the Loeffler mansion, happened to spot Sailor and Cas emerging from the house. She quickly set her coffee thermos on the bench next to a homeless man and hurried to duck behind a huge azalea bush.

"Thanks," the man said, and she nodded then put her fingers to her lips. Peeking out from behind the bush, she zeroed in on Sailor. She wore a shirtdress this morning with ruffled shoulders and an orange floral print. *Erdem,* Ingrid thought automatically, *around twelve-hundred dollars.*

In contrast to Sailor's polish, Cas looked positively ragged in rumpled chinos and a faded black Henley shirt, his shaggy blond hair curling over his ears and neck. The combination took her breath away. Oh, was he a beauty, like an angelic carving of stone. Except for those eyes. They were nothing like stone. They were alive. Like the rich brown eyes of a deer.

Her sinner. She missed him almost as much as she did Sailor.

As soon as they were safely past her, she scooted out from behind the azalea and followed them, being careful to stay far enough behind not to be noticed. They headed north, through Madison Square, then Chippewa, all the way up to Wright, where they ascended the steps of the Lutheran Church of the Ascension. A half a minute later, Ingrid followed them inside and up the stairs to the second-floor sanctuary. She slid into a back pew and scanned the space.

The sanctuary was lovely. Peaceful and bright, with a sparkling arch of jewel-colored stained glass behind the altar as well as down either side of the pews. The pastor, an older woman with short, bristly, gray hair, was dressed in a robe with a colorful stole around the neck. A choir sang a rousing hymn.

She searched the pews for Sailor and Cas, spotting them on the opposite side of the aisle, a few rows up. She fixed her eyes on them, telling herself to stay calm. To breathe. She reviewed all the things she wanted to say to them:

I'm sorry for what I did to your mother.

It was a mistake, a misunderstanding, and I will do anything to fix it.

She would stop Cas and Sailor outside the church. Make them listen to her. Remind Sailor how she'd made her feel seen and understood. How she'd given Cas a safe place to start to explore his shadow-self, even though she wouldn't say that part out loud. She imagined the moment when their faces froze first in shock, then softened with compassion.

She imagined Sailor, reaching out to her. Gathering her into her gentle embrace and telling her how much she'd missed her one true friend. And Cas. He wouldn't say anything, not in front of Sailor. But later, when they'd found a place to be alone, he would plead for the saint to absolve the sinner. She felt revved up and jittery, right here in the back pew, just thinking about it.

During the opening bars of the last hymn, Ingrid slipped out and was heading out the front doors when she was caught by something. Someone who reached out and took Ingrid's hand in both of hers.

"Peace be with you," the older woman said.

"Oh," Ingrid said. "Thank you. You, too."

"Are you visiting with us?"

"I . . ." In the spill of congregants, Ingrid noticed Cas and Sailor walk past her, out the doors, and down the steps. "Yes. I just wanted to try it out."

"Well, I hope you'll come back."

Ingrid nodded and pulled her hand away. Sailor and Cas were headed toward the square, cutting through it toward Bull Street. She should follow them.

The woman looked over her shoulder and greeted the person behind her. "Judge Norwood. Welcome back. You're looking tan and well rested. I hope your vacation was a pleasant respite from this heat."

Ingrid nearly jumped out of her skin. *Norwood.* The judge who'd handled Scoot's case.

Who'd sent her to the luxury rehab instead of charging her with a crime.

"Eighteen holes of golf in hundred-and-one degree weather isn't exactly a respite," boomed the man behind her.

She melted back into the well-dressed crowd, trying to get a glimpse of the judge and his wife, Patti Jo. Ingrid watched them separate from the crowd—with much waving and air-kissing—then head south toward Bull Street just like Sailor and Cas. She followed them, an alternate idea forming in her mind. One better than approaching Sailor and Cas directly.

On Oglethorpe the judge and his wife turned right and disappeared into an elegant restaurant called Husk. Ingrid stood on the corner of Oglethorpe and Bull, gathering her courage. This may not be an entirely conventional approach, but she couldn't stand silently by any longer. She had to own up to her responsibility. She had to at least try.

She entered the restaurant, momentarily taken aback by the opulence, the crowd, the huge paintings. She suddenly became aware of the existence of the striking host who was giving her a quizzical look.

Ingrid imagined Sailor standing beside her, as she had so many times when they'd walked into restaurants. *Leimberger for Loeffler,* Sailor would always say, and not once would the host even skip a beat. They would always nod briskly and cheerfully and tell Sailor and Ingrid *right this way*.

She lifted her chin now. "I'm with the Norwood party," she announced in a voice she hoped sounded confident.

"Yes, of course," the woman said. "Just there by the window."

Ingrid was glad she didn't offer to show her to the table. She really didn't prefer an audience for this. As she walked up, she fixed a smile on her face.

"Excuse me," she said to Patti Jo Norwood. "I'm so sorry to interrupt."

Patti Jo looked up from her menu. "I'll have an unsweetened iced tea, dear. And a lime, if you don't mind."

"Oh . . . no. I'm sorry. I'm Ingrid White. The, ah . . . Sailor Loeffler's psychic."

Patti Jo seemed to be reaching back into her memory. The judge had a wary look in his eye.

"We met at the party. Sailor's engagement party," Ingrid added, smiling at them both.

"Oh, that's right." Patti Jo was pointing at her now with a short, pale pink fingernail. "Clemmie Fairburn's been to see you a few times. She said you're absolutely marvelous. Dead-on, every time." She sent her husband a wry smile. "I've been dying to make an appointment with you, but the judge over here has been keeping me busy with all this traveling—"

"I'd be happy to make time for you this week, if you like," Ingrid said.

"Oh, that's sweet." Patti Jo looked distracted now. "I'll have to check my calendar."

"I just was having brunch with my"—Ingrid waved her hand vaguely in the direction of some nonexistent table across the restaurant—"and I saw you, Judge, and wondered if I might speak to you about . . . about a legal issue."

Judge Norwood raised his eyebrows.

"Honey, talk to her," Pattie Jo said, and rose from her chair. "I'm going to run to the little girls' room." She bustled off and the judge sat back in his chair.

"It's about Scoot Loeffler," Ingrid said to the judge quickly. "I have something to tell you about her case."

"There is no case," he said gruffly. "Not anymore."

"But they sent her away to some kind of rehab."

"I can't discuss the details of a private legal matter, Miss—"

"White. Ingrid White." Ingrid gulped. "It's just that I'm not only a psychic, I'm a witch, too. I . . . I do spells and things like that, on occasion . . ."

He was looking up at her, a look of intense alarm on his face.

"Only white magic, mostly," she said hurriedly. "For things like healing and success and peace. Positive things . . ."

His eyes were darting around now, possibly hoping his wife was on her way back.

Ingrid went on. "I think I . . . well, I know I did a spell against Scoot that night. The night she had her accident. I didn't mean to, but I think I inadvertently did some kind of black magic spell, a curse or a hex—"

His face had gone pale and slack. "Young lady—"

"Anyway, it's my fault." Ingrid felt her armpits grow damp, a bead of sweat rolling down her spine. "It's my fault that she got in her car in her . . . condition. That she hit that man—"

"Young lady." The judge's voice was firmer now. He stood, glancing around the room surreptitiously before gently, but firmly, taking her arm and propelling her toward the door.

Ingrid tripped along beside him, words pouring out as fast as her feet were moving. "I hexed her and that's what made her do that. It was because of me, and that's why I should be held responsible, not Scoot—"

"Hush," he growled at her as he manhandled her past the host stand and the woman standing beside it, staring in curiosity. "Do not say another word." He yanked her arm, hard and fast, and her mouth clamped shut. In an instant they were out the door and on the busy sidewalk. He still didn't release her but held her close enough to hiss in her ear.

"I know who you are."

"I'm—"

He held her even tighter. "I'm talking now."

She found his eyes. The look in them—recognition—turned Ingrid's legs to water.

"I knew Edith White," he said in a low voice. "Your grandmother. She was a good woman. The kind of woman who would look out for someone's child if they were in trouble. And you, my dear, are in trouble."

Ingrid felt her face go hot.

"But I did a—"

He gave her arm a little shake. "No spell made Scoot Loeffler order too many drinks at the Perry Lane rooftop bar with some young beefcake and then get in her car and drive out to Tybee Island. That was her ridiculously poor decision, and only hers. You hear me?"

Ingrid swallowed the rest of what she'd been about to say and nodded.

He inhaled then spoke in a measured tone. "You have no idea of the family you're dealing with, Miss White. The absolute and unbeatable power. So, on behalf of your grandmother, I will tell you that the best thing you can do right now is go home and shut your mouth. Stop this nonsense before Rill Loeffler hears about it and decides you really are somehow responsible."

He turned her loose. Her legs felt weak. Her heart pounded against her ribs with sickening thuds.

"Go home, Miss White." He turned and walked back into the restaurant, but she couldn't move. People streamed past her on the sidewalk, skirting her or bumping into her, all oblivious to her distress.

The judge was right. He was. All Sailor had to do was spread the word about Ingrid's spell, and the only customers she'd be left with were tourists. If Rill found out what Ingrid had done, she'd be finished in Savannah, Ingrid was fairly certain of that. Norwood was kind to tell her to go home. He was trying to help her.

Still . . . how could she just let this go? None of it added up. Sure, Scoot drank a lot, but it was always at home or on family outings. And the woman had a full-time chauffeur to take her everywhere. So why would she go out and drink in public with some young guy? Why would she go to Tybee, a place Sailor said she stayed away from? It made no sense.

Ingrid had to find out what had happened. If her spell had really caused this, maybe, somehow, she could figure out a way to fix it. Judge Norwood's warning still ringing in her ears, she cast one look back at the entrance of the restaurant, then headed east, in the direction of the Perry Lane Hotel.

Chapter 38

The only time Ingrid had set foot on a Savannah rooftop was once a year on St. Patrick's Day as a guest of her friend Zoe, who worked as a nail tech at a spa on Broughton Street. That roof, a flat expanse of asphalt with a handful of lawn chairs, was a premium spot for watching the parade. Nothing like Peregrin, the rooftop bar at the Perry Lane Hotel.

This place was a different story altogether. Even walking through the hotel lobby, Ingrid felt like a stray dog who accidentally wandered in from outside. Upstairs, the view took her breath away. At least five degrees cooler than down at street level, there was a clear view to the river and the ocean beyond, where tugboats puffed and barges hauled their goods. The Talmadge Memorial Bridge with its clean, modern lines stretched over the river and crawled with traffic.

The bar was scattered with plush seating and wide umbrellas. A cooling breeze ruffled palm fronds as a handful of patrons sipped Bloody Marys and mimosas. She hadn't really planned how she was going to do this, and she glanced around uncertainly. There was one girl behind the bar. She had thick eyelash extensions and was deeply tanned, her dark hair slicked back into a low bun.

"Hi there," the girl called out to Ingrid. "What can I get you to drink today?"

Ingrid perused the menu, trying not to curse at the prices. Even with the money she'd been saving since Sailor had taken her on, she'd never drop twelve dollars on a cocktail. "I'll have a glass of chardonnay, I guess."

"Great." The bartender turned back to the bar and opened a bottle.

Ingrid leaned against the bar. "Hey, I'm Ingrid."

"Darya."

"Darya, I'm wondering . . . by any chance were you working here on a day in August? Saturday, the seventeenth?"

"No." The bartender set Ingrid's glass on a napkin. Poured in a generous amount of wine. "That would've been before I started."

"Do you know who was working here that night? Right before closing? I wanted to ask if they saw someone up here. A friend of mine."

The girl corked the bottle and started cutting lemons on a board. "Who?"

"Scoot Loeffler."

The girl's eyes flicked up to meet Ingrid's then back down to the fruit. "You friends with the Loefflers?"

"Yes. I was . . . I'm their psychic. Just trying to help them out with a few things. I wondered if you heard who Scoot was drinking with that night. I heard it was a guy. A young guy."

"Why don't you have a seat over there?" She jutted her chin at a deserted corner of the rooftop. "When I get a sec, I'll stop by with another drink."

Ingrid chose a plush chair by the edge of the roof that was covered in shade, and settled in to sip the chilled wine. She took off the mohair sweater. The church had been cold, but out here under the blazing sun, she'd started to warm up. Just then, her phone trilled. It was a number she didn't recognize.

"Ingrid White?"

Ingrid sipped her wine, which was making her feel at peace with the world. "Yes?"

"This is Poppy. Duncan. Sailor's friend."

Ingrid nearly choked on the wine and set down her glass. "Oh, hi. Hi, Poppy. How are you?"

"I'm fine," Poppy said. "Can you talk?"

"Sure." Ingrid's heart had started up a jagged, irregular beat.

There was silence for a moment. "Sailor doesn't know I'm calling you," Poppy said. "But I just didn't know where to turn."

"Do you want a reading?" Ingrid held her breath.

"No . . . ah." Poppy was obviously having difficulty getting the words out. "I wanted to call you to let you know, as Sailor's friend, that she's have a really difficult time. With what happened to her mom and the wedding coming up and everything."

Ingrid's head felt floaty from the wine. She realized she hadn't eaten anything that morning. "What do you mean?"

"Her mother had an accident and got arrested."

"I know about Scoot—" Ingrid had said it a little too loud and now the bartender, Darya, was looking at her. She lowered her voice. "I mean, what's Sailor doing?"

"She fired her wedding coordinator, for one thing. I think they worked it out, but there's other stuff, too. Jude's in Singapore and somebody saw Sailor out with this guy she used to date."

Ingrid's heart did a sudden sideway jag. "A guy? What guy?"

"This guy she dated in high school and, I don't know, he was like a big-deal football player when he was eighteen, but now . . . he works crew on a shrimp boat, you know? Like he's blue-collar."

Ingrid couldn't help but roll her eyes, but she held her tongue.

"And he has a wife, supposedly, somewhere, and kids. Like *multiple* kids."

Okay. This was not good. "She didn't break up with Jude, did she?"

"God, no," Poppy said. "No, I don't think so. It's probably just . . . with her mom gone and everything blowing up the way it is . . . I think she's like reaching out to people from her past to kind of, I don't know, anchor her. But like, not an ex, you know? Not the right support system."

"Yeah." Ingrid was thinking.

"We don't know what to do, frankly," Poppy said.

"Why can't you just talk to her?" Ingrid said impatiently. "You and Calla and Madeline?"

Poppy huffed. "Okay, but it's not like we can just drop everything and hold her hand twenty-four seven. My marketing company is taking off right now. Madeline's traveling constantly for her work. And Calla's . . . you know . . . got stuff, too." She hesitated. "Look, I don't know why Sailor's mad at you, Ingrid, but whatever it is, y'all need to work it out. Like, just set up a lunch and have a conversation. I'm sure you can work through whatever bad blood there is."

Someone was heading toward her now. Not Darya, the bartender, but a young man, tall and muscled, with thick red hair and a growth of reddish whiskers along his jaw. He was holding an amber cocktail with a rim of brown sugar and a purple flower peeking over the edge. He stopped in front of her chair.

"Courtesy of the house," he mouthed.

"Oh." Ingrid glanced over at the bar.

"She's training," the redheaded guy said. "Made one for everybody."

He was right. The other guests were toasting with a variety of fancy cocktails. He put the glass down and backed away.

"Ingrid?" Poppy. "Are you still there?"

"I appreciate the call, Poppy." Ingrid picked up the drink

and took a sip. It was fruity and tart and delicious. She licked a bit of sugar off the rim and took one more pull on the straw. "I'll see what I can do."

"Oh God, Ingrid, thank you," gushed Poppy. "Thank you so much. We all just, like, really need this wedding to go off without a hitch and, to be honest, it's not looking like that's going to happen if Sailor doesn't pull herself together. Okay. Gotta run. I'll see you soon. Bye!"

Ingrid tapped out of the call, set her phone down, and took another sip of her cocktail. She closed her eyes, leaning back against the cushion, letting the heat of the sun soothe her.

What an interesting development. Poppy, Madeline, and Calla on their knees, begging for her help. It was no wonder Sailor had kept her so close that night of the engagement party. These women were like a herd of gazelles. They only cared about their own survival. And they didn't hesitate to leave behind their wounded.

Time passed and she slowly drained the drink. She studied the empty glass and considered having another. She looked around, noticing the other patrons were gone, and now she had the whole rooftop to herself. She stood up, feeling herself wobble and the sky spin above her. She closed her eyes. Held her arms out and found her equilibrium. Focusing on the bar, she started toward it but stumbled over her own feet. She stopped, waiting for her balance to catch up with her. Waiting for the sky to stop that annoying spinning . . .

She gulped in a breath of air. It was so hot, and Goddess help her, it carried with it a whiff of trash. She tried to take another step toward the bar. Then one more . . . Now Darya the bartender was watching her with a strange expression. Ingrid lifted her finger. *I want another,* was what she thought.

What came out was "Somethin' in my drink . . ."

Darya's eyebrows shot up and her slim body went stiff. Ingrid's mind zigzagged from thought to thought:

One, she seemed extraordinarily drunk for only having had two drinks.

Two, this had to do with her questions about the night Scoot was here.

Three, that man, the good-looking redhead, was heading toward her now, his muscular arms outstretched toward her.

Four, she had to get away from him.

Chapter 39

"Miss." The redhead was getting closer.

She stumbled backward. "Don't touch me!"

"If you'll allow me, I can get you out the back way. You won't have to go through the lobby."

"No, no, no, no . . ." She was backpedaling now, faster than before.

"Miss!" He lunged for her.

She didn't know how she did it, with the dizziness and the heat, but she ducked and pivoted, dodging him and running past the bar. Darya was just a startled smear in her peripheral vision, but she could feel the guy gaining on her. Wherever he had wanted to take her—down some shadowy corridor, over the side of the railing down to the street below—she sure as hell wasn't going.

Inside the hallway, she tore open the stairwell door and clattered down the metal steps.

"Stop!" the guy shouted above her, but she was flying now, down more steps, bursting out into the lobby, running past surprised guests, bellboys, then the doorman. Out on the crowded sidewalk, she slowed her pace, weaving in and around the people. She had no plan, no idea where she was headed. She just knew she had to keep upright, keep her eyes open, keep her legs moving. Moving, moving away from that man. Up one street, down the next. Cutting through an alley, crossing a busy avenue against the light.

Only one thing brought her to a standstill.

Sailor.

Sailor Loeffler, in the flesh, standing right in front of her like the Goddess had just dropped her there.

A gift.

She had changed out of her church dress and now wearing a skintight spaghetti-strapped black bodysuit and jeans whose frayed hems dragged the pavement. Her hair was pulled up in a smooth bun, her eyes hidden by huge amber aviators, but Ingrid knew it was her. Without question.

Her friend. Her best friend, walking beside a guy Ingrid didn't recognize. He was young, dressed as sloppily as Sailor was, also with sunglasses covering his eyes. He had a sparse, oily-looking goatee. A sharp chin and stringy hair. This had to be the guy Poppy had been talking about. The high school ex, married with kids. He held the door of a restaurant open for Sailor, and she stepped past him.

"Sailor!" Ingrid's voice sounded strange. Like someone who hadn't used it for ages and ages.

But Sailor didn't hear her. She disappeared inside the restaurant followed by her companion. Ingrid stopped, swaying slightly on the sidewalk. There was only one thing to do; it was obvious. She followed them.

The small restaurant, Lombardy's, was warm and homey, all red-checked tablecloths, timber and plaster, and bottles of wine in baskets. A woman, hair shaved off one side of her head and ears full of piercings, stopped her just beyond the door. "Reservation?" she asked.

"No," Ingrid mumbled. "But I'm going to be sick." It wasn't exactly a lie.

"Jesus," the woman groaned.

Ingrid fixed her with a pleading look. "Please, your bathroom."

The woman pointed over her shoulder. "Past the bar on the right."

It must've been the power of suggestion. On her way past the bar, she did indeed feel a wave of nausea, and when she pushed open a stall door, she vomited violently. When she was done, she felt drained and weak, but still strange. Hazy and disconnected. Maybe the bartender really had put something in her drink.

She rinsed out her mouth, splashed her face, and washed her hands. She looked in the mirror. Her eyes looked strange, pupils dilated, and glassy, but she couldn't just hang out here and wait out the effects of the alcohol or drugs to wear off. She was running out of time. She smoothed her hair and headed back out.

She peered around the bar into the cozy dining room. The Loeffler family, minus Scoot, plus Sailor's male friend with the goatee, was sitting at a large round table in the far corner. Two bottles of wine decanted on the table, a basket of bread and a bottle of olive oil beside them. Rill picked up one of the wine bottles and poured it for Cas. That's when Ingrid finally understood what was wrong with the tableau.

Cas was dressed in a suit and tie.

She'd never seen him in a suit, not on his way to church, not even at Sailor's party.

Rill lifted his wineglass. "A toast to Casimir," he said. Sailor, Mr. Goatee, and Cas lifted their glasses. "My son—my searcher and pilgrim—has finally found his way home."

They all murmured *To Cas*, clinked glasses, and drank.

"When do you start, bro?" asked Goatee.

"Monday morning, bright and early," said Rill. "See you at sunrise in the C-suite, Mr. Vice President of Operations."

Cas sent his father a tight smile. Sailor looked miserable.

So Rill had finally gotten his way and persuaded Cas to join Savannah Sauce, clearly in an effort to prepare him for the role of CEO one day. The job Sailor wanted—and had earned. Ingrid trembled with fury. Because she knew Rill had only done it for one reason. He wanted to keep Cas under his thumb. To control his son, for now and always.

It was so unfair. Cas was a quiet, contemplative person, a searcher. He was into the church, not running a multinational corporation. Sailor was the one with the head and heart for business. But Rill only cared about his own image and legacy. He expected his children to serve his purpose. He wanted them to carry out his wishes.

And the icing on top? Sailor wasn't even VP yet in her own department, only a director. It was a slap in the face, and Ingrid had to help. She had to stop this. She had to help her friends.

"Sailor!" she cried, then, "Cas! Hi!" She stepped forward, out from behind the bar. Out into the open where everyone could see her.

Cas straightened. And then, to Ingrid's amazement, his face lit up and he smiled the widest, most genuine smile Ingrid had ever seen on his face. Her heart surged with joy. With hope. Cas was truly happy to see her. He *did* like her. She felt it.

Beside him, Rill flashed an expression of his own, a look like a thundercloud. He put a hand on Cas's arm and moved as if he meant to stand, but Sailor stopped him, holding out one finger to him and rising out of her seat.

"Stop right there," she said to Ingrid, venom in her voice.

Ingrid stopped. "Sailor, it's me." She turned back to Cas, imploring. "It's Ingrid."

But now Cas was looking down at his plate of bread.

"We see you," Sailor said with a snide glance at her father. "What we want is to *not* see you."

Her words hit Ingrid in the gut. She turned her gaze to Cas, opening her mouth, ready to offer something of value—an apology, a promise, anything.

"He wants you to be something you're not," Ingrid said to him. "He doesn't see the real you. He's planning on getting you into the company and training you to take over. To be CEO."

Cas's face turned a shade of red in proportion to the amount of color that drained out of Rill's.

Sailor narrowed her eyes at Ingrid. "No, he's not."

Rill sent Ingrid a level look. *Shut your mouth*, it said.

"He doesn't care what either of you want," Ingrid said. "He only cares about his plan. What he thinks is best."

"She's drunk." Rill stood with a flash of danger in his eye. "Ingrid, let's get you out of here."

Ingrid stepped back, bumping into one startled customer then spinning around and crashing into a server carrying a tray of food. Ingrid heard a yelp, and then everything seemed to jumble together in a cacophony of color and sound. She felt herself go down, along with the dishes and glasses, food and cutlery. She felt herself lifted, then pushed and pulled, carried out of the restaurant to some other dark, fetid place. An alley.

Her back slammed against a brick wall, the breath forced out of her. Hot breath blew in her face, and she tried to twist away, but hands pushed her back and her spine ground helplessly into the mortar. A hand pushed the side of her face against the rough wall. She gasped and struggled against it, but it held her firmly.

"Stop it, Ingrid," came a firm voice. "I don't want to hurt you, but you've got to calm down."

She obeyed. It was the only thing to do. He released her face, and she felt something drawing close—a blessed end to this strange way she was feeling. Relief. Unconsciousness. But she couldn't pass out in an alley. She clawed at the shoulders and arms holding her, this time for help. She couldn't . . .

The face came near again, and this time, she smelled the wine on his breath. Wine and garlic and expensive cologne. Rill Loeffler's cologne. *Fig and cognac.* He spoke again in a soft, coaxing tone.

"Ingrid," he said. "Listen to me. You have to stop all this . . . this pushing. Wanting something you can't have will make you bitter. And bitterness makes you sick." His face softened. "And I couldn't bear it if you got sick."

She frowned at him. Was that a threat? Had he sent Darya and the hot, redheaded guy at Peregrin after her? It could've been Patti Jo Norwood. She could've called Rill from the restaurant.

"Did you follow me to Peregrin?" she mumbled. "Did you tell them to put something in my drink?"

"Honey," Rill said. "Baby. You're not making any sense. I'm just saying that when your grandmother died, it ncarly killed me. I would never let anything happen to you."

"I wanna go home," she moaned.

But he held her fast against the wall. "Ingrid . . . Ingrid . . ." Her name was a whisper in his mouth. He didn't look angry now or threatening, just strangely tender. She felt something ripple through her. The way he was looking at her felt wrong, but she stopped pushing against him.

"Stay with me," he said. "Just a second, okay?"

He was staring at her so intently. And the look in his eyes . . . she'd seen it a few times before, the night of the engagement party, that first family dinner, but now it was different. It was so plain . . .

Rill spoke softly. "It's amazing how much you look like her. Like Edie. You both have the exact same freckles . . . here . . ." He ran the side of his thumb over the bridge of her nose. ". . . and here . . ." Now the side of his thumb across her upper lip.

She couldn't move. She felt a glimmer of desire inside her, a spark that ignited something she didn't want ignited. A tear gathered in her eye then fell down her cheek.

He brushed his cheek along hers and whispered, "That night at Sailor's party, it was like I was seeing a ghost. Ever since then, I've been your friend. Your advocate. Did you know that? I've been the one on your side, helping you out, all along."

She shook her head.

"I was the one who found the jade flowers. Just a quick phone call to an old friend in Mexico. And the dress, the harpist? Those were just a couple of calls, too, Ingrid. Because I wanted to help you. I wanted to make you look good so Sailor would keep bringing you around."

He looked so pleased with himself, but she felt like her brain was knocking around her skull from all the information bombarding her. Rill had been the one who'd made Sailor's perfect wedding possible. Not her. Not her magic.

It had never been her magic . . .

Rill stared into her eyes and gave her a smile. The same slow, lopsided smile Cas had. "Hey. Don't you want to thank me for how good I made you look?"

"No . . . I . . ." She struggled against him, again, but now it felt half-hearted. She was so tired.

"We could work something out, Ingrid. All you have to do is say the word."

She couldn't speak. She pushed him away again, and this time, he actually released her.

"If you want to go, go. But I don't think you do. I think you want to stay. I think you appreciate me for what I've done. I think you want me, Ingrid—" He took hold of her arm.

She wrenched away from him, stumbling.

He put his hand out as if to catch her. "Whoopsie-daisy."

She let out a sob as she staggered down the alley toward the street. She didn't know where she was going, she just knew she had to get away.

"Ingrid!" she heard behind her, but she didn't stop. She just ran.

Chapter 40

She woke, her faced smashed into her pillow. The pillowcase was wet with drool and smudged black with mascara, but it smelled gloriously like home.

She was home. In her own bed. In her own room, in her own house. Edie's house.

Morning light streamed in through the windows, and she smelled coffee brewing downstairs. She rolled over to see Miles, standing beside the bed, holding a damp washcloth and a bottle of yellow Gatorade. He peered at her with a worried expression. She cracked a smile.

"Oh, thank God," he breathed.

"Goddess," she croaked.

"When you came home, you were babbling all this crazy stuff about the Loefflers. About Rill."

A fragment of a memory. *We could work something out . . .*

Had she let something slip to Miles about Rill? She couldn't remember.

"I didn't know what to think so I just put you to bed."

"Thanks."

She let him fuss over her with the washcloth and Gatorade, then managed to convince him to leave her alone while she cleaned herself up. When he was finally gone, she got out of bed and showered away the grime, the memory, and the shame of the previous day. Wrapped in a towel, she walked down the hall into Edie's room. As always, Edie's scents enveloped her, reassuring her as she inhaled.

I gather, I gather, I gather . . .

She opened the closet and selected another of Edie's shapeless linen shifts, this one apple green. She took Edie's Birkenstocks and a stack of her bangle bracelets and even clean underwear from the dresser drawer, granny panties and a stretched-out old bra. They smelled comfortingly of old laundry detergent, perfume, and sunshine.

Downstairs, at the door of the altar room, she hesitated. She hadn't been in it since that night, the night she'd done the karma spell for Sailor. She inhaled, drew herself up to her full height, and pushed open the door. Inside, the room was quiet and still. The Cotillion box with blobs of black candle wax and smashed glass encrusting Scoot's picture sat on the altar.

"I know you're there, Edie," she said. "Go ahead and say it, whatever it is you're going to say."

Silence.

"I thought I was doing the right thing." She gathered the detritus off the altar and dumped it into the trash can. "I was trying to help Sailor." She gathered the tablecloth and shook it into the can. "I thought I might even be righting the balance for you."

No answer. *Fine. Be that way.*

She cast her circle, called the corners, then did a cleansing ritual over herself and the room, ridding herself not only of any residual chemical toxins from the drug in her drink, but also of the bad energy she'd taken on in the last twenty-four hours. Judge Norwood, Darya, and the guy at Peregrin.

Rill Loeffler . . .

She remembered the way he pressed against her in the alley. His face so close to hers. His wife had almost killed someone, she was locked up in a rehab somewhere, and this was what he did—tried to seduce his daughter's friend. And Sailor had no idea. She worshipped her father. Everyone did. To all of Savannah, Rill Loeffler was a god.

But Ingrid knew the truth. He was a despicable human being. She'd thought she had to protect Sailor from her mother, but now she realized Rill was just as bad. And yes, she had been tempted by him, but she was only human. It had only been a momentary lapse, and she knew it was wrong.

She had to stop him. But she wouldn't do black magic, not after what had happened with Scoot. She had to keep things positive and only cast white magic spells. At least until Edie and the Goddess gave her guidance otherwise.

She closed her eyes and began chanting, sending her intention into the air around her. Up to the sky above . . .

Gather strength,
As the clock waxes.
Gather courage,
As the day wanes.
I gather, you gather,
And what we gather shall grow,
So in the bloom of night, we shine forth.

She did every spell of protection that she could think of. She felt the agreement of the stars and planets and moon as she chanted. Her will aligning with the greatest Will. The only Will.

She gathered the energy of all the elements into her body. She lit all the candles Sailor had ever given her and arranged all the relics she'd collected from her time with Sailor in a circle spiraling away from her body. It was a waxing moon, so she did white magic—invoking Venus and Jupiter, pulling all good things to herself, through herself and then outward to Sailor, Jude, and Cas.

When she was done, she opened her eyes and looked around the altar room.

Everything looked exactly the same, and yet everything was different. She didn't know how to explain it, but she felt safe now. Safer than she'd ever been. And maybe more powerful, too. Powerful enough to stand up to Rill. Powerful enough to keep fighting for Sailor. To make her believe that Ingrid was truly her friend.

Her first appointment of the day showed up at eleven and, for the first time in weeks, the reading was what Ingrid considered successful. The woman, in her fifties, had never been to a psychic, and when Edie traced her palm, she'd cried. She'd also tipped generously when the session was up and made an appointment for three months down the road.

There were several more drop-ins, so it was past seven in the evening when Ingrid finally trudged back upstairs, exhausted to the bone. She found Miles in the kitchen eating a peanut butter sandwich and drinking a glass of milk.

"What have you been up to all day?" she asked.

"Helped this girl with her new window unit."

She smiled and, taking the other half of his sandwich, bit into it.

"How are you?" he asked.

"Better." Her mouth was sticky with the peanut butter. She motioned for the milk, and he handed it over.

He caught her eye. "Do you remember anything from yesterday?"

"I saw Judge Norwood at Husk and told him I thought I was responsible for Scoot getting arrested."

"Oh no, Ingrid, you didn't."

"He told me she was drinking at Peregrin that night, so I went there to ask around if anybody saw someone with her. And then I'm pretty sure somebody roofied my drink."

"Roofied you?" Miles went stiff, his eyes blazing in surprise and anger.

"And then tried to . . ."

"Tried to what?"

Throw me off the roof? Assault me in an alley? If she'd been muddled then, she was even more so now. Had the redheaded man really tried to throw her off the roof, or was he just trying to escort her off the property? Maybe she'd misunderstood the whole situation.

"I don't know."

Miles was quiet for a moment. "Ingrid, look. The Loefflers own this town. If you were at Peregrin asking about Scoot, somebody probably put a call in to Rill." He shrugged. "That's just the way it works around here. And at the very least, they would want to shut that down and get you out of there. I'm telling you, you've got to move on. These people are trouble."

She moved to the sink to automatically start rinsing dishes and load them into the dishwasher. "Sailor needs me, Miles. Her mom is in rehab and her father is . . . well, he doesn't care about her at all. He's made Cas a vice president at Savannah Sauce because he thinks all Sailor is good for is being some man's trophy wife. I'm telling you, she's in a vulnerable place, maybe about to mess up her life. One of her friends even called me."

"But she won't see you."

"I know." She kept her voice light. "That's why I was thinking I could do a spell. I did one for protection, for all of us, earlier today. But maybe I should do more."

"Do you really think that's a good idea? After what happened with Scoot?"

Annoyance prickled over her. "Whose side are you on?"

"I'm just worried about you." He tilted his head. "You're a sweetheart, you really are, Budge. After all they've done to you." He hopped up, gave her a hug, and then gulped his milk. "I've got to go. I've got a tour."

"Okay." She kissed him on the cheek. "Thanks, Miles, for looking after me."

He licked his thumb and swiped at the corner of her mouth. "Peanut butter."

She jerked back and made a face. "Gross."

But he just grinned at her. She really did love him, even with all his irritating qualities. He was a true friend.

Now he was looking at her thoughtfully.

"What?" Ingrid said.

"Is that what you really want? Sailor Loeffler back in your life?"

"Yes. Why? What are you thinking?"

"I don't know." He lifted one eyebrow, one of his jaunty, mischievous, pirate expressions. "What if something happened to Jude?"

"What do you mean?"

"I don't know. Just . . . what if he happened to get mugged or something and you somehow saved him?"

She gave him a wry look. "I'm a witch, Miles, not Spider-Man."

He laughed. "No bad ideas in brainstorming." He headed toward the door. "We'll think of something that'll convince her. Don't you worry, Budgie."

"Seriously, you've got to stop calling me that!" she yelled after him, but he just laughed again and clattered out of the house.

Chapter 41

Every day after that, Ingrid followed the same routine.

In the morning, she would select one of Edie's dresses to wear, grab coffee and a muffin, go downstairs, and do a series of protection rituals in her altar room. She would then spend the day doing readings.

By the end of the week, she couldn't believe she hadn't figured this out years ago. She felt so at home in Edie's clothes. Protected and powerful. Like she'd taken on the literal mantle of her grandmother. Like they were working together at last. She decided she might as well move all of the contents of Edie's entire closet into hers.

When she asked Miles to help her, he gave her a quizzical look. "Why don't you just move into her room?"

It was the perfect solution. It would enable her to align with Edie, to get in her skin, so to speak. She was convinced that Edie had intended her to get close to the Loefflers so she could right the balance, but she couldn't do that unless she could find her way back to Sailor. She couldn't believe she hadn't thought of it herself.

Ingrid gave the Daffodil Room a rigorous cleaning, vacuuming the rug, dusting the chandelier, polishing oak, mahogany, walnut pieces. She shook out the heavy curtains, wiped the dust and streaks from all the windows, and even though it was hot out, threw them open to let the fresh air in. She felt guilty that she'd let Edie's room get so filthy, but now she was putting everything to rights.

The cleaning also cleared Ingrid's mind. There was so much Edie hadn't told Ingrid about her past. About her thorny relationship with Rill. While it made sense that Edie had kept all that information private, it was crucial now that Ingrid understood fully who she was up against.

Know thy enemy. It was the way she was going to win Sailor back. She was going to find out who Rill Loeffler really was, what he'd done, and then she would beat him at his own game.

On the occasional Sunday morning, E. Shaver, a bookstore on the east side of Madison Square, had a sensory friendly hour of shopping. They dimmed the lights and turned down the music in the shop, requesting customers keep silent as they browsed. The bookstore cats that typically roamed each nook and cranny were crated. This particular Sunday, the quiet was exactly what Ingrid needed.

Ingrid bought two books, one for Miles about navigating by the stars, and for Cas a book about the Salzburgers, the religious exiles from Austria who settled in Savannah. Tucking them into her tote, she headed to the back of the store, to the tiny alcove dedicated to witchcraft, occult, and hoodoo literature.

In the cramped space, sitting on a crocheted puff, was a little woman in a man's glen plaid blazer with red glasses hanging around her neck on a beaded chain. She was reading a book, holding it so close to her face the pages almost touched her nose. *Potions for Beginners.*

Ingrid grinned. "Miss Paulette," she chided. "You're no beginner."

The woman looked up, and her face split into a wide smile. "Sugar! Come down here and hug my neck. If I get up, I'll pop a ligament."

Ingrid dropped down on the floor beside the puff and reached over to hug the older woman. Miss Paulette groaned theatrically.

"It never hurts to brush up on the basics. Sometimes we can outthink ourselves." She put the book aside.

"You have the best job in the world," Ingrid said. "Hide back here, read all the books you want. And you only have to point some poor seeker of good literature in the right direction if they accidentally trip over you. Plus, you get paid for it."

The woman laughed. "Not enough to keep me in the manner to which I've never been accustomed. Good thing you and me had kin with the foresight to get into real estate back in the old days. Otherwise, our butts would be out on the street."

Miss Paulette lived in a ramshackle town house on Washington Square that had been built back in the late 1700s and left to her by her aunt. Still, with nothing but a job at the bookstore, Ingrid couldn't imagine how Miss Paulette paid her tax bill either.

"Amen to that," Ingrid said.

"Praise the Lord," Miss Paulette said absently. She was not only a witch and connoisseur of all things occultic, she was also a deacon at her church. Ingrid wasn't sure how the woman reconciled the conflicting dogmas, but Ingrid appreciated her ecumenical bent. Plus, she'd been Edie's closest friend.

Miss Paulette playfully swatted Ingrid's leg. "Haven't seen you in an age. Too busy hobnobbing with the hoi polloi, I hear."

Ingrid laughed. "What does that even mean?"

"You Gen Zers. Y'all have lost the art of the idiom." Miss Paulette stuck a bookmark between the pages and closed the book, setting it aside. She turned back, arranged her glasses at the end of her nose, and eyed Ingrid. "It means hanging out with the richies," she said flatly.

"It's fine," Ingrid began. "I'm fine . . . and not really doing much hanging out. Anyway, speaking of that, I wanted to ask you something. About Edie and somebody she might've had a relationship with after my grandpa died."

Miss Paulette wrinkled her nose and squinted over at the shelves.

"Rill Loeffler," Ingrid said, "is who I'm talking about."

Miss Paulette waited a beat, then turned back to Ingrid. A look of trepidation was on her face. This scared Ingrid. To the random person, Miss Paulette might seem like an eccentric, but Ingrid knew better. Miss Paulette saw things. She knew things—both in the material world and the spiritual.

"Tell me everything," Ingrid said. "I need to know."

Miss Paulette huffed. "Well, there's nothing to tell. The man was plumb lovesick over Edie, even though she was a good twenty years older than him. But nothing happened. She didn't take him seriously."

"She didn't feel the same way about him?"

"Well, she was flattered, of course. Who wouldn't be? And her husband, your grandpa, was long gone, so she was free as a bird. Rill Loeffler was young and handsome. Rich as Croesus. He was a king, by the way, Miss Gen Z."

"I know," Ingrid said impatiently.

"Anyway," continued Miss Paulette, "back then, if a woman was forty years old, she might as well have one foot in the grave. So, yes, Edie was flattered. And she probably entertained Rill's nonsense more than she should have—let him make a pet out of her. Flirt with her and overpay her, but she always kept him at arm's length. She knew better than to get tangled up with him."

"Because he was engaged to Scoot?"

"That." Her eyes shifted back to the shelves. "And just because he was plain trouble."

"What do you mean, 'trouble'? What kind?"

Miss Paulette shifted her position with a bit of difficulty and another groan. "She told me once that he gave her a bad feeling. She called him a pirate. She said that he didn't think the rules applied to him, that he made his own laws."

A pirate . . .

"She said it would be doing goety if she messed with him."

Ingrid's stomach twisted. She had heard Edie use the term. Goety was necromancy, black magic done by summoning an evil spirit. So Edie had compared being involved with Rill Loeffler to being involved with a pirate and an evil spirit. Not good.

"What do you think made her say all that?"

Miss Paulette sighed and shook her head. "There were rumors."

Ingrid waited. She could tell Miss Paulette was reluctant to bad-mouth a Loeffler, and she understood why. It was a heady thing to have the family as an ally, a fearsome thing to have them as an enemy.

Miss Paulette struggled to her feet, going to check outside the alcove. She turned back to Ingrid with a grim expression, her body blocking the entrance in case any oblivious customer should accidentally intrude.

"There was talk about Rill back then."

"What kind of talk?"

"That he liked to mess around with girls. Young girls."

Ingrid frowned. "He liked Edie, though. She was so much older than him."

"I think Rill just liked women he couldn't have. For him, I think it was all about breaking the rules."

"What girls did he mess around with?"

She spoke slowly. "When Edie turned Rill away for good, he

moved on to someone else." Miss Paulette blinked a few times. "I only know this because I accidentally stumbled on them one day. Edie had asked me to drop off some candles I'd made for her. For her rituals. I knew where the key was hidden, Edie's key to the garden level of the house. I let myself in and took the candles back to one of Edie's storage rooms. I heard something in the house. Music playing. I went upstairs and found them—in the living room—together."

Ingrid felt sick. "Who?" she asked, even though she already knew the answer.

"Tess." Miss Paulette grimaced. "I interrupted things, that was for sure. Sent that grown-ass man running for his life." She shook her head. "Tess was just sixteen. A child. He was in his mid-twenties. I couldn't ignore it. She begged me not to tell Edie, and I'm ashamed to say I agreed."

"Paulette," Ingrid said reproachfully.

"I know, I know. You can't make me feel worse than I have for all these years. It was the wrong thing to do, but I was scared of him. Those Loefflers did what they wanted back then. Ran over folks. Took their property and ruined their businesses, if it benefited them."

"Did anyone else know?"

"I confess that I did confide in Dean Remington. I had to tell someone; I was so upset. He told me to tell Tess she had to end it with Rill. For good. And I did."

"Did she?"

"She did. And she left town soon after that. It was too big a secret for a girl that young to bear, I think. She had to get out of Savannah. Away from Edie. Away from him."

Ingrid felt the horror of this revelation creep up her like a vine growing up her legs and over her body. It curled around her limbs, the nasty, snaking knowledge. And then another thought occurred to her . . .

Miss Paulette noticed Ingrid's expression. "Oh, honey. No.

The math isn't right. He's not your daddy. That's another man Tess met when she was living down in Florida."

The woman couldn't have known that wasn't what Ingrid was worried about. In fact, it hadn't even occurred to her. All she could thing was *he was in love with my grandmother . . . he had sex with my mother . . . and then, decades later, he came on to me . . .*

Rill Loeffler acted like Cas sexting women was the end of the world. But he was the sick one. He was the one with the problem. She wanted to scream, ball her hands into fists, and knock every last book off every last shelf in this room and throw them to the floor.

"Darlin', what's wrong?" Miss Paulette said.

But Ingrid shook her head. "Nothing. I'm just surprised, is all."

"Well, I expect you got a right to be. I guess your generation doesn't know about the Loefflers the way us old folks do. And we were used to keeping their nonsense quiet on account of . . . well, on account of them being Loefflers." Miss Paulette moved close to Ingrid, gathering her hands and looking deeply into her eyes. "Anyway, you got nothing to worry about. Rill married Scoot, and Tess left town, and your grandmama minded her own business. All was well that ended well."

Ingrid nodded, but she knew nothing had ended. It had just begun.

Chapter 42

As she headed out of the store, she felt something catch hold of her and reel her back, like a fish on a hook. The fisherman, Gloria Ledieu, leered at her with her painted clown face.

"Ingrid White." Gloria now had a grip on Ingrid's other arm, imprisoning her. "Honey. I'm so glad we ran into you. You know we saw you in church last week. You should've told us you were coming. We would've saved you a seat."

Ingrid's nose detected sickly-sweet perfume. She tried not to physically recoil.

"We like the eight-thirty. That way we can beat the crowds to brunch. Were you at the early service?"

"No. Not this week. I was just . . ." She gestured limply at the bookstore. She wished she was still hidden between the stacks, in the dim quietude of the books, ignored by everyone around her.

"Well, praise the Lord anyway, is all I have to say." Gloria said, then looked sharply at Harmon, her husband, a teddy bear of a man squeezed into a summer seersucker suit with a tie so tight it was causing him to tug at his collar and contort his neck in order to get a proper lungful of air.

"Praise the Lord," Harmon echoed wheezily and looked at his watch.

"We've been praying for you, you know." Gloria's aquamarine-blue-lined eyes searched hers.

Ingrid set her teeth. "You mentioned that. Several times." She had that automatic Southern-bred instinct to add *thanks,* but clamped her mouth shut. She didn't have to be polite. She didn't owe this woman anything.

"It must've been so hard to lose your grandmother. And with Tess run off to Florida, too . . ." Gloria trailed off, but her eyes had gone watery and were darting around nervously. "I almost couldn't bear the idea of you keeping up with that big old house all by yourself. And carrying on your business. And with nobody to help but that little boy . . . that friend . . . of yours."

Ingrid frowned in surprise. "That's why you were praying for me? Because I lost my grandmother?"

Gloria looked affronted. "Well, why else, hon?"

Ingrid glanced from Gloria to Harmon, both of them now regarding her with expressions of curiosity. "I don't know, I guess."

Gloria sought Harmon's hand. "After the funeral, I wanted to have you over, but you seem to prefer your space and, listen, hon, I understand. When my mother passed, I was just a wreck. So we left you alone. But I have prayed for you, every day, that you would have some sort of comfort in your loss."

Ingrid shook her head, a laugh bubbling up in her throat. "I thought you were praying for me because I'm a . . ." She swallowed.

The skin between Gloria's penciled-on brows creased.

". . . a psychic."

Gloria barked out a laugh. "Oh, Lord, no. That was before, in the nineties, you know, back when we went to that charismatic church out on Highway 16." She stretched out a hand to her husband. "Harmon, tell her. Those folks were very strict about psychics and tarot readers and all that. But they were up there, calling people down to the altar, telling people's fortunes, too . . . only they called it prophesying."

Harmon nodded. "They did say pretty frequently that psychics were an abomination unto the Lord."

"Harmon." Gloria shook her head. "I'm sure I probably said something in poor taste to poor old Edie, now that you mention it—"

Harmon chimed in. "Oh, Glo, you *definitely* said something in poor taste—"

"Anyway"—Gloria spoke over him—"that's the past. We left that church, and now we're here with the Lutherans, and we accept all lifestyles and choices and preferences, don't we, Harm?"

"That we do," Harmon agreed.

"Even psychics," Gloria said. "And witches," she added with a lower, more playful tone of voice. She patted Ingrid's arm. "You'll come to lunch with us, won't you?"

"Oh." Ingrid was already shaking her head, scrambling for an excuse. "I don't—"

Gloria wrapped her skinny arms around Ingrid and squeezed. "You can't say no. I'm not gonna let you. Dean Remington's asked Harmon and me over for brunch. A whole summer spread. You can ask your boyfriend . . ."

"Miles. But he's not my—"

"The more the merrier. Sheffield always has a collection of collectibles over, whenever we go. It'll be a party."

Chapter 43

Sandwiched between Gloria, Harmon, and Miles, and standing in front of Dean Remington's glossy black door, Ingrid felt queasy. Edie and Dean had always been cordial with one another, nodding politely and commenting in passing about the humidity and the number of tourists on the street, but Edie didn't exactly pal around with him.

Ingrid wasn't sure what she was about to encounter.

She tried to remember if she'd actually ever been inside Dean's house. Not one instance came to mind. The closest she'd come was peering out her window into Dean's courtyard garden, which was planted with lush azaleas, gardenias, camellias, and jasmine, all white, surrounding a small, aquamarine plunge pool. She used to watch Dean and whoever he happened to be dating at the time laze around it.

She'd spy on them as they drank cocktails and smoked. Sometimes when she was lucky, she got a front-row seat to epic arguments between Dean and whoever was his current paramour. In these interactions, the boyfriends either sulked or went on Oscar-worthy rampages, sputtering and pacing and screaming expletives. Sometimes they even threw bottles of sunscreen, glasses of fizzy drinks, or paperback novels. Dean always maintained admirable calm, standing with one elbow resting on the other arm, forefinger pressed against his lips during the show. Ingrid could never imagine what it was about Dean that made them so angry. He seemed like such a mild-mannered person.

Nothing like that had happened in the two years since Sheffield moved in. Sheffield was a gorgeous man, over six feet, with the face of an impish Greek demi-god. Like the previous boyfriends, he spent a lot of time oiling himself by the pool, firing up a bubbling bong, and talking nonstop on the phone, but whenever Dean came out, they never fought. Dean always just planted a quick kiss on Sheffield's head, then took a quick tour around the garden to deadhead brown blossoms.

The front door swung open, revealing Dean, resplendent in peach trousers and a marigold-yellow jacket with a multicolored silk cravat tucked into a crisp button-down shirt. He reached past Gloria and Harmon and gathered Ingrid's hands into his own.

"You're here," he said, looking deeply into her eyes with his own owlish green ones behind his horn-rimmed glasses. "Come in, come in, my little lamb."

Ingrid let herself be led into Dean's opulent town house, taking in its silks and taffeta, tassels and fringe, buttons and baubles. Delicate antiques glowed in the soft light from crystal chandeliers and gold sconces. He took them all into a back conservatory where a round wicker table sat beneath a bower of orchids and ferns. Sheffield appeared and hugged Ingrid, then gave Miles a lingering, wistful once-over.

"Sit down, everybody," Dean said expansively.

As they sat, Ingrid glanced at Miles. He smiled back at her, and she felt her heart swell with love. She felt so thankful for him. And for Gloria and Harmon, who had turned out to be nicer than she'd expected.

"Harmon, say grace," said Gloria, slapping him on the arm.

Harmon blessed the food, and they proceeded to feast on course after course that Zelda, the chef, brought in from the kitchen. There were platters of brown sugar scones with clotted cream and clementine jam; a Dutch baby with fresh cherries; individual ramekins of Eggs Florentine with goat cheese, dusted with sourdough crumbs; and flaky caramelized bacon tarts.

Dean plied them with hot coffee and mimosas, and an hour and a half later, they moved the party outside, where they sprawled poolside on chaises. They were drowsy with the sunshine and the scent of gardenia, all laughing at Sheffield's impression of Dean's timid way of tiptoeing into the pool. Harmon fell asleep and the bells of St. John's rang. Miles and Sheffield took turns doing flips off the side of the pool into the crystal blue water.

After a while, Dean held up his drink. "A toast to neighbors."

Gloria and Ingrid lifted their glasses. Harmon snored peacefully on his chaise.

"It's been too long since we were all together like this," Dean said.

Ingrid's eyebrow raised. She eyed Dean, then Gloria. Why did the two of them look like they were sharing a secret? "Y'all used to get together a lot? Was Edie ever included?"

"Always," Gloria said with a furtive glance at Dean. "Before she and Dean had their falling-out."

"Let's not dig up old bones," Dean admonished.

Ingrid sat up. "I never realized Edie was friends with you. She never said. What happened?"

"Oh, lamb." His expression went soft. "Back in the nineties, things around here got really wild. The city was changing. We could all feel it."

Ingrid nodded. She'd heard the stories from Edie.

"Well, you know how it went. The tourists read the book— "

"The book," everyone tutted, like they always did in conversations like these.

" —and they came down to see what all the fuss was about . . . and it was like some folks here wanted to put on a show for 'em. You know, with the wild parties and over-the-top behavior. People acted the fool, playing into the mythology. Rill Loeffler took it to a whole other level." Dean rolled his eyes. "Rich kid, maybe the richest in Savannah, fresh out of . . ."

"Virginia," Gloria supplied.

"I can't blame him. He saw an opportunity with the influx of new tourists. For Savannah Sauce and himself. He was always having these parties— "

"Out on Tybee," Ingrid said. "In the house on the beach."

"That's right." Dean inhaled, lost in the past. "A lot of people came through that place. From New York, LA, Miami, London, Paris. A lot of drugs went through it, too. Basically, if you were a person of influence back then, any kind of mover and shaker, you partied with Rill Loeffler at his beach house."

"The Sargassum Sling," Ingrid said.

"Named after a drink Rill invented for the parties." Dean looked off into space. "Lots of secret ingredients in that one."

"Lots of bad behavior resulting from drinking too dang many of them," Gloria said.

"And you were mad at Edie for going to the parties?" Ingrid asked.

"Let's just say we disagreed about them," Dean said simply.

Ingrid felt the fear creeping up. "Did something bad happen at one of those parties? To Edie?"

Dean heaved a sigh. "Nothing that she ever mentioned. Or that I ever found out about. I'm not one to blame the victim— but I think all of us thought Edie had put herself in a tricky position. She was hanging around Rill Loeffler, a man from one of the most powerful families in Savannah. A man who was engaged to be married to a young woman from an equally powerful family, and a man who clearly had an enormous crush on Edie. It was a situation that Rill created. One that would hurt people. That would bring a storm of epic proportions." Dean shook his head wearily. "And then, out of nowhere, Edie started having these debilitating health problems. She was coughing constantly, tired all the time. Losing weight."

"Already just a slip of a thing," Gloria interjected.

"She went to the doctor," Dean continued, "but they couldn't find anything wrong with her. We were talking once, and I repeated a rumor that she was either depressed because she was actually in love with Rill, too, or . . ."

"Or what?" Ingrid asked.

Dean stroked his jaw. "That Scoot Loeffler, or Fairburn as she was then, was poisoning her."

Ingrid sat bolt upright. Her eyes darted from Dean to Gloria. It was like her dream. That day in the doctor's office. Scoot, mixing a milkshake made with volcanic ash. "Poisoning her?"

On his chaise, Harmon snorted and flopped onto his side. Across the garden, on a bench entwined with jasmine, Miles and Sheffield were sharing a smoke and giggling. Gloria lowered her sunglasses over her eyes and lifted her face to the sun.

"It was a rumor," Dean said. "Which I thought was a joke. I regretted the moment I said it. It hurt Edie."

"But was it true?"

"Of course not," Dean said. A little robotically, Ingrid thought.

"Of course not," Gloria echoed.

"But she got cancer," Ingrid said. "Later, anyway."

"Well, that was just bad luck," Dean said.

"It happens, hon," Gloria said.

Ingrid wasn't ready to let it go. "But you're telling me that people were saying Scoot Loeffler tried to poison my grandmother? And then years later, she gets cancer, and nobody thinks anything about it?"

Edie's doctor had really listed those possible causes that day. *Contaminated soil. Volcanic ash. Kitty litter.* She thought of all the photos from Rill's Tybee Island house, the Sargassum Sling. Rill hanging all over Edie. He'd been in love with her. *Enamored*, he told Ingrid. And then he went and slept with Tess. Scoot had probably found out about that, too.

And she still wasn't over either betrayal.

"It makes perfect sense," Ingrid said. And it did. Everything was starting to align. Everything was clear now.

Ingrid really *had* cast a simple karmic spell on Scoot. Her only mistake was that before doing it, Ingrid hadn't known how many despicable things Scoot Loeffler had actually done in her life. If the woman had really poisoned Edie . . . well, then, inviting Scoot's karma had been like inviting a category five hurricane right in the front door.

Miles had walked over and was standing beside her now. Looking at her with that protective, worried expression he occasionally got. He reached for her. "Ingrid—"

She brushed him away. She was filled with something hot and molten, something that seeped through her body, the way a comic book supervillain got infected by alien ooze. And like those stories, she could feel the substance inside her was going to bring a new level of strength. Of vision and power.

This was it. The wrong that had been done to Edie. The heart of the false balance.

Scoot Loeffler poisoned and killed Edie.

And it was up to Ingrid to right the balance.

She stood abruptly. "I have to go," she said, more to herself than any one of the startled people sitting in Dean Remington's garden, and headed toward the gate.

"Sweetheart?" Gloria called after her.

"Ingrid," Miles called.

But Ingrid didn't stop. She ran out the gate, letting it swing open behind her, and down East Taylor, running, running, running. Blind with rage and disbelief but also with a new purpose. She was heading to some destination she couldn't name but was confident she would recognize when she found it.

Edie would show her.

Chapter 44

No one could run forever, especially in Savannah in the double digits of August, so eventually Ingrid slowed down to a brisk walk.

She walked aimlessly, boiling in a ninety-eight-degree cauldron of anger, panic, and elation. As she went, the hair on the back of her neck prickled. She felt eyes on her. Watching her. She wondered if Sailor or Rill were having her followed. Maybe by the redheaded goon from Peregrin.

She eventually found herself south of Forsyth Park, in the Starland district. Down here, away from the area swarmed with tourists, the streets were empty. On Bull Street between 39th and 40th, she happened upon a neighborhood pub called The Wormhole, which felt like an appropriate place to hunker down for the rest of the afternoon. No chance anyone from the Loeffler family or their crew would pop in.

Inside, the bar was neon-blue dark and mostly empty. A couple played pool at one of the tables and a tall guy stood at one of the pinball machines at the far end of the room. Ingrid found a seat at the bar and ordered a Chatham Artillery punch, a drink that contained rum, whisky, brandy, and champagne. She saw on a laminated sign over that bar that there was trivia later. She'd be drunk by then.

"Ingrid? Hey, girl."

She twisted around to see Boney, UGA baseball cap turned backward over his stringy black hair, grinning at her. "Oh, hey."

"You saving this seat?" He waggled his eyebrows in a lascivious way.

"No." Goddess, what a pest.

He nodded at the bartender in whatever shorthand they had and sat on the stool beside her. She sucked a fortifying inch and a half from the liquid in her glass. Positively lethal. Just what she needed.

"Ladies' night while the old ball and chain works the evening shift?" Boney asked. "I like it."

Feeling her chest burn pleasantly, she bestowed on him a condescending smile. "It's the afternoon, Boney."

"Or were you just really in the mood for a Chatham Artillery mixed up by Percy?"

She rolled her eyes and sucked down another inch of the drink. Boney got his beer and tipped it back. "No, really. What are you doing here?"

"I like this place. Haven't been here in forever." In spite of her reluctance to talk to Boney, her tongue felt loosened by the alcohol. "And Sailor's furious at me. It's a matter of time before everyone knows that I put a spell on Scoot."

"You put a spell on Scoot?"

Well, that cat was out of the bag. She sighed. "It was just a karma spell." She didn't mention she'd done it at Sailor's request.

"I wouldn't worry about it." Boney's half-lidded eyes closed as he drank. "That family cares too much about their reputation. They're telling everybody Scoot was tired from all that doing nothing she does and went to a rejuvenation center in Charleston to rest, and I don't know, get her blood de-toxified or something."

Ingrid regarded him doubtfully. "Really?"

"You think they're going to let it get out that she maimed a homeless guy while she was driving sloshed? No way."

"Is she really in Charleston?"

"Who knows? Who cares?"

Ingrid did, but not because she felt bad for the woman. Scoot Loeffler needed to be kept somewhere safe. At least until Ingrid figured out what to do about her.

"Ingrid," Boney said. "Why is that girl is looking at you?"

Ingrid turned. Sure enough, at one of the tables in the corner, there was a family: a square-jawed, muscular man feeding French fries to a toddler with a pink beret angled jauntily on her curly red hair. On the other side of the toddler was a woman about her age, long red hair, wearing a Ralph Lauren Polo logo cap and a crisp white button-down unbuttoned over a bandeau top. The woman was staring at her.

"Oh, shit." Ingrid flushed and stared down into her glass, wishing she could somehow shrink down to the size of a tree frog and dive into it.

"Who is that?" Boney said. "She's gorgeous."

"Disney villains usually are," Ingrid muttered.

Boney grinned, making him look like a male model, a look that got him way more attention than he deserved. He contorted his wiry torso to get a better look. "Look at that hair. That Instagram outfit."

"Boney. Don't," Ingrid said. "And stop smiling at her."

But he kept at it, grinning away and stealing looks at the girl, who obviously took this as a welcome mat. She got up and began walking toward them.

"Shit, shit, shit," Ingrid muttered, and inhaled two more

inches of Artillery. She was buzzing now with the dangerous stew of alcohol she'd imbibed, feeling spiky and spiteful.

"Ingrid? Ingrid White?"

Ingrid whipped around, a bright smile stretching her lips. "Destiny Amos! Well, hi there!"

"Long time no see." Destiny's eyes slid over to Boney, and she did that self-conscious little shimmy women always did in Boney's presence. "And it's Garcia now. Amos-Garcia, actually. I did the hyphenate thing. Well, not at first. At first, I was like, a major trad-wife, rolling deep with the sourdough and shit. But recently I started this whole lifestyle, wellness business thing and with the branding and then the rebranding and the soft launch, I was just like, 'Hold up! I'm an Amos but I'm also a Garcia,' you know?"

Ingrid snorted softly.

"We all have to be true to ourselves." Destiny directed this to Boney.

Boney twinkled. "One hundred percent."

He held out his hand and with a giggle, Destiny took it in hers.

"Tristan Anderson," Boney said.

"Destiny."

"Amos-Garcia."

Destiny twinkled.

"Everybody calls him Boney," Ingrid said.

Destiny pointed at Boney. "Oh, you do the ghost tours."

"That's me." Boney propped one elbow up on the bar. "You should bring the fam one night. Or date night." He gave her a look that said everything opposite of date night, and Ingrid frowned. He made a face back at her. She had the impulse to smack him right off his stool.

Destiny Amos-Garcia tore her eyes from Boney and addressed Ingrid. "So what are you up to, girlie?"

"Drinking here with my friend," Ingrid said coolly. She glanced over at the muscular guy and toddler. "What a cute kid."

Destiny threw a look over her shoulder. "Thanks. She's almost two. Quite a handful. Like we were, you know? Back in the day." She beamed and winked at Ingrid.

"Ho, ho," laughed Ingrid. "*You* were certainly a handful."

Destiny's smile tightened. Her eyes darted to Boney, then back to Ingrid. "What do you mean by that?"

"Nothing," Ingrid sang gaily and bypassing her straw, gulped the remainder of her Artillery.

"No, seriously." Destiny squared up to Ingrid. "Is there something you want to say to me?"

"Destiny, it's fine." Ingrid waved her off, held her glass up to the bartender. From the far end of the bar, he nodded.

"I mean, it was a long time ago," Destiny's mouth was still stretched into a semblance of a smile. "We were just kids."

"Sounds like a story there," Boney commented.

"Oh my God, not really," Destiny said, flipping her hair back.

"I mean, if you want a story," Ingrid swiveled on her stool, fully facing Destiny. "I have a story. When I was a thirteen-year-old girl, this one tied me to a chair and tried to cast a demon out of me. At a sleepover."

"We were children," Destiny protested. "It was a joke. And a very long time ago." She focused on Ingrid, picking at a strand of her hair. "Anyway, Ingrid. I heard you were like, hanging out with Sailor Loeffler and doing events for her and stuff. And I, like, had this flash of, like, brilliance? That you and I could maybe do some kind of collab. Maybe fold it into a chamber of commerce thing? Or possibly a charity—"

The bartender set a fresh Artillery in front of Ingrid. She nodded her thanks and took a long pull.

"I know Sailor's got tons of connections so I thought we

could do like a Savannah Sauce-D.A.G. Glow event where you could tell fortunes or something . . ."

"It wasn't funny to me, just so you know." Ingrid put her drink down carefully and edged off her stool. She could feel her internal engine revving, gearing up for a fight. "In fact, I was so upset, my grandmother took me out of school."

"Oh wow." Destiny took one step back. "I hadn't . . . I had forgotten that."

"And I don't *tell fortunes,* FYI."

"Listen, Ingrid—" Destiny started to say. "Let's just move on. That was a long time ago. I just came over here to see if you wanted to do some kind of collab—"

"No, you listen to me." Ingrid jammed a finger in Destiny's face. "You said I worshipped the devil. You tried to exorcise me. You humiliated me and made me feel like a terrible person."

Destiny huffed impatiently. "That's what my mother told me you were supposed to do if somebody was . . . if somebody was a witch. She's very religious, and that's how she taught me. I didn't know any better. I was actually trying to help you."

Ingrid yelped with laughter. "No, you weren't. You were trying to make all those girls scared of me. Like I was some kind of character out of a horror movie. And that's exactly what you did."

"Ingrid, why would I do such a thing—"

"I'll tell you why." Ingrid felt a flash of anger.

It was like she'd opened a window in the dead of winter and a wall of cold hit her, shocking her and waking her up. This woman standing in front of her had been nothing but a bully to her, but now that she believed Ingrid was running with Sailor Loeffler, she was trying to suck up to her.

She took a step toward Destiny. "Because it made you feel powerful to put me down. To scare those girls. To push me outside the group. And I get it, Destiny, I do. Power feels good.

It feels like everything. In fact, I won't lie. I love power." A singular thought occurred to her. A thought that gave her a sudden feeling of calm.

With just one spell, she had been able to land Scoot Loeffler in rehab.

Destiny Amos-Garcia would be a breeze.

Ingrid sucked in her cheeks, made the sign of the horns with her fingers and, coolly, calmly, pointed them at Destiny. "I know because I have it."

Chapter 45

Destiny's eyes popped wide.

"Hey, Ingrid . . ." she heard Boney say, but his voice sounded muffled, like he was underwater.

"Your business is cursed," Ingrid said quietly to Destiny.

Destiny let out a dismissive huff, but in the neon-blue glow of the bar, her eyes looked wild.

"You'll lose everything you've invested and more," Ingrid said. "Everything."

"Ingrid, come on," Boney said.

She ignored him. Pivoted away from Destiny and fixed her eyes on the table across the room. The square-jawed husband. The child with the pink beret.

Destiny let out a squawk. "What are you— " She grabbed Ingrid's arm. "Don't you dare, you bitch— "

"Your marriage is never going to make you happy," Ingrid said softly, her eyes gone soft and dreamy. "He'll never love you the way you want. He'll never fully see you, never fully hear you— "

"Stop it, Ingrid." Boney was off his stool now, crowding her with his body, pushing her arm down, shuffling her toward the door.

She didn't stop. There was something flowing through her, the current of some divine river that she couldn't resist even if she wanted. It felt inevitable. Sacred. There was a droning in her ears that reminded her of a medieval chant. The songs of acolytes, filing toward worship. She liked it. It reminded her of the middle C hum she'd heard when she met Sailor.

Her gaze settled on the little girl. She stretched out her hand. Destiny let out a panicked wail.

"Jesus, Ingrid, no!" snapped Boney and then, grabbing her by the wrist, threw a bill on the bar and dragged her out of the place.

Outside, Boney opened the door of his car and shoved her in. "Stay," he ordered, and went around to get in the other side. He started the car, as Ingrid blinked in her seat. "Strap in," he said as he peeled out of the parking lot. He glanced in his rearview mirror. "Great, the husband's coming out."

He gunned it and glanced at her. "I said seat belt!"

Ingrid buckled herself in as they streaked down the highway.

"What the hell was that?" Boney shouted at her.

"I wouldn't have done it. I wouldn't curse a baby."

"I don't know. It looked to me like you were pretty much on your way to doing that. And her husband was jacked."

"She's a bad person."

He sent a swift look at her. "And you're good? Randomly cursing someone you don't like?"

Ingrid said nothing. She'd finally started to come down from the high she was riding, and now tears had started to slide down her cheeks.

"Oh God, don't do that." Boney wheeled the car onto another road and patted her shoulder. "Come on, Ingrid. Pull it together."

"Where are we going?" she croaked.

"We're taking a field trip."

He took a couple more turns, finally pulling down the road that ran parallel to the Bonaventure Cemetery. He opened the door for her.

"Get your ass out."

She wiped her face. "Boney, it's closed— "

"Out!" he snapped.

She climbed out of the car and grudgingly followed Boney to the chain-link fence. He climbed it, then motioned for her to do the same. Once she was safely over and standing at the edge of the cemetery, he straightened her dress.

"Now where is it?" Boney asked her.

She sighed. She was calmer now, gazing out over the white gravestones. The breeze swayed the moss on the branches of the trees. The crickets sang. She could hear the low hum of the river at the back of the property. She had forgotten how peaceful it was here.

"I'm not kidding," Boney said. "Tell me where she is."

Ingrid, resigned, drunk, and spent from her spiritual exertion, beckoned him to follow her. They walked down the sandy path all the way to the rear of the cemetery where the Wilmington River flowed. She took him to the small gravestone, still smooth and unsullied by the humid salt air and the creeping fungus, glowing pale gray in the dusk.

Edith Sossaman White, 1950 – 2016, She Gathers the Light.

Ingrid swallowed a sob down her already-clogged throat. This was where she should have come in the first place. Edie's grave. But the truth was she hadn't visited in years. She was too busy pretending that wearing Edie's clothes and sleeping in her bedroom meant her grandmother was actually with her.

But Edie wasn't with her, was she? She was here, under this stone, buried under the sandy dirt.

"'She gathers the light,'" Boney said behind her. "I like that. You should do that," he added. "Gather the light."

She sniffed, wiped under her eyes, and folded her arms. "Spare me the lecture, if you don't mind."

"Just trying to help." Boney gave her a look, then ambled off between the headstones.

Ingrid gazed down at the smooth slab of granite. She wanted to say so much, but the words just weren't there. How could she make Edie understand that she'd tried to follow her guidance, but that all it had ever gotten her was bullied and used and blamed for every bad thing that happened?

Even now, she could imagine the argument as it would go between them.

They said it wasn't my magic that got Sailor the things she wanted for her wedding.

Why does it matter what they say? You know what's true. Just stay in the light, my Budgie . . . don't stray from the path . . .

But how could Ingrid stay in the light after all the terrible things Scoot and Rill Loeffler had done to so many people? She was duty-bound to wield her magic against them. To avenge Edie and to save Sailor and Cas.

To right the fucking balance.

But she couldn't do it the way Edie had wanted. The Loefflers didn't play fair.

She finally found her voice. "They destroyed you, Edie, and then they tried to do the same to me. I can't change what they did to you, but I won't let them take my power. I know who I am, and I know what I have to do. I want to save them, Edie—Sailor and Cas—but your way won't work."

Ingrid strained to hear Edie's answer, but all she heard was the wind blowing through the trees, ruffling the Spanish moss.

"I still need your help, though. I need you to be with me."

Nothing. If Edie wouldn't answer, if she wouldn't send her

help, what could Ingrid do? She would be on her own. She would have to come up with her own plan.

She felt Boney's soft footfalls behind her, and he came to stand beside her at the grave.

"Were you following me?" she asked. "Earlier, when I was walking around town?"

He was quiet for a moment. "Miles was worried. He's been scared you were going to . . . I don't know, do something stupid."

She nodded.

"He loves you, Ingrid. He's worried about you. You should give the guy a break."

"I know." She felt him lean down, press a kiss on her temple.

Boney said in a low, gravelly voice, "Your grandmother loved you, too. She would hate to see you so messed up over the Loefflers. They're not good people."

"Sailor is." *Cas is.*

"Maybe." He held her as they both looked down on Edie's grave. "But it's not your job to save her. You could get hurt."

"Maybe it is, though. My job, I mean." She was saying it as much to herself as to him. "Maybe I'm the only one who can do it." She took a breath. "I feel like if I don't do something soon, I may never get another chance to help her."

Just then, her eye caught sight of another gravestone, taller than the rest, just a few yards away from Edie's. It was half-shadowed, half-illuminated in the fading light. On the base, carved in granite, stood an angel. At her side she held a ship's anchor.

It reminded her of something . . .

Something Miles had said not long ago.

Boney was pressing himself against her now. "Been a while, you know . . ."

She wiggled away from him. "You'll survive." She gave him a wry grin, but her mind was racing now.

For reasons Ingrid could not understand, Edie had chosen not to come to her tonight. But it didn't matter. She would do it on her own. Because something had to be done, and quickly, about Sailor refusing to see Ingrid. Or she worried Sailor and Cas would be swept away by the tidal wave that was Scoot and Rill Loeffler. Lost to Ingrid forever.

Chapter 46

Back at home, Miles took one look at Ingrid and sent her upstairs to take a hot bath. When he brought up some of Edie's milk thistle and ginger root tea, he didn't press for information. Later, warm and dry in one of Edie's flannel nightgowns, she joined him in the living room to watch an episode of *The Twilight Zone*.

Litha jumped onto her lap, and she stroked the cat, thinking through her plan. The first step had to happen under the cover of darkness. She was glad for the full moon that night and the protective eye of the Goddess. Both would strengthen her magic. But that bright moon would also make it difficult to go unnoticed.

Up to this point she'd tried to keep her relationships with Miles and Sailor separate, but now she realized how desperately she needed Miles's help. She paused the show and told him her plan—at least as much as she'd been able to lay out in her own mind. He listened quietly, but when she was done, he had a look on his face she couldn't interpret.

"Say something." She elbowed him.

"You're going to make up with Sailor and dump me again."

"I didn't dump you," she said, only a hint of impatience in her voice. He hadn't even made one comment about her plan. "You're being ridiculous."

He scoffed. "It got . . . weird between us. You were different."

She sighed. "How was I different?"

He shook his head. "You were so busy."

"Busy making money. For us."

"We didn't hang out as much." He laced and unlaced his fingers, staring at them. "You didn't talk to me."

"You're right," she said contritely. "You're right, Miles, but it was your idea for me to move in with Sailor. And being there was kind of overwhelming. I know I neglected you, and I'm sorry. I promise, when everything's back to normal—when I've got Sailor back—it'll be different."

His eyes roved her face. "Maybe it's the money, maybe it's just that you want a family to belong to . . . but they have some kind of power over you, Ingrid. And it scares me."

"Miles," she said gently. "I love you. You know that. You're like a brother to me. I'll never allow anything to pull us apart. We will always be *us*."

He shook his head. "I'm low-class to them, Ingrid. They'll never accept me."

"Are you kidding me? If they accept me, they have to accept you. We're a package deal, Miles. That's all there is to it." She picked up his hand and ran her thumb across the mountain range of his knuckles. She rubbed his knuckles against her cheek, and he slumped against the cushions of the sofa.

"I'm sorry," he said. "I want to help you with your plan."

"You mean . . . ?" She widened her eyes meaningfully.

He nodded. "Yes."

She watched him closely. "Are you sure?"

"You can't do this alone, Ingrid. It's too dangerous."

She lunged at him, grabbing him into a fierce embrace. "Thank you, thank you, thank you. I love you so much." She released him. "Let's get started," she said, and picked up her phone to dial Sailor. When she got the voicemail, she locked eyes with Miles, then spoke in a small, frightened voice into her phone.

"Sailor, call me, please. There's something I really need to talk to you about."

She dressed in a dark hoodie, black yoga pants, and beanie. Miles borrowed Boney's car and drove them out to Whitemarsh Island. They parked on a quiet neighborhood street near the entrance of the yacht club and climbed the low brick wall. They split up, Ingrid picking her way down the muddy bank of the river while Miles ambled casually up to the guard house.

From her spot down near the boat slips, she saw him rap on the door. Saw the guard rise and open it for him. He stepped into the small room, and she could see them talking. Miles was good at this kind of thing—shooting the shit with regular people, making friends. Right now he was probably asking the guard how he could get into the security business. If there was a spot open for him at the club. The guard would be filling him in on all the details. She should get moving.

Pulling the beanie down low over her eyes, she hurried along the shoreline, then down the dock, past the row of yachts. She found the *Do Not Disturb* easily and, with a quick glance over her shoulder, climbed aboard. She slipped into the galley, staying close to the wall out of sight of the onboard cameras, and was immediately enveloped in the smell of wood polish and leather upholstery.

There were six cameras in all: two on the forward and aft decks, two in the living cabin, one in the bridge, and another in the galley. They were all wirelessly connected to a hub in a cabinet under the built-in sectional sofa, which she found easily, then unplugged. The water lines she didn't have to worry about.

Many times she'd seen Jude's crew turn the lever to switch off the supply line when they left the boat.

She crept back to the galley. At the row of hooks over the dining table, she pawed through ball caps, visors, and rain jackets, finally locating the straw hat with the pleated brim and Sailor's Hermès scarf tied around it. She stuffed it under her hoodie and looked around the silent, finely appointed vessel.

It would be so easy, she thought then, to just help the magic along . . .

She looked over at the stove. She could wad up some paper towels, put them in a pan on one of the burners. They'd catch quick. Spread to the cabinets nearby. Or she could soak dish towels in olive oil and stuff them under the curtains in one of the bedrooms. She could even go down to the engine room and start it there. Jude had showed her once where it was.

But that would be cheating. Admitting that she didn't trust in her own power or the power of the universe. That wouldn't be magic. That would be a crime.

Back at the house, shadows danced along the walls of the altar room. In the center of the room, the altar glowed with candlelight. Ingrid knelt before it in silence.

She had changed out of the yoga pants and hoodie and put on one of Edie's older dresses, a caftan in watercolor shades of blue. She'd let her brown hair loose, the way Edie had always worn hers. She had told Miles to stay upstairs. She needed the mental space to take the next step in her plan.

A snow-white cloth covered the brass table and quiet cello music played. She cast her circle, called the corners, then cleansed herself. She called out to Edie to help her and protect her. Her pulse was thrumming through her veins, her heart in her throat. She'd never done this before.

Baneful magic.

But it wasn't exactly against Edie's teaching. She was only

hexing an object, not a person, and objects could be replaced. Especially when you had lots of money like the Loefflers. Like Jude Etris. Besides, he would definitely have insurance on the boat.

She rose, cleared the energy around her, and faced north to start.

"*Do Not Disturb*," she said in a low voice, then turned east. "*Do Not Disturb, Do Not Disturb, Do Not Disturb* . . ."

She closed her eyes and pictured what she wanted.

Flames licking . . .

Consuming it all . . .

FireFireFireFireFireFireFire . . .

Chapter 47

"The blaze swept through the Savannah Yacht Club at Whitemarsh Island in the hours just past midnight, destroying at least four yachts and a portion of the dock. So far, no word on possible injuries or the origin of the fire."

The WSAV News 3 Today's six-a.m. anchor breathlessly turned it over to the reporter on the scene at the yacht club. The camera showed B-roll of an inferno, as firefighters hosed down multiple boats engulfed in flames.

In the Daffodil Room, Ingrid and Miles were lying side by side in Edie's bed, snuggled under the chenille bedspread, watching the report. They exchanged wide-eyed looks then turned back to the footage. In fact, there was the *Do Not Disturb* on camera now, a smoking, ruined wreck with only the hull still intact. The interior of it was destroyed, and most of the outside, a sad, charred skeleton.

Ingrid sat up and let out a high-pitched, manic giggle. "Oh my God—"

"Goddess," Miles corrected.

"I did it!" she crowed. She grabbed Miles, squeezing him until he gasped for breath. "I can't believe it! The hex worked! It actually worked!"

She released him and jogged in place like a maniacal sprinter, chopping her arms and pumping her legs, then stopped abruptly and lifted her face to the ceiling and yodel-screamed at the top of her lungs.

Miles laughed. "You did it."

Ingrid's eyes had gone blank. "She'll let me back in her life now. It's a done deal." She snapped out of her daze and looked at Miles. "I've got to shower. Got a few appointments and then . . ." She inhaled deeply, with anticipation and waved her hands. "Tuesday night family dinner!"

She skipped into the bathroom and slammed the door. She ran the shower and stared at herself in Edie's gilt-framed mirror. As steam billowed around her, the mirror fogged and her reflection blurred until she could no longer see her face. She reached out with her hand and wiped the condensation away.

Her grandmother's face looked back at her.

She flinched, but if there was a scream, it died in the back of her throat. What was happening? She couldn't move, but she wasn't afraid. Not anymore. One tear rose in her eye—Edie's eye—and slipped down Edie's cheek. She reached up and touched it. She felt the wetness between her thumb and middle fingers. Edie's fingers.

"Edie," she said in a hoarse whisper. "You came. You're here."

Edie looked back at her with a soft, knowing expression.

I was always here, my little one. My Budgie . . .

Somewhere, from the Edie looking back at her in the mirror, came Ingrid's voice. "I'm going to have everything, Edie. So soon. Everything I've always wanted."

And what might that be, sweet Budge? Edie's face looked amused now.

"Friendship, family. Enough money that I won't ever have to worry again." Ingrid made Edie's head nod. Which, for some odd reason, made her laugh. Then Edie spoke again.

And what about the light? Will you have the light?

Edie's eyes stared into the mirror. Into Ingrid's eyes.

You've strayed from the path—

"I haven't. I mean, not that far—"

Miles pounded on the door. "You okay in there?"

Ingrid sucked in a lungful of steamy air. The mirror had fogged again, and she wiped it, but now it was only her own face she saw looking back at her. White skin wreathed by light brown hair and ears that stuck out. Spray of pale freckles over her slightly crooked nose and along the line of her upper lip.

This was all in her mind. Just a trick her own mind was playing on her. Edie wasn't mad at her. She couldn't be. She understood that Ingrid had done what she had to do.

"I'm fine," she yelled, and turning, she headed for the shower.

Ingrid decided she would catch Sailor just after predinner cocktails, after she'd had one drink. One drink that would soften her up and lower her defenses and make her open to everything Ingrid was about to say.

But Ingrid had to be careful. If word had gotten out that Jude Etris's yacht was one of the boats damaged in the fire, people would be hanging around the mansion. Reporters hoping for a comment on the record from him or one of the Loefflers.

She left her house, the straw hat nestled safely in a canvas tote bag. She practiced her speech silently all the way through Taylor Square, across East Gordan toward the Loeffler house. As she approached the house, her breath sped up and her heart hammered.

But there were no reporters. Just the house, rising from the mounds of velvety gardenias in bloom around it. A queen on her majestic throne. Ingrid noticed, as if for the first time, the masses of jasmine that twined around the iron fence and foundation of the house. The tendrils of glossy English ivy, which had made its way up to the second story. She noticed for the first time the cracks there, in the plaster, one running almost all the way up to the roof. Smaller cracks branched off it, and she thought of the old Edgar Allan Poe short story Edie had assigned her to read when she was a kid, *The Fall of the House of Usher*.

She climbed the wide front steps that led to the looming double doors of the house and turned the knob, pushing open one of the heavy doors. The front hall was cool and dim, and the air smelled like roast chicken and . . . well, money.

She heard voices in the second drawing room to the right. Male voices. Rill. Cas. Jude. And now she heard footsteps coming into the hall. Sailor's voice—"I'll let them know"—talking to Freddie or Sarita back in the kitchen where she'd be collecting the limes and olives for the drinks.

Sailor stopped just at the carved newel post, tray of garnishes in her hand, and regarded Ingrid with a mixture of surprise and iciness. She looked coolly elegant in white trouser jeans, crisp, blue button-down and loafers. Ingrid straightened, smoothing her dress, pushing her hair behind her shoulders. She held the tote bag in both hands like a shield.

"Who let you in?" Sailor asked, and then without waiting for a reply said, "Please don't make me throw you out, Ingrid. I'm really not up for it."

She looked tired, Ingrid thought. There were shadows under her eyes. In the light of the entry hall, Sailor looked eerily like Scoot.

"How is your mother?" Ingrid asked.

Sailor set the tray on a console table and began to mix drinks for her family. Rill's Dark and Stormy first, Ingrid noticed. "I don't know. I haven't been to visit her . . . yet."

Ingrid swallowed. "I'm so sorry."

"Yes. Me, too." She slumped, hands in her pockets, but she didn't call out to everyone in the drawing room. Ingrid took this as a good sign.

"I could go with you, if you wanted. To see her."

Sailor scoffed as she started on Cas's drink. "No, thanks."

"Okay, that's fine," Ingrid said quickly. "I just came here because I wanted to give you something."

Sailor's face took on a guarded expression.

"I heard about Jude's boat. The fire."

Sailor said nothing.

"Do they know who started it?"

Sailor cleared her throat carefully, pouring gin into a tumbler. "They think it might've been faulty wiring in the boat next to Jude's and somehow it spread. The security system on the boat must've been destroyed in the fire and the security guy actually forgot to hook up the system last night so it didn't record."

Ingrid straightened. *Thank Goddess.* She hadn't even thought of that.

"He's been fired. He might be charged with negligence." Her voice was hollow.

Ingrid pushed away the jab of guilt and shifted, gripping the straps of the tote. "I need to talk to you about something. About the fire."

Sailor cocked her head. "Do you know something about it?"

"No." Ingrid took an involuntary step backward. "No. I just . . . well, that's not true."

Sailor's face drained of color. "What?"

"I do . . . actually . . . know something about it."

Sailor advanced on Ingrid, lifted a finger to her face. "If you had anything, *anything* at all to do with this, I will make sure you never, ever see the light of day again." Venom dripped from her voice.

"Sailor, no. It's just something very strange happened to me yesterday, and I think I should tell you."

"What?" She had Sailor's full attention now.

"It was around lunch, right after one of my appointments. I was in my altar room. I was doing a healing ritual. And that's when I got this . . . sort of . . . download."

"Download." Sailor narrowed her eyes.

"Yes, like this intense knowing. It happens sometimes when—"

Sailor made an impatient face. "I remember, Ingrid."

"Right. It's just . . . this one was so strong. So powerful. I just *knew* that something bad was going to happen. To Jude."

Sailor frowned.

"I didn't know if it meant he was going to get sick or be hurt in some way. Maybe it was more that something bad was going to happen around him. I wasn't sure, so I just kept meditating and calling in the light." Ingrid looked at her expectantly.

"And?"

"Eventually I saw a boat. The *Do Not Disturb*. And I saw fire."

Sailor's eyes flashed fear, then disbelief. "You did not."

Ingrid nodded. "I did. So I called you."

Sailor was quiet.

"I left a message and then I called Jude. When I couldn't get either of you, I went to the yacht club. To his boat, and took something off of it . . . the hat his wife—"

"Stop right there!" The finger was up again and dangerously close to Ingrid's nose. Sailor trembled with anger. "Ingrid? So help me, if I find out you are connected in any capacity to this fire—a *devastating fire* that destroyed three boats and damaged two more—and you haven't marched your silly little psychic ass over to Bull and Habersham and told the police everything you know, then I will *destroy* you."

"That's the thing," Ingrid said quickly. "I didn't know-know anything, I just *felt* it."

Sailor rolled her eyes. "You need to get out, right now." She spun Ingrid around and pushed her toward the door. Ingrid stumbled and turned back.

"Sailor, just let me—"

"Get out!" Sailor pushed her again but this time, Ingrid shoved her back. She dropped the tote, more in an effort to fend off Sailor's swinging hand now, when Jude, Cas, and Rill ran into the room.

Ingrid felt a sting and she stumbled, stars swimming into her vision. She caught herself and straightened. Touched her cheek and looked at Sailor. Sailor was panting, red-faced.

"I swear to God I'll do it again if you don't leave," Sailor gasped. "Don't push me, Ingrid!"

"What the hell—" Rill shouted.

"Sailor!" the voice boomed.

Everything slowed down as all eyes turned to Jude. In one hand he was holding the canvas tote that he'd picked up off the floor. In the other, the straw hat. He was looking at Sailor. "What is this?" Jude faced Ingrid, holding out the hat. "Where did you get this?"

Ingrid was suddenly breathless. Her cheek burned where Sailor had slapped her. "I . . ." She looked quickly at Cas, then Rill. They both stared at her, uncomprehendingly.

Sailor cut in. "She says she saved this from the boat. Before the fire. Because she had some kind of psychic *feeling*." Her voice was disdainful.

Jude turned to look at Ingrid. "Is that true?"

Ingrid nodded wordlessly. "I don't know how to explain it, but I felt like I was supposed to save it. Before something bad happened."

"Bad like what, specifically?" Jude asked.

Ingrid shook her head, feeling everyone's eyes on her. "I didn't know for sure, but when I was doing a ritual, I saw fire." She held his gaze. "I tried to call you, but you didn't answer."

"Why didn't you leave a message? 'Um, hello there. Your boat is about to catch fire.' "

"I did."

Jude pulled out his phone and scrolled then tapped a button. Ingrid's voice, hesitant and tinny, came from the phone.

"Hi, Jude? I'm sorry to bother you. It's Ingrid . . . White. I know this is going to sound really strange, but today I had this feeling . . . this sense . . . that something might happen to the boat. Your boat. It's just that . . . I saw fire, is the thing. And I don't know if it's like literal fire or something else, but I couldn't just ignore it. I had to let you know so you could . . . I don't know . . . go check on things maybe? Okay. That's all. Take care. Bye."

The room was silent. Ingrid glanced quickly at Cas. He caught her eye then looked at the floor.

Sailor glared at Jude. "You could've told me."

He shrugged. "Sorry. I don't listen to voicemails from numbers I don't recognize."

Ingrid held her breath.

Sailor turned to her, arms folded. "Did you also happen to get a download about how the fire started?"

"No. I'm sorry." Ingrid hesitated. "When I went to get the hat, I didn't see anything unusual. I just . . . knew I had to save something that important . . . to you both."

Jude turned back to Sailor. He held the hat out to her. "I think it's pretty obvious what's happened here, darling. Ingrid took a risk here and did something really meaningful for us."

Sailor stepped to him. She took the hat, turned it around in her hands. She seemed to be fighting something within herself, but then she made a snuffling sound, and Ingrid realized she was trying not to cry.

Jude draped his arm around Sailor. "Let's calm down, why don't we? Invite Ingrid in for a drink and supper. You two can kiss and make up and be friends again, yeah? And I can get my fiancée back."

"Sounds good to me," Rill said mildly.

Jude gave Ingrid a saucy wink, but she saw something more behind it. A real, deep gratitude. She turned questioning eyes to Sailor, and, after a moment of hesitation, all the anger and resistance seemed to seep out of her. She moved to Ingrid and took her hand.

"I'm sorry," she managed. Her eyes were red and now swimming in tears. "Thank you. I've missed you."

"I've missed you, too." Meeting Sailor's gaze, Ingrid's eyes filled reflexively.

Sailor didn't say any more, but she held tight to Ingrid's hand as they walked toward the sitting room. And at last, Ingrid allowed herself to catch Cas's eye. He was smiling.

Chapter 48

Just as quickly as she had been pitched out of it, Ingrid was welcomed back into Sailor Loeffler's orbit. It felt like she'd been trapped in cold, dark space for a time and was now finally being enveloped once again in the verdant warmth of planet Earth.

Her whole being relaxed in relief.

Although she was living in her own house, she was over at the Loeffler mansion more frequently than ever, and, so acutely aware of all she had regained, Ingrid soaked everything in. The lunches, brunches, and dinners. The invitations to spa days and shopping excursions. Every minute she spent in Sailor's bright light was a moment of pure joy.

Sailor no longer asked Ingrid to do any spells, and occasionally, Ingrid would catch the girl watching her with a pensive, thoughtful expression, but she never said anything. The weekly deposits reappeared in her bank account, and Ingrid continued to do post-yoga psychic meditations and the odd reading whenever Sailor had time. So all was well that ended well, as Edie might have said.

Miles seemed glad to have things back to normal. He couldn't argue with having the bills paid and a full fridge, and all he ever said before Ingrid walked out the door to see Sailor was "Be careful."

She wasn't sure what she was going to do about Rill. As best she could, she tried to avoid him, but it wasn't entirely possible. Sailor kept inviting her to Tuesday dinners, to cocktail hours at the Fairburns' or the Hawkes' or the McIntyres', and even Cas's birthday dinner out at the yacht club. And Rill was always certain to be in attendance.

There were other moments, too, when their paths crossed. Times at the mansion when Rill would be coming down the stairs or rifling through the fridge or on the phone in the front hall, when he and Ingrid would bump into each other. In those instances, their eyes would catch, and Ingrid's mouth would go dry.

He always said something innocuous like *Nice to see you, Ingrid* or *Fancy meeting you here,* but his eyes sent an entirely different message.

As for Cas, now that Rill had installed him in the Savannah Sauce offices, on track to become CEO of Savannah Sauce, he was hardly ever around. Ingrid wondered if Rill had succeeded in pulling Cas away from everything else he loved, like his church. It was impossible to know. Like Scoot, the subject of Cas seemed to be off-limits with everyone.

She periodically tried texting her sinner.

Where are you? I miss talking to you.

There was never any reply.

On an early weekday evening, Ingrid was over at the house helping Sailor decide between the dozen dresses her stylist had pulled for the rehearsal dinner. She was heading down the front steps of the house, on her way back home, when she spied Cas stepping out of the family Rolls. Dressed in a charcoal suit and sky-blue tie, hair combed neatly, he was almost unrecognizable to her. She stopped, gripping the handrail.

"Hi, Cas."

"Ingrid." He crossed the sidewalk. She was a few steps above him, looking down at him. The sunlight hit his brown eyes, turning them molten. "How are you?"

"I'm well. Just helping Sailor pick out a dress." All of a sudden, she felt like she had the worst case of heartburn in the world.

"Another dress," he said. "Just what she needs."

She regarded him coolly for a long moment. "It's her wedding, Cas. It's an important day to her."

He shook his head. "Sorry. That was rude. I'm nervous, I guess."

She felt a stab of annoyance. "Why would you be nervous?"

He gave her a sidelong look. "I haven't exactly . . . treated you the best, I guess."

She lifted her shoulders, neither in agreement nor disagreement.

"I guess I was thinking . . . I've been worrying you might want to get back at me."

"Get back at you?" She caught his gaze. "You mean with magic?"

He swallowed. "Would you? Could you?"

"No." She shook her head emphatically. "Cas, I would never. I don't know . . . maybe if you got to know what I actually do, I wouldn't seem like some kind of green-faced monster out of a child's fairy tale to you."

He shook his head, and now he was looking at her in a new way. "I doubt it."

"Excuse me?" She lifted an eyebrow.

"I think you are what you are, Ingrid, and you should stop

trying to make yourself smaller. Or more palatable. To anyone." He took one step up. One step closer to her. "I think you *are* scary, actually. But not like a monster. You're scary in the most interesting way imaginable. And I think you should embrace it. That's all."

She felt the slam of her heart against the wall of her chest with so much force that she thought it might knock her over.

"You like that? To be ordered around by someone?"

"By you." Now he smiled—the old, familiar grin that transformed him from sad man to sunny, carefree boy.

But he'd made his choice. He was living the life Rill had chosen for him. And she was not part of it.

"I should go," she said abruptly. She stepped down to the sidewalk just as he stepped up.

"It was nice to see you," they said at the same time, then both smiled.

"We should go to dinner sometime," he said.

"Should we?" Ingrid bit the inside of her lip. "What would your dad say?"

"Maybe I don't care what he says." He looked a bit sad. "Will you go to dinner with me?"

She smiled. Her heart soared now, even though she knew she should be careful. "I'd love to."

With the wedding just around the corner, preparations were moving at a fast clip. It seemed like there was still an endless list of things to do. Thankfully, Sailor had rehired the wedding coordinators she'd fired, a harried, hapless woman named Francesca and her alarmingly haughty assistant Courtland. They promptly assigned Ingrid a list of errands to run.

With the mayor's blessing, they planned to close down the entire northern half of Forsyth Park for the ceremony, with a cocktail hour immediately following. The reception dinner was to be held at Saint Bibiana at the Bardo Hotel. Dancing would take place later on Monterey Square, which the mayor had also agreed to rope off from the public, but only until three a.m. the next morning.

Months earlier, Francesca the coordinator had floated the idea of several high-profile celebrity pop stars performing, but both Scoot and Rill had vetoed the idea. As far as Scoot was concerned, no one was going to outshine her daughter. And Rill wasn't about to shell out the equivalent of a medium-sized Eastern European country's GDP to some diva flown in for the night. They'd compromised with three alternatives—Chicago (Rill's favorite) would play a half-hour set, then Earth Wind & Fire (Scoot's favorite), after which a celebrity DJ whom Jude knew would take over for the remainder of the night.

Ingrid's task was to ensure Sailor finished the seating chart for the twelve-course dinner, an event which was to include something called an amuse-bouche and a mignardise. Each of the twelve courses was to be accompanied by a red or white wine, diner's choice, plus all manner of coffee, tea, waters, and after-dinner brandies, sherries, and liqueurs. Point being, if you were going to be served a three-hour meal, getting very drunk in the process, you had better enjoy who you were sitting next to.

Which meant Ingrid was forced to trot behind Sailor almost every day, cajoling, begging, pleading her to "just please sit down for a half hour so we can knock this out!" At last, one morning before Sailor planned to go with Jude down to a shipyard to look at new yachts, Ingrid cornered her in the kitchen.

The job finally completed, a relieved Ingrid poured them both orange juices, generously spiked with champagne. They clinked glasses and drank.

"What would I do without you, Ingrid?" Sailor sighed.

Ingrid tilted her head. "I don't know. What *did* you do when I wasn't around?"

Sailor looked thoughtful. "I kind of lost my mind a little bit, to tell you the truth."

Ingrid took a sip of her mimosa.

Sailor brushed her hair over her shoulder and looked down at her hands. "I know what kind of person my mother is. She drinks too much . . . way too much. She's cruel and she takes pleasure in making people suffer. Instead of actually talking to her, Dad throws money at her business to give her some sort of structure so she doesn't flame out and make him look bad . . ." She trailed off.

Ingrid touched her arm.

Sailor gave her a frank expression. "I know it wasn't your fault, what Mom did. I knew it then, too; I just couldn't bring myself to admit it. I was so hurt and angry, but I just couldn't face the reality that my mother is . . . that she's not really a mother. So I took it out on you." She gazed at Ingrid, her eyes clear. "I was wrong, Ingrid. And I'm so sorry. You truly have a gift. And even after how I treated you, you used that gift to benefit me. I can't thank you enough. You're the best friend I've ever had."

Ingrid blinked in surprise. An image flashed before her, rose-tinted and in slow motion, like a dramatic movie: The three of them, Sailor, Cas, and Ingrid, gathered around a massive, twinkling Christmas tree in the Loefflers' drawing room, toasting their friendship. Thanksgiving, in the kitchen with the chef, sampling endless dishes, laughing and sipping cocktails. Lazing on the deck of the Tybee house, lulled to sleep by the sound of the rolling waves.

She had won. She had aligned herself with the power of the universe and manifested her will. She would always love Edie, but now, at last, she was a part of a real family.

She sat in the chair, so close to Sailor, feeling every inch of her body pulsating with that power. Her veins pumped it through her body, her lungs breathed it like air. She moved in alignment with the universe and with the Goddess. There was nothing she couldn't do.

Cas was right. She *was* scary.

Scary enough to face down both Scoot and Rill Loeffler. To protect Sailor and Cas, when the time was right. And to finally fix the things that had been broken when Edie was in her place, in the Loefflers' world. To finally make things right.

She was ready to do it all. More than ready.

Chapter 49

Ingrid knew she would have to be a lot smarter about how she orchestrated Rill's fall from grace than she'd been with Scoot—but the solution continued to elude her. In the meantime, she kept her head down and tried to be helpful to Sailor.

The answer would present itself in time. She truly believed that.

One sweltering afternoon, after a day spent giving readings, Ingrid changed into shorts and a tank top and walked up to the river. Despite the searing heat and thick humidity, the sidewalks were clogged with tourists. They carried water bottles or colorful drinks in plastic cups, or ice cream cones from Leopold's that melted as fast as they could lick them. As she neared the river, the breeze picked up, washing scents of salt, motor oil, and candy over her. She inhaled contentedly. She loved the riverfront.

Ingrid climbed the stairs to Boney's apartment. The door was unlocked and she walked in, surveying the filthy kitchen, the counter and sink stacked with dishes. She crept down the narrow hall and found Boney asleep on the sad mattress in his room. She shut the door behind her, latched it with the hook and eye latch, and took off her clothes. She dropped them on the bare wood floor along with the other items of clothing strewn around, eased herself under the sheet, and curled around Boney's sleeping form. He started, jerked awake, then rolled over to face her.

"Hi," he murmured. "I thought you were done with me."

She didn't answer, just settled into his arms and let the nerve endings register the cool smoothness of skin over muscle. He kissed her deeply. As she opened her mouth to him, her brain went pleasantly blank, and her body took over.

Afterward, they lay side by side in companionable silence. The noise of River Street floated up to them. Day-drinking tourists. Music from the restaurants. The horn of a container ship.

"Wanna smoke?" Boney asked.

"No." What she wanted was for him not to talk, but when she cracked open one eye, he was up on his side, propped on his elbow, watching her.

"You're back in the Loeffler fold, I hear," he said.

"Mm."

"How's Miles taking it?"

"He's taking it fine. He's happy for me."

Boney traced a finger along her collarbone. "He's not jealous?"

"He has nothing to be jealous of."

"What about Casimir?" He drew out the name in a sing-songy way.

She gave him a sharp look. "What about him?"

"Nothing. Just that I think he's got a crush on you."

She closed her eyes again. "Even if he did, Miles wouldn't care. You know that."

"I'm just worried about you."

"Why?"

"Because you've done all this magic you believe has actually had an effect on this family, and I think you're being completely delusional."

She sat up, glaring at him. "Excuse me?"

He gave her a sexy smile. "I said I think you're cuckoo for Cocoa Puffs, drinking your own Kool-Aid, and I'm worried what you're going to do next."

For a moment she searched his face, then turned away and scoffed. "You don't know anything."

"I'm sorry to break it to you, Ingrid, but Miles tells me—"

"What?"

"Enough to make me suspect he's given some of your spells a little extra . . . you know, zhush."

"A what?" She sat up.

"He's supplemented your spells with some extra help."

She felt cold all over. "You're crazy. He hasn't done that." She paused. "What did he say?"

"Nothing. Not in so many words. I'm just connecting the dots."

"What dots?" She stood up and stretched, feeling Boney's eyes on her naked back. She willed herself to stay calm as she sauntered across the room and picked up her underwear. What did Boney know that she didn't? What had Miles done?

Boney sat up and leaned against the dingy wall. "Come on, Ingrid. He definitely set fire to those boats down at Whitemarsh Island. And I'm pretty sure he got Scoot drunk at Peregrin and into her car."

"Scoot didn't need anybody to get her drunk." She pulled on her shorts. She picked up her top, but didn't put it on, enjoying the way she so easily held his attention without it. "She did that all on her own."

"Yeah, but some people said there was another person with her in the car when they ran off the road. A guy."

Right. The "young beefcake" Judge Norwood had mentioned who'd supposedly been drinking with her at Peregrin. It could've been Miles. If you considered him a beefcake.

"Scoot's not saying that."

"Well, she wouldn't, you know? Tell people that she was

drinking with some guy and then got in a car with him. She's no idiot."

Ingrid gave him a scornful look. "Scoot Loeffler would never drink at some random hotel *bar* with Miles Drummond. She's met him. She knows he's my roommate and my friend."

Boney lifted his eyebrows. "She's never met me."

She went quiet. Stared at him, dumbfounded. "Boney. What are you saying?"

He gave her a sheepish look. "Scoot likes to sneak out and drink at Peregrin with the tourists. No locals to snitch on her. Everybody who works at the Perry Lane knows about it. Mari has seen her there plenty of times."

"I've never heard that."

"You're friends with Sailor."

"Boney, what did you do?" Her voice trembled. Unbelievable that a few minutes ago she'd been pulling him deeper into her because now she would've liked very much to kill him.

He shrugged. "Miles asked me to buy her drinks for a couple of hours. Keep her occupied. So I did."

"Boney! Why the hell would you do something like that?"

"Miles is my brother, man. He's done a lotta shit for me. But all I did was buy her drinks and flirt with her. And then escorted her out a back door to her car, which I guess Miles had figured out how to get out of the garage where she keeps it—"

"What?" she shrieked.

"I didn't ask how he did it and I did not get in the car with her. I swear. Ingrid. I had no idea what he was planning."

She pressed the heels of her hands into her eyes and let out a growl of frustration.

"Also, Mari told me that a couple of weeks ago she let Miles into an empty room at the Doubletree where she works to use the shower. She said he was all sweaty and covered in grease, which I am now guessing was because he had been down in the engine room of a boat, fucking around with the wiring."

She pulled her top back on and scowled at him. "That doesn't mean shit. He could've been doing anything."

"At three o'clock in the morning?"

She felt weak all of a sudden, like her legs no longer wanted to hold her up. She dropped into the lone piece of furniture in the room, a lawn chair and looked out the window. A small prop plane buzzed the bridge. On the windowsill there was a picture of young Boney, maybe twelve or thirteen, his arm draped over a blond girl's shoulders. A sister maybe. She had the same sly, troublemaker smile.

"Why would he do that, though?" It was as if she was asking herself. "Help me? He's been so against them this whole time. So jealous of them."

Boney shifted uncomfortably. "You know I love the guy to death, but he's a tough nut. He's got, you know, this thing about the big-money people."

"All you guys do—"

"Right." He got very still. "And he worries about you, too, I guess."

"Yeah."

"I just thought you should know."

Even if Miles had set the fire or had gotten a blitzed Scoot behind the wheel, it didn't matter. She hadn't asked him to do any of those things so she couldn't be blamed, not by the police. And she had still nailed all that other stuff. The dress, the harpist, the flowers. That was all her.

She wasn't exactly happy about it—and yes, maybe it bugged the fuck out of her—but if Miles wanted to support her with a little boots-on-the-ground support, she didn't see why anyone had to know. If she had to, she would make it clear to him that he needed to stop. He would do whatever she asked. She was sure of it.

She glanced over at Boney. He was watching her.

"You know, I care about you, but I wouldn't commit a

bunch of crimes to make you think you were more powerful than you really are. I respect you too much for that."

Ingrid looked away, staring at the picture of little Boney with his smirky-looking sister. Lucky them. They had each other.

"I guess the question here is, what spell you're going to cast next, and are you okay with Miles helping to make it come true?"

"Fuck off, you jerk." She gathered her long hair up in a top-knot and stood. "I don't need to do any more magic, not for the Loefflers. And Sailor's forgiven me. I'm helping her plan her wedding. We're very close."

He sent her a resigned smile. "Great. That's great. I just think you better watch your back whenever Scoot gets cut loose from that rehab. If she happens to remember that Miles really was the guy who got her behind the wheel of her car that night, I guarantee she'll assume you were in on it—or at least know about it. And she'll be out for blood."

Ingrid swallowed nervously. "Sailor said she's allowed to come to the wedding before she goes back to a sober living house."

"If Miles is your plus-one, you could definitely give Scoot a heart attack at her own daughter's wedding. Which might be fun. Or, who knows . . . maybe she blacked out and has no memory of it."

She grabbed her fanny pack, and he waggled his fingers at her in a sarcastic goodbye. She considered one last parting shot . . . something full of snark and sarcasm, but when she turned back, he'd already buried his face back in his pillow. She sucked in her cheeks and headed to the kitchen, where she opened the fridge and took one of his beers. She left by the back door.

Miles wouldn't have dared to intervene in her spell work and not told her, would he? Letting her think she'd worked powerful spells when he'd gone behind her back and made it all happen? She didn't need her ego boosted like that. She could take the truth.

She cracked open the beer and gulped it as she strode up the cobbled alley toward the steep stairs. Edie had always said that magic was mostly dependent on your state of mind. Setting your intentions with care, believing in the things you want, giving yourself fully to the workings of the craft.

Ingrid had worked her whole life to fine-tune her practice. She didn't need Miles butting in. Her magic had done what it was supposed to do. When it was time to take care of Rill, she would be very careful. Her magic was powerful.

She was powerful.

But now, if Miles really had interfered and planned to again, she could find herself in a dangerous situation. If he was caught—she could be blamed for his actions—and everything she'd worked so hard for would be ruined. She couldn't allow that to happen. There was too much at stake.

Chapter 50

It turned out that Cas's schedule was booked solid until the wedding, so his and Ingrid's dinner date had to be indefinitely postponed.

Ingrid was disappointed, and part of her worried that Rill had gotten to Cas again, but she decided she wouldn't jump to conclusions. And besides, maybe he really was just busy. She didn't mind waiting. It would only make it sweeter when she and Cas finally got together.

In the meantime, she needed to figure out what she was going to do about Miles going to the wedding. She couldn't exactly wiggle out of inviting him—and it was as good a time as any to introduce him to the rest of the Loefflers—so one morning as they drank coffee in the kitchen, she plunged right in and asked him if he wanted to go with her.

He seemed genuinely excited about it. She did her best to seem upbeat as well. The fantasy of slow dancing with Cas would have to take a back seat to friendship and loyalty. It was a good thing, though. She really did want Miles to get to know the Loefflers. To love them as much as she did.

She offered to buy him a new suit, but he said that was a waste of money since he'd only wear it once, and the day before the wedding, he pranced through the living room, modeling her grandpa's collection of sixties and seventies-era suits. She tried to pay attention, to ignore the knot in her stomach, but she couldn't help worrying. Two days earlier, Scoot had been released from the rehab facility, and thus far, Ingrid hadn't heard much from Sailor about how things were going.

Was Scoot drinking or making trouble? Had there been any discussion between them about what happened that night at Peregrin? Had Scoot told anybody about the guy she'd been drinking with? About who'd been in the car with her? Did she even remember?

"What about this one?"

Ingrid turned her attention back to Miles, who had struck a dramatic model's pose by the fireplace. He did look nice in her grandpa's old deep burgundy suit with the light blue shirt, even if the lapels were a little too wide to be fashionable and the ruffle on the shirt was definitely over the top.

She considered once again asking him straight out if he'd been helping her spells along, but what good would that do? If he said yes, they'd fight. If he denied it, she'd know he was lying to her, and they'd fight about that. And did she really want to know? Maybe it was better she didn't. It would only mess with her confidence.

She smiled up at him. "You look great."

"You think?"

She headed to the stairs. "Of course."

"Thanks, Budge," Miles called after her. She gritted her teeth. She would not pick at him, not now. Tomorrow was the most important day of her life. Sailor and Jude's wedding was her chance to be there for Sailor. To show her that, in the end, no matter what sort of obstacles had been thrown in their way, their friendship was a lasting one.

Back in Edie's room—her room, Ingrid kept reminding herself—she studied the dress Sailor had helped her pick out for the wedding and, naturally, paid for. A black, strapless, taffeta gown, its full skirt printed with one enormous white peony. The expensive black stiletto sandals beside it made her sigh. As did her bedraggled reflection in the full-length mirror. All she wanted was to feel like she belonged. But what she saw in the mirror was an imposter.

"Beautiful." Miles stood in the doorway, nodding. He had taken off her grandpa's suit and put his shorts back on. His chest was bare, the blond curls on his head sticking up all over.

"The dress is," Ingrid said. "But I'll still look like a poor, low-class psychic even when I'm wearing it. Because that's exactly what I am."

"It's nothing to be ashamed of, Ingrid." Miles had a serious look on his face. "Being a psychic. Being poor. They're the ones who should be ashamed. The way they treat other people. The way they treat their own children."

Her stomach twisted. Miles didn't even know the worst of it. What Rill had done to Tess and to her. But she couldn't think about all that now. The wedding took precedence over everything, and she wasn't going to risk ruining Sailor's day. One thing at a time. After the wedding was over, when everything had calmed down, she would figure it out.

Miles fixed her with an unwavering look. "They're lucky to be graced with your presence."

She laughed. "Please."

"I'm serious." He took a step into the room. "But I don't know why you're acting like you can't do something about those people. Because I know, and you know you can. You can do whatever you want."

"No," she protested. "No more magic with the Loefflers. It's too risky. Something always goes wrong." She studied him, searching for a sign, but his face looked like it always did. Like an innocent but wild young pirate.

"What about a spell that would bind Rill and Scoot . . . just at the wedding?" he suggested.

"I don't think I can be that specific. I cast the spell, but it's the universe and the Goddess who truly control it."

"Then cast the spell," Miles said in an even voice, "and trust whatever happens next. Ingrid, you know who these people are. They won't be negotiated with. They have to be stopped. Especially Rill."

He was looking at her now, intently, like he knew something. Something he wasn't supposed to know.

"What do you mean?" she asked.

"I mean . . . because of what he did to Tess."

The dress felt like it was squeezing her now. She sat on a chair, a hand on her chest. "Who told you?"

"Dean. At brunch, after you left. He heard it from Miss Paulette, a long time ago."

Against her will, she felt tears threaten. "Yeah. That's who told me."

"Ah, Ingrid." Miles sat on the bed. "Why didn't you say anything?"

"I don't know." She shook her head. "It was just so awful.

"Rill Loeffler had no right to do what he did. To *your* mother. She was just a teenager. He needs to pay." Miles looked angry. And he was right. Rill *was* a terrible person and should pay for what he did to Tess.

But . . .

But she'd really liked the attention he'd shown Ingrid. At Sailor's party, at all the family dinners. All the times he would run into her in the house. He'd always looked at her like she was something out of his reach. No one had ever looked at her that way.

And part of her had liked it. Really liked it.

Miles spoke again. "Look, we have to go with what we know for sure. Scoot poisoning Edie was just a rumor. But we know for sure that Rill messed around with your mother when she was an underage girl. The last thing Edie asked you was to right the balance, right?"

Ingrid nodded.

"And that you should watch out for pirates. You can't tell me that she didn't know exactly what she was saying. She knew you were the only one who could stand up to the Loefflers. She knew that Rill Loeffler was a pirate, as mean and dirty as fucking Blackbeard himself, and she made you promise to make him pay."

Ingrid was quiet. He widened his eyes at her.

"You have to do it, Ingrid. She was counting on you to take care of him."

She hesitated. "I mean, I guess I could do a protection spell or a warding thing—"

"It has to be a hex," he said in a calm voice. "A death hex."

Her eyes widened then she shook her head. "Miles. No . . ."

"Why not?" He had a belligerent look in his eye, and his jaw was clenched. "You take him out, you solve everyone's problems. Sailor can be CEO. Cas can go live with his monks or whatever. And Scoot can inherit all his money and go work on her sobriety in peace."

"I've never done anything like that." She couldn't even say the words out loud, *death hex*. "I don't know if I can do it, to be honest." She spoke carefully. "And if I did, I wouldn't want anybody helping me."

Miles folded his arms. "What do you mean by that?"

She felt a nervous thrum inside her. "Nothing. Just that I would want it to be left up to the universe to decide . . . whatever fate was right for him." She swallowed with difficulty.

Miles stared at her. She stared back. The moment seemed to last forever, and then, at last, he lifted his chin and spoke in a low, fierce voice.

"If your spells needed help, Ingrid, you would not have the

thriving business you have. You got Sailor because you are good at what you do. And Edie knew how good you were, too. You have the power to fix everything, Ingrid. Never believe anything different."

She put the tips of her fingers to her mouth and let herself consider it, just for the briefest moment . . . Rill, six feet under at Bonaventure Cemetery. Sailor and Cas, free from their father's manipulations.

Still, she didn't want Rill dead, not really. There was good in him. Maybe he just needed a chance to be truly sorry for what he had done. Maybe all Rill Loeffler needed was a chance to see that Ingrid had come into the Loefflers' lives to right the balance.

"Ingrid." Miles squinted at her. "What's your deal with this guy? Why are you protecting him?"

"I'm not protecting him." She felt herself grow uncomfortably warm.

"Did he do something to you, too?"

"No. Miles. No."

His eyes flashed. "I swear to God, if he—"

"Miles, stop! Rill Loeffler hasn't done anything to me." She cleared her throat. "Maybe I could do a spell that lifts the veil of protection."

"What's that?"

"It would leave him open to . . . anything really . . . whatever—"

"Like what?" Miles demanded. "Like sickness or something? A heart attack?"

"Sure . . . or just doubt. Lack of confidence."

"Fuck that. What about a straight-up assault?" Miles's eyes gleamed. "Or jail."

Ingrid sent him a reproving look.

"I'm just kidding."

But she could tell he wasn't.

"We have to leave it up to the universe," Ingrid said.

Miles nodded. "Fine."

He hugged her and she clung to him tightly. He smelled like his usual mix of sweet and sour, and she suddenly wished she was a more experienced witch. That she could see more clearly into the future. She didn't know how she was going to balance her love for Miles with her need to be in the world of the Loefflers.

And there was a part of her—a small flashing light of warning buried deep in her gut that made her think they were all heading for a collision. A disaster of unexpected proportions.

Still, when she went to her old room, to the mantel where she found the red-and-gold fountain pen she'd stolen from Rill's desk the night of Sailor's party, she tried to believe this was the right thing to do. She would lift the veil from Rill and let Edie and the Goddess decide his fate. And, most importantly, she would not allow Miles to interfere in any way.

Gripping the pen tightly in her fist, she headed down to her altar room.

Chapter 51

The morning of the wedding dawned dew-washed and glistening. The scent of salt and pine and sunbaked surfaces rode the breeze. There were hardly any people out as Ingrid, dressed in Edie's old pajama pants and GREETINGS FROM SAVANNAH, GA T-shirt, emerged onto her front stoop.

Next door, on his own stoop, Dean Remington watered his begonias with a hose. He pushed his tortoiseshell glasses up his nose and waved at Ingrid. "Wedding day, is it?"

She smiled and waved back. "It is."

She'd been so busy since Sailor was back in her life that she hadn't seen much of Dean and Sheffield or Gloria and Harmon either. She felt bad about that. Later, when she was more secure in her place in the Loeffler family, she'd have all of them over for a wonderful dinner. Introduce them to the new and better generation of Loefflers.

"I thought the festivities started in the evening," Dean commented over the splash of the water.

"Sailor asked me to come by earlier, to be with her while she gets ready. It's a very stressful time."

"Ah." Dean looked at her with an expression she couldn't read. "I take it you've worked out . . . the other issue you were having. With the Loefflers."

"I think I probably overreacted that day in your garden," she said. "About all of that."

He looked doubtful, but thankfully let it go. "I hear Scoot's back home."

"Yes." Ingrid really didn't want to talk about this. "Sailor's very relieved. She really wanted her mother at her wedding."

"Good," he said. "That's good. Just . . ."

She lifted her eyebrows.

"Have fun," he said even though she was fairly certain that's not what he intended to say.

"Oh, I plan to," she replied.

He gave her a look of consternation, but she didn't stop. She needed to stay positive and focused. Today was an important day, in more ways than one.

The Loeffler mansion gleamed in the morning sun. It appeared that sometime in the night, a cleaning crew had washed the whole exterior. Now the place swarmed with a different sort of staff. Stylists, glam squad, caterers, photographers, and assistants buzzed through each room, up and down the stairs, communicating solemnly with one another on slim headsets. They were all dressed in black, all focused on one goal: preparing Sailor Loeffler for the moment when she and Jude would become husband and wife.

"She's been asking for you."

Ingrid turned to see the one person she'd hoped to avoid being alone with.

Scoot, the Great and Terrible.

The woman looked impossibly healthy, fresh-faced and clear-eyed, barefoot in silk pajamas and a matching kimono. Her toes were painted an extraordinary shade of bright blue.

Ingrid sucked in a deep, fortifying breath. "Nice to see you, Scoot. How have you been?"

Scoot gave her one of her signature sweeping looks, mentally tabulating every flaw Ingrid possessed. "I don't think we want to get into that, do we? I mean, we should focus on the future, right? On making sure today is a perfect day for Sailor, don't you think?" She smiled, maybe the most genuine smile Ingrid had ever seen on her.

Thank the Goddess.

She must not know about Ingrid's spell—and she must not remember that it was Miles who had been with her in the car that terrible night. Ingrid was in the clear.

Scoot leaned toward her and kissed the air beside her cheek. "On that subject . . . she's up in her room. That's all I'll say." The woman sailed off in the direction of the kitchen. "Good luck."

That definitely didn't sound good. Ingrid hurried up the stairs, nerves jangling. She knocked softly on Sailor's bedroom door then pushed it open a crack. "Sailor?"

The door flew open. "Ingrid!" Sailor was standing before her, also in pajamas, red-nosed and watery-eyed. Her hair was wet. "I'm so glad you're here!" She launched herself at Ingrid, clutching at her.

Ingrid hugged her back. "Sailor, what is it? What's wrong?"

Sailor didn't release her grip. "Poppy's sick."

Ingrid's brows knitted. "Sick? What do you mean, 'sick'?"

Sailor finally let go. "They admitted her to the hospital. Walking pneumonia."

"Oh no. That's awful."

"I know." Sailor wiped her eyes. "And she's my maid of honor. My lifeline. She knows everything. The order of the ceremony. Where the bouquets are, the rings—Mom's already sent Mrs. Leimberger over to her apartment to collect everything. It's fine. It's just . . . I'm really freaking out." Sailor glided across the room to an antique dressing table and sat.

Ingrid felt the sudden break in their connection. "Sailor, whatever I can do to help, just tell me. I'm here for you."

Sailor picked up a brush and started running it through her already combed out hair. She watched herself in the mirror.

"Sailor?"

The brushing continued. "Did you do something, Ingrid?"

"Do something?"

"Cast a spell." Sailor twisted in her seat to face her.

The shock of the accusation shot through Ingrid. She tried to swallow, but her throat had suddenly become uncomfortably dry. "No. No, Sailor. Of course not. I wouldn't—"

Sailor tilted her head, not smiling.

"I wouldn't do that again. I swear to you. I swear." Her voice broke.

Sailor's expression remained grim. "Ingrid, I have to know. You have to be honest with me."

"Sailor, I promise. I didn't do a spell."

Not on Poppy.

"Because if you did, I don't know what I'd do—"

Ingrid knelt on the rug at Sailor's feet. "Sailor, I'm begging you—"

She turned her face away. "Ingrid, stop—"

"I am begging you," Ingrid repeated. "You have to believe me. I did not cast a spell on Poppy. I would not do that. I know she's your friend. That you love her. I will do anything to make this day perfect for you. Anything. Just say the word."

Sailor heaved a sigh. "Get up."

Ingrid scrambled up. "I'm sorry," she repeated helplessly. She couldn't think of anything else to say.

"Don't be," Sailor said at last. She stood and went to Ingrid, clutching at her. "I'm the one who's sorry. I shouldn't have doubted you. I'm just . . ." Her breath hitched. "Ingrid, I really need you right now."

"Anything . . ." Ingrid said in a breathless voice.

"Be my maid of honor." Sailor looked into her eyes and Ingrid felt something leap inside her. It was triumph, she recognized. She had finally worked her way to a place right beside Sailor. She was almost there.

"Yes."

Chapter 52

Other than dragging on the floor a good four inches, Poppy's tiered, tulle-and-lace gown in a delicate shade of buff fit Ingrid perfectly. The length was easily remedied, thanks to the stylist, whose assistant promptly swooped in armed with needle and thread.

"Size seven, right?" The assistant handed Ingrid a pair of sky-high, silver stilettos she'd seemingly conjured from thin air. Ingrid slid her feet into the strappy platforms and wobbled across the room, holding up the dress. Her ankle turned and she swayed precariously.

"Perfect," pronounced the stylist.

"Perfect," echoed the assistant.

"Hem it, steam it, then get her into hair and makeup," the stylist ordered the assistant.

"Me?" Ingrid asked.

Sailor, on the other side of the room, having her hair blown out by a curvy brunette in a black jumpsuit, nodded. "We're all getting glam today, babe. And you should definitely get started. Madeline and Calla won't be here for another hour."

* * *

Getting glam, Ingrid discovered, was actually kind of a soothing process. She was patted, poked, and dabbed at with brushes, sponges, and fingers. She had her hair pulled and brushed and heated and curled then pinned and pinned and pinned. Her nails were shaped to points and polished with a glossy pink. Throughout the process, people kept offering her tidbits to eat: bagels with salmon, breakfast casserole, cheese biscuits with ham. Soda and water and glasses of champagne with straws in them so she wouldn't smudge her lips.

Two photographers snapped pictures of the entire process from every angle, sometimes including Sailor, but Ingrid felt almost too nervous to smile. These photos were going to be part of Sailor's wedding album, keepsakes she'd treasure forever . . . and Ingrid was included in them. It was almost too much to comprehend.

She was so overwhelmed she almost forgot about Miles, finally thinking to text him to explain she was in the wedding party, and he might not want to come since she would be busy helping Sailor and the other girls. She secretly hoped he'd decide to stay home, but he texted back that he still wanted to come, as long as that was all right with her. She assured him he was welcome, of course. What else could she say?

Madeline and Calla arrived with news of Poppy's condition—the poor girl was hooked up to an IV and by all accounts improving, but it was serious enough that her mother was flying in from Portugal where she'd been vacationing. The conversation quickly pivoted to eyeshadow shades, contour sticks, and illuminating drops. Scoot made an appearance, ignoring Ingrid and air-kissing Madeline and Calla. She inspected Sailor's intricate updo and suggesting a few adjustments, then took the seat her daughter had vacated.

Scoot gently stretched the skin of her face as she looked in the mirror. "You've got your work cut out for you," she said to the makeup artist.

"Mom," Sailor said. "You look beautiful."

"You've got to erase the weeks of absolute torture I've just gone through," Scoot said to the artist.

Sailor sucked in her cheeks but held her tongue.

After everyone was done, there were more rounds of photos of the party in various stages of undress, and then the squad hurried Sailor off to the adjoining bedroom to dress her and Scoot left to go put on her gown. Ingrid, too, was put back into the newly altered dress and stood before the mirror as the assistant fussed with the hem.

After what seemed like an eternity, the door of the bedroom opened again. There was a hushed gasp, then Madeline and Calla slowly rose from their seats.

Sailor stood in her dress, her eyes bright with tears, a smile lighting her face. The gown was simple yet stunning. An off-the-shoulder, pearl silk wool, with draping at the center front that fell into two swagged sleeves. At the center of the dress's neckline, a platinum, diamond, and ruby brooch in the shape of a bouquet of flowers was pinned—her something borrowed. Ingrid had never seen anyone who looked more elegant or more beautiful. Ingrid burst into applause and the others joined her.

After another endless round of photos, the group made their way downstairs and piled into the fleet of limousines waiting at the curb ready to whisk them the one block down to Forsyth Park. As they extricated themselves from the limos, Ingrid took note of it all.

The police barricades and velvet ropes cordoned off the north end of the park. Soft evening light filtered through the oaks and the lacy moss. A gentle breeze blew in from the river, with just enough force to produce a continual gentle shower of flower petals that drifted down on everyone's heads. Violetta, the harpist, played. The gathering crowd was seated in gold chairs lining the walk leading up to the fountain and the bower of blooms that arched over it.

Look, Edie. Look how far we've come . . .

From his seat on the back row, Miles, in her grandpa's old burgundy suit, spotted Ingrid and gave her his familiar grin. She smiled back at him, the fullness of her heart almost too much to bear. Hadn't he always been there for her? Always believing and trusting in her? If he really had helped her spells along, he'd only done it to help Ingrid get what she wanted. Because he loved her.

She should hold onto that love as tightly as possible.

"Ingrid?"

She turned. Rill, in his elegantly simple tuxedo, was standing a few feet away, gazing at her with an inscrutable look on his face.

She gave him a nod. "Hello, Rill. You're looking handsome."

His eyes lit up. "You're looking lovely yourself, if you don't mind me saying." He thrust his hands in his pockets. "I wanted to apologize for the other day. At Lombardy's. I got carried away. I hope you're not angry."

"No," she said. "I'm just very happy for Sailor. That's all."

"Good." He looked into her eyes, letting the gaze linger too long. "That makes two of us."

He was pulled away by one of the coordinators, and she caught sight of Cas then, standing apart from the wedding party. She inhaled swiftly. His trim tuxedo fit him like a second skin and his usually ruffled hair had been carefully styled. Scoot was standing beside him. She had her hand on his back and was whispering up into his ear, but Cas wasn't looking at his mother. His eyes were roving the crowd, searching. When they landed on Ingrid, he straightened, his eyes locking on hers.

She felt a thrill as he took in the sight of her, then broke into a smile. The next second, he was easing around Scoot and making his way in her direction.

"Beautiful," he said when he reached her. He leaned in and kissed her cheek. "You look incredible, Ingrid."

"Poppy was sick— " she began.

"I heard," he said. "Lucky Sailor, that you were there for her. Lucky all of us." He took her hand. "You're walking with me. I'm the best man." He led her toward the spot at the rear of the chairs where everyone was gathering, and she told herself to breathe.

Because there was Miles again, twisting in his seat, watching Cas lead her by the hand. He frowned momentarily, then turned back to face the fountain. Cas deposited her at the group where the coordinators Francesca and Courtland were organizing the processional. They distributed the bouquets of rare jade vine flowers, while bridesmaids and flower girls—who'd appeared from nowhere, looking adorable with their baskets of jade vine flower petals—cooed over each other and swapped compliments. No one spoke to Ingrid, but she was fine with that. Being quiet calmed her jitters.

The harpist launched into a new piece—"Hey Jude"—and Ingrid saw Jude, Cas, and two other men she'd never seen before step out in front of the fountain beside the purple-robed pastor. Jude looked handsome in his tuxedo, but nervous.

Courtland herded the trio of little girls toward the aisle and Francesca waved for the party's attention. "Ladies, over here please." Ingrid followed Madeline and Calla into position. At Francesca's nod, she started down the aisle toward Jude, mindful of the towering heels she was wearing. Beside Jude, Cas was now not even attempting to hide his delight at the sight of her, grinning like a kid. Ingrid felt the eyes of every one of the guests focus on her, and as if the sun was coming out from behind a cloud, she felt the light inside of her now begin to radiate outward. She felt its beams shooting in every direction, bathing the crowd in her happiness and glory.

Because it was glorious, this moment. It was everything she'd fought for in the past months. She'd sacrificed her own feeling of safety. She'd risked it all. And she'd done it for

Sailor. As she neared the fountain, she caught Cas's eye and smiled at him.

I gather you, Cas Loeffler.

I gather you to me.

I gather you for all time . . .

How could he resist the power coming from her? How could he resist the light? He couldn't. That was the answer, plain and simple. He was hers, and the details of what that meant were unimportant.

She had won.

Chapter 53

After the ceremony, friends of Scoot and Rill surrounded Ingrid, kissing and hugging her and admiring her beautiful dress. They exclaimed how glad they were that she was able to fill in for Poppy. How proud Edie would've been of her. How blessed Sailor was to have a friend like her.

In the clamor, she lost track of Miles, only to find him later at the dinner, at the Hotel Bardo, in the upstairs private club. He was surrounded by a group of strangers, definitely not guests of the wedding, doing shots. She hurried back downstairs before he saw her, secretly grateful she didn't have to babysit him.

After that she was swept back to the Loeffler mansion, up to Sailor's room to be fitted into Poppy's black satin and white lace reception dress. Assistants fluttered around her and the other women again, her hair and makeup retouched and re-fluffed, while photographers documented everything. When Sailor appeared in her grandmother Louise's remade dress, she squealed along with the others.

The silk shantung shortened to a structural mini was a show-stopper. When Sailor came over to give her a quick kiss on the cheek and whisper in her ear, "Nice dress you got me," Ingrid nearly bubbled over with joy. She practically floated downstairs and onto Cas's arm, who was waiting with Jude and the rest of the groomsmen to escort the women to the square for their introductions.

It was their first moment alone, since before the wedding, and he swallowed nervously, his voice almost so low she couldn't hear it.

"I need to tell you something, Ingrid."

Ingrid stilled. The look on his face made her heart swoop down in a dangerous arc.

"I wanted to tell you, face-to-face. Not ghost you, like before." Cas swallowed with difficulty. "It's going to be a while before we can see each other. I just have so much to do at the company. And I promised my dad . . ." His eyes went cloudy and skittered away. "I told my dad I would give my new job all my attention. Because that's what our family's company deserves."

"If that's what you want," she said.

He hesitated, seeming to search for words. "His support means everything to me. He's my father and I love him."

Ingrid waited. "So it's just for a little while, then? Later on we can hang out?"

His eyes locked onto hers. "Actually . . . he asked me to stay away from you. For good."

"Oh."

Cas nodded once then ducked his chin.

"You could still text me. I wouldn't mind that." She held her breath, willing away any tears, but she shouldn't have worried. There were no tears, just a blank, sort of disconnected feeling that enveloped her now.

He shook his head, blushing an intense pink. "We shouldn't do that either. I'm really sorry, Ingrid. I really am."

She stared at him, disbelieving. Rill had been right after all. Cas was immature and untrustworthy, and he would hurt her. He was doing it now.

Coward. He would never fight for what he wanted. He would never fight for her.

"Sure." She turned away, floating in that numb state, and let herself be pulled into the crowd.

After the official introductions of the wedding party and the bride and groom, and all the family dances, the two marquee bands took the stage.

Ingrid had been to a handful of concerts before, but only in the cheap seats in the nosebleed section of Enmarket Arena. Nothing could compare with the feeling of being right there in front of a band, feeding off the energy they were putting out and sending it right back to them. In spite of the hole that Cas just blown through her, Ingrid could still feel the electricity.

She joined Sailor and the other women on the dance floor, determined to forget her troubles and celebrate her friend. Drink in hand, she let out every ounce of her frustration to the pounding beat of the music. She drank and danced and drank some more, even taking a turn around the floor with Scoot during Earth, Wind & Fire's "September." The whole time she never caught a glimpse of Cas in the melee of bodies in the square—and she was grateful for it. She only wanted to think about happy things tonight.

I gather the light . . .

I gather the music . . .

I gather every single thing in this good world that I deserve . . .

When the DJ took over, she realized she was reeling and should probably find some water. She saw Boney, dressed in jeans and a T-shirt, signature top hat on his head, dancing with Calla. She pointed a playfully accusatory finger at him. He grinned, sent her an innocent look that said, *who, me?*

Back on the dance floor, Ingrid found herself once again spinning around the room, bouncing from group to group, dancing with all. At one point, she thought she saw Miles, dancing with a girl who looked familiar. A lot like the bartender from the Peregrin. *Dara, Danny* . . . she couldn't be bothered to remember. She danced on, and toward the end of the song, she abruptly found herself caught in a man's strong, assured arms.

Jude.

He smiled down at her and swung her into a dip. Ingrid yelped then burst into laughter.

"I think I'm drunk," she said.

"I was hoping I'd get a chance to talk to you," he said in his crisp accent. "Before Sailor did."

Ingrid frowned. "Why?"

"She's a bit nervous about giving you the news."

Her legs suddenly felt heavy and wooden. She was glad Jude was holding her. "What news?"

"She and I are going to London for a year after the honeymoon. I'm opening a new line of boutique hotels and she's going to help me."

Ingrid absorbed his words. Sailor, in England? It couldn't be true . . .

"Ingrid?"

"Oh, sorry. Congratulations." He spun her around.

"She knows how you depend on her." He gave her a little pat on the back. "But she'll be back. And you know, getting married does change things. See those blokes over there?" He nodded at a cluster of men in tuxedos, laughing and drinking. "I barely see them anymore. They've got their wives—husband, in one case—and children, and it's just what happens. But Sailor loves you, and you've an open invitation at our house in London, yeah?"

Someone pulled at Jude's arm, one of his friends, and Jude

released Ingrid. He nodded at her and she back at him, and then he was sucked back into the crowd. She watched him go, her heart knocking in her chest.

Sailor, gone . . . for a whole year?

She felt the long-awaited, hot tears pressing her eyes at last. A sob choking her throat. Why couldn't Sailor have told her this? They'd had all that time at the house before the wedding. And she wasn't even supposed to be there. When had Sailor planned to tell her?

First Cas, now Sailor . . .

She started back toward the house—to hide her tears, to hide herself—when she felt herself grabbed again, then enveloped in strong arms. Rill Loeffler was now holding her close, expertly maneuvering her to the edge of the square.

She clung to him. There was nothing else to do.

"Why, hello there." He encircled her lower back with one arm and spun her farther away to a secluded, shadowy corner of the park.

"Hi," she said in a hollow tone, lowering her chin against his shoulder.

He held her close. "My little, tipsy, pirate wench."

She said nothing. Figs and cognac mixed with pain overwhelmed her.

"Come on, it's a compliment, Ingrid." He whirled her around, deeper into the shadows. "You look like a fucking dream, you know that? In that little dress."

She couldn't even work up the emotion to enjoy the compliment. To be mad at him. She was empty inside. "You should keep your eyes on your wife," she said.

"I can look more than one direction at once. I don't wear blinders."

"Maybe you should."

He laughed. "Saucy, drunk, little wench. I guess you've heard the news about Sailor and Jude." He tightened his grip on her.

"Don't be sad about it, Ingrid. I've had an idea. A you-me-fly-to-Scotland kind of idea."

"What are you talking about?" She knew she sounded annoyed. Snippy, even, but she didn't care.

"My grandfather—the one who invented Savannah Sauce—joined a golf club in St. Andrews back in 19-whatever so he could play the world-class courses there. We own a cottage in Strathkinness . . . well, it's technically more like a castle than a cottage, but, whatever, semantics. We wouldn't have to play golf. In fact, I'm assuming you don't play—"

He guided her easily on the dance floor with strong, practiced arms. "I'm thinking a little hiking, sitting by the fire, reading books, and drinking good, single malt Macallan. We could sleep late, going to bed early . . ." He nuzzled his cheek against hers. And then this, softly, in her ear, "It's a surprisingly cozy castle."

She shook her head, but she had to repress the manic laughter that almost came bubbling up her throat. Maybe it was just a hysterical response to being propositioned right after she'd had her heart broken by both of this man's children. Maybe she secretly liked the idea that Rill wanted her.

Or maybe she was just a very bad person.

"Ingrid?" Rill said softly into her ear. "Are you mad at me? Don't be mad at me. Say something."

She steeled herself. If he wanted to play this game, she would. "You said you were the one who found the flowers Sailor wanted. And the harpist and the designer."

"Did I?" He looked amused. "I don't remember saying it exactly like that. You were pretty out of it that day at Lombardy's. I don't know if you remember."

"I remember," she said evenly.

"Okay, look. Fine. If I took credit for your work, Ingrid, I apologize. But I do like to think I had a hand in making this day perfect for my daughter. There's something else bothering you, I think," he pressed. "Is it Cas?"

She said nothing. He wouldn't get that from her.

He gathered her even closer. "Haven't you wondered why all he ever did was text you?"

She avoided his gaze.

"It's not because he's shy. It's because he has trouble with the real thing. The thing that no one should ever have a problem with when it comes to you."

"'The real thing.' What's that?" she asked, sending him a caustic eye roll.

"Sex," Rill said simply.

Chapter 54

"Normally, I would try to persuade Cas to be the one to tell you all this, but he's never going to be honest about it. He's a coward."

She had thought that less than an hour ago. Still, it angered her to hear him say it.

Rill shook his head. "Scoot and I have dealt with several other . . . situations. Jams he got himself into, associating with women he had no business with. Flying them to Europe for brunch . . . sending them designer clothing. And then there was the texting. Always the texting."

Ingrid felt so faint that she realized she was leaning on Rill's arms for support.

"Sexual stuff, yes, but more importantly, more dangerous to our family, promises. Promises he could never keep."

Promises. The word was like a knife. Cas had never made any promises to her, had he?

"At one point or another, when the time would come to follow through on those promises, he would run like a scared little boy. There was Finley, Sailor's friend . . ."

She stiffened. *Finley.* Of course.

"He promised her a family diamond. Then there was the daughter of a big coal family in Alabama. He told her she could have a job at the company . . . vice president of something, I don't know. Six-figure salary. Stock options. It was a mess. But yeah . . . in the end, all he wanted to do was to talk. He refused to lay a hand on her." He rolled his eyes. "My son, the celibate." He sent her a sidelong look. "The young lady was quite angry, to say the least. It got nasty, extremely complicated, and, in the end, very, very expensive for me."

She felt her lip quiver.

He looked resigned. "I love my son, and in no way do I judge him for his hang-ups, but I can't have him getting himself or this family dragged under a microscope. My job, the job my grandfather entrusted me with, was protecting Savannah Sauce. And to do that, I have to protect my family." He touched her cheek. "He hasn't been texting you again, has he?"

"No." It was true. Since the night in mid-August there'd been nothing.

"But you've talked since then, right?" Rill watched her closely.

"He's not going to do anything to displease you," she said bitterly. "Trust me."

"But I don't trust him. I see the way he looks at you. And I don't know how to stop this thing without turning it into some kind of Romeo and Juliet deal."

She held her breath.

"The strange thing is, I find, Ingrid . . ." He stopped moving and looked intently at her. "I find that I am unwilling to let my son break your heart."

Too late for that.

"I find"—Rill continued—"that I want you for myself."

She froze in his arms. It was as if her entire brain had just shut down.

"You can't be surprised. I told you at Lombardy's."

She nodded dully.

"Do you . . . have a reaction? Anything at all?"

Did she? How did she even feel about this man? She knew he was a bad person. Had done bad things. She also knew how other people would react if she took up with him. Even though he'd sent her away, Cas would be hurt. Sailor, too. But she'd be in London. Busy with her new husband.

But Rill Loeffler was here. Standing before her, offering her an alternative.

He was handsome. Charming. And incredibly rich. And she couldn't lie; she had always enjoyed the attention he gave her.

So what if this was the answer to everything?

The man who had started it all.

He was even closer to her now, his face inches from hers. "Just so you know, Scoot and I have an agreement. When she's released from sober living, she'll be moving to Tybee. To a condo I bought for her there. She won't make a fuss about anything I do. About us." His eyes looked like they'd been ignited by a blue flame. "I'm the one who can make you happy, Ingrid. I can and will take care of you forever."

She was quaking. And now realizing that she was also shaking her head. *No, no, no . . .* how could she do this? Even though Tess had abandoned her, could she really betray her own flesh and blood this way?

"What is it?" he demanded. "Tell me."

"Just something I heard," she said faintly.

"What?" He looked vulnerable, if that was even possible. "What did you hear?"

She closed her eyes. "That you slept with my mother when she was a teenager, and that's why she left Savannah."

He drew back, seemingly knocked off-balance. "Who told you that?" He held up a hand. "Wait. Don't. It was Dean Remington, wasn't it?"

Her heart was racing. She opened her eyes.

"Ingrid." He laughed but it was a hollow sound. "That man despises me. He always has. I won't bore you with the details but his family and mine . . . well, a long time ago there was a big kerfuffle over the origins of Savannah Sauce. His grandfather and my grandfather, they really had to duke it out. There was a settlement, but I think there's hurt feelings on his side. I'm just saying, he's seen how we've welcomed you into our family. He wouldn't hesitate to try and poison you against me."

At that word *poison* she extricated herself from his arms.

"Ingrid," he said softly, shaking his head.

Fix her little red wagon . . .

Ingrid pressed her fingers to her temples. Her thoughts whirled, crowding in on each other. Confusing her. "Dean wasn't the one who told me about you and Tess . . . but he did tell me something else. Something that Scoot did to Edie."

"That vicious little . . . still, after all these years with that fucking rumor." Rill shook his head, then lifted a finger. "Ingrid, listen to me. Scoot has her faults, believe me, but she would never do anything like that. She did not hurt Edie. Poison her, whatever Dean told you. And, for the record, I didn't sleep with Tess. Whoever told you that lied, too."

"I don't know who to believe." It was the truest, realest thing she'd said up to this point. She looked down at herself. The expensive dress that didn't quite fit her, the borrowed shoes. "I don't even know what I'm doing here."

He fixed her with an intense look. "You're here because I want you here. It's that simple. I've wanted you from the first time I ever laid eyes on you, that night at Sailor's party. I can't defend it, Ingrid, and maybe it's not right, but it's the truth."

He took her upper arms in his hands and searched her eyes. In the dim light his were a blue fire. His expensive fig and cognac smell overpowered her. He pressed his palm to her cheek. The palm where she'd seen the Via Lascivia. The line of lust. She imagined it burning a furrow into her skin. Branding her.

His voice came out silken and persuasive. "One word is all I need, Ingrid. One word and everything could change . . . for both of us."

She didn't know what she was feeling.

No, that wasn't right. She did know. She just didn't like it. Didn't want to admit it.

She was feeling relief.

Relief that if she agreed to Rill's proposition, she wouldn't be left out in the cold. She would be safe forever. From bills, from taxes, from any and every disaster that lurked just around the corner. She would never have to worry about money again. About *anything* ever again.

The thought of that, the reality of it, was overpowering, like a wave that knocked you over as you waded into the surf. That first bloom of well-being you felt with alcohol or weed when the chemicals flooded your brain. Her legs had gone weak and watery.

Fig and cognac . . .

They represented safety and strength, she realized. She imagined what it would be like to be enveloped in that fragrance forever—and instantly she knew.

It would be wonderful. Perfect.

This is what Edie should have done when she had the chance. Accepted Rill's love, his care and his offer of protection. Everything would've been different. Rill wouldn't have turned to Tess. He and Scoot wouldn't have spent a lifetime torturing each other and their children.

Edie wouldn't have died.

Ingrid felt her thoughts slow, to begin to reorder themselves. The light was piercing through the alcoholic fog in her brain.

She saw it all so clearly now. She hadn't been brought into the Loefflers' lives for Sailor or for Cas.

No.

It had been for Rill. Rill, all along.

All she had to do was say yes and she knew that would right all balances, once and for all.

"Ingrid? What's your answer?"

Chapter 55

"I have to think."

She heard herself say the words and was surprised that she was being so measured. But it was the right thing to do. This was the biggest decision she'd ever made in her life.

She felt strangely torn when he released her. Like already they were a whole.

"Meet me in thirty minutes, in the house. In my study," he said. "No one will be there. We can discuss the particulars."

She nodded and he gently pushed her away. She turned and began to walk away, feeling him watch her go. She could feel how serious his face was in the soft moonlight. How good it felt to be the one who was desired above everyone else. She'd never experienced that before. Not in this way.

She went to get water, and as she drank it, she almost choked.

Oh Goddess . . .

Oh shit.

She'd cast that spell on Rill—the lifting of the veil of protection. Which wasn't exactly the worst thing in the world, but it wasn't the greatest either. She should undo it. Fast. And talk to

Miles so he didn't do anything stupid and try to help her magic along—

Oh shit, shit, shit. Miles . . .

Her brain finally pushed past the alcohol and now, her heart skittering, panic level rising, she scoured the square. Miles was nowhere in sight. She was already chanting under her breath: *uncross, uncross, uncross . . .* remembering something Edie told her once. How to undo this particular spell. There were purifying baths, rituals involving black salt and hyssop and mirrors. She also said you could recite the 37th Psalm. Ingrid googled quickly and read off her screen.

. . . better the little that the righteous have than the wealth of many wicked; for the power of the wicked will be broken, but the Lord upholds the righteous . . .

She should have Rill recite the psalm later when they talked. She'd make up some kind of reason for it. Right now, she had to find Miles. Find him and stop him before he possibly did something stupid.

It was fully dark now, the shadows obscuring the square, making it almost impossible to see anyone's face clearly. Ingrid wound her way through the crowd, searching for Miles, asking everyone if they'd seen a guy in an old-fashioned, burgundy suit.

When she was near one of the outdoor bars, she saw Cas.

"Hi, you," he slurred.

She met his eyes. He looked sweaty and flushed. She stepped away from him.

"I'm heading over to the house to use Sailor's bathroom. Bridesmaid privilege."

"Come find me when you're done. You owe me a dance."

"Leave me alone, Cas."

His mouth opened, a crestfallen look on his face.

"You said we're done, so we're done. And now you have to leave me alone."

He lifted his hands. "Fine." He turned his back on her and stalked away.

She stared after him. It didn't matter. How many women had he toyed with before her? How close had she come to being just another piece of trash to be lied to, then discarded, by Cas Loeffler? She'd wasted enough time. She was finally on the right path.

She sped up her search, scouring every corner of the square. After what seemed like forever, finally pointed her to the Temple Mickve Israel, where she found Miles, sitting with Boney on the imposing stone steps. As she approached them, giddy with relief, Boney waved, and she saw they were passing a joint between them.

"Princess! What a wonderful party your darling richie friends have thrown for the proletariat."

"Guys, really? The temple steps?" She scanned the area for cops, then glanced at Miles. He'd taken his jacket off, her grandpa's jacket, and it was balled up beside him like an empty bag of potato chips. She couldn't make out the expression on his face. He looked strange. She hoped he hadn't seen her dancing with Rill. She wasn't ready to explain that situation.

"It's fine," Boney said, leaning back and inhaling with deep concentration. "Seems like lots of rules are being broken tonight."

She gave him an *eat shit* look. "Just can't stay away from the richies, can you, Boney?"

"Not when they're providing free libations." He lifted up his glass of brown liquor and elbowed Miles, who passed him the joint. "And I'm Tristan tonight, by the way. Upstanding citizen of Savannah, Georgia."

Miles was studying her. "Where have you been?"

"Around." She tilted her head, eyeing him back. What was

wrong with him? He looked so glum. "Can we talk? In private?"

On the other side of the square, a uniformed cop was heading in their direction. Boney pinched the joint and dropped it on the step. Miles smoothly pocketed it, as Boney stood and saluted them.

"I'm off to find my own princess. Wish me luck."

The cop was closer now and laser-focused on Boney. "Sir, I'm going to need you to move along now."

"I'm a guest," Boney protested.

The cop jutted his chin. "Move it, Boney."

"I'm going, I'm going. Jesus." Hands jammed in his pockets again, he started off toward the river. The cop watched for a few seconds, nodded at Miles and Ingrid, and ambled back toward the square.

Ingrid shook her head. "I told you not to bring him."

"He just showed up. What was I supposed to do?" He leaned back on both elbows and his head lolled back, as if taking in the stars over the square in the Savannah night sky. He was slurring the slightest bit. Sweat glistened on his temple.

"Fine, whatever." She swallowed nervously. "I need to talk to you, Miles."

"What about?"

"About the spell I did yesterday."

"Now what spell would that be?" He sounded a million miles away. Or just really high.

She lowered her voice. "You know."

"Oh, right." His heavy-lidded eyes found hers. "The death hex on Rill."

"No," she said slowly. "It was a lifting of the veil of protection. Not a death hex, Miles."

"'*Not a death hex, Miles,*'" he mimicked in a high-pitched Southern drawl, then smiled dreamily at her. "You really are a budgie, aren't you, Ingrid?"

What was this horrible, sinking fear making her heart skitter and her mouth feel full of sand? "What's that supposed to mean?"

"Budgies are little birds. Little pets." His eyes bored into hers. "Pets that mimic their masters."

She felt her throat constrict. "I'm no one's pet."

Miles shrugged. "I tried to tell you that you were better than them. That you should take what you could and not get so involved. But now"—his gaze swept over her dress, which probably cost more than anything she'd ever worn—"look at you. You've gone and become one of them."

Chapter 56

Miles hummed quietly to himself as he picked at a fingernail.

She sat beside him and studied his face, slack and cold. What was wrong with him? Why was he being this way?

"I'm not one of them. And it was a spell I cast on Rill," she repeated. "Not a hex."

"I guess we remember it differently."

A sick feeling settled in the pit of her stomach. "Why are you being this way, Miles? What's going on?"

He leaned back on one elbow, his gaze roving the crowd before them. "You came looking for me, so why don't you tell me?"

She concentrated on keeping her voice steady. "I think the spell I did was wrong. *I* was wrong. I shouldn't have done it."

He got a weird look on his face, then turned away from her. "Why would you say that? I thought we agreed. Rill slept with your mother when she was a minor. He's a fucking pedophile."

"Miles." The sick feeling in her stomach was hardening into a knot.

He shrugged. "Why are you telling me this, Ingrid? Tell your Goddess or whoever. Or go back home and reverse the spell. If you can."

He turned back to her. His eyes were cool and blank. It was a look she'd never seen. Miles always had that innocent, eager to please, puppy-dog appearance that lit up his whole face. Now she felt like she didn't recognize him at all.

She clenched her jaw, willing herself not to shout at him. Or to burst into tears. "Are you mad at me?" she asked.

"So what if I am? Why would you care? You have plenty of new friends."

"Miles, stop being like this. If you're mad at me, say so."

He was quiet for a moment. "No, I'm not mad at you. I would be afraid to be mad at you."

Her mouth opened then shut. "Afraid? Why?"

"Of what you'd do to me."

She shook her head. "I would never do anything to you. You know that."

Now he turned to her, gazing at her fully. "Do I?"

"Of course, I'm sure. Miles. You know I would never . . . I don't even think I have the ability. Come on. You *know*."

"What do I know?"

"That it's not all me," she said hotly. "That you sometimes like to help me out. With the spells."

He studied her face for a moment, then let out a harsh laugh. "I don't know what you're talking about."

She tilted her head. "You do. Miles. Boney told me everything. About Scoot at Peregrin. That you set the fire at the marina."

He was shaking his head. "I had nothing to do with that."

"Miles, it's okay. I'm not mad at you. I appreciate everything you've done for me, I do—"

"I haven't done anything for you, Ingrid," he said evenly. "It's *you.* All you. All your magic. *Your* spells. You've done it all. Alone, start to finish."

Ice filled her veins, raising goose bumps all over her body. "Miles, I don't understand."

He regarded her coldly. "What I don't understand, Ingrid, is why you're chickening out after how far you've come. After everything Sailor's done for you and everything you've learned about her family."

"I'm not chickening out—"

Miles appraised her coolly. "I saw you two dancing."

Ingrid froze. "Miles—"

He blew out air through his lips and shook his head. "I knew he was going to do something like this. I bet he really laid it on thick, didn't he? I bet he told you you were beautiful and said you two could work something out on the side."

She rolled her eyes.

"You think you're so hot because Boney sleeps with you. Because Cas has a crush on you. But you're not. You're just a circus freak to them. They want to sleep with a witch, Ingrid, because they think it's kinky or something. And Rill. Jesus, you gotta know it's just some disgusting fetish to him, trying to get you . . . to whatever. He went after your mother and your grandmother, that sick fuck. And now I guess he's going for the grand slam—"

"Shut up!" Ingrid yelled. "Shut up!"

"Don't go to him, Ingrid," Miles said in a low voice. "Don't do it." His eyes were locked on her, and she felt suddenly as if she was standing before him naked. Stripped of any pretense or lie.

"But Miles." Her voice was a plea. "Don't you see? It will fix everything."

Then, in some imperceptible but real way, his face changed. It was as if he became a stone replica of the Miles she had known and loved. He was a stranger to her now.

Fear coursed through her. A deeper fear than she'd ever known. "Miles, please. I'm begging you—"

"What?" he snapped, eyes flashing a warning. "What are you begging me for, Ingrid? What do I have to give you?"

"Please . . . just stay away from Rill."

They locked eyes.

He stood.

"Miles."

He turned away from her and sauntered into the street, backlit by the fairy lights and the throng of dancing people. He was leaving the party but not headed back to the house. He was headed up toward Broughton Street. Back to town. But he'd left his jacket on the steps.

She grabbed the coat and ran to him. "Miles!"

He turned back, his face hard again, and stiffly took the jacket from her. "You better run home and undo your spell before all hell breaks loose," he said. "Before he changes his mind about you."

He walked away. All she heard was the DJ's music—a Drake song now—and the screeching of the drunk, dancing guests. A faraway siren, coming from down by the Riverwalk, wailing on its journey to someone in need of help. She felt the sudden absence of air in her lungs, and dully wished the ambulance was coming for her. She reached for something to steady her. There was nothing around her, so she clasped her own hands.

But they were wet. Tacky from Miles's jacket. It was too dark to see what the substance was, but she recognized the smell. The scent of copper.

She looked across the square, over at the Loeffler mansion. Its newly washed walls gleamed in the dark, its windows glowed. She looked back at the dancing crowd. Everyone was doing a line dance now. She caught sight of Sailor at the lead, in her grandmother's dress, shimmying beside Jude. He had one arm around his bride and with the other was waving his jacket over his head. Scoot was standing nearby, beside a gray-haired man Ingrid didn't recognize. Maybe her lawyer. Her hand was on his arm, her lips close to his ear. Rill was nowhere to be seen.

Oh no. She looked at her hands again just as light flashed from someone taking a picture with their phone. Her hands were streaked with blood.

No, Miles . . .

She sprang up from the temple steps and, skirting the edge of the square, she sprinted in the direction of the Loeffler house. Running up the front steps, she threw open the door and stepped inside. The front hall was dark. Shadowy and still. So different from the wild celebrating taking place just steps away. She shut the door carefully behind her and walked quietly through the two drawing rooms to Rill's study.

She pushed the door open.

One lamp burned on the far end of the room, making the room look dramatic, like a scene set up for a movie. On a small table beside a leather wing chair, she saw an uncorked bottle of wine and two filled glasses.

She glanced around the room. "Rill?" Her voice sounded small and scared.

There was no answer.

She walked to the table. Looked at the glasses. "Rill, I'm alone. It's safe."

She looked out the large bay window, noticing the odd way one panel of curtains was pushed back against the wall. She walked around the end of the tufted chesterfield and felt her legs buckle under her and her vision swim.

It was hard to believe what she was seeing.

The horror.

The curtain had been snagged, caught and held by one of the two bodies that lay on the floor, draped over each other, face up, in the shape of an X. A bloody X, as two thick rivers of blood ran from each of their heads, splitting into two branched waterfalls that splashed over their skulls and pooled on the rug beneath them.

Chapter 57

Ingrid remembered her screaming. Her panicked hyperventilating. The way she began darting around the library as if she was searching for something or someone to wake her up and banish the bad dream in which she was locked.

She also remembered Mrs. Leimberger, shouting in her face. Arms holding her, a blanket thrown across her shoulder. Police. Flashing lights and sirens that had come for her after all. That was when she heard Sailor's and Scoot's screams. Those were the worst.

The seeds of an unfolding nightmare she couldn't escape.

In the end they had to give her a sedative—the paramedics who were working in the room—because no one could contain her. She kept running, screaming incantations. Calling for Edie, calling the corners, and casting imaginary circles. All she knew was that she had to do something. Do some ritual, gather the light from somewhere in this vast house of shadows and sin.

When she felt the pinch of the needle, there were more arms to take her to a bed.

She woke a long time later in her old room, how many hours

or days had passed, she couldn't say. She was wearing crisp, men's-style pajamas. There was a carafe of water with a glass over the opening. She poured and drank two glassfuls then struggled up to lean against the pile of pillows.

That's when she remembered the gory X. Two bodies, lying over each other. Blood, rivers of it, soaking tuxedos and the fine, antique rug beneath them like someone had emptied buckets of it over them. And they *were* dead. She'd seen a dead body before. Edie, gnarled and twisted from the pain of the cancer, skeletal and clenched from her fight. She knew what death looked like.

Both of their eyes had been open, like Edie's, staring out of blook-soaked faces. Staring at her, she felt. Father and son, Rill and Cas, and she knew . . . she knew Miles had done it.

He'd done it because of her. To avenge her mother. To prove his loyalty. To help her spell along.

Except she'd changed her mind and told Miles she was going to undo the spell.

And she hadn't hexed Cas at all. She would never . . .

Even after she'd begged him not to, Miles had gone and done it anyway . . . that's what she couldn't understand. But then she realized her mistake. No. He'd obviously done it even before she'd found him on the synagogue steps, smoking the joint with Boney. He'd done it, not for her, but for himself, because he'd seen her dancing with Rill. He'd seen and known what was happening. That he was about to lose her.

She was suddenly overcome with the weight of all of it. The image of the bloodied bodies. The neat holes in their heads spouting those twin rivers of blood. Their staring eyes. She felt something rising in her, a swirl of panic and terror. The same feeling she'd had last night—the urge to run and run, away from the looming horror of what she'd set in motion. Of what would most certainly be coming back on her. She could never escape the Law of Three. She may not have hexed Rill, but she'd wished harm on him. She'd opened him up to harm, and already she had received the first of the consequences of her actions.

The vortex of horror in her chest moved up her throat, and she was unable to deny the force. She opened her mouth and an unearthly sounding howl came out. The door flew open and Mrs. Leimberger, in her usual gray suit, sleek bob, and glasses, appeared. Her face was shocked and pale. Her glasses slipped down her nose.

"Miss White?"

Ingrid dissolved into sobs and turned her tearstained face away from the woman. "They're dead," she moaned into the pillows.

Mrs. Leimberger moved to the bed and was quiet for a moment. "I'm afraid so."

Ingrid twisted to her, her face wet and red and contorted. "Where's Sailor? I have to see her."

Leimberger shook her head. "She's with her husband. Downstairs. Miss White, please. You have to calm down. You're not the only one in this house."

Ingrid absorbed this. "Scoot?" she asked in a more subdued voice.

Another shake of the head. "Mrs. Loeffler was escorted back to the . . . facility last night."

Oh Goddess. How cruel. Even Scoot didn't deserve that . . .

"The police are here," the woman said.

Ingrid lay back on the pillows, distraught. Sailor was alone. Yes, she had Jude, but she was without a single member of her family. And it was all because of her. This was Ingrid's doing.

"I'll send up breakfast." Mrs. Leimberger moved to leave.

"I want to see her." Ingrid flung off the covers and swung her legs around to the side of the bed. She felt dizzy; maybe the drugs they'd given her hadn't fully worn off. "I want to see Sailor right now. Where is she?"

Mrs. Leimberger hurried to her, arms outstretched as if to put her bodily back in the bed. "Oh no, Miss White. You need to rest. To eat. And to let Miss Loeffler—Sailor—do the same."

"But she's all alone."

"She has her husband."

Ingrid's body sagged and she returned to her spot against the pillows. "I just want to help."

Mrs. Leimberger straightened the covers over her. "Soon enough. One step at a time. First, breakfast. And then, the police. They want to speak to everyone. Particularly you."

She left, and Ingrid lay back, her pulse racing. She had to see Sailor. Was her friend thinking Ingrid had had anything to do with Rill's and Cas's deaths? Was she somewhere in this house, hysterical, blaming Ingrid like she had with Scoot's accident? She had to find out what was going through Sailor's mind before Leimberger sent one of her minions up with a breakfast tray.

She jumped out of bed and hurried to the door, slipping out into the hallway. She felt jittery and lightheaded. She was on the top floor, down the hall from the room where she'd first met Cas at Sailor's engagement party. Where she'd had that first conversation with him. A sob made its way up her throat, and she clapped her hand over her mouth to stifle it. She didn't have time to carry on.

She ran down the stairs, keeping close to the wall, listening for any approaching footsteps. On the second floor, she could hear voices. The police in Rill's study on the floor below. The crime scene investigators. Finding Sailor's bedroom door, she knocked but there was no answer. She pushed the door open and peered inside. The room was dim and in disarray, strewn with clothes and dishes of half-eaten bagels and flutes of flat champagne. Sailor and Jude must've slept somewhere else.

There were four bedrooms on this floor, each occupied by one member of the family. Sailor might be in either of the other three, though she couldn't imagine which one. She slipped down the hall, peeking into Scoot's room, done all in lavish golds, then Rill's, with its masculine plaids. Sailor wasn't in either. She tapped softly on Cas's door then slowly pushed it open.

Jude, shirtless but still wearing his tuxedo pants from the previous night, slouched in a chair by the window. He looked up when Ingrid entered the room.

"You just missed her," he said tonelessly. "She went upstairs looking for you."

Ingrid ran back up the stairs. At the landing between the floors, she saw Sailor and flew into her arms. The two clung to each other, trembling and crying. Sailor was in a T-shirt and leggings. She smelled rank, like sweat and alcohol and dirt. Smeared makeup creased her forehead and ringed her eyes. She hadn't even washed her face. She was heaving out sobs and fragments of sentences.

"I can't . . . they don't . . . why would . . . ?"

Ingrid held onto her as tightly as she could. "I'm here, Sailor. I'm here. I'm not going anywhere. We're going to find who did this. We're going to make them pay."

Sailor finally turned her loose. This close, in the light of the window on the landing, Ingrid could see how puffy and red her face was. How huge dark circles ringed her eyes. Ingrid had never seen her look this destroyed.

"The police want to talk to us," Sailor croaked.

"I know. Mrs. Leimberger told me. Will we have to go down to the station? I need to go home. Shower and dress and feed Litha— "

"No," Sailor said, a wild, unhinged look in her eyes. "They won't make us go to the station. They'll talk to us here. But Ingrid, please . . . I don't want you to leave. I need you. I need you here with me. Can Miles take care of the cat? Can you stay?"

There was a loud bang, like a piece of furniture had been

toppled, then the slamming of a door. Startled, Sailor jumped, then burst into a fresh round of hacking, hiccupping wails. Ingrid embraced her.

"Of course," Ingrid said. "Of course I'll stay." She held her friend at arm's length and looked deeply into her wrecked eyes. "I'm not going anywhere, Sailor. I'll never leave you."

Chapter 58

Back in her room, Ingrid found her phone charging on the desk. She checked her messages. Only a few potential clients, asking for appointments next week. Nothing from Miles.

She choked down the eggs and bacon and toast Mrs. Leimberger sent up, chugged the coffee, then took the hottest shower she could stand. She found the clothes she'd worn the previous morning laundered and folded neatly on a chair. She dressed as a knock sounded at her door.

"Come in," Ingrid said, and a group of three men and one woman entered. She recognized two of them. Judge Norwood, the man who'd handled Scoot's case, and Brooks Glover, the family's lawyer. The two others she didn't know.

"Ingrid," the judge said, offering his hand. She reached out, grasped it, and shook it limply, even as his eyes darted away from hers. "This is Detective Ray Shannon with the Savannah PD." He indicated a middle-aged man, portly and bald, bursting out of an ill-fitting blazer and tie. "His partner, Detective Heather Lowe." This was a tall woman, younger than her partner, and a lot prettier, with blond hair in a ponytail and no trace of makeup on her angular face.

Ingrid nodded at both detectives.

"Ingrid, hello," said the third man, about the same age as Norwood, slim and distinguished, with silver hair and a tasteful waft of aftershave emanating from his expensive suit. His accent was thick Southern molasses, like Clemmie Fairburn's and all the other Savannians of that older generation. "I'm Brooks Glover of Glover Gilchrist Townsend."

"We've met," she said.

He sent her a blank, bland smile, the kind of smile men in his position bestowed on forgettable, lower-class, young women like her. Of course, Brooks Glover didn't remember her.

"Brooks is going to sit in while the detectives interview you about last night," said Judge Norwood. She noticed he was in golfing attire. He'd been called in at the last minute by Sailor or Scoot, no doubt. "I'll be here, too, as a friend of the family. Just to make sure all the i's are dotted and t's crossed."

The detectives exchanged a look in which Ingrid thought she detected barely suppressed annoyance. Or possibly resignation.

"Shall we sit?" asked the woman.

They sat on the chairs arranged around the fireplace. Shannon pulled out a notepad. Lowe just crossed her legs and stared at Ingrid.

"So you're a psychic by trade?" Detective Shannon asked.

Ingrid smoothed her jeans. "Psychic-witch, technically. I do readings—palm, aura. I took over my grandmother's business when I was eighteen years old. After she was diagnosed with cancer."

Everyone was quiet.

"I don't mean to speak out of turn," she went on. "But I'm happy to be of assistance in the investigation in whatever way possible. I know quite a few police forces use psychics to solve cases." She shut her mouth, wondering where that had come from and suddenly feeling like she'd accidentally blundered over some sort of invisible etiquette line. She was nervous. She should be more careful.

"Never used a psychic in one of mine," Shannon said mildly as he jotted something down. "But thanks for the offer."

Ingrid nodded.

Lowe studied her thoughtfully. Detective Shannon was obviously the straight guy. Lowe, the reader. The one who picked up on a vibe, who noticed the shifting of eyes or the slight hesitation before an answer. The woman was probably psychic and didn't even know it.

In that moment, Ingrid's head cleared, and she knew exactly how she was going to play this interview. This *reading*. Because that's what it was.

She cleared her throat and turned to Shannon. The guy in charge. "I know you're probably wondering what I was doing in Rill's study during the reception."

She saw Brooks Glover and Judge Norwood both stiffen as if choreographed. The fixers. They were the ones who were going to have to clean up this mess. They just didn't know how big a mess it was going to be.

"I just want to come right out with it because it feels wrong to hide anything."

Alarm filled Glover's face. He opened his mouth to say something, but she continued before he could, focusing on Shannon.

"Rill Loeffler and I were acquainted. I met him earlier this spring, through his daughter, Sailor. He was always kind to me. Thoughtful. He included me when many people of his . . . position in society probably wouldn't." She cleared her throat. "Unfortunately, Scoot wasn't as welcoming. I think there's some history with her and my grandmother . . ."

"Go on." Shannon was scribbling furiously.

"For the past few months, I have been carrying on a relationship . . . of sorts . . . with Cas Loeffler. Not dating exactly, but something close. Sailor and Scoot both knew about it, and I believe it gave Scoot another reason not to like me. I'll admit it's been kind of"—she glanced at Glover—"sexual in nature, our texting, but nothing physical actually developed. You'll find it in his phone if you look. Not under my real name but probably 'Saint.'"

"Your generation," mumbled Detective Lowe, "y'all don't really go in for the in-real-life thing, do you?"

She turned her eyes to study Lowe's aura. In the spirit world, she saw a small group of people circled tightly around the detective. The woman didn't have much family left, but the ones she did have were important to her. *She'll do anything to protect them.*

"If Rill and Scoot Loeffler were your parents," Ingrid said to Lowe, "I'd imagine you'd have your share of neuroses as well. I try not to judge people who are just trying to make it through their lives as best they can."

The room went quiet. Ingrid resettled herself.

"Go on," Shannon said.

"Recently . . . well, a couple of weeks ago, I was made aware . . ." She slowed her words. "I was made aware by Rill Loeffler that he . . . that he was actually attracted to me himself."

Shannon's head jerked up. One side of Lowe's mouth curved up in a disbelieving smile. Brooks Glover looked startled. Judge Norwood let out a long sigh and turned to the window.

"When he first told me of his feelings, I declined his offer. He's married. But then, last night, at the reception, he said his situation had changed. He said that Scoot was moving out permanently. He suggested that I accompany him to Scotland for several days so we could explore the possibility of starting a relationship."

Now everyone was openly goggling her. Even in the midst of her grief, she felt an inappropriate burst of laughter trying to escape her. It was so strange, this feeling of swooping through the air, suspended by only a wing and a prayer. She felt high.

"He said his grandfather belonged to a golf club over there." She looked around. No one was moving, but now Judge Norwood's and Brooks Glover's expressions had both gone sour, their eyes narrow in disbelief.

"He mentioned a cottage . . . a castle . . . where we could stay."

"No kidding," Lowe said.

Ingrid glanced at Judge Norwood. "In Strathkinness. Yes."

Glover coughed.

Ingrid addressed Lowe. "I knew it was wrong, and I know I'm airing dirty laundry here, but I think it's best to tell the truth. He said he and Scoot had an agreement, that she was moving to Tybee when she got out of her . . . current situation . . . and he wanted me as his mistress."

"And what did you say to him?" Lowe asked.

"I said I had to think about it."

"What about Cas?" Lowe asked.

Ingrid went quiet. Looked down at her fidgety fingers. "He didn't want me."

"And you were in love with him?" Lowe asked.

"With Cas?"

"No," Lowe said steadily. "With Rill."

Ingrid hesitated. "No. I was not in love with Rill, but I was attracted to him. And I believed that it could possibly turn into more, on my end."

"How romantic," Shannon muttered.

"Not every relationship has to be romantic. Lots of situations are arranged or just decided on for pragmatic reasons."

"And what about Miles Drummond?" Shannon asked.

"Oh." Ingrid looked around at the men. "You know him?"

"We know him," Shannon said flatly.

"Miles and I aren't . . . we're just roommates. Friends. Not romantically involved."

They watched her. She resisted the smile that was trying to spread across her face. They had come into this interview expecting to have to ferret the truth out of some trashy, low-class, sidewalk witch, but she'd turned the tables on them.

She'd told the truth, given them everything they could possibly want, and more, and now they had nowhere to go. She might technically have secrets, but she had no motive to kill either one of the Loeffler men. She was innocent.

Shannon's phone bleeped, and he stepped out into the hall to answer it.

Ingrid eyed Detective Lowe. "Can I ask you a question?"

"Sure."

Ingrid hesitated. "If there was suspicion that a cancer patient had gotten sick because someone poisoned them, could they dig the remains up and do an autopsy to prove it?"

Lowe's face softened slightly. "You think someone you know was poisoned?"

Ingrid shrugged. "I don't know. I might."

"What type of poison was it? Some kinds stay in the body forever. Others eventually dissipate."

"Beryllium. That's one of the causes of lung cancer, the doctor said. I wonder if my grandmother was poisoned back in the nineties and then got sick for real years later."

Lowe paused a long time. "Well, private exhumation costs a lot. And to be honest with you, I'm not sure that kind of metal is still going to be present in the body after three decades, but I'm no expert."

"Okay." Ingrid bit her lip.

"I did know of a case once over in Charleston. Double homicide. They used a psychic to find the bodies." She regarded Ingrid thoughtfully.

But Ingrid did not have a chance to decide because just then Shannon stuck his head around the door. "Lowe," he said. "Downstairs. They found something."

Chapter 59

Later that afternoon, after the police had cleared out of the house, word on the street was that an arrest had been made.

While Sailor scrolled for news, Ingrid searched the multiple fridges in the kitchen, pantry, and working pantry, gathering vegetables for a salad. She chopped it all robotically—Sailor liked her salads chopped fine—then dumped everything in a Waterford crystal bowl and mixed up a mustard vinaigrette to dress it. She hoped Sailor would eat something. She had refused breakfast.

"Oh my God," Sailor breathed now, staring intently at her phone. She read, "'Tristan "Boney" Anderson, twenty-four, a local ghost tour guide with a prior record for petty theft and drug possession, was arrested in connection with the double murder of Aurelian Stokes Loeffler III and Casimir Stokes Loeffler during the wedding reception of their daughter and sister Sailor Loeffler-Etris, held last night in Monterey Square in front of the Loefflers' residence, the Noble Hardee Mansion.'"

Ingrid's entire body tensed, becoming a live wire that surged with a dangerous current. She told herself not to move.

Boney?

It couldn't be. Why . . .

Sailor read on. "They've put him in jail. No bond. That's all it says."

"They're not going to put any more than that in the media," Jude said in his clipped accent.

Ingrid's hand sought the edge of the counter. She was trembling. Sailor and Jude were now discussing what they'd been able to glean that morning from Judge Norwood and Brooks Glover. Apparently, the crime scene techs hadn't found a weapon. Instead, they'd discovered that one of Rill's glass display cases had been broken and the antique pirate dirk was missing. They hadn't found any prints other than Rill's and Cas's in the room; however, the butt of a joint had been discovered nestled in the potting soil, which, when tested for prints, had led them to Boney.

What Ingrid had realized in the hours since she'd been interviewed was that she remembered something else as well. Something she'd seen in Rill's study but not registered until now. Both Cas and Rill had similar gashes in their heads. Holes, to be specific. It was as if someone familiar with fishing—and how to quickly kill a fish with a spike to the head—had done the same thing to them.

"Who is this Boney bloke anyway?" Jude stared glumly at his salad.

"I have no idea." Sailor was still reading. "It says he's a ghost tour guide, that's it." She looked up at Ingrid. "Ingrid?"

"He's a friend of Miles," Ingrid blurted out.

Now Jude was staring at her. Both their mouths dropped open.

"Do you know him?" Sailor asked.

Ingrid's mouth opened, too, but nothing came out.

"Ingrid!"

"I mean, a little. Just in passing."

"Do you know why this guy would want to hurt Dad and Cas? I don't understand." She put a hand on Ingrid's arm. "Why would he do this?"

"I really don't know." Ingrid just shook her head, feeling trapped. Anything she said at this point could incriminate Miles. Or herself.

And Miles couldn't have meant for this to happen . . . for Boney to be arrested for this. Could he? She couldn't make any sense of it. She needed time to think. To get Miles alone and grill him.

"Let's just try and keep calm—" Jude started to say.

Sailor rounded on him. "Don't tell me to keep calm!" she snapped. "Don't ever say that to me again! My family is destroyed! Murdered on our wedding day!"

Jude and Ingrid stared at her in silence. She was shaking. Trembling with fury and grief.

"Death is all around me, when I'm awake and when I'm asleep, so don't you dare ever say that I should calm down!" Now Sailor whirled on Ingrid. "Miles knows this guy, so you have to tell me what's going on. Tell me the truth right now, Ingrid. I mean it."

"I truly don't know, Sailor, I swear." Ingrid stood. "Not yet. But I'll find out, I promise you that."

She hurried out of the kitchen and down the dark hallway, Sailor on her heels. At the door, Ingrid turned to her friend and offered her hand. Sailor took it in both of hers, clinging like Ingrid was the only one keeping her from plummeting to the chasm below.

"I told you once, Sailor," Ingrid said, her voice low. "I will never leave your side. And I won't."

Sailor's eyes filled with tears once again.

"But now you've got to trust me. Trust me that I will find out what happened to your family."

Sailor was gripping her hand so tightly, Ingrid could barely separate them, but at last she did and stepped out onto the front porch.

"Go back inside," she instructed Sailor. Ingrid looked over her shoulder. "There are going to be reporters and busybodies and vultures everywhere. Savannah Sauce is yours now. That means everybody's going to want a piece of you. Don't give it to them."

Sailor shook her head, her eyes full of fear. "I'm scared. I'm really scared, Ingrid."

Ingrid bit her lip, and Jude came up behind Sailor, gently pulling her back into the dark house and shutting the door behind them. Ingrid turned to face Monterey Square. The police barricades and velvet ropes were gone. The bandstand and dance floors and bars were gone, too. The strung lights had been taken down and all the trash swept and bagged.

It looked like nothing had ever happened there.

And then, for the first time, Ingrid thought of something and immediately hated herself for even thinking it. With Rill and Cas gone, not only would Sailor have to take over Savannah Sauce. There was no way she was still going to move to London.

Chapter 60

Inside Ingrid's house was dim and quiet. The familiar musty smell Ingrid thought the renovations had eradicated rose over the smell of new fabric and fresh paint and wallpaper now, hitting her nostrils. She closed her eyes and breathed it in: Edie's brewed tea, her smudges of lavender, the smell of her warm, sweet, wrinkled hands.

Home.

Ingrid switched on a lamp. The living room was strewn with clutter. A wadded-up Arby's bag. A handful of Miles's Warhammer figurines. Empty Coke Zero cans. Pretty much like she'd left it before the wedding.

Before the wedding.

When everything had been different. When her life had been simple, her future assured. Now, all that was over. Rill was dead, Cas was dead, and Boney was in jail. And she had promised Sailor she would fix it all.

She found Miles upstairs in Edie's room. In her bed, sprawled out in the middle, his blond curls on her pillow, Litha stretched out luxuriously beside him. Ingrid pounced on him, rousing Litha, who sprang off the bed and out of the room.

"Miles! Wake up!"

He groaned and flung a hand at her, shooing her away.

She threw open the closet door and started rummaging in the back. "You have to get up. You have to get ready."

"No," he groused.

"Miles!"

He sat up, yawning. "Hey."

"You have to get up."

"Ingrid, look." He rubbed his eyes. "I'm sorry for how I was to you at the wedding. I saw you dancing with Rill, and I got jealous. Like, scared, I guess. I thought you were going to ditch me. I don't know— "

She brought out an old Samsonite suitcase, splitting it open on the bed. "Cas and Rill Loeffler are dead."

Miles stared at her, blinking slowly.

"And they've arrested Boney," she said.

"What?" He looked away from her. "Whoa."

Her heart hammered painfully. "You don't look surprised."

"I'm not, I guess," he said quietly. "Not really."

She stilled, feeling her gut twist ominously. "Miles. What the hell? *What the hell?* Talk to me. What's going on?"

He rested his arms on his knees and stared at the tangled bedding. "I always worried something like this was going to happen."

"Miles! What are you saying?"

He looked at her, eyes full of pain. "I didn't want to tell you, Ingrid. Because I know how you . . . how y'all are . . ."

She reddened.

He shifted his eyes away from her. "I ran into Boney last week, over in Tybee. He was selling drugs to some guy."

"No." Boney had never been into that kind of stuff. Yes, smoking it, but not selling. At least she didn't think he had.

"I felt bad for him, so I took him to get breakfast. We were talking about Sailor's wedding, and, you know, I mentioned I was going to it. He asked if he could come so I said yes. And like, I don't know. We might've talked about how the house would be empty. No alarms set, that kind of thing—and he knew how to get in through that back door, the one that led to the kitchen, where we got the food that time—"

"Oh, Miles, no," she said softly. "What have you done?"

Miles cracked his knuckles, looking pained. "I was just trying to help him out. We only ever go to these things for the leftovers, you know? I thought at the most he'd take some booze or a ham or something." He paused. "Okay, maybe a laptop at the most."

She said nothing, feeling the enormity of what he was saying crashing down on her. On both of them. How would they keep this from the police? Those two detectives who had interrogated her at the mansion were smart. They knew who Ingrid was—and that she hung around with Boney. They'd start to put things together soon enough.

"I need to think." She gazed out the window. The birds were almost dementedly cheerful this morning.

"I know it was a bad idea," Miles said. "I admit that in hindsight. But those people have so much. They don't need it all. And I didn't think he was going to kill them. I swear to God."

"Shut up, Miles! I said I have to think!"

He looked abashed. Hurt.

"You were threatening me last night," she said. "Don't act like you weren't."

"I was mad."

"WHAT DID YOU DO?" she screamed.

He leaped off the bed, eyes blazing. "I didn't do anything, Ingrid! It was you! All you! Your curse on Rill!" He was shouting now, too.

She glared at him, tears spilling in anger and desperation. "It wasn't a curse. It was a spell. Only a spell. It couldn't have . . ." She gathered herself. "It's not just Rill, Miles. All the other things . . . Scoot's accident and the fire at the marina . . . those weren't me either. It was never me, was it, Miles? It was you. You all along."

"No—"

"I saw you with her at the wedding. With the girl from Peregrin."

He frowned. "I don't know who you're talking about."

"The bartender who spiked my drink at the Peregrin, Miles! Darya! You were dancing with her at the reception."

"Who cares? We don't know that she was the one who did that to you. And I wasn't with Scoot that night, I told you. It wasn't me."

Ingrid blinked. "I know because Boney told me you got him to do it. To get Scoot drunk at Peregrin and into her car. For you."

Miles looked away from her. "That doesn't mean I did this Rill and Cas thing."

She wanted to grab him and shake him. *This Rill and Cas thing*? How dare he? What was he thinking?

"You know it wasn't Boney," she said bitterly. "He could never do this."

"And you're saying I could?"

"I don't know. I don't know," she wailed. "Their heads . . . they had these holes—"

"You're tired, Ingrid. And probably hungry." He sent her a patient smile. "Come on. Let's just table this, get some dinner, and we can figure this out."

She turned back to the closet and started hauling clothes out and dumping them into the suitcase.

"Wait, what are you doing?" Miles asked.

"Packing."

"Where are you going?"

"Back to the Loefflers' . . . until the estate is settled and Sailor has a firmer foundation under her feet."

"All right. That's nice of you. I guess I'll stick around here and keep the home fires burning." He sounded petulant.

"If you don't mind, yes." She threw in another armload of clothes.

"I don't mind." Now his voice was soft. Sincere. "I'd do anything for you, Ingrid. You know that. I told you. I'm sorry for being a dick last night. But, honestly, Ingrid, I don't feel bad for them and neither should you. They don't deserve your pity."

"Cas does. Cas never hurt anybody." She started crying and sat on the bed. Miles rubbed her back.

When she finally quieted, she could hear a bird sing just outside Edie's window. Could hear people talking and laughing on the street below. A dog barked. Life was continuing on all around them. No matter that Cas and Rill were dead and Boney was in jail. The birds and the dogs didn't know. They didn't care. They would all die soon. And so would Ingrid. They all really only had just a little bit of time here, didn't they?

"Best to use it wisely," Ingrid said absently.

"What?" Miles asked.

She sighed. "I said, we should make the most of our lives."

A slow smile spread across his face. "I couldn't agree more. Why not, after how hard you've worked. After all you did for us. To take care of us."

She nodded. "I better go."

"I love you, Budgie."

It pained her to say it back to him, but she couldn't let him know how much she distrusted him now. There was no predicting what he'd do.

"I love you, too. But you should take a shower and get dressed. The police are probably on their way here soon. To talk to you."

She would not be here when he told his story about Boney to the cops. She couldn't bear to hear it again.

Chapter 61

Adrian met her and Litha on the sidewalk in front of the Loeffler mansion. "I'll get that for you, Miss White. And the cat."

She handed over the leash, giving him a grateful smile. "I've got to run a quick errand. Thanks, Adrian."

She hurried through the square, north, toward the river. At the tourist shop, she climbed the back stairs to Boney's apartment. It was locked. She reached up for the key on the ledge and let herself in. The place was quiet. On the dirty linoleum floor of the kitchen sat a large duffel bag, stuffed full.

She pushed open Boney's door and saw the stripped mattress and bare floor. She walked into the room and looked around. All his clothes were gone. Even the framed picture from the windowsill. She turned to see a girl standing in the doorway.

Mari, in underwear and a Savannah Bananas T-shirt, eating a bowl of Honey Nut Cheerios. "He was on his way out of here this morning. The police made him leave his bag."

Ingrid tried to compose herself. "Where was he going?"

"He said he was heading north. He has family in Boston, I think."

Ingrid looked around again. "Did he tell you why?"

"No." She slurped a giant spoonful of cereal. "He got home pretty late from the wedding last night—this morning—but I was asleep." Mari gave her a wry look. "Look, Ingrid. I don't know half of what he and Miles get up to, and I'm pretty sure none of it's on the right side of the law, but Boney's solid. You know that."

"Yeah."

"I never thought he would do something like that."

"No."

She slurped milk. "Oh my God, just think about it. All that Savannah Sauce money is going to the daughter now, right? Your friend."

"Right."

"And her mom, too, I guess. Some reward for being a wino and a hit-and-run driver, huh? Winding up with a gajillion dollars."

"Yeah." Ingrid moved back toward the kitchen and the door. "Thanks, Mari. Sorry to barge in on you."

"No, I get it. If you hear anything, let me know. A couple of us were going down to the jail to see him, but they said we weren't allowed." She set the bowl down. "You know, he was the one who set Scoot Loeffler up."

Ingrid kept her expression neutral. "No way."

Mari nodded. "When he came in that night, the night she had her accident—he was crying in his bedroom. I mean, sobbing like a baby. I asked him about it the next morning, but he blew me off, but my friend said she saw him at Peregrin. Buying Scoot drinks."

Ingrid shook her head. "Wow."

"I don't know what those guys have against the Loefflers."

"Yeah. Me neither."

Mari gave her a brief, one-armed hug, and Ingrid clattered back down the stairs to the cobbled street, letting herself be carried away by the current of tourists. She was too tired to cry.

* * *

When she got back to the Loeffler house, overheated and pouring sweat, she was greeted in the hallway by Sailor. Barefoot, she looked pale and tired in a T-shirt and shorts, her hair tied in a knot. Ingrid gave her a gentle hug. She worried that if she held her friend too tightly, the girl might shatter.

"I'm so glad you're back," Sailor said.

"What's going on?"

"It's the will," Sailor said. "Usually there's this whole probate period before they can read it."

Ingrid nodded even though she wasn't sure what that meant.

"But Brooks says since most everything is held in trust, we don't have to go through probate." She sighed. "I don't know. It's a legal thing."

"Of course," Ingrid said.

"Brooks wants to read the will tomorrow because so much of what Dad wanted for the company—the leadership and everything—isn't known. He wrote it all in there."

Ingrid nodded.

"Mom will be there, and Jude, but I want you to come, too, Ingrid. I need you. Promise you'll be there with me."

Chapter 62

The reading of Aurelian Stokes Loeffler III's will took place on the top floor of the Savannah Sauce headquarters—in the CEO's office, as it was a more discreet space than the glass-walled conference room.

Brooks Glover, the family's lawyer, concerned about privacy, had requested the entire staff of the company be given the day off. As a result, the top two floors of the high-rise building were eerily quiet as Ingrid, Sailor, and Jude rode the elevator to Rill's office.

On a good day, the corporate headquarters of Savannah Sauce were intimidating. Now the oppressively elegant interiors seemed to close in around Ingrid. It didn't help that she hadn't slept a wink the night before. She'd had terrible dreams.

A knife, punched into a skull.

Rill, letting out a last, gurgled, dying gasp.

Cas, grunting in pain.

And so much blood. Blood everywhere . . . on the carpet, on her shoes. Slicking her fingers. Blood from a crumpled burgundy suit jacket.

Now she clenched and released her fists, trying to settle her nerves. Sailor was pale and quiet, but when Ingrid asked her if she needed anything, she just shook her head. When the elevator doors slid open, they entered the large suite that overlooked the river, and Ingrid felt another wave of smothering panic. Everyone was already there.

Glover, dapper as always, stood by Rill's vast desk, flanked by one of his associates from his firm, a young man who had well-bred fraternity brother written all over him. Scoot, looking sleeker and more svelte than ever in a sedate brown dress, was seated beside a waifish, colorless man with wisps of brown hair wrapped around his scalp. Her lawyer.

The company's lawyer and acting CEO, a woman named Priscilla Feng, perched on a leather chair. Behind the vast desk, Rill's leather chair was empty. Sailor walked around and sat in it, looking like a traumatized child. Jude positioned himself behind her.

It was just what she'd seen in the reading she'd done for Sailor when she first moved into the house.

A top-floor office . . .

Sailor, in a dark suit, sitting behind Rill's desk . . .

But it hadn't meant what she thought. Not even close.

In a grave voice, Glover greeted everyone, then took his seat at a side table and opened a leather folio. He introduced his associate, then ran through the details of the probate process and the exemption of the will, as a result of Rill putting most of his estate into a trust. At the end of his spiel, he adjusted his glasses and glanced over at Sailor.

"Are we ready to begin?"

"Of course we're ready, Brooks," Scoot snapped. "Get on with it."

"I was addressing Mrs. Loeffler-Etris," Glover said mildly, lifting an eyebrow at Sailor.

Sailor drew herself up and nodded back at him. Behind the chair, Jude put a hand on her shoulder.

"Regardless of the . . . ah . . ." Glover cast his eyes around the spacious office. "Situation?"

Scoot let out an annoyed huff. "What situation? Why are you stalling? Just get on with it."

Glover was looking intently at Sailor, who held his gaze just as steadily. She nodded again, with one, almost imperceptible jut of her chin, and he widened his eyes ever so slightly. What was going on? Something, Ingrid thought, between Glover and Sailor, that much was obvious. Something no one else seemed to be in on. Judging from Sailor's pallor, it was serious.

Ingrid tried to catch Sailor's eye with no luck. Anger flashed through her, and for a moment she wished she'd never agreed to attend this thing. She was already upset enough from finding Rill and Cas, wasn't she? How was she to be of any help to Sailor, if her friend kept secrets from her?

"Well, then," Glover said, looking back down at the folio on Rill's desk. "Let's proceed."

Glover cleared his throat. Nodded at his associate, who proceeded to distribute copies of the document. "As you all know, many years ago, Rill named me as executor of his will. Or in this case, trustee, as most of his assets went into a trust. You also know that, in this day and age, there are no longer formal readings of wills. That's the stuff of television shows and movies. But to every rule there is an exception."

He surveyed the room, his eyes landing on Ingrid. She felt her nervous system buzz. Why was Glover looking at her? What was going on?

"Just read what my father wrote," Sailor said in a quiet voice.

"Very well." Glover examined the document as everyone else scrambled to find their place. "'As a result of the events of this August, I found it expedient and within the family's interest to amend the distribution of assets, namely the diminishing of monies and property going to my wife, Laura Fairburn Loeffler, also known as Scoot, and redistributing them among my children.

" 'Therefore, I have awarded Laura Fairburn Loeffler a monthly stipend of fifty thousand dollars, a condo on Tybee Island which has been recently purchased, as well as the unlimited use of a car service. Her business, Loeffler Interiors, will retain occupancy of the Bull Street and West Jones building for ten years from the date of my death, at which she is free to continue paying the rent on her own or vacate the premises.' "

Scoot's lawyer nodded once. Scoot held her chin high, her expressionless gaze fixed on some spot on the wall beyond Glover. She'd obviously been aware of the changes Rill had made to his will. If she felt any anguish over the situation she was now in, she wasn't giving anyone the satisfaction of seeing it.

Glover flipped a page. " 'As for the leadership of the company, I nominate my son Casimir Stokes Loeffler for the office of CEO. A majority vote by the board will confirm the office, and I have ultimate confidence that all members will, in this way, respect my wishes. In the event that he is no longer living or unable to take over those duties, I name my daughter, Sailor Fairburn Loeffler.' "

Sailor stared down at her hands, folded in her lap.

Glover read on. " 'There have been additional revelations in the past months, requiring a redistribution of my remaining assets. I have learned that instead of being the father of two children, I am the father of three.' "

Ingrid's head jerked up. She felt her lungs expel air as a series of gasps came from around the room.

What?

" 'I was entirely unaware of this fact until recently,' " Glover forged on. " 'The third child, a son, born in the state of Florida without my knowledge to a Tess White, formerly of Savannah, Georgia, lately of Tampa, Florida—' "

Ingrid's eyes went wide, her entire body flooding with adrenaline. She heard her heartbeat thunder in her ears—a roar like the crashing ocean. She looked at Sailor, who was still staring down at her hands. Scoot, ramrod straight in her chair, seemed to have turned to stone.

"'—was given up for adoption to a local couple, Randall and Raina Drummond, also of Savannah, Georgia—'"

"I'm here," came a voice from the doorway of the office. "Better late than never."

Chapter 63

Everyone twisted in their seats.

Miles, dressed in faded jeans, a wrinkled button-down shirt, and his scuffed loafers, flashed a smile. "It's only fifteen past. You could've waited."

Ingrid could barely move. Barely breathe. She felt her vision swimming, blurring the people in the room. She felt dizziness rise inside her like a wave and then crash down again, submerging her.

Miles's eyes roved the room until they met Ingrid's. They were flat blue. Cold, clear turquoise water.

"Hi, Budgie."

So ridiculous for him to use her nickname here. Had he lost his mind? Ingrid opened her mouth to speak but nothing came out.

"I know this is all a big surprise for you," he said to her. "And we're going to talk about it all, I promise."

Ingrid glanced at Sailor, then back at Miles. "What's going on?"

Miles sent her an apologetic look. "I couldn't tell you. It's so complicated. I was dealing with so much." He hesitated. "See, your mother, Tess . . . was my mother, too. She had me before she had you, but she came back up here and left me with the Drummonds when I was a baby . . . because Edie wouldn't take me. Because of who my father was."

He looked at Sailor. She lifted her chin, her face a blank.

Ingrid flushed, now with anger and confusion. She could feel Sailor's eyes on her. Everyone's eyes on her. She wanted to scream.

"Who your father was?"

"Oh. It's Rill." Miles grinned sunnily. "Rill Loeffler . . . was my father."

Ingrid's mouth dropped open. She looked at Sailor, addressing her in the calmest voice she could muster. "You knew about this?"

Sailor nodded. "Just yesterday. Brooks told me."

Ingrid turned to Miles. "And you? How long . . ."

"Oh. A long time. Years. My adoptive parents told me I was adopted when I was ten or so. They used to let me call Tess down in Florida. We talked all the time. She told me Rill was my dad when I was like fifteen, I guess?"

He said it so casually. In such an offhand manner. It almost, but not quite, covered that brief flash of shame Ingrid caught in his eyes. Because he had to know how much that hurt her. Tess had never called her. Never told her who her father was.

"Tess said she felt like she owed it to me to tell the truth about my lineage. She didn't say anything about you, Ingrid—about my having a younger half sister—until right before she died."

Ingrid let out something between a laugh and a sob and gripped the arms of her chair. Her brain scrambled to fit the pieces together. The years, the recent months. Everything she and Miles discussed and planned and promised each other.

All of it lies.

"So . . . you knew when we first met?" she asked him. "On

the ghost tour? That you were my brother? That *he* was your father." The room was so quiet that her voice echoed in the immense space. "But you never told me."

He hesitated, as if he was searching for the right words.

"I don't understand, Miles. Why didn't you just tell me?"

He glanced at Sailor again.

"Don't look at her!" Ingrid snapped. "Look at me."

He obeyed, a sheepish expression on his face. "I wasn't ready. I had to decide how I was going to . . . you know, handle it. What approach was best for me to take."

She let out a raw laugh. "Tess dropped me off at Edie's when I was six years old. And that was it. I got nothing after that. I take that back. I got two birthday cards, that's it. No letters, no phone calls. Did she ever tell me who *my* real father was? No! I still have no idea who he is! Or was!"

"Ingrid—" Miles said.

She was screaming now, everyone's eyes wide and mouths in little O's, but she didn't care. If she'd had a match, she would have burned the place down.

"But that was because my father was just some nameless nobody with no company and no fancy house and no money to be had." She jabbed a finger in Miles's direction. "She told you. She told you who your father was because you could make her rich!"

"Ingrid," Brooks Glover's voice was calm but firm. "Let's take it down a notch."

Ingrid ignored him, her gaze sliding back to Miles. She felt the hatred emanating in waves from her body toward his. He felt it, too, she knew, because he visibly flinched.

Good, she thought. *You know you've made an enemy. And what an enemy I will be . . .*

"Ingrid," Miles said quietly. "I didn't plan to lie to you. Tess told me Edie wanted nothing to do with me because of who my father was. How do you think that made me feel? And I figured if I told you the truth, you might turn against me, too."

"That's bullshit. Edie was a loving person. If she knew you existed, she would've never refused you. Tess kept you away from us on purpose. She had a plan. A plan to get money from Rill Loeffler."

"Oh my Lord," Scoot said.

"I promise, Ingrid," Miles said, undeterred. "It all started—our friendship—because I wanted to get to know my sister. I wanted to know *you*."

Ingrid lifted her eyebrows. "While you figured out how exactly you were going to blackmail Rill?"

"Blackmail?" Miles asked.

"Or murder him, I don't know—" Ingrid shot back.

"What?" Sailor shrieked.

"What is she saying?" Scoot demanded.

"Everyone," Glover said. "Let's just take a moment—"

"Yes!" Ingrid was shouting now. "Murder him because he had sex with Tess, *our mother*, when she was sixteen years old! You wanted to get revenge for her, didn't you? Just say it, you piece of shit!"

Scoot stood, pushing her chair back and pointed at Miles. "That's enough. I want this person out of here! Out!"

Glover put a calming hand out. Not that anyone was paying attention to him.

"And her." Scoot whirled, pointing now at Ingrid. "Get her out of here, too. I can't stand the sight of her. Of either of them!"

Pandemonium broke loose. Miles started talking over Scoot, and Scoot screamed even louder. Scoot's lawyer stood, trying but failing to placate his client. Glover and his associate were yelling over the fray. Sailor and Jude watched silently. At the window, Ingrid glowered, her eyes fixing on a massive container ship moving upriver.

Tess had known better than to just knock on Rill Loeffler's

door demanding a payout. Rill was too smart to be the target of some amateur paternity shakedown, especially one that had included the element of sex with an underage girl. So she confided in her son and together they came up with a plan.

She used Miles to gather intel on the Loefflers so she could figure out their strategy. She told him about Ingrid, his half sister, a witch-psychic who was running a nice little business over on Taylor Square and who might be the best, safest way into the Loeffler family. And who knows? Ingrid might even want to help Miles out. Help him take what they had decided was rightfully his. He should get Ingrid on his side.

Tess had been the one to suggest Miles put his ghost tour flyer on her door, Ingrid had no doubt about that. Tess instructed Miles to get close to Ingrid. To make himself indispensable to her. To pretend he loved her. And then, no doubt, with one more well-placed flyer—*Miss Edie's Palm and Aura Reading*—in Sailor's door, to subtly steer Ingrid in the direction of the Loeffler family.

Unfortunately for her, the woman had died before she could enjoy the fruits of her labor.

Ingrid could see everything so clearly. When Sailor had come into Ingrid's life, Miles had played the part of jealous friend. But it had all been an act to keep her from suspecting him. In truth, he been right beside her the whole time, whispering in her ear. Suggesting, coaxing, encouraging her to get close to the Loefflers. To move in with them. To pick them off, one by one. Destabilize them. Diminish their ranks, so he would have a clear way in.

So he, Miles, would be the last man standing.

He convinced Boney to get Scoot drunk and he helped her wreck her car. He set fire to Jude's boat. And then . . . then he stabbed Rill and Cas, his father and half brother, to death with a pirate's dagger, framing Boney for it . . .

. . . and all because of what was going to happen in the next hour in this room. The distribution of Rill Loeffler's substantial assets. Assets that were even more substantial now that Scoot was basically cut out of the will and Cas was dead. Assets that would be divided now between Sailor and Miles, her recently discovered half brother.

Ingrid had only been the means to an end.

But what could she say now, to these people? If she told the truth about Miles, she would tell on herself as well. She would have to tell the truth about cursing Scoot. Cursing Jude's boat. Casting the spell on Rill.

Turning a blind eye on Miles adding his help to her magic.

"We're just work colleagues, me and that guy Boney." Miles was saying now to the lawyer in a clear, confident tone. A tone she didn't recognize. "You can check my phone and his. I'm an open book. I didn't know him that well. I will admit, I did want to get to know Ingrid, my sister. And I was curious about my biological father, too. My other family. But that's all I've done."

Glover raised his hand and nodded wearily.

But Miles wasn't finished. He turned to Sailor. "I did happen to mention to Boney about your wedding, but it was just an offhand comment. Sometimes the caterers give us leftovers after events. It helps to make ends meet, you know. Ghost tours don't pay that well."

Ingrid glared at him, astounded at his lies.

Fucking snake . . .

Ghoul . . .

Miles continued. "I had nothing to do with the tragedy that occurred the other night, I swear this to you, Ingrid. To all of you. I swear it on my life that I'm completely innocent. I'm only to blame for one thing—being acquainted with a guy who obviously was extremely troubled."

He faced the room, his arms spread wide, his face as open and vulnerable as Ingrid had ever seen it be. And now, much to her horror, silent tears were falling down her own cheeks.

She brushed them away, hating how they made her look weak. Hating him.

Miles turned to Sailor. "I can't tell you how sorry I am for what that awful person did to your family."

Sailor was sobbing into a tissue now as Jude rubbed her back. Miles watched her with a compassionate look on his face.

"Shall we continue?" Glover motioned for his associate to bring the chair that had been waiting by the wall closer to the desk. Miles sat.

"Continue," Sailor sniffed to Glover.

Glover resumed his reading. Rill had divided the remainder of his ample estate between his surviving children, Sailor, Cas, and Miles. This included his majority stock holding in Savannah Sauce; his houses in Scotland, Spain, Uruguay, and France; his various holdings in real estate, stocks, and bonds. There was also a Manhattan apartment, a quail hunting club in Thomasville, and jewelry, rare coins, and gold bars locked away in several safe deposit boxes scattered at banks throughout the state. The Tybee House, known as Sargassum Sling, would be sold, the proceeds evenly distributed between the three children.

Except there were only two now.

More for them.

Glover went on to read that in the event of one or more of his children's deaths, Rill stipulated that the assets be divided equally between the surviving number. "'. . . and I would ask Cas or Sailor, whichever of my children who is head of the company my grandfather started with a mere ten dollars in his pocket and the grit of a man with no choice other than succeeding, to take care of their younger half brother, Miles Drummond.

"'I, unfortunately, cannot claim him at this time. The Loeffler family has already suffered enough scandal and upheaval, and I'm unwilling to put them through additional pain. After I am gone, I do not feel I can deprive him out of what he rightfully deserves.

"'He is my son. I ask that my children, Sailor and Cas, welcome him to the family, share with him the nobility, dignity, and privilege of the Loeffler name, as well as allow him to participate in our precious organization. Be patient with him. Treat him as blood. Accept him as I was not able to. I love you all. Your father.'"

Chapter 64

Miles hadn't been back to Ingrid's house since the reading of the will, and Ingrid wasn't about to call him. For now, she was safe. If Miles threw her under the bus, he threw himself, too. And right now, as far as Sailor was concerned, it was merely an odd coincidence that her personal psychic and newly revealed half brother just happened to have been roommates. Ingrid didn't dare rock that particular boat.

Sailor hadn't contacted Ingrid either, not since they'd said goodbye outside the Savannah Sauce headquarters. They had embraced, Sailor so pale and distracted.

"You know they found texts on his phone," she said to Ingrid. "My father's. To Finley. I just assumed she was texting Cas, but she wasn't. She was texting those disgusting pictures to my *father*."

Ingrid flushed. "I'm so sorry."

"Men." Sailor sighed then added, "Women, too. Frankly, I'm sick of everyone."

"Yes," Ingrid said, then, "Speaking of . . . you should keep an eye on him. Miles, I mean."

Sailor gave her a long look. "Why?"

Ingrid shook her head. How could she tell Sailor the truth about Miles without implicating herself? She didn't want to think it was her fault Rill and Cas were dead, but she couldn't escape the hard truth that she was inextricably linked with everything terrible that had happened to Sailor's family.

Sailor regarded her with a pitying expression. "Miles is family. The only real family I have left now. I have to give him a chance. And"—she added hesitantly—"I'm married now. Running the company. I'm not going to have time for all the stuff we used to do. I don't even think I'm going to be much of a friend. But I'll keep up your payments. Don't worry about that."

Sailor's gaze had skipped past Ingrid, toward the rest of them—Glover and his associate, Jude and Miles—as they crossed the street in the direction of the waiting Rolls and an additional sleek, black car. "It's nothing personal, Ingrid. I just have so much on my mind right now."

"Of course."

As Ingrid watched her walk away, Scoot appeared. The older woman lit a cigarette and sucked on it, hard.

"Looks like you and I are in the same boat," she said with a delicate little sneer. "And it's certainly no yacht."

Ingrid leveled a look at her. "If I found myself in a boat with you, Scoot, you better believe I'd be man overboard."

Scoot laughed like it was the funniest thing she'd ever heard. "You better watch your step, missy. You're on the outs now."

"Tell me something, Scoot," Ingrid said.

"Anything, *Ingrid.*" Scoot said dramatically and blew smoke over her shoulder.

"How did you do it?"

Scoot lifted her eyebrows.

"Was it kitty litter in her drink? Poisoned water from the Savannah Sauce factory? The volcano ash from Rill's desk?"

Scoot stared at Ingrid, her cigarette burning to ash, and then she burst into gales of deep, rolling laughter. "Oh my God! You're a hoot and a half, aren't you? Is that what you've been thinking all this time? That I poisoned your grandmother . . . with volcano ash?"

Ingrid regarded her coolly. "And caused the cancer that ultimately killed her? Yes. Yes, it is exactly what I've been thinking."

Scoot's laughter dwindled, and Ingrid saw an almost imperceptible flicker of fear in her eyes. "That would make me quite the supervillain, wouldn't it?"

"Or just a pathetic, sad woman, desperate for some happiness."

"You know, Ingrid, it's best to let resentments go," Scoot said. "If not, you risk becoming bitter. And I don't know if anybody's ever told you, bitterness gives you wrinkles. Wrinkles that only poison from a needle can smooth out." She gave Ingrid a little squeeze on her arm. " 'Bye now, sweetheart. You take care." She dropped the cigarette on the sidewalk and sauntered off toward her lawyer, waiting beside yet another black car.

With a savage jab of her shoe, Ingrid stamped on the smoking butt. Then, fuming, she walked all the way back to East Taylor Street, where she burst into her house, collapsed on her fancy new sofa, and drank the rest of Miles's Bud Lights while watching endless episodes of *The Twilight Zone*.

She'd been so gullible. So weak. She really had lost herself, just like Miles said. In becoming Sailor's friend, in falling for Cas—and being prepared to accept Rill's debasing offer to be his mistress—she had lost herself. Their money and power and glamor had blinded her. Blinded her as well to the pirate waving a false flag whom she'd invited into her home. And then . . . oh Goddess . . . she'd ignored Edie's warnings, turned to baneful magic, and in that moment of indiscretion, let the pirate take everything away from her.

At some point later in the evening, Gloria Ledieu and Dean Remington knocked on her door, asking in hushed tones if she needed company. Word had gotten out, apparently, about Rill Loeffler's will and its terrible revelations. She thanked them, but said she wanted to be alone. She went upstairs then, climbed into Edie's bed, and cried herself to sleep.

Chapter 65

October arrived bringing chilly mornings and crisp blue skies. It was the witch's month, with the Harvest moon and Samhain. Ingrid's favorite month, back before her life had been upended.

Scoot, now persona non grata in town, closed her business and left for Tybee. Ingrid was relieved, but she doubted the woman was gone for good. Scoot Loeffler was no quitter.

Miles collected all his belongings from Ingrid's place and moved into the Loeffler mansion. He had gone to work in the gleaming glass tower by the river. Word on the street was that Sailor had taken him under her wing. He would eventually end up as a vice president in some random department, Ingrid figured, not that Miles cared. The day-to-day of Savannah Sauce was an afterthought to him. He owned half of the Loeffler fortune now.

He texted and called incessantly.

I want to see you, Ingrid.

I miss you.

Why are you so mad at me?

Sailor would love to see you, too.

Please, can we just talk?

I DID THIS FOR US!!!

Ingrid never answered them. How could she sit across from him at a table at Saint Bibiana, sipping a twenty-dollar cocktail and eating tomato toast? She couldn't believe a word he said. She knew he'd planted that joint and betrayed Boney with barely a thought. She did not believe for one minute that he wouldn't do the same to her. Or even Sailor.

Sailor was still CEO and in possession of half of the Loeffler fortune, but if Miles was still plotting, if he planned to go after Sailor somehow, how could she not protect her friend? The thought of what Miles might do now kept her awake most nights.

She attempted to go see Boney. He was still in the Chatham County Jail, awaiting his hearing, but she was told she wasn't on his visitors list. "He's got his lawyer and one other family member, that's it," the woman said, probably divulging more than she was supposed to. Up in her bedroom, Ingrid sat at Edie's desk and wrote him a letter, asking what she could do to help. She mailed it but never received a reply.

One bright, brisk day, though, an invitation dropped through the mail slot on her door. A Halloween party thrown by Savannah Sauce to benefit the unhoused population of the city. A costume ball hosted at the Loeffler mansion by "Sailor Loeffler-Etris and Miles Loeffler."

She was invited. Merely a guest, like everybody else on the list. Which probably numbered in the hundreds. In spite of that, she decided to go. It had been exactly one month since the wedding, and she could not deny she was yearning to see Sailor again. To draw a little nearer to the warmth of her light.

Ingrid found her costume from the back-back room, the same ensemble Edie had worn in the snapshot of her and Rill standing on the deck of Sargassum Sling. The tiered skirt. Peasant blouse. Headscarf and hoop earrings. She didn't care if it made anyone uncomfortable with its obvious stereotyping. To her, the costume was Edie. And Edie was power and love, light and strength—all things she desperately needed.

After she dressed, she did a cleansing ritual in her altar room, calling on Edie to be with her at the party. At the end, when she paid respect to the light, to the elements, and closed the circle, her whole body hummed with the positive vibrations. Edie was with her.

But as she walked down East Taylor toward Monterey Square, she felt a hint of cold in the breeze coming up from the river. The kind of wind that buffeted Savannah right before late fall. That wind spoke to her of a different kind of possibility. A possibility of danger and desolation.

She would need to keep her eyes open.

The double front doors of the Loeffler mansion were flung open and flanked by two security guards. Inside, Ingrid clocked more guards stationed at strategic points throughout the rooms and even on the first landing of the staircase.

Sailor and Miles weren't playing around.

The hall was packed with family friends and business associates, all dressed in elaborate costumes. There were superheroes and characters from fantasy books and TV shows. Ghosts and cowboys, witches and milkmaids, ex-presidents and porn stars. There was something different about this particular party, though. This time the guests included regular, everyday people. Local shop owners, professors from the art school, real estate agents, and even the bartender from the Wormhole.

It made sense. Now that Miles Drummond was a Loeffler, he was their connection to the common man. And that was the thing about the common man—and woman. They had plenty of cash to buy every flavor of the Loeffler sauces and chutneys, marinades and jams. These people worshipped wealthy families like the Loefflers. They longed to brush shoulders with them. They aspired to be them. They might not be capable of large donations, but even their small ones would add up.

Miles was no dummy.

To her right, in the front drawing room, she spotted Dean Remington and Sheffield talking to Gloria and Harmon Ledieu. She made her way over to them, finding herself enfolded in their protective embrace.

"Hey there, hon," Gloria said, as Harmon dropped a peck on her cheek. "It's been too long. We've been worried about you."

"Poor little lamb," Dean said. "How are you?"

"I'm fine."

Sheffield took her hand. "I'm sorry I said ever said that guy was pretty. He's such a bitch. A heartless, heinous bitch. I can't believe he didn't move you immediately into this house with him. After all you did for him."

Gloria pursed her lips. Harmon muttered, "Damn straight."

"Please come over for dinner," Dean said to her. "Any day of the week. We all want to fuss over you, Ingrid."

Ingrid nodded. She was finding it hard to speak without crying. She wasn't totally alone. These people, her neighbors, cared for her. Even though she hadn't been especially kind to them. "I will," she finally blurted. "Thank you."

Turning away to search for the bar, she stopped at the pocket doors that led to Rill's study. She inhaled and pushed them open.

The room was empty. Dim, except for the lights in the cases. The glass had been replaced in the one that had been smashed. The one that had held the dagger. But no artifact sat under the pinpoint of light.

Ingrid stepped into the hushed room and pulled the doors closed behind her. She crept across the room, glancing once at Rill's desk, now cleared of his papers. There was a lamp. A framed picture of Cas and Sailor. The beaker of volcanic ash. And an old book with a blue cover, faded and frayed at the corners, sat before the chair. She walked behind the desk and touched the gilded lettering.

A General History of the Robberies & Murders of the Most Notorious Pirates. She opened the book to a page with an illustration of a small ship following a larger one. The caption read, *A pirate brigantine flies the King's Colour, the flag of Great Britain, to disguise its dastardly mission.*

She closed the book and walked away from the desk, over to the end of the sofa. She stopped there, reflexively looking down. The rug under her feet was new—a modern shag in a muted, beige shade Scoot would hate. Clenching her fists, she held her breath and peered behind the sofa.

There was nothing to see. Just the empty space between the sofa and the window.

She didn't know what she'd expected. To see an apparition of the bloody X of Cas and Rill? Some sort of clue the police had overlooked?

She was a fool to come back here.

She left the room.

Ingrid slipped through the crowd, weaving around more costumed guests. She climbed the massive staircase to the second floor and wandered down the hall. There were scattered knots of guests, these mostly surreptitiously snooping in the Loefflers' bedrooms. Ingrid skirted one such group, entered Cas's room, and shut the door behind her.

Like Rill's study, the room had not been changed. At least there was that. It looked the same as the first time she'd gotten a glimpse into it—at Sailor's party when Cas was kneeling in prayer before the old wingback chair.

She walked to the chair now and ran her fingers over the back. What an oddball she had thought he was then. At a party, with his bedroom door wide open, praying. What had he been asking God for that night? For guidance? For help? She'd never asked him. She would never know.

"Champagne?"

She turned to see Miles standing in the doorway, holding a flute of fizzing gold out to her like a peace offering.

Chapter 66

She hadn't heard him enter the room, but that didn't surprise her. These days her senses were definitely off. Her eyes swept over him. Even though he wasn't in costume, she almost didn't recognize him.

He wore his hair differently now, gelled and combed back. He was dressed in a pair of slim, perfectly tailored gray pants, and a navy shirt unbuttoned one button too low. His belt was Hermès. Shoes, Gucci. He smelled good, too. Rill's cologne. Fig and cognac.

No, she thought, Miles *was* actually in costume.

He was dressed up as a Loeffler.

"Come on," Miles said, thrusting the champagne at her.

Unsmiling, she took the flute and drank down the entire thing.

"Okay." He watched her with an amused look. "How have you been?"

"Fine. Busy," she said in a clipped, cold voice, setting down the flute. "Lots of appointments."

A brief flicker of something inscrutable crossed his face. He shrugged his shoulders, then seemed to study a painting of a ship on Cas's wall.

Ingrid watched him. "How's everything with you?"

"God, I can't even tell you." He dropped his hands in his pockets. She spotted the chunky silver watch on his wrist. Cas's Omega. She wanted to rip it off his arm and smack him across the face with it.

"The company is insane," he said. "You'd never imagine how much it takes to run a place like that. But Sailor's been great, showing me the ropes, giving me some real responsibility. It's just all such a ride, you know?"

She hated how glib he was being. But two could play at that game. "Sounds fascinating."

"You've been avoiding me."

He said it in such an innocent tone, like he had no idea why she would be doing such a thing. What a liar.

"You know you're always welcome here," he said. "I want you around. Sailor wants you around."

Ingrid folded her arms. "Sailor wants nothing to do with me."

"She's grieving. She does want you around. She talks about you all the time. You're our sister."

"I'm *your* sister."

"And she's mine. That's the thing. I'm trying to build a bridge between you two."

She glared at him. There wouldn't have needed to be a bridge if it hadn't been for him in the first place. Everything had been perfect between her and Sailor. And Cas. And Rill. She had had it all under control—

She couldn't go there. Couldn't think about it.

"I like your costume," he said.

She shrugged. Shook her head.

"I miss you. Talk to me."

She moved to the window and turned to look out over the rooftops, saying the next words in a barely controlled growl.

"You murdered Rill and Cas. You set up your friend, an innocent man. You used me to get close to them."

He stepped closer to her. His voice was low. The fig and cognac smell was overpowering. "You have that all wrong, Ingrid. All wrong. I took care of everything. Everything you were trying to do with your magic, I did with good, old-fashioned work. Just so you know, all of it was for us. You and me. But you can't see that. You can't just take the gift that I'm holding out to you— "

"I don't want your fucking *gift*— " she hissed.

"Yes, you do." Miles's gaze was steady. "You want it so bad you can taste it."

He was infuriating. So sure he knew her. So sure he knew what was best.

"It's just . . ." She clenched her fists in pure frustration. "Why did you have to lie to me? Why did you have to make me feel bad for months for wanting to be a part of this family?" Her voice cracked. "I loved them, and you made me feel like a terrible person for it."

"I was jealous. I didn't want to lose you. Before we met, I just wanted to know you, more than anything. You're my sister, Ingrid. But after everything Tess told me about Edie, I was scared you would reject me, so I thought it was best to take a different approach. Maybe it was wrong, not telling you everything, but after we met, I realized we were a perfect pair. Us, you and me, working together, I realized that was the best way, the *smart* way, to get close to the Loefflers."

"You used me," she snapped.

"And you used the magic." He shook his head. "Or the light or Goddess, whatever you call it. But what I'm trying to say is that what I did, I did for *us*."

"What you did was wrong," she said.

"I could say the same of you."

"I didn't kill anyone." Her voice shook.

"Didn't you?" Miles's blue eyes were open. Clear. "You're the one who removed the veil of protection from him, Ingrid. You wanted him out of the way just as much as I did."

"I didn't want him dead."

"Yes, you did," he snarled, his face turning red, a vein on his forehead bulging. He ran a hand across his brow. Settled himself. "You did want him dead, Ingrid. Whether you admit it or not, we were on the same page."

She threw up her hands. "Well, I changed my mind, okay?"

"Because he offered you money." He spat the words out. "But if you'd just trusted me, I was going to get us the money anyway—"

Ingrid blinked at him. Felt herself sway. There it was. His confession.

"Baby!"

Miles's head swiveled in the direction of a woman—gorgeous, blond, and dressed in a gossamer sequined slip dress with wings attached at the back. She was grinning at the two of them. He reached for her, and to Ingrid's amazement and shock, pulled her to his side.

"Ingrid, this is Poppy."

"Oh my God, Ingrid. How are you?" Poppy bent and kissed the air beside Ingrid's cheek.

"You already know each other," Miles said. "What was I thinking? Of course you do."

Poppy caught Ingrid's forearm in her soft hand. "I never got a chance to thank you for filling in for me as maid of honor at Sailor's wedding. And all you went through that night. Awful. Just awful." Now she took hold of Miles's arm. "But look at all that happened as a result. Miles finally finding his family. Sailor getting back her long-lost brother. Talk about silver linings, right? And then, meeting this guy . . ." She leaned into Miles and planted a soft, tender kiss on his lips. His hand snaked around her waist. "He's so incredible. So open to living intentionally. Holding space for me when I'm overwhelmed with my company." Poppy giggled. "But of course, you know all about how great he is."

Ingrid swallowed down the rage that was bubbling up from her gut. She had to. Otherwise, she was going to lose her shit. Do something she regretted.

"Grab you another beer, babe?" Poppy asked Miles.

"I'll come with you. I need to check in with Sailor." He turned to Ingrid and gave her a hug. "Talk later, okay?"

Ingrid clamped her hand on his arm. "Give it to me."

Miles furrowed his brow.

"The watch," she said in a low voice. "Give it to me now."

Poppy blinked in surprised dismay. He unclasped the Omega and shook it off. He dropped it into her hand. "See you later, Ingrid."

"Bye, Ingrid." Poppy took Miles's proffered hand, and the couple left the room.

Ingrid closed her eyes. She stood still for a few seconds, then, opening them and taking a deep breath, slid the watch onto her own wrist. She fastened the clasp. It was too big and hung halfway over her hand, but she didn't care. She liked feeling the weight of it on her skin.

She went back downstairs. At the open front doors, she stepped back outside and breathed in again, this time the tranquil, briny night air. She pulled her phone out of her bag and ordered an Uber.

Five minutes later, she was climbing out of the car, just outside the gates of Bonaventure Cemetery. As the car drove off, she glanced around. The cemetery closed at five every night, but she knew how to get around that, thanks to Boney. She missed the guy, missed his bed, the feel of his skin against hers. She worried for him.

She scaled the fence and dropped down onto the sandy path that led into the heart of the cemetery. As she walked past the large marble statues and markers that marked all those who'd been laid to rest, drawing closer toward Edie's grave, she silently gathered the light to her.

Gather strength,
As the clock waxes.
Gather courage,
As the day wanes.
I gather, you gather,
And what we gather shall grow,
So in the bloom of night, we shine forth.

Edie's granite marker glowed like a beacon, shining from among the sea of other stones. Someone had left a bunch of peonies, tied with a black ribbon, on the ground. They were withered now, desiccated brown petals parchment, just awaiting a strong rain or the touch of someone's hand to release their hold on the stem and fall to the ground.

Miss Paulette? Maybe Rill, even.

She picked up the cadaverous bouquet and flung it away, then kneeled and grasped the small marker with both hands.

"Edie," she said.

There were no tears now. There were none left in her. She would just tell the truth now, straight out. No hiding.

"I've lost," she said to her grandmother's grave. "I *am* lost."

She waited, feeling the embrace of the moonlight. Feeling the breeze trail its fingers along her face and lift her hair. She heard an owl hoot from somewhere in the cemetery, calling to its mate. She felt the synchronicity of the universe open up before her. She felt the spirit of her grandmother rise and wrap around her. She closed her eyes and smiled in relief.

Edie . . .

She thought about what Edie had taught her. Goodness and strength and honor. She would hold to them, to her new friends and neighbors. She would depend on the people around her, Dean and Gloria and Sheffield. She would let them help her. She would respect the Goddess, trust in the benevolence of the universe and her place in it. She would not fail. She could not.

Edie . . .

And then, it was all gone—Edie, the owl, the sense of unity she had felt. She was alone once again, just a girl kneeling at a grave in a Savannah cemetery. She was on her own, fighting for the scraps that life might throw her way.

She let go of the granite marker and lay down, curling up on the root-rippled ground. She stayed that way a while. She was tired, after all. Confused and empty. When she looked to the future, she couldn't see a thing. It was no longer open to her.

With her head down on Edie's grave, she let out a long sigh and closed her eyes.

Chapter 67

Ingrid dreamed of a city of castoffs. The debtors, the thieves, the confidence men, and witches. She dreamed of the homes they cleaned. The offices in which they answered phones and filed documents. The restaurants where they scooped up the coins tossed their way. The alleyways where they told the wealthy the truth of who they were.

The castoffs gave themselves away to the people of Savannah, over and over and over again, but they danced while they did it. They danced all through the streets of the town, forming an endless, shambolic parade. Like boats on a river that wound their way up and down the blocks and slipped past the squares, on their slow journey toward the sea.

The wealthy watched the procession from the porches of their mansions, admiring the show. What they didn't know, what they didn't see, was that the castoffs were the blood of the city, pumping through its system of gridlike veins. The wealthy in their houses, they were the pirates, perched in their crow's nests, shadowing the castoffs. Watching and waiting, false flags flying. Waiting and watching for the moment when they could slip alongside one of the castoffs and take everything.

A breath, a whisper, tickling her ear. Edie. "Look."

She turned and there was Miles, standing in the window of the Loeffler mansion as the parade passed. He was dressed in her grandpa's old burgundy suit with the blue ruffled shirt. He held a knife, Rill's Khanjali dagger. The suit, she realized, was wet, liquid dripping from it to the floor beneath Miles's feet. The liquid ran under the massive front door of the house. It leaked over the porch and down the steps, pooling on the sidewalk as the parade danced on.

Blood.

Miles, with his lithe body, ocean eyes, and perpetual tan. He'd always looked to her like a poor unfortunate boy taken at sea, but now she knew she'd been wrong.

"You know what I always say." Edie's breath tickled her ear again. "Pirates fly flags that belong to another."

He hadn't been kidnapped by Blackbeard.

He *was* Blackbeard.

She woke with a gasp, the dew blanketing her skin and hair and clothes. Then, just as quickly, as she lay motionless on the ground, she felt the Goddess dry it again with the warm beams of her sunlight. She felt washed clean and tenderly dried as if by an invisible mother.

Ingrid sat up and scrubbed at her eyes, Cas's watch clanking comfortingly against her arm. The cemetery glimmered in the morning sun—a peaceful sanctuary of stone and moss, serenaded by choirs of birds. She kissed the tips of her fingers and pressed them against the headstone. Right on the carved name *Edith*.

"Good morning," she whispered.

She stood. Smoothed her blouse and straightened her skirt, which had twisted halfway around her waist. She picked her headscarf up from the ground, brushed the dirt from it, and tucked it into her pocket.

She had dreamed a dream of her city, and now she knew what she had to do.

But first, breakfast. She was craving chocolate chip pancakes, extra-crispy bacon, and as many cups of piping hot coffee as she could down. She would stop by Clary's Café on her way. She found her phone, which thankfully showed just enough battery to call a car, and then headed toward the gates of the cemetery, which were flung wide open now.

After paying for her breakfast, she headed south on Habersham. Through Lafayette Park, past East Taylor and Dean Remington's house and into Taylor Park. On the light, she crossed busy Oglethorpe, spotting the person she'd come to see.

The woman stood right there on the sidewalk, just outside the red brick police station. Tall, rangy, and blond, dressed in dark trousers and a crisp blue shirt, she could have been a model in her younger days. She turned, saw Ingrid, and smiled in recognition.

"Hi, Detective Lowe." Ingrid offered her hand. "Ingrid White."

"That's right." Lowe clasped her hand. "The psychic-witch."

"Yes. I was just heading over here to talk with you."

"That so?" Lowe tilted her head. "What about?"

"I keep thinking about something we discussed the day you and Detective Shannon interviewed me at the Loeffler house."

"The thing about exhuming a body?"

Ingrid smiled easily. "No. Not that. It was something else I mentioned—that I might be of some help with the investigation. If you were interested."

Lowe's eyes lit with interest.

"I'd like to offer my services to the Savannah Police Department . . . to help you find Rill and Cas Loeffler's killer."

Lowe's face went stony. She pressed her lips together. "They've arrested someone."

"I know, but he didn't do it. That guy. Boney."

Lowe inhaled and smiled in a perfunctory way. "Well, I appreciate the offer, but unfortunately, I'm no longer on the case."

"Wait, why?"

"Why don't you call Detective Shannon? He'd be happy to talk with you." She gave Ingrid a brisk nod and turned toward the station.

Ingrid grabbed her arm. "But I really want to talk to you."

"Sorry. I can't help you."

Ingrid held her breath. Tried to focus on Edie and the light.

I gather, I gather, I gather . . .

She saw Edie, standing before one of the sunny windows of their house, positioning Ingrid's small body in the block of light. Explaining its properties.

That's how magic works, Budgie.

Being a witch is learning how to pay attention and connecting to everything and everyone around you.

And then she saw it.

A photograph, sitting on a windowsill. A window that overlooked the river and Talmadge Bridge. Two kids, arms draped over each other, grinning an identical, troublemaker smile.

She looked at the woman's left hand and saw the wedding band.

"Oh," she said, her voice full of wonder. Her eyes locked on the detective. "It's Boney. Tristan Anderson. He's your little brother. That's why they took you off the case."

She hesitated. "He told you?"

"No, but . . . I did see a picture once. But that's it. He and I never talked about you. I just made the connection. Just now."

She let out a caustic laugh. Nodded. "We haven't really been on speaking terms lately. Diametrically opposed life goals and all," she said wryly. "But he's in trouble now, Ingrid. Big trouble."

"He didn't do it," Ingrid said. "But I guarantee he knows who did. You'll never find Rill Loeffler's stolen pirate's dirk.

Dagger, whatever, that was taken from his study. I'm guessing it's probably at the bottom of the river."

Lowe watched her.

"But not everything sinks. Some things float . . . or could wash up on shore . . . so they would have to be burned."

Lowe's eyes were flashing now. "I'm listening."

Ingrid only paused for a second, maybe two, but it felt like an eternity. It wasn't that she didn't still love Miles. Maybe she always would, but she had been wrong about so much. It had been Sailor all along—the girl with everything—whom the universe had brought to Ingrid's doorstep.

But now Sailor was living with Miles, the very person who had murdered her father and brother so he could inherit the family fortune. Sailor wasn't safe—she never would be, not with Miles free.

Ingrid would have to be her ballast.

She swallowed uneasily and looked at Lowe. The woman was waiting patiently for her to speak, unaware that the next thing Ingrid said was going to change everything.

"There's a spot I know about," she said quietly. "A spot I think you should check. The knife won't be there, nor will the suit he wore that night because he's probably already burned it by now. But . . ." She caught her breath, willing herself not to cry.

Oh, Miles, Miles, I'm sorry . . .

But this wasn't her doing. No. This was his responsibility. Miles had done all this and now his fate was locked in.

". . . I'm pretty sure he stored the jacket there for a little while because it was covered in blood, and he couldn't carry it around town with him . . ."

Deep breath.

". . . he's messy. He won't have cleaned the spot very well . . ."

Another breath. It was getting easier now.

"There will be traces of blood. Cas and Rill Loeffler's blood."

Lowe's lips partly slightly. "Where is this spot exactly?"

"The Lucas Theatre," Ingrid said. "Down below the screen. At the edge of the stage. There's a secret compartment there that Miles Drummond showed me once. Big enough for him to have hidden his clothes and the murder weapon before he got rid of them. You should test the compartment. Test it for blood."

Epilogue

Scoot Loeffler, dressed in pastel-toned, luxury athleisurewear, poured her morning coffee, dosed it with a generous splash of Kahlúa, then pushed open the sliding glass door and walked out onto her balcony. It was another glorious fall day on Tybee. Sun shining. Seagulls wheeling and crying above. Waves crashing on brown sand.

She hated it here.

She sipped her coffee and closed her eyes. These days she didn't see anything around her, only images of her darling Casimir. Right now, for instance, she was seeing a boy of three with white-blond curls and big brown eyes running after a soccer ball in Forsyth Park, chubby hands outstretched.

After that it was only a short segue to another image. This one a flash of Rill's smile as she walked down the aisle of First Presbyterian Church toward him wearing her mother's wedding gown. And then a flash of his body on hers in their lavish bedroom on the second floor of the mansion . . .

And then came the jarring image that followed. The one that always overlaid the good memories . . .

Both bodies, her son's and husband's, arranged over each other on the floor of Rill's study. Blood everywhere. Mrs. Leimberger scurrying around. And that girl . . . that witch . . . screaming and screaming—

She gulped her coffee and squeezed her eyes shut. No. If she thought of that, she'd lose her absolute marbles, strip naked, and run out onto the beach like a madwoman, plunge into the cold surf and let it sweep her under. She had to think about something else.

Something nice . . .

The young man at Peregrin who bought her drinks. Yes. The sexy, dark-haired one wearing a backward baseball cap. The young man who had, briefly, ended up sitting in a cell, charged with the murder of her family. He had followed her into the ladies' room and kissed her beside the stall. She could think about that, thank God.

It had been so long since she'd kissed a man.

But this memory was ruined, too, because there were other things she was starting to recall as well. At first, she had thought it was the sexy, dark-haired man who had somehow located her little BMW and eased her behind the wheel. *Let's go to the beach,* he'd said in a suggestive drawl once he was sitting in the passenger seat. But now she was almost certain she'd gotten it wrong. The young man in the car with her had been shorter, with tanner skin and strong hands. And wasn't that blond hair curling out from under the backward baseball cap he wore?

He had seemed so familiar to her at the time even though she'd been too out of it to place him, and it had taken her a good few weeks in the second visit to the rehab to place him.

The witch's roommate.

Rill's bastard son.

That nasty little thieving pirate who took everything. Who kept her and Sailor apart.

But he was in trouble now, wasn't he? Arrested, then let out on bail, and under investigation. His trial wasn't until next year, but he'd get what was coming to him, she was confident of that. He'd get his, and then she could finally see her precious daughter again.

Show her that her mother wasn't the villain in this story . . .

There was knocking then at the condo door. Polite but insistent. She went back inside and opened the door to the sight of two uniformed police officers and another dumpy, middle-aged man wearing a tragic suit and whom she instantly recognized.

The detective.

He nodded a greeting at Scoot. "Morning, Mrs. Loeffler. Detective Ray Shannon."

"I remember. Is this about the trial? I told my lawyer I'd rather not testify—"

"No, ma'am. I'm actually here for another reason." He glanced at one of the cops. "Officer."

She caught the exchange and tensed, gesturing with her coffee. "I don't—"

Before she realized what was happening, the officer had deftly removed the mug from her hand while the other officer clamped metal handcuffs on her free wrist.

"Excuse me—"

A second set of cuffs *chinked* on the second wrist.

"Laura Loeffler, you are under arrest for the murder of Edith White. Your Miranda rights will be read to you when you are in police custody at the station."

Scoot bristled. "What? What in the world—"

"You'll be able to make a phone call at the station—"

She let out a screech of outrage. "This is about that witch. Ingrid White! What did she tell you?"

"—and we'll take your statement about your activities concerning Mrs. White."

She drew herself up to her haughtiest height. "I will have all your jobs, every last one of you! I will sue you into the ground!

I will sue the entire department into the ocean! I will take Ingrid White for everything she has and then I will bury her—"

"Ma'am, if I were you, I would not be making threats—"

Now came the dragon fire. "I am a *Fairburn* and a *Loeffler*! I pay your salaries, and this will *not* stand—"

Detective Shannon jutted his chin tiredly at the officers. "Take her to my car. Put her in the front seat. No use in making a show of it."

She looked wildly around at the group. "You sniveling, taxpayer-funded bunch of second-rate toy soldiers-for-hire! Have you ever heard of Brooks Glover? Well, you're about to, you filthy, poorly dressed *terrorists*—"

Gingerly, the officers guided Scoot out of her apartment and toward the elevators at the end of the hall. For a moment, Detective Shannon stood very still, watching a block of light as it shimmered on the walkway, as if it was a living thing.

He heard the faint, melodic sound of a guitar. It was coming from one of the other units, probably. The old John Denver song, "Sunshine on My Shoulders." For a moment, he felt himself swaying along to the tune, then, catching himself, he pulled the door of the condo shut and made his way down the hall after them.

ACKNOWLEDGMENTS

Thank you, readers, for buying my books, checking them out from libraries, writing reviews, posting on social media, telling your friends, showing up to events, and sharing what they meant to you. I love writing for you.

Thank you to the many booksellers I met on tour. You are truly building hope, joy, and community in what feels like desperate times. You are heroes.

This particular book would not have been possible without the incredible support of my editor Elizabeth Trout, who was willing to allow me to pivot from a previous idea I had pitched to Ingrid's story. I'm so grateful for the creative freedom and trust she gave me. Thanks also to the incredible team at Kensington for loving books and authors: Steve Zacharius, Adam Zacharius, Jackie Dinas, Susanna Grüninger, Vida Engstrand, Kait Johnson, Kristin McLaughlin, Robin Cook, and Kristine Mills.

A million thanks as well go to:

My agent Samantha Fabien, who remains a north star of wisdom and encouragement, as well as Gabrielle Greenstein and the rest of the team at Root Literary. Y'all absolutely rock.

Megan Beatie and Stephanie Elliot at MB Communications who have been tireless, upbeat promoters of my books. I'm so lucky to have you in my corner.

Zach at Computer Advantage in Savannah, Georgia, who found the edited manuscript that my dastardly computer ate. You probably won't see this, but that doesn't make you any less of a lifesaver.

Dawne McCurry and Annissa Armstrong, who supported my books in the early days and introduced me to their wonderful book club who wrote hilarious and heartwarming things in the ARC of my last book.

My family—Rick, Everett, Noah, Madi, Alex, and Haley—who are always so understanding and my biggest cheerleaders. I love y'all.

AUTHOR'S NOTE

I was raised in the 1980s in America, during the "Satanic Panic," a widespread moral panic that took the Christian community by storm. In those days, many people believed, among other things, that the role-playing game *Dungeons and Dragons* was occultic, rock and roll records contained "backmasked" messages worshipping the devil, and Satanists were abusing children in daycare centers.

It's fascinating to look back on that time as a sociological phenomenon. In the context of American history, I can see how it happened. The popularity of late '70s movies like *The Exorcist, Rosemary's Baby,* and *The Omen,* the anti-cult movement, the Protestant spiritual revival known as the "Jesus Movement," along with the creation of the Moral Majority, all set a very gothic stage.

Interestingly, the warnings I received had the reverse effect on me. I might've toed the line at the time, but the dire threats of danger lit up a part of my brain that has never dimmed. To this day, I'm more than slightly obsessed with everything to do with "the other side." Give me a ghost story or haunted house tale and I'm yours. Nearly every book I write involves some sort of element that can either be explained as para—or, conversely, perfectly normal.

As the years passed and the accusations of that period were debunked, I embarked on a journey to assess what my own spirituality and beliefs were, apart from the teachings of my childhood. Above all I tried to keep an open and fearless mind, and, not unexpectedly, I did evolve in my beliefs.

For me, writing a book about a psychic-witch was a step of that journey. While working on the novel, I visited two psychics. Three books in particular were invaluable in my research:

The Witching Year: A Memoir of Earnest Fumbling Through Modern Witchcraft by Diana Helmuth, *The Dabbler's Guide to Witchcraft* by Fire Lyte, and *Psychic Witch: A Metaphysical Guide to Meditation, Magick & Manifestation* by Mat Auryn. I read excerpts of numerous other books and did plenty of lurking on online forums. I am grateful for the open discussions there.

I do not practice witchcraft or paganism, and the book is not meant to be a precise representation of anyone's real-world practice or spiritual worship, though Edie and Ingrid's craft could probably be categorized as some version of chaos magic, and they do employ some basics of witchcraft. For the most part, though, I invented their specific beliefs—hopefully with honor, respect, and plausibility—so as not to misrepresent anyone's actual practice. For example, Ingrid does not read tarot, as it is a complex skill that requires years of training, and I did not feel I could accurately and responsibly represent it in the book.

Discussion Questions

1. At the opening of the book, Ingrid has a looming tax bill, as well as multiple costly repairs of the townhouse that she worries she can't pay. Discuss the impact money worries have on her and how they affect her actions throughout the book.

2. As a child, Ingrid was abandoned by her mother and bullied by classmates. How do you think this sets her up to be vulnerable to both Miles and Sailor?

3. Ingrid uses her witchcraft in many ways, both positively and negatively. What do you think is at the bottom of her need to continue the practice her grandmother taught her? Do you personally think witchcraft works? And if so, is it a force for good or evil?

4. Have you ever been to a psychic? Was it a helpful experience or not?

5. Sailor finds Ingrid to be a better friend than the women in her wedding party. What do you think has prevented Sailor from finding true friendship, reaching her goals, and becoming the person she wants to be?

6. The Southern Gothic genre deals with sins of the past in the American South and typically includes eccentric characters, derelict settings, and sinister or ghostly events, as well as crime and violence. What elements of the book would you say fit this description?

7. How are the concepts of friendship, family, and control explored in the book?

8. There are two Savannahs in this book: the one the Loefflers experience and the one Ingrid and Miles and their friends experience. What are the differences between the two?

9. If you were as wealthy as the Loefflers, how would you live your life differently from them?

10. Who would you cast as Ingrid, Sailor, Miles, Scoot, and Rill in a TV show or movie?